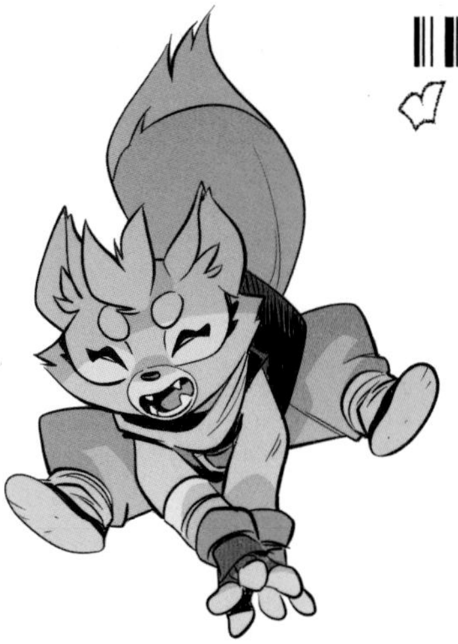

SUMMONERS WAR
LEGACY

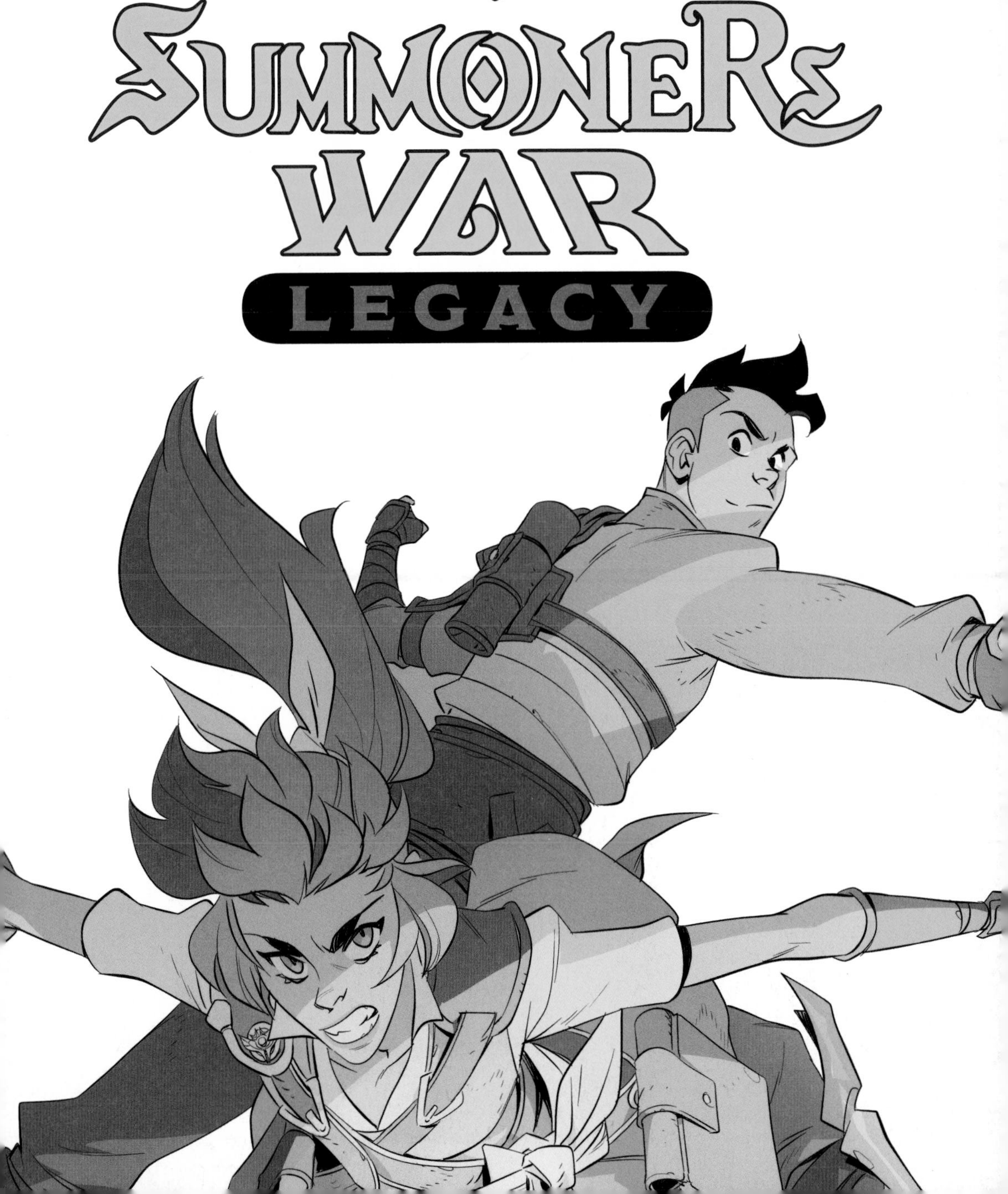

JUSTIN JORDAN
WRITER

LUCA CLARETTI
ARTIST

GIOVANNA NIRO
COLORIST

DERON BENNETT
LETTERER

ARIELLE BASICH
& JON MOISAN
EDITORS

CARINA TAYLOR
PRODUCTION DESIGN

SKYBOUND ENTERTAINMENT | SKYBOUND.COM
ROBERT KIRKMAN, CHAIRMAN | DAVID ALPERT CEO | SEAN MACKIEWICZ, SVP, EDITOR-IN-CHIEF | SHAWN KIRKHAM, SVP, BUSINESS DEVELOPMENT | BRIAN HUNTINGTON VP, ONLINE CONTENT | ANDRES JUAREZ, ART DIRECTOR | ARUNE SINGH, DIRECTOR OF BRAND, EDITORIAL | ALEX ANTONE, SENIOR EDITOR | JON MOISAN, EDITOR | AMANDA LAFRANCO, EDITOR | CARINA TAYLOR, GRAPHIC DESIGNER | DAN PETERSEN, SR. DIRECTOR, OPERATIONS & EVENTS | FOREIGN RIGHTS & LICENSING INQUIRIES: CONTACT@SKYBOUND.COM

COM2US | SUMMONERSWAR.COM
JOHN JOOHYUN NAM, VP OF IP STRATEGY | KRISTEN SIMON, MANAGING EDITOR | ADRIANO BAEK, CREATIVE MANAGER | AMI KIM, WORLD BUILDING EDITOR | SEUNGPIL BAEK, WORLD BUILDING WRITER | JIHOON JEON, PRODUCTION SPECIALIST | LESLIE NESBIT, PRODUCTION SPECIALIST

IMAGE COMICS, INC. | IMAGECOMICS.COM
TODD MCFARLANE, PRESIDENT | JIM VALENTINO, VICE PRESIDENT | MARC SILVESTRI, CHIEF EXECUTIVE OFFICER | ERIK LARSEN, CHIEF FINANCIAL OFFICER | ROBERT KIRKMAN, CHIEF OPERATING OFFICER | ERIC STEPHENSON, PUBLISHER / CHIEF CREATIVE OFFICER | NICOLE LAPALME, CONTROLLER | LEANNA CAUNTER, ACCOUNTING ANALYST | SUE KORPELA, ACCOUNTING & HR MANAGER | MARLA EIZIK, TALENT LIAISON | JEFF BOISON, DIRECTOR OF SALES & PUBLISHING PLANNING | DIRK WOOD, DIRECTOR OF INTERNATIONAL SALES & LICENSING | ALEX COX, DIRECTOR OF DIRECT MARKET SALES | CHLOE RAMOS, BOOK MARKET & LIBRARY SALES MANAGER | EMILIO BAUTISTA, DIGITAL SALES COORDINATOR | JON SCHLAFFMAN, SPECIALTY SALES COORDINATOR | KAT SALAZAR, DIRECTOR OF PR & MARKETING | DREW FITZGERALD, MARKETING CONTENT ASSOCIATE | HEATHER DOORNINK, PRODUCTION DIRECTOR | DREW GILL, ART DIRECTOR | HILARY DILORETO, PRINT MANAGER | TRICIA RAMOS, TRAFFIC MANAGER | MELISSA GIFFORD, CONTENT MANAGER | ERIKA SCHNATZ, SENIOR PRODUCTION ARTIST | RYAN BREWER, PRODUCTION ARTIST | DEANNA PHELPS, PRODUCTION ARTIST

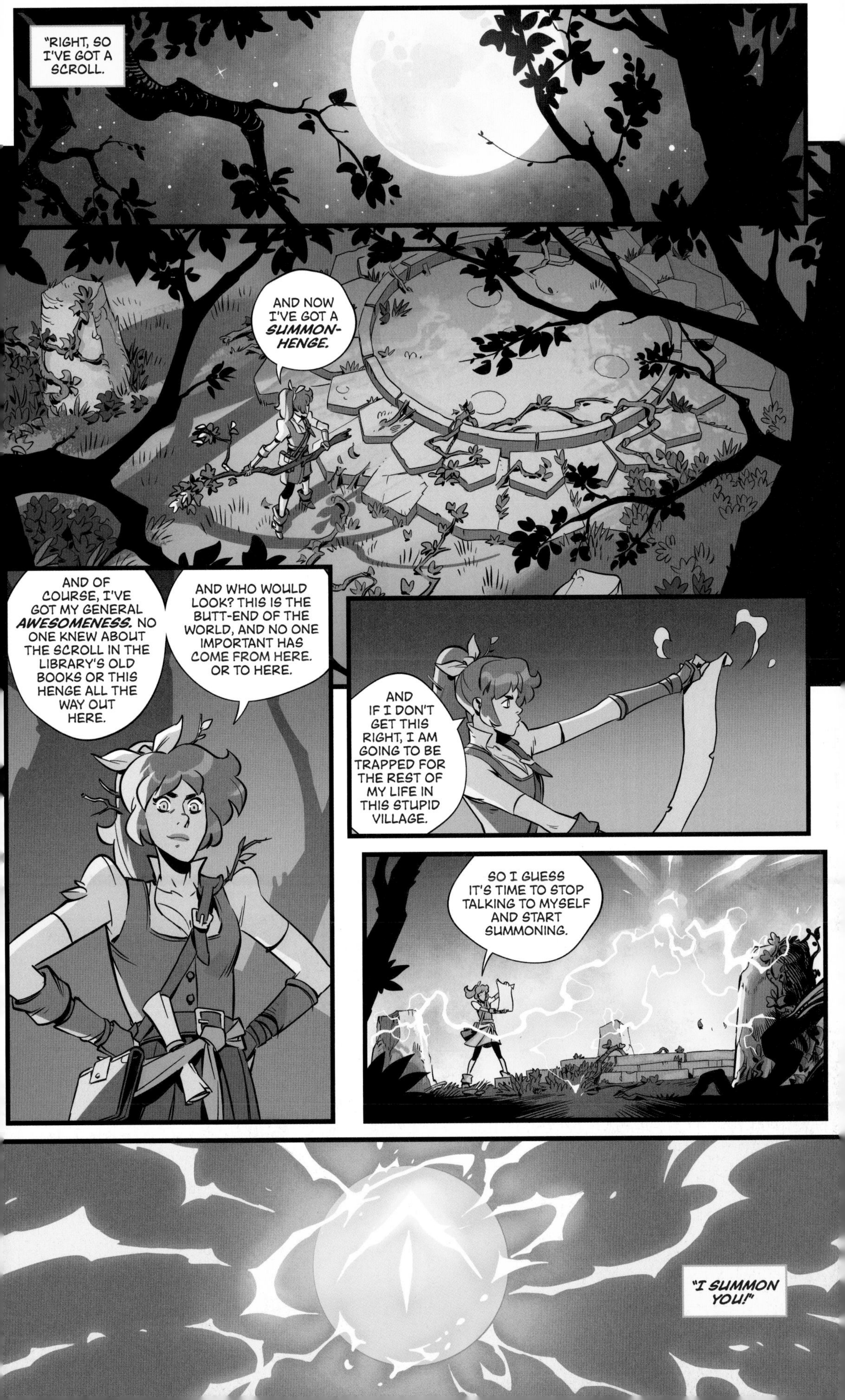
"RIGHT, SO I'VE GOT A SCROLL.
AND NOW I'VE GOT A SUMMON-HENGE.
AND OF COURSE, I'VE GOT MY GENERAL AWESOMENESS. NO ONE KNEW ABOUT THE SCROLL IN THE LIBRARY'S OLD BOOKS OR THIS HENGE ALL THE WAY OUT HERE.
AND WHO WOULD LOOK? THIS IS THE BUTT-END OF THE WORLD, AND NO ONE IMPORTANT HAS COME FROM HERE. OR TO HERE.
AND IF I DON'T GET THIS RIGHT, I AM GOING TO BE TRAPPED FOR THE REST OF MY LIFE IN THIS STUPID VILLAGE.
SO I GUESS IT'S TIME TO STOP TALKING TO MYSELF AND START SUMMONING.
"I SUMMON YOU!"

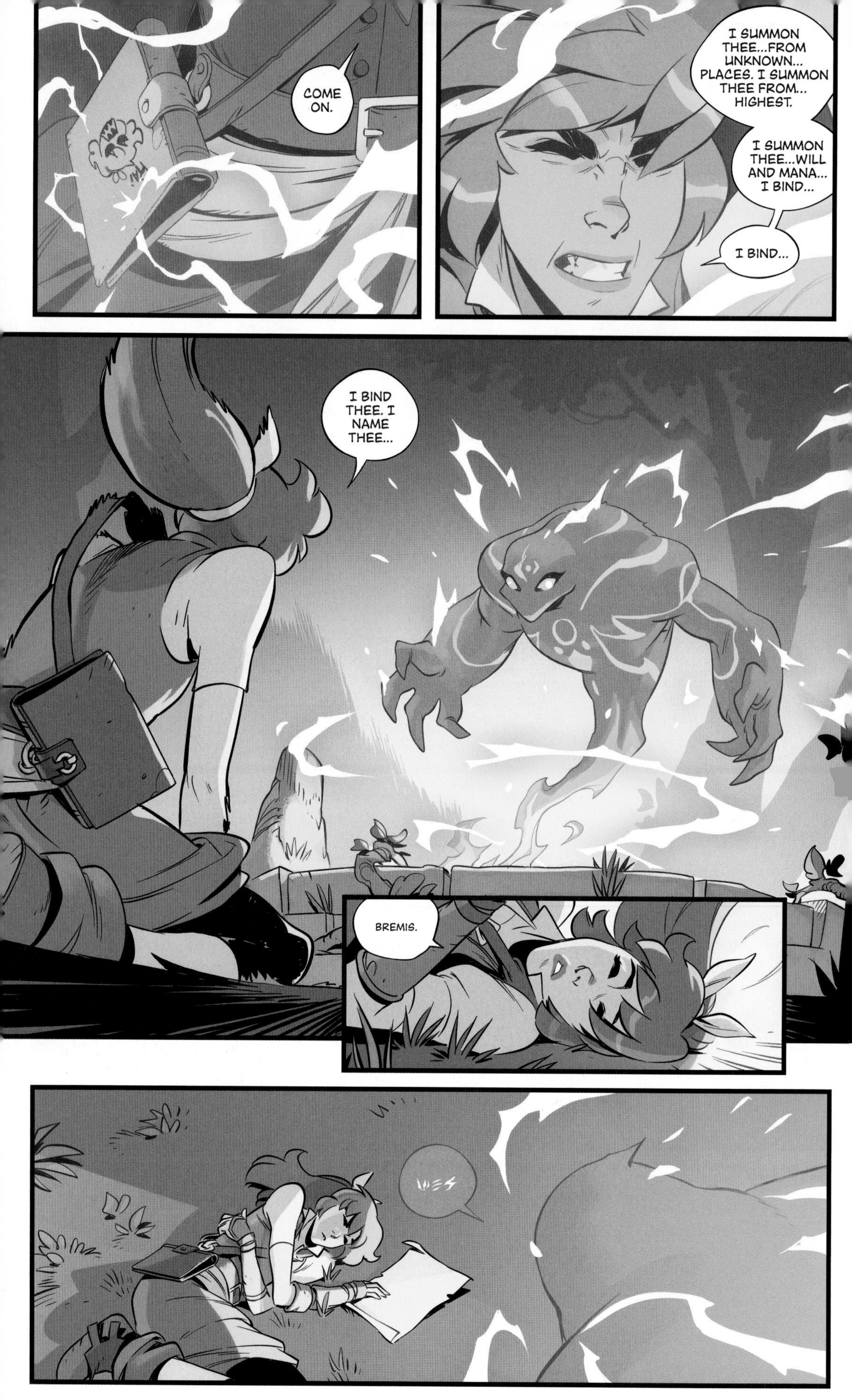
COME ON.
I SUMMON THEE...FROM UNKNOWN... PLACES. I SUMMON THEE FROM... HIGHEST.
I SUMMON THEE...WILL AND MANA... I BIND...
I BIND...
I BIND THEE. I NAME THEE...
BREMIS.

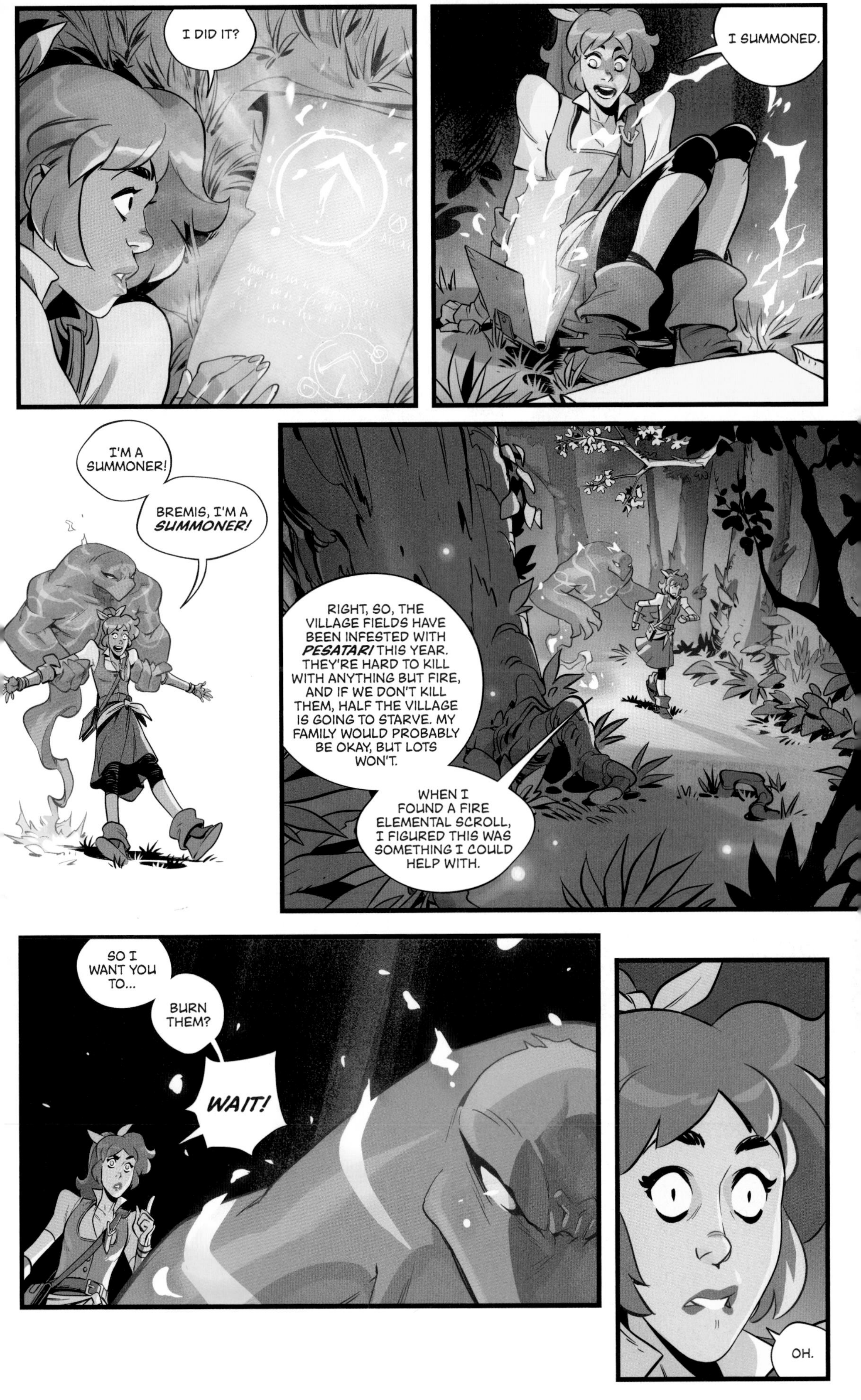
I DID IT?
I SUMMONED.
I'M A SUMMONER!
BREMIS, I'M A *SUMMONER!*
RIGHT, SO, THE VILLAGE FIELDS HAVE BEEN INFESTED WITH *PESATARI* THIS YEAR. THEY'RE HARD TO KILL WITH ANYTHING BUT FIRE, AND IF WE DON'T KILL THEM, HALF THE VILLAGE IS GOING TO STARVE. MY FAMILY WOULD PROBABLY BE OKAY, BUT LOTS WON'T.
WHEN I FOUND A FIRE ELEMENTAL SCROLL, I FIGURED THIS WAS SOMETHING I COULD HELP WITH.
SO I WANT YOU TO...
BURN THEM?
WAIT!
OH.

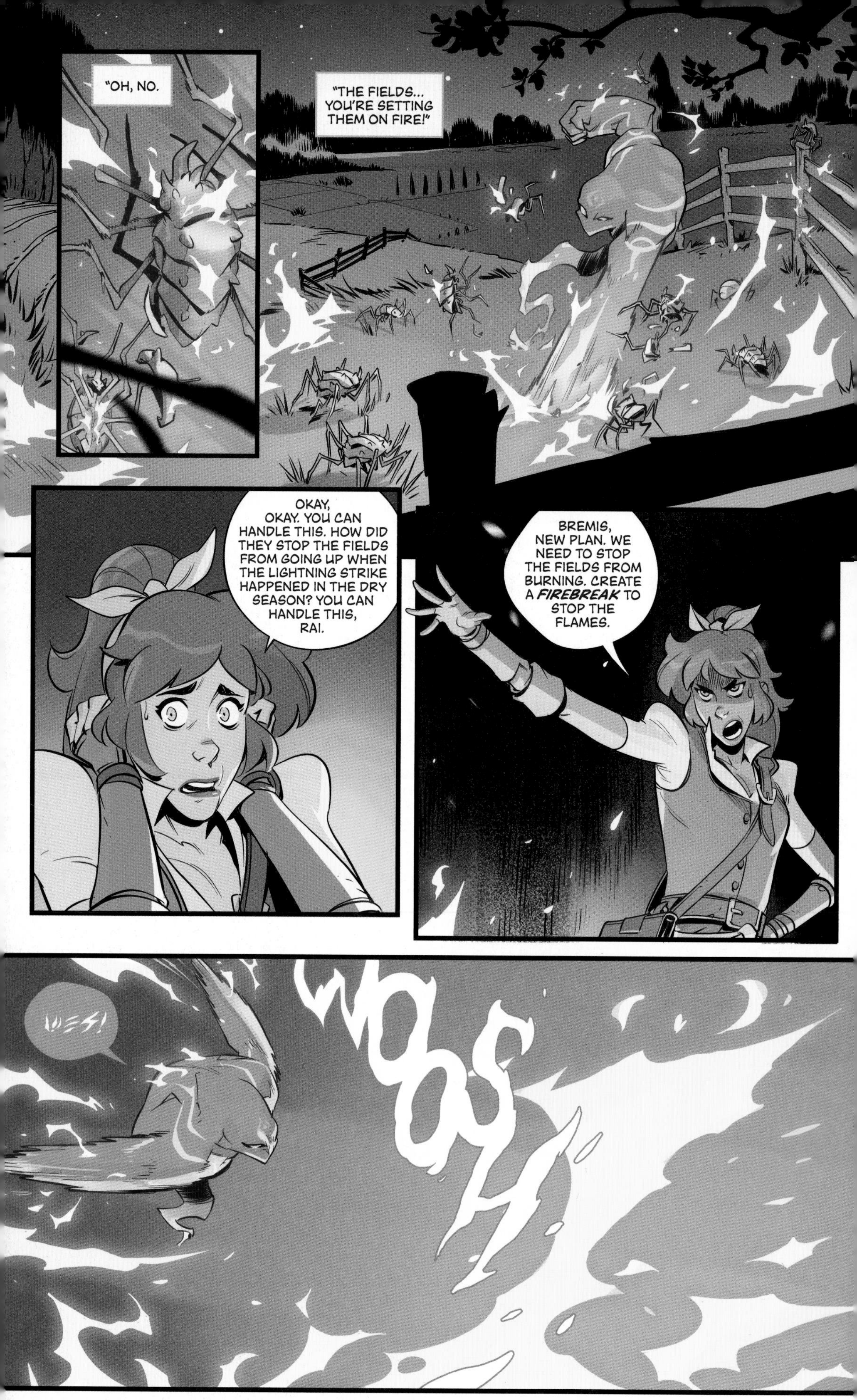
"OH, NO.
"THE FIELDS... YOU'RE SETTING THEM ON FIRE!"
OKAY, OKAY. YOU CAN HANDLE THIS. HOW DID THEY STOP THE FIELDS FROM GOING UP WHEN THE LIGHTNING STRIKE HAPPENED IN THE DRY SEASON? YOU CAN HANDLE THIS, RAI.
BREMIS, NEW PLAN. WE NEED TO STOP THE FIELDS FROM BURNING. CREATE A *FIREBREAK* TO STOP THE FLAMES.
WOOSH

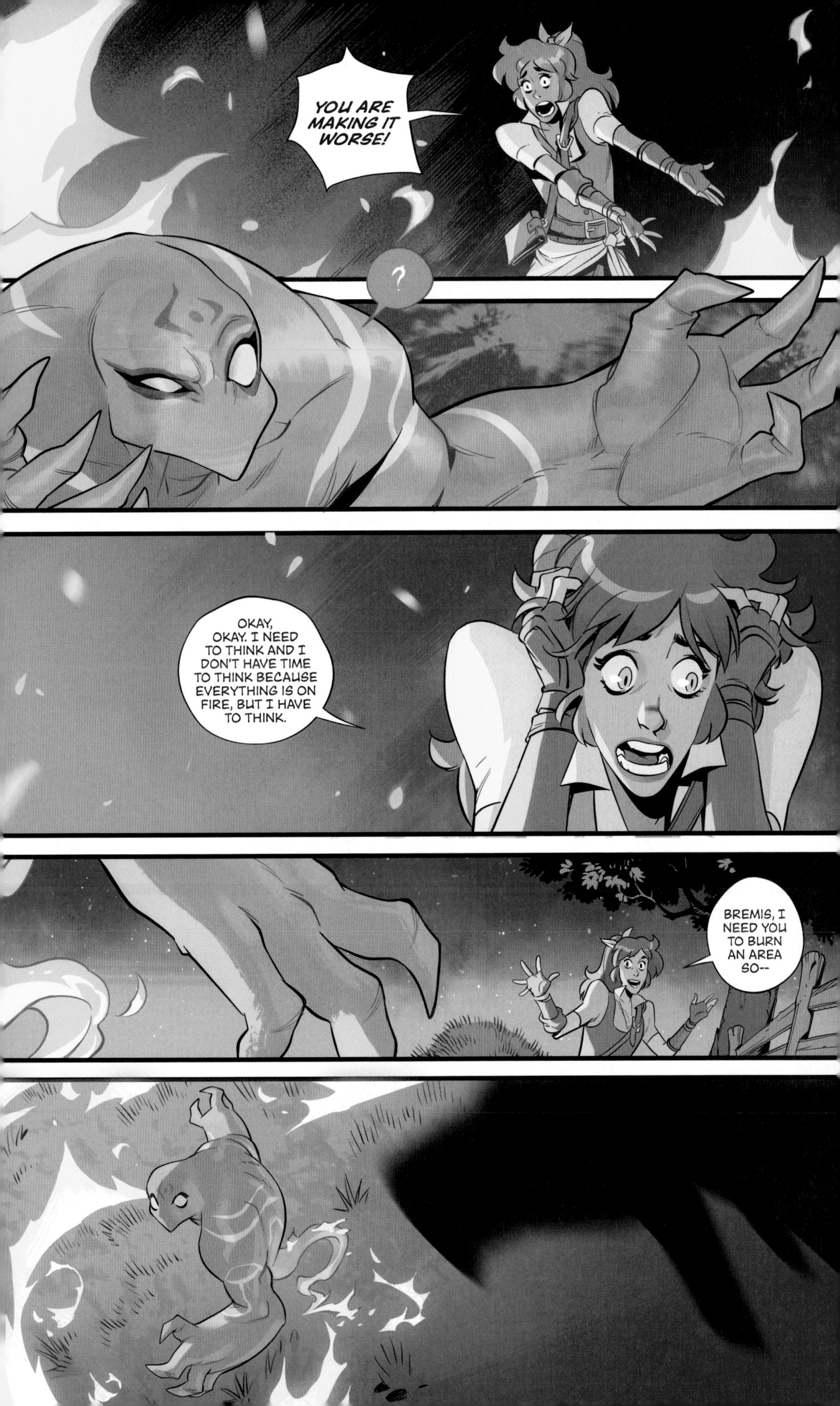
YOU ARE MAKING IT WORSE!
?
OKAY, OKAY. I NEED TO THINK AND I DON'T HAVE TIME TO THINK BECAUSE EVERYTHING IS ON FIRE, BUT I HAVE TO THINK.
BREMIS, I NEED YOU TO BURN AN AREA SO--

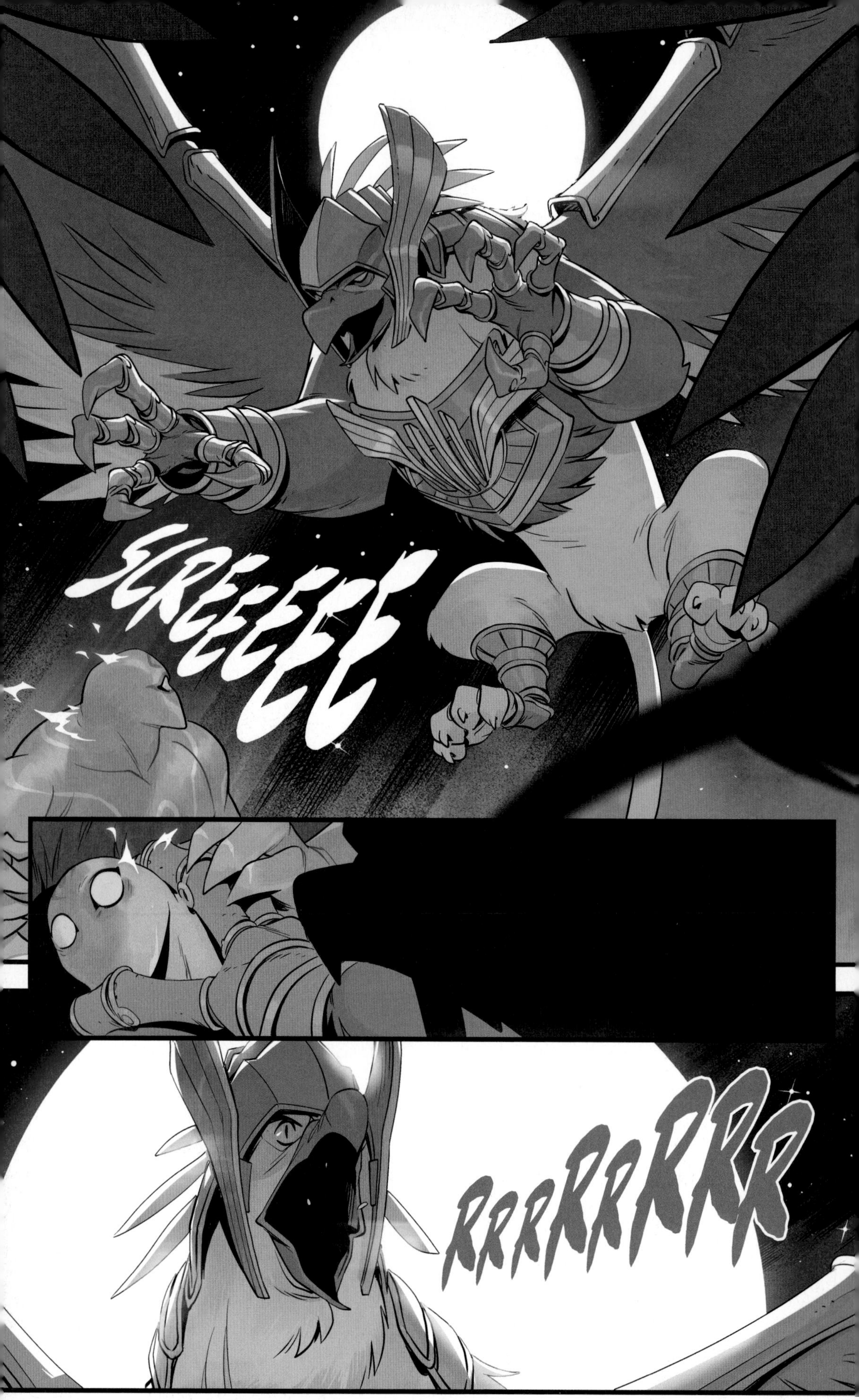
SCREEEEEE
RRRRRRRR

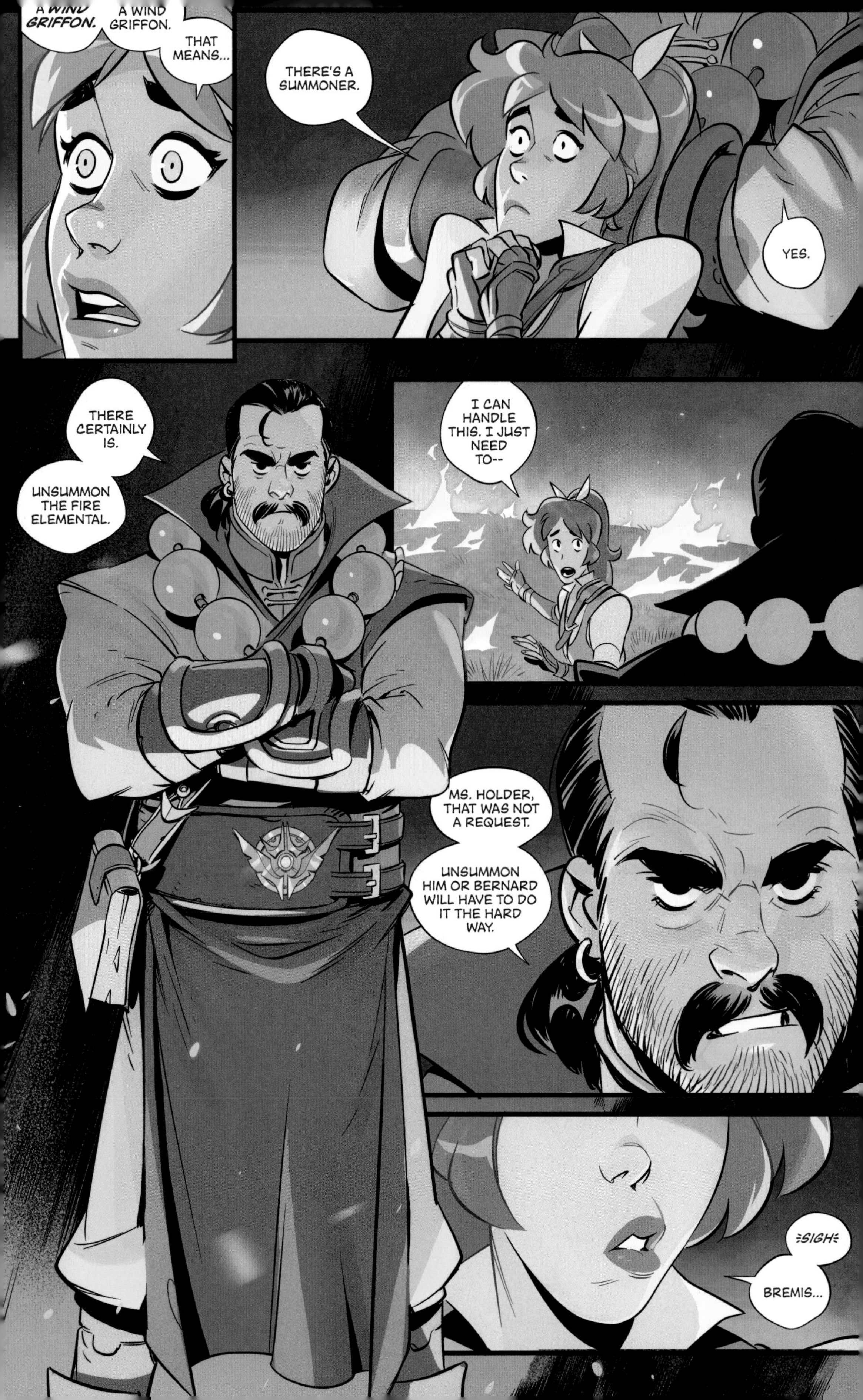
A WIND GRIFFON.
A WIND GRIFFON.
THAT MEANS...
THERE'S A SUMMONER.
YES.
THERE CERTAINLY IS.
UNSUMMON THE FIRE ELEMENTAL.
I CAN HANDLE THIS. I JUST NEED TO--
MS. HOLDER, THAT WAS NOT A REQUEST.
UNSUMMON HIM OR BERNARD WILL HAVE TO DO IT THE HARD WAY.
SIGH
BREMIS...

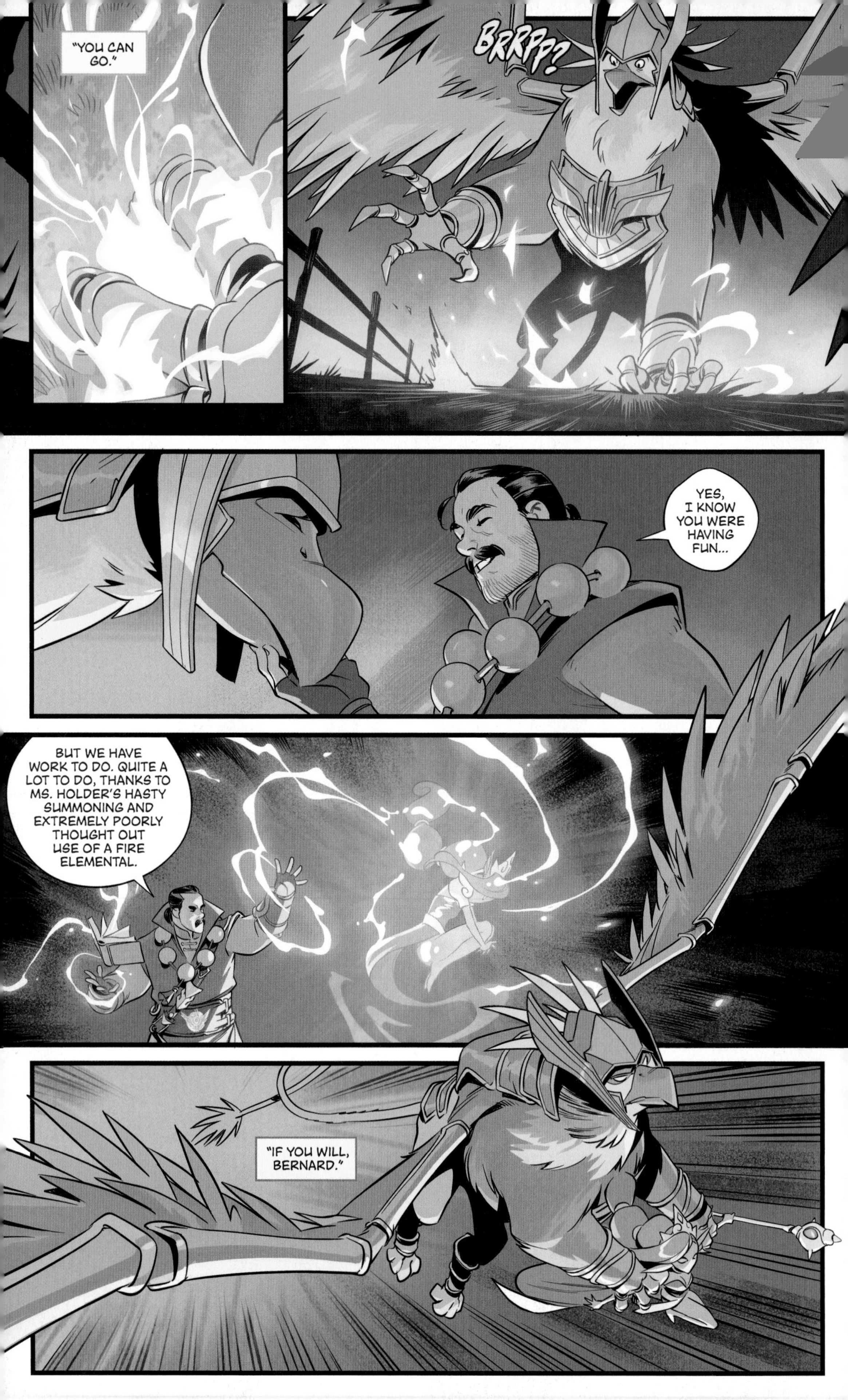
"YOU CAN GO."
BRRPP?
YES, I KNOW YOU WERE HAVING FUN...
BUT WE HAVE WORK TO DO. QUITE A LOT TO DO, THANKS TO MS. HOLDER'S HASTY SUMMONING AND EXTREMELY POORLY THOUGHT OUT USE OF A FIRE ELEMENTAL.
"IF YOU WILL, BERNARD."

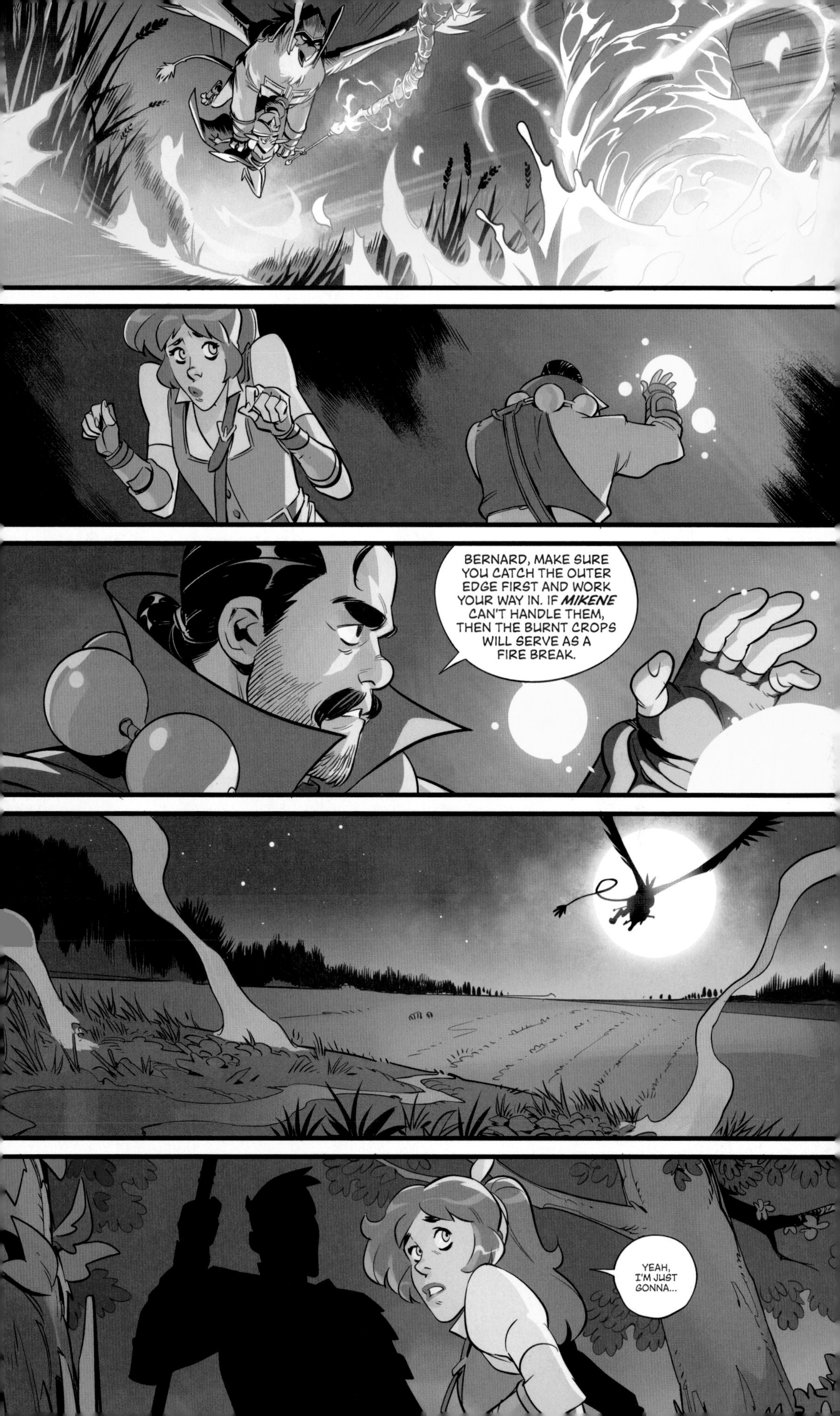
BERNARD, MAKE SURE YOU CATCH THE OUTER EDGE FIRST AND WORK YOUR WAY IN. IF MIKENE CAN'T HANDLE THEM, THEN THE BURNT CROPS WILL SERVE AS A FIRE BREAK.
YEAH, I'M JUST GONNA...

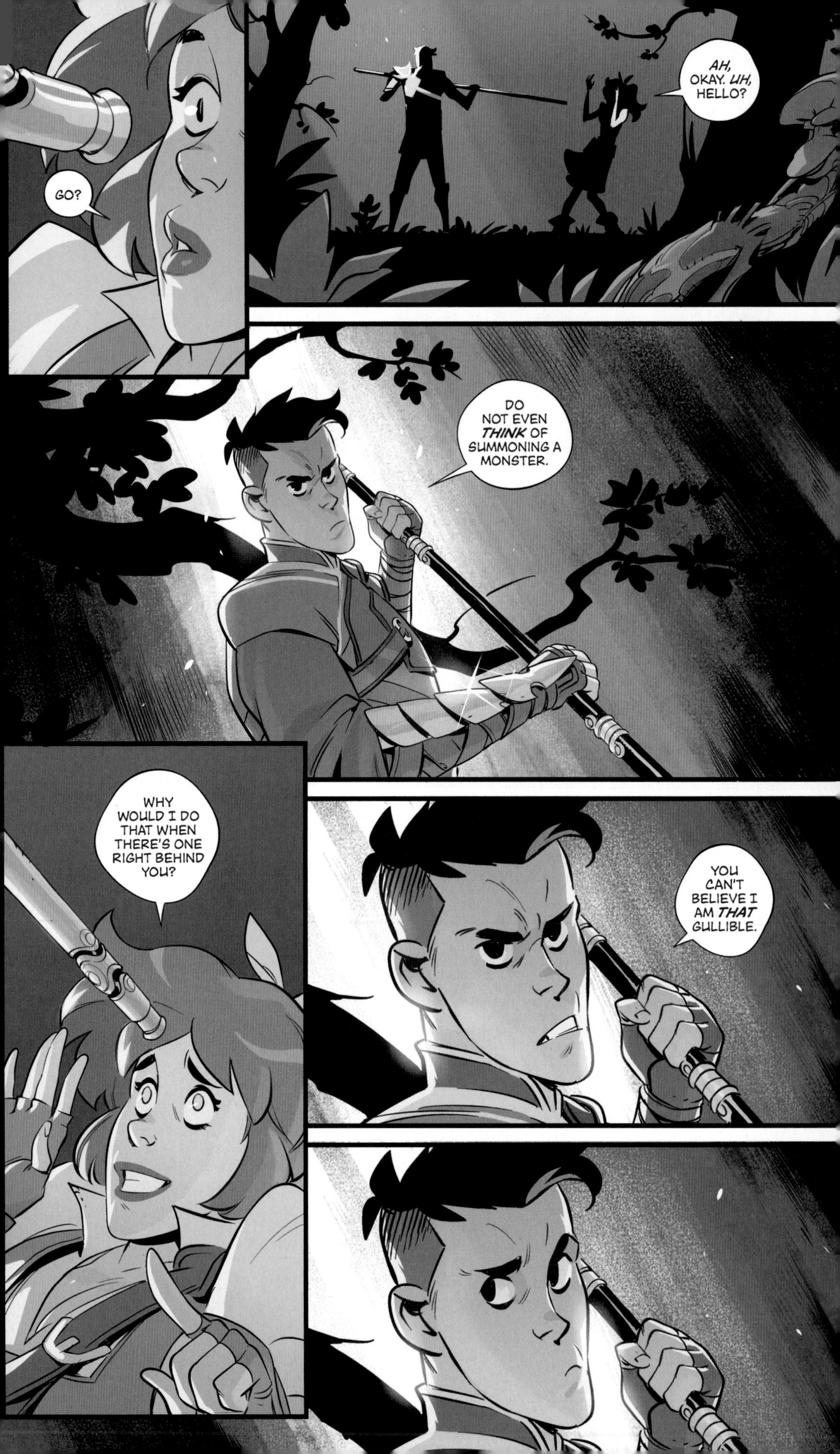
GO?
AH, OKAY. UH, HELLO?
DO NOT EVEN THINK OF SUMMONING A MONSTER.
WHY WOULD I DO THAT WHEN THERE'S ONE RIGHT BEHIND YOU?
YOU CAN'T BELIEVE I AM THAT GULLIBLE.

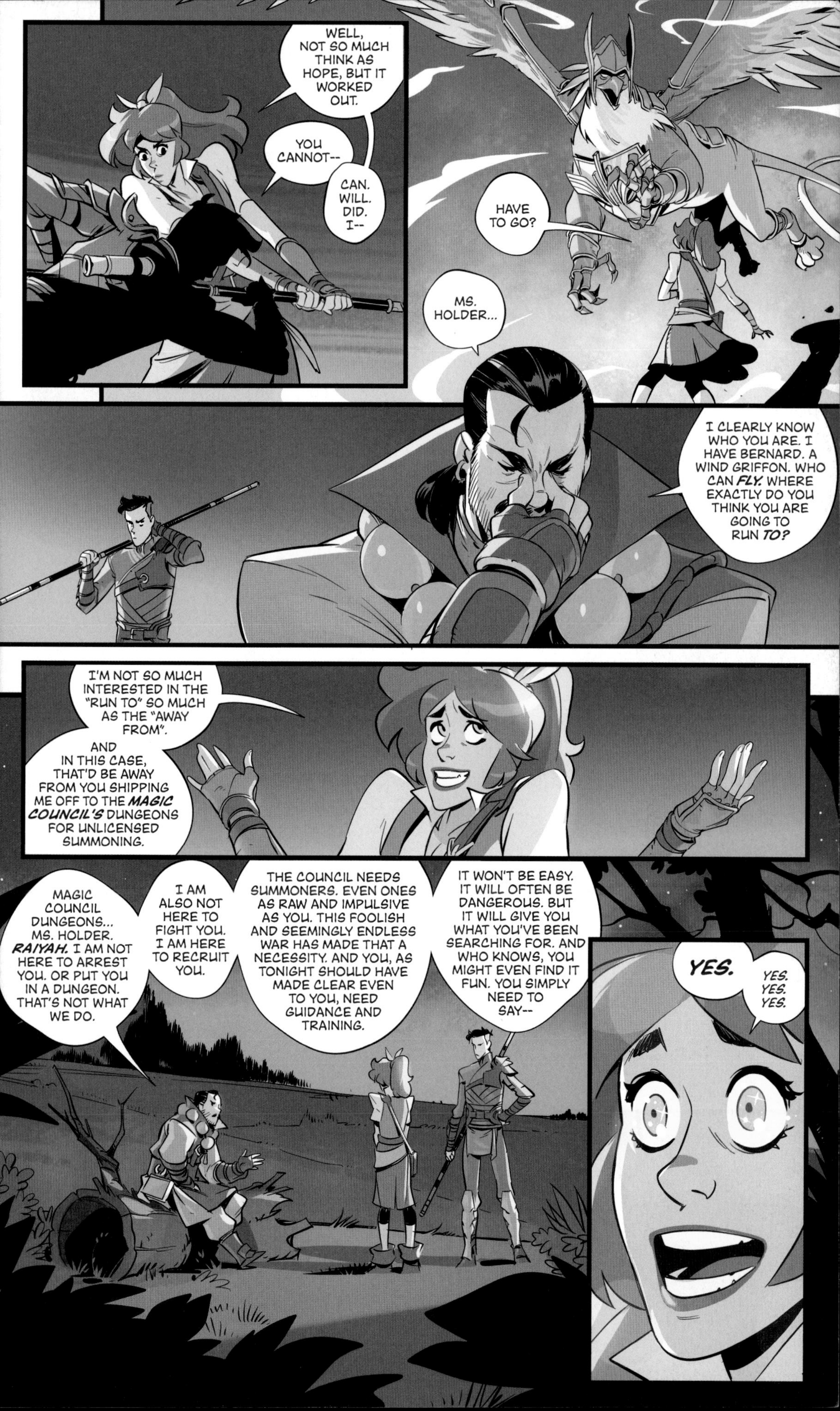
WELL, NOT SO MUCH THINK AS HOPE, BUT IT WORKED OUT.
YOU CANNOT--
CAN. WILL. DID. I--
HAVE TO GO?
MS. HOLDER...
I CLEARLY KNOW WHO YOU ARE. I HAVE BERNARD. A WIND GRIFFON. WHO CAN FLY. WHERE EXACTLY DO YOU THINK YOU ARE GOING TO RUN TO?
I'M NOT SO MUCH INTERESTED IN THE "RUN TO" SO MUCH AS THE "AWAY FROM".
AND IN THIS CASE, THAT'D BE AWAY FROM YOU SHIPPING ME OFF TO THE MAGIC COUNCIL'S DUNGEONS FOR UNLICENSED SUMMONING.
MAGIC COUNCIL DUNGEONS... MS. HOLDER. RAIYAH. I AM NOT HERE TO ARREST YOU. OR PUT YOU IN A DUNGEON. THAT'S NOT WHAT WE DO.
I AM ALSO NOT HERE TO FIGHT YOU. I AM HERE TO RECRUIT YOU.
THE COUNCIL NEEDS SUMMONERS. EVEN ONES AS RAW AND IMPULSIVE AS YOU. THIS FOOLISH AND SEEMINGLY ENDLESS WAR HAS MADE THAT A NECESSITY. AND YOU, AS TONIGHT SHOULD HAVE MADE CLEAR EVEN TO YOU, NEED GUIDANCE AND TRAINING.
IT WON'T BE EASY. IT WILL OFTEN BE DANGEROUS. BUT IT WILL GIVE YOU WHAT YOU'VE BEEN SEARCHING FOR. AND WHO KNOWS, YOU MIGHT EVEN FIND IT FUN. YOU SIMPLY NEED TO SAY--
YES.
YES. YES. YES.

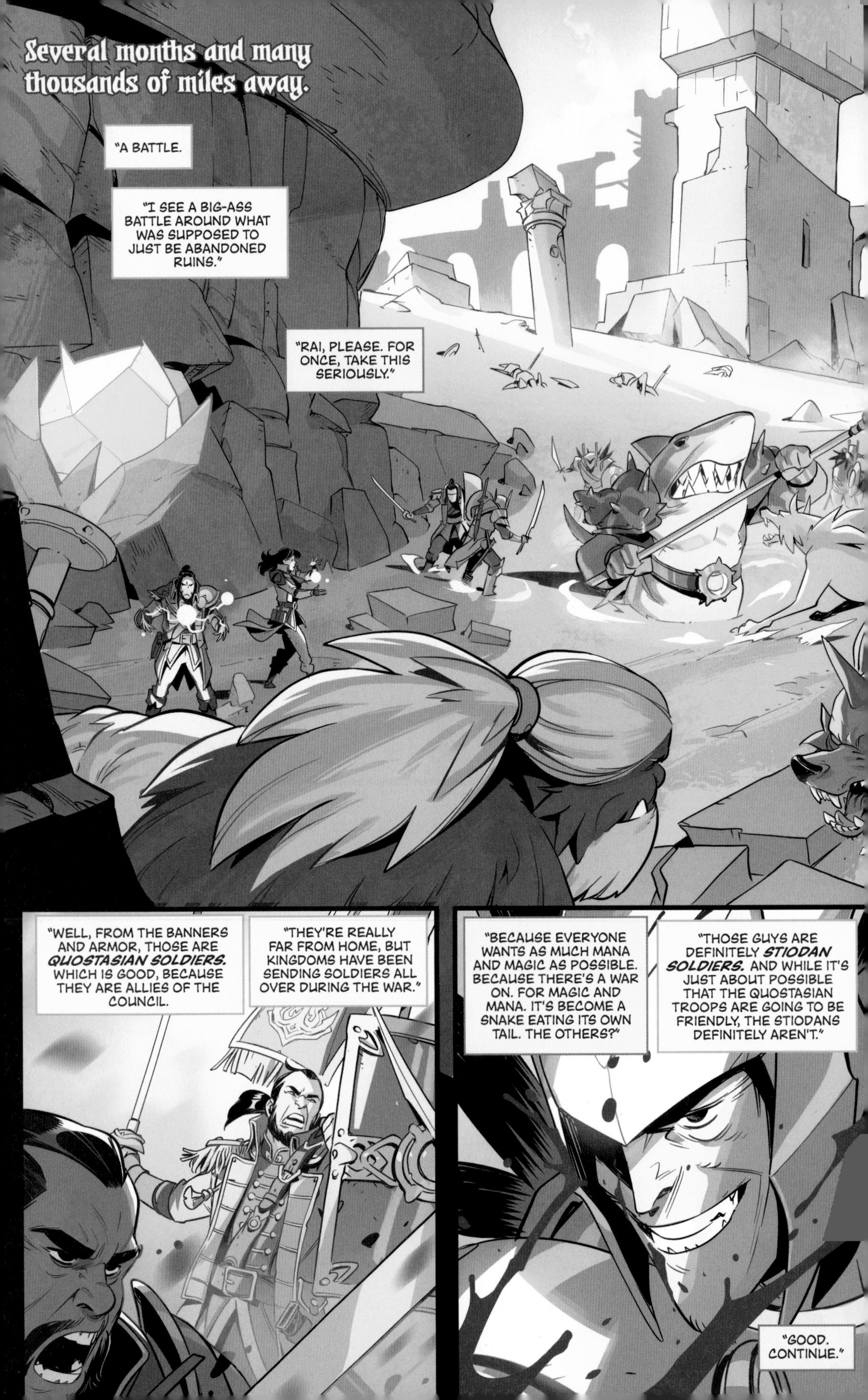
Several months and many thousands of miles away.
"A BATTLE.
"I SEE A BIG-ASS BATTLE AROUND WHAT WAS SUPPOSED TO JUST BE ABANDONED RUINS."
"RAI, PLEASE. FOR ONCE, TAKE THIS SERIOUSLY."
"WELL, FROM THE BANNERS AND ARMOR, THOSE ARE QUOSTASIAN SOLDIERS. WHICH IS GOOD, BECAUSE THEY ARE ALLIES OF THE COUNCIL.
"THEY'RE REALLY FAR FROM HOME, BUT KINGDOMS HAVE BEEN SENDING SOLDIERS ALL OVER DURING THE WAR."
"BECAUSE EVERYONE WANTS AS MUCH MANA AND MAGIC AS POSSIBLE. BECAUSE THERE'S A WAR ON. FOR MAGIC AND MANA. IT'S BECOME A SNAKE EATING ITS OWN TAIL. THE OTHERS?"
"THOSE GUYS ARE DEFINITELY STIODAN SOLDIERS. AND WHILE IT'S JUST ABOUT POSSIBLE THAT THE QUOSTASIAN TROOPS ARE GOING TO BE FRIENDLY, THE STIODANS DEFINITELY AREN'T."
"GOOD. CONTINUE."

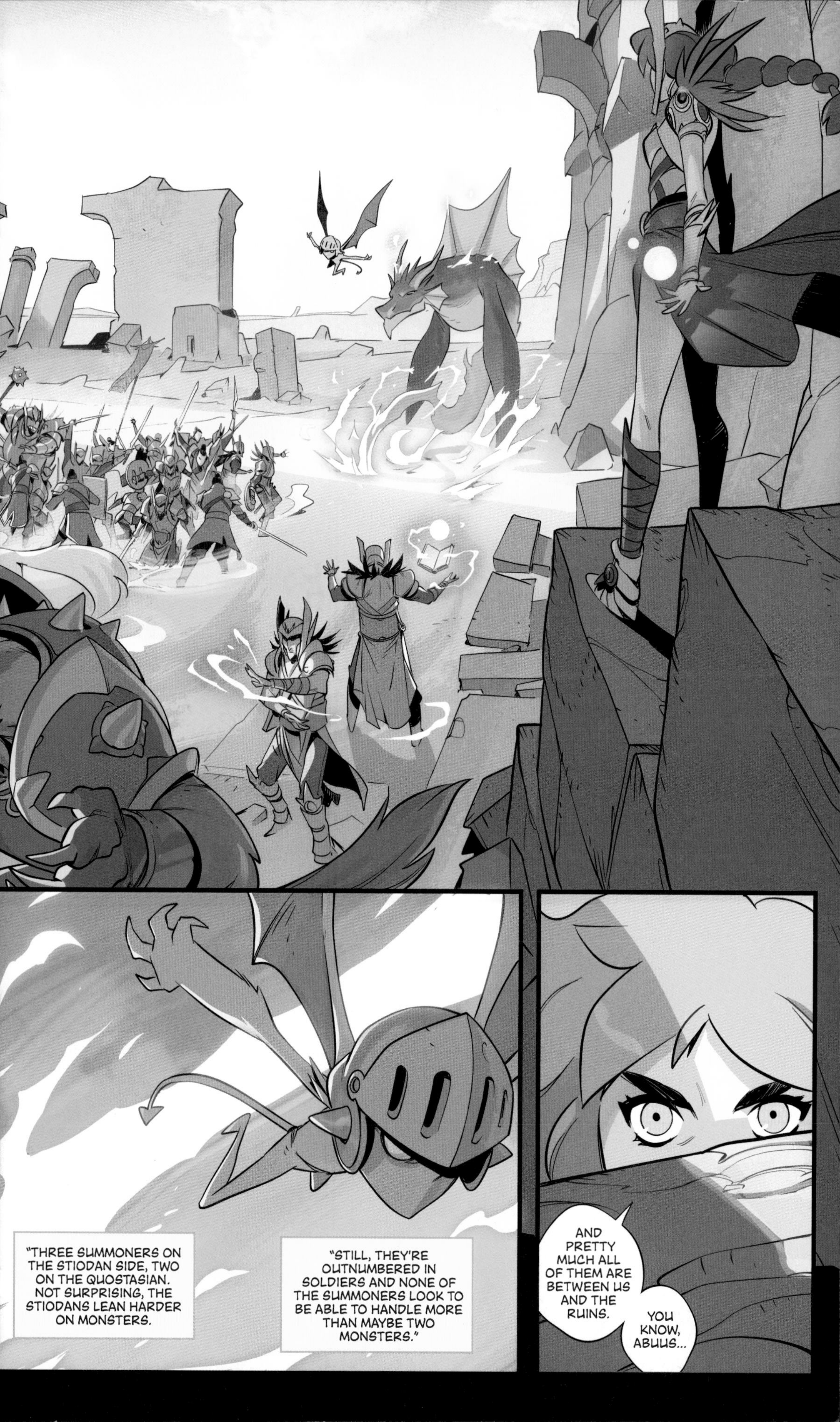
"THREE SUMMONERS ON THE STIODAN SIDE, TWO ON THE QUOSTASIAN. NOT SURPRISING, THE STIODANS LEAN HARDER ON MONSTERS.
"STILL, THEY'RE OUTNUMBERED IN SOLDIERS AND NONE OF THE SUMMONERS LOOK TO BE ABLE TO HANDLE MORE THAN MAYBE TWO MONSTERS."
AND PRETTY MUCH ALL OF THEM ARE BETWEEN US AND THE RUINS.
YOU KNOW, ABUUS...

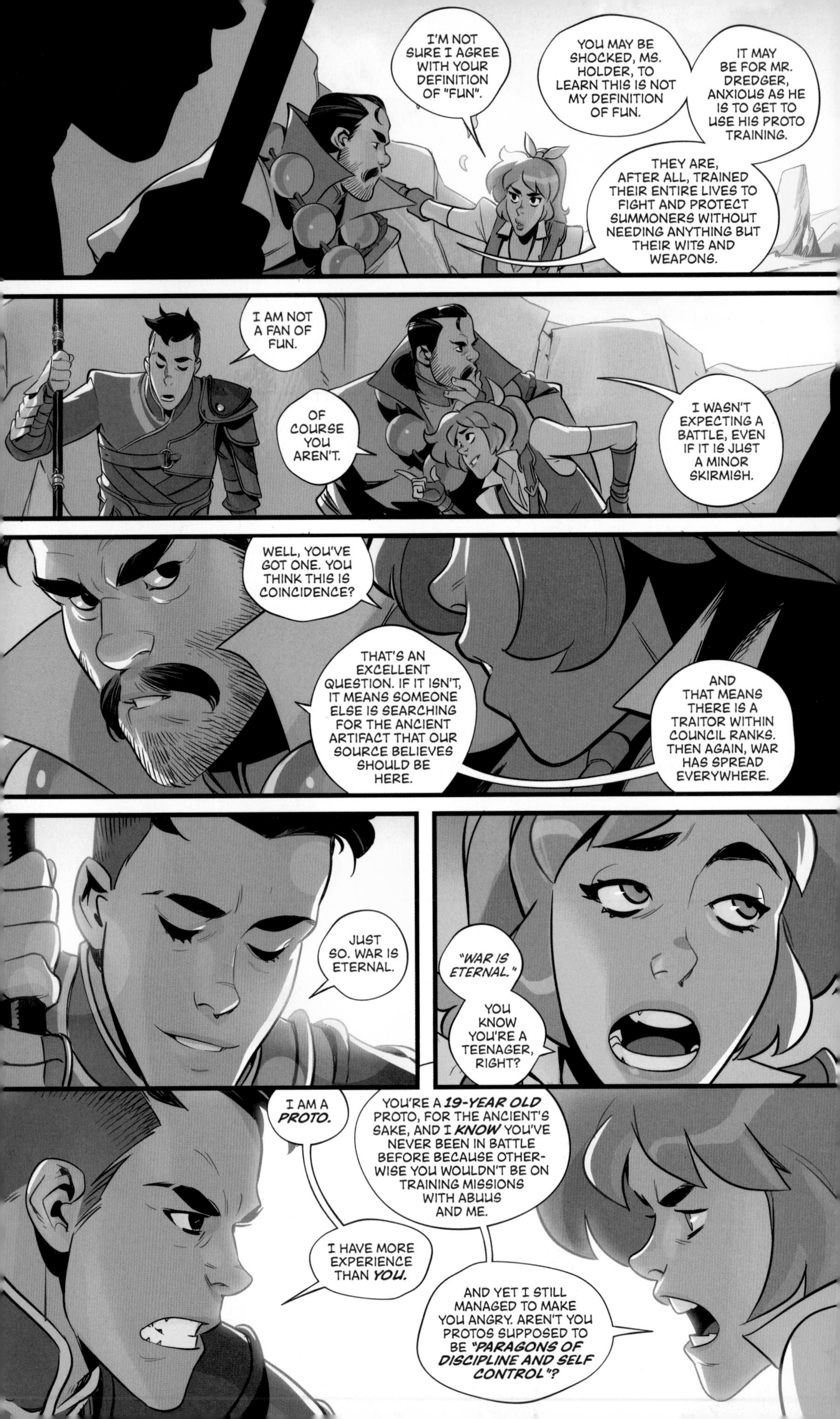
I'M NOT SURE I AGREE WITH YOUR DEFINITION OF "FUN".
YOU MAY BE SHOCKED, MS. HOLDER, TO LEARN THIS IS NOT MY DEFINITION OF FUN.
IT MAY BE FOR MR. DREDGER, ANXIOUS AS HE IS TO GET TO USE HIS PROTO TRAINING.
THEY ARE, AFTER ALL, TRAINED THEIR ENTIRE LIVES TO FIGHT AND PROTECT SUMMONERS WITHOUT NEEDING ANYTHING BUT THEIR WITS AND WEAPONS.
I AM NOT A FAN OF FUN.
OF COURSE YOU AREN'T.
I WASN'T EXPECTING A BATTLE, EVEN IF IT IS JUST A MINOR SKIRMISH.
WELL, YOU'VE GOT ONE. YOU THINK THIS IS COINCIDENCE?
THAT'S AN EXCELLENT QUESTION. IF IT ISN'T, IT MEANS SOMEONE ELSE IS SEARCHING FOR THE ANCIENT ARTIFACT THAT OUR SOURCE BELIEVES SHOULD BE HERE.
AND THAT MEANS THERE IS A TRAITOR WITHIN COUNCIL RANKS. THEN AGAIN, WAR HAS SPREAD EVERYWHERE.
JUST SO. WAR IS ETERNAL.
"WAR IS ETERNAL."
YOU KNOW YOU'RE A TEENAGER, RIGHT?
I AM A ***PROTO.***
YOU'RE A ***19-YEAR OLD*** PROTO, FOR THE ANCIENT'S SAKE, AND I ***KNOW*** YOU'VE NEVER BEEN IN BATTLE BEFORE BECAUSE OTHERWISE YOU WOULDN'T BE ON TRAINING MISSIONS WITH ABUUS AND ME.
I HAVE MORE EXPERIENCE THAN ***YOU.***
AND YET I STILL MANAGED TO MAKE YOU ANGRY. AREN'T YOU PROTOS SUPPOSED TO BE ***"PARAGONS OF DISCIPLINE AND SELF CONTROL"***?

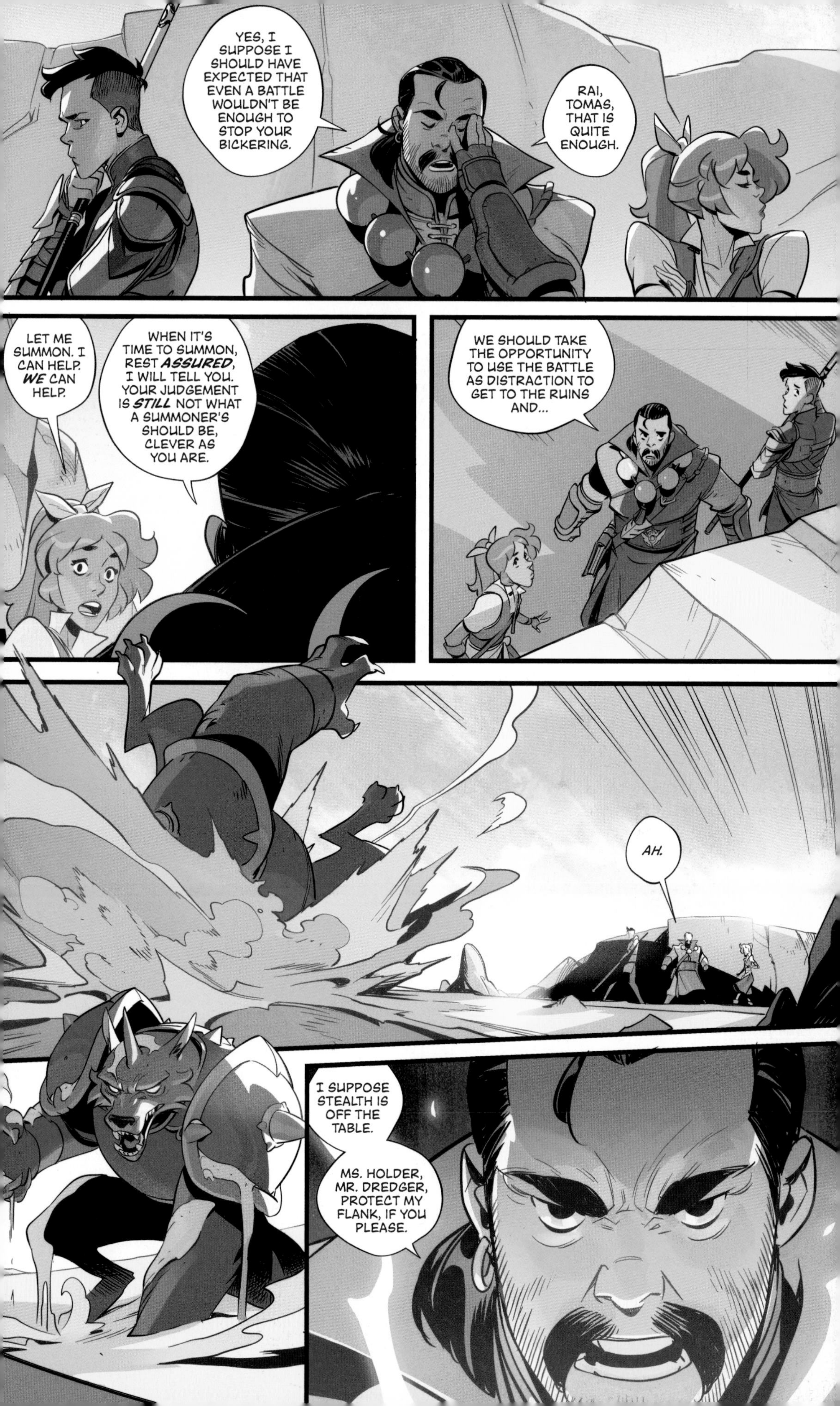

YES, I SUPPOSE I SHOULD HAVE EXPECTED THAT EVEN A BATTLE WOULDN'T BE ENOUGH TO STOP YOUR BICKERING.
RAI, TOMAS, THAT IS QUITE ENOUGH.
LET ME SUMMON. I CAN HELP. *WE* CAN HELP.
WHEN IT'S TIME TO SUMMON, REST *ASSURED*, I WILL TELL YOU. YOUR JUDGEMENT IS *STILL* NOT WHAT A SUMMONER'S SHOULD BE, CLEVER AS YOU ARE.
WE SHOULD TAKE THE OPPORTUNITY TO USE THE BATTLE AS DISTRACTION TO GET TO THE RUINS AND...
AH.
I SUPPOSE STEALTH IS OFF THE TABLE.
MS. HOLDER, MR. DREDGER, PROTECT MY FLANK, IF YOU PLEASE.

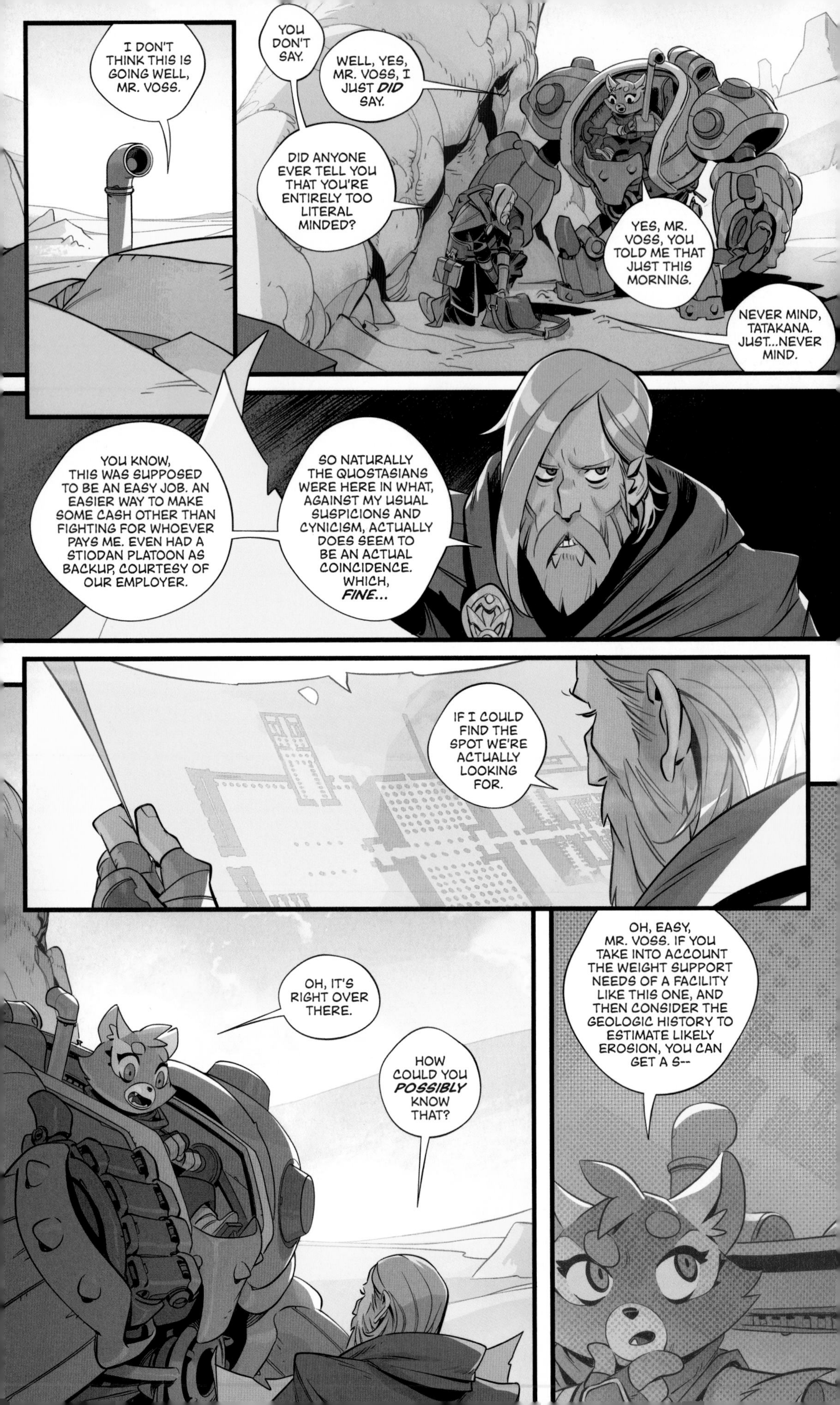
I DON'T THINK THIS IS GOING WELL, MR. VOSS.
YOU DON'T SAY.
WELL, YES, MR. VOSS, I JUST *DID* SAY.
DID ANYONE EVER TELL YOU THAT YOU'RE ENTIRELY TOO LITERAL MINDED?
YES, MR. VOSS, YOU TOLD ME THAT JUST THIS MORNING.
NEVER MIND, TATAKANA. JUST...NEVER MIND.
YOU KNOW, THIS WAS SUPPOSED TO BE AN EASY JOB. AN EASIER WAY TO MAKE SOME CASH OTHER THAN FIGHTING FOR WHOEVER PAYS ME. EVEN HAD A STIODAN PLATOON AS BACKUP, COURTESY OF OUR EMPLOYER.
SO NATURALLY THE QUOSTASIANS WERE HERE IN WHAT, AGAINST MY USUAL SUSPICIONS AND CYNICISM, ACTUALLY DOES SEEM TO BE AN ACTUAL COINCIDENCE. WHICH, ***FINE...***
IF I COULD FIND THE SPOT WE'RE ACTUALLY LOOKING FOR.
OH, IT'S RIGHT OVER THERE.
HOW COULD YOU ***POSSIBLY*** KNOW THAT?
OH, EASY, MR. VOSS. IF YOU TAKE INTO ACCOUNT THE WEIGHT SUPPORT NEEDS OF A FACILITY LIKE THIS ONE, AND THEN CONSIDER THE GEOLOGIC HISTORY TO ESTIMATE LIKELY EROSION, YOU CAN GET A S--

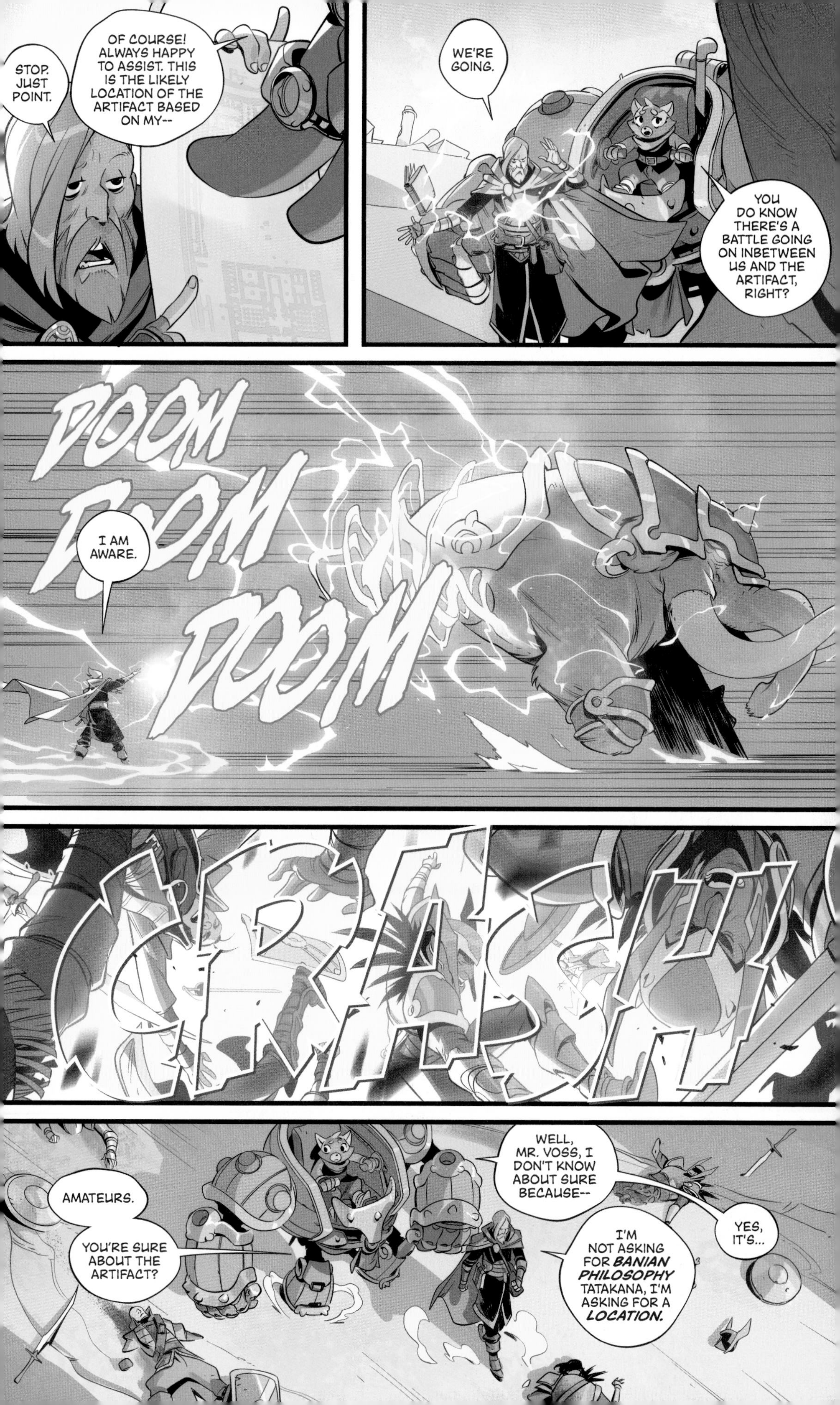
STOP. JUST POINT.
OF COURSE! ALWAYS HAPPY TO ASSIST. THIS IS THE LIKELY LOCATION OF THE ARTIFACT BASED ON MY--
WE'RE GOING.
YOU DO KNOW THERE'S A BATTLE GOING ON INBETWEEN US AND THE ARTIFACT, RIGHT?
DOOM DOOM DOOM
I AM AWARE.
CRASH!
AMATEURS.
YOU'RE SURE ABOUT THE ARTIFACT?
WELL, MR. VOSS, I DON'T KNOW ABOUT SURE BECAUSE--
YES, IT'S...
I'M NOT ASKING FOR ***BANIAN PHILOSOPHY*** TATAKANA, I'M ASKING FOR A ***LOCATION.***

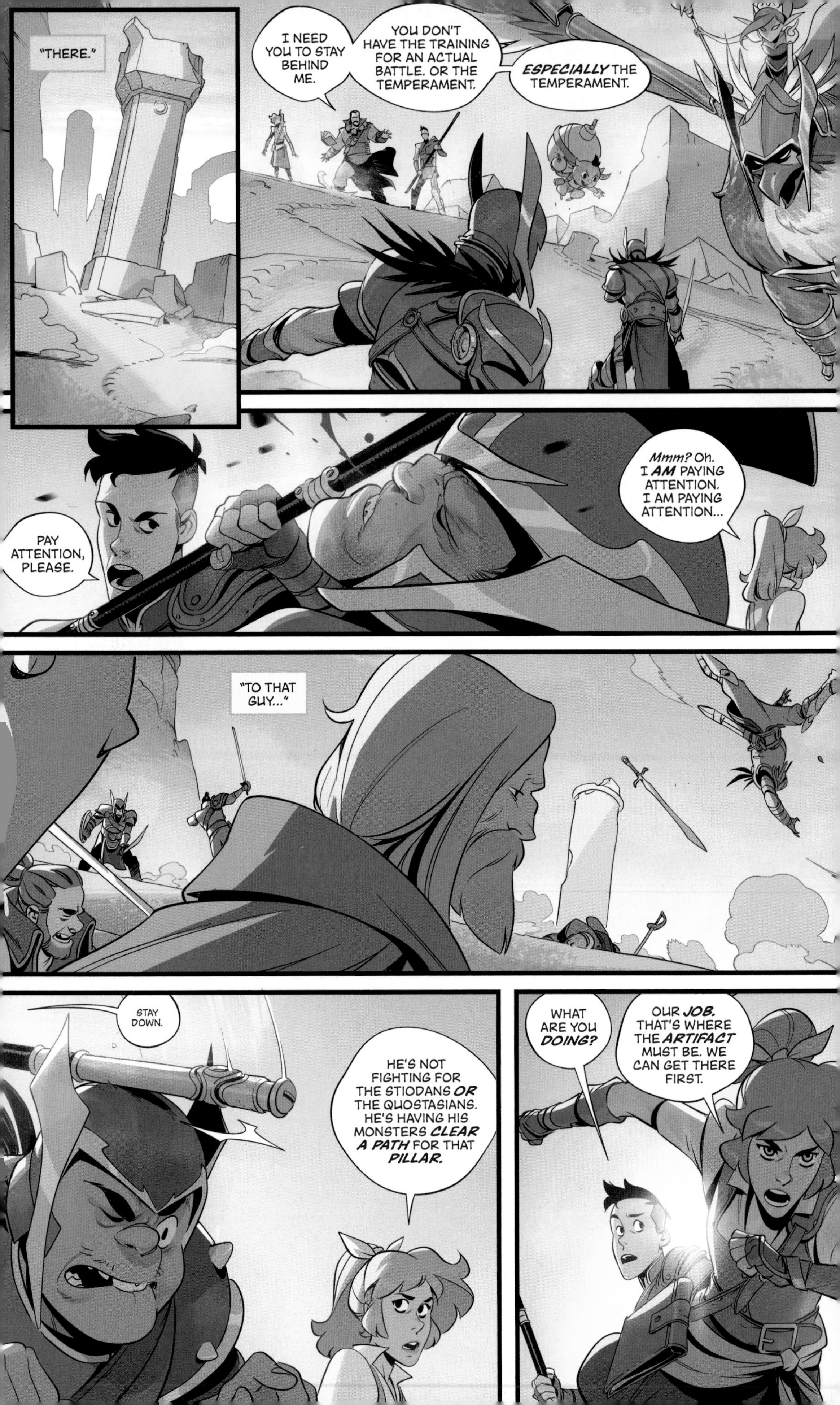
"THERE."
I NEED YOU TO STAY BEHIND ME.
YOU DON'T HAVE THE TRAINING FOR AN ACTUAL BATTLE. OR THE TEMPERAMENT.
ESPECIALLY THE TEMPERAMENT.
PAY ATTENTION, PLEASE.
Mmm? Oh. I AM PAYING ATTENTION. I AM PAYING ATTENTION...
"TO THAT GUY..."
STAY DOWN.
HE'S NOT FIGHTING FOR THE STIODANS OR THE QUOSTASIANS. HE'S HAVING HIS MONSTERS CLEAR A PATH FOR THAT PILLAR.
WHAT ARE YOU DOING?
OUR JOB. THAT'S WHERE THE ARTIFACT MUST BE. WE CAN GET THERE FIRST.

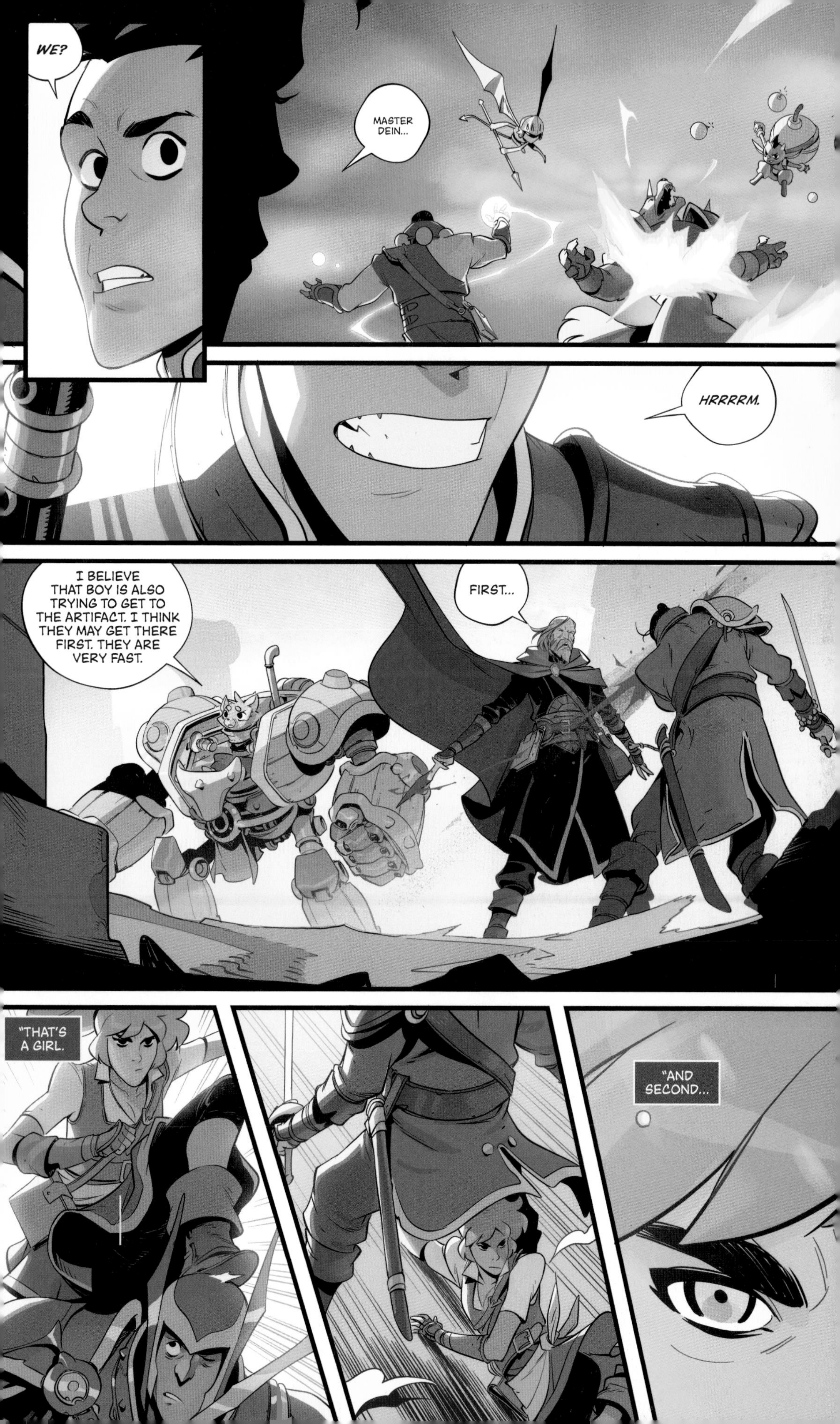
WE?
MASTER DEIN...
HRRRRM.
I BELIEVE THAT BOY IS ALSO TRYING TO GET TO THE ARTIFACT. I THINK THEY MAY GET THERE FIRST. THEY ARE VERY FAST.
FIRST...
"THAT'S A GIRL.
"AND SECOND...

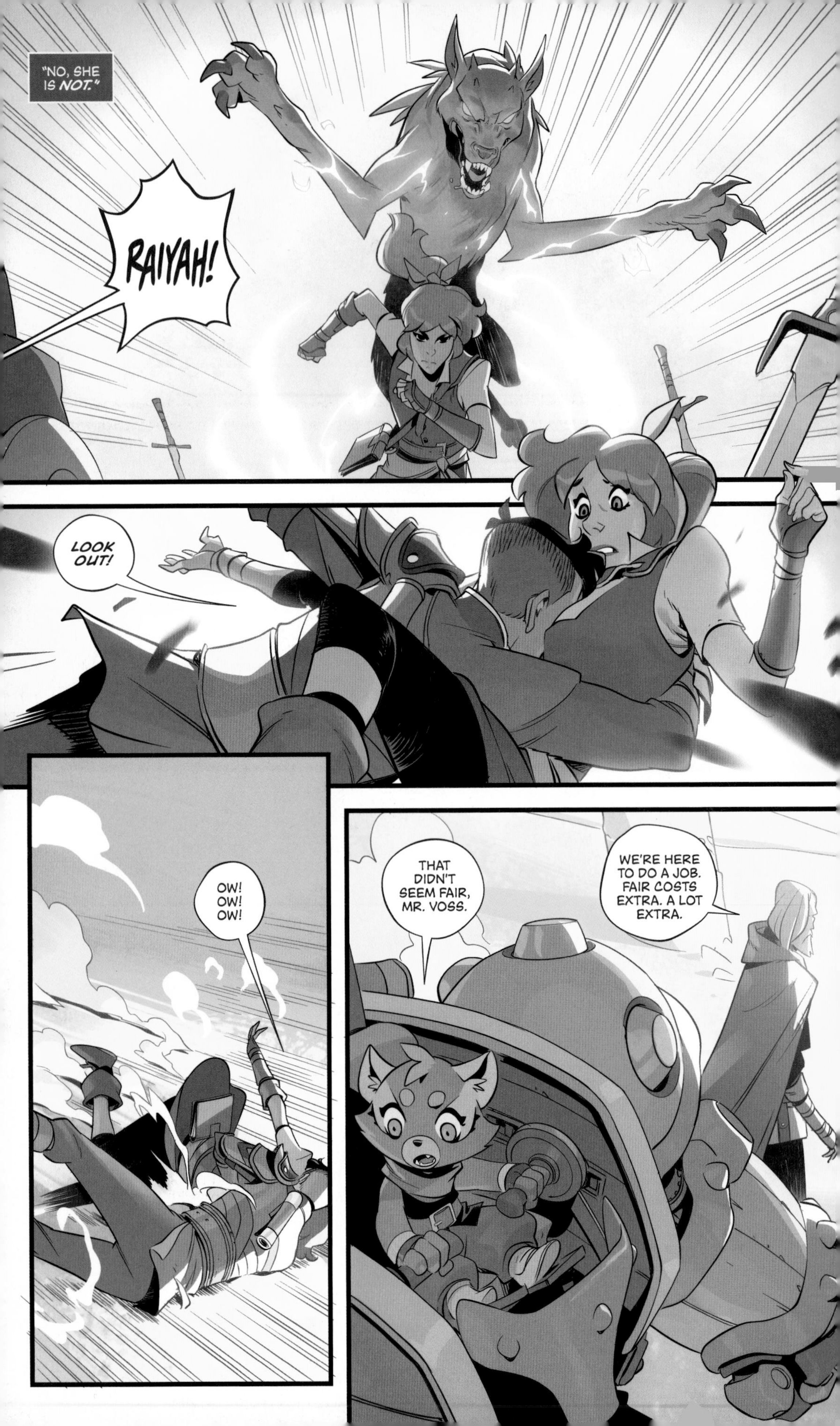
"NO, SHE IS *NOT.*"
RAIYAH!
LOOK OUT!
OW! OW! OW!
THAT DIDN'T SEEM FAIR, MR. VOSS.
WE'RE HERE TO DO A JOB. FAIR COSTS EXTRA. A LOT EXTRA.

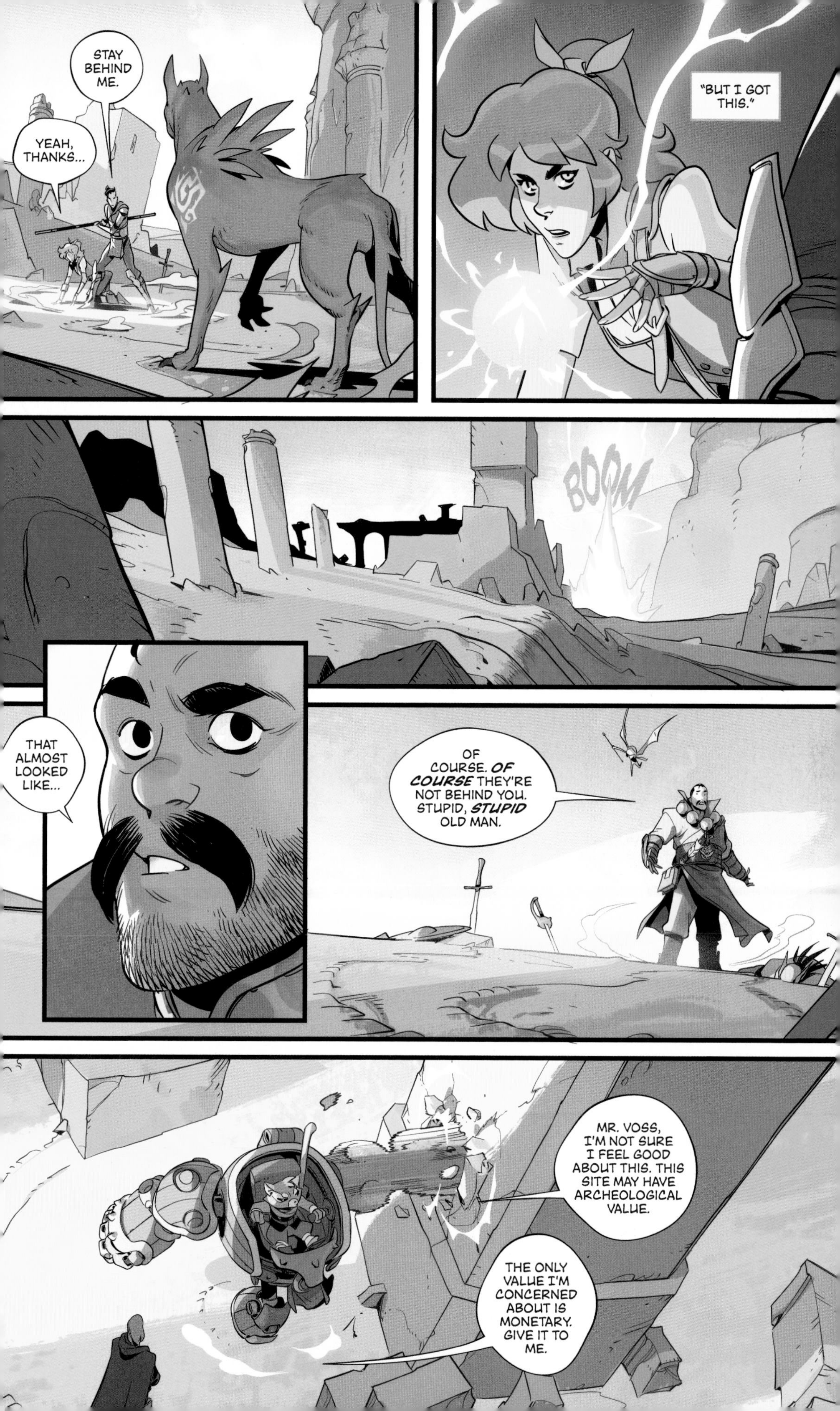

STAY BEHIND ME.
YEAH, THANKS...
"BUT I GOT THIS."
BOOM
THAT ALMOST LOOKED LIKE...
OF COURSE. OF COURSE THEY'RE NOT BEHIND YOU. STUPID, STUPID OLD MAN.
MR. VOSS, I'M NOT SURE I FEEL GOOD ABOUT THIS. THIS SITE MAY HAVE ARCHEOLOGICAL VALUE.
THE ONLY VALUE I'M CONCERNED ABOUT IS MONETARY. GIVE IT TO ME.

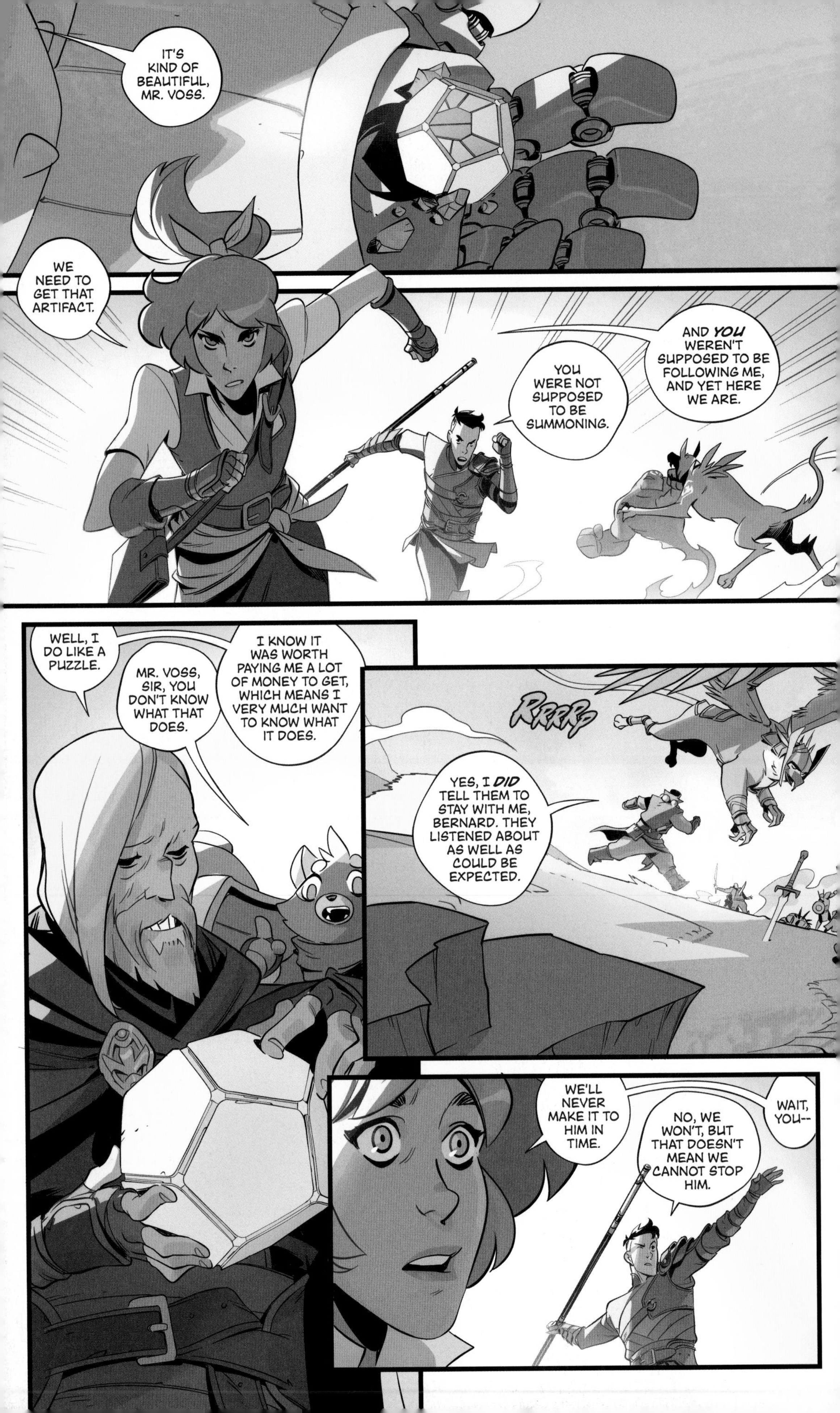

IT'S KIND OF BEAUTIFUL, MR. VOSS.
WE NEED TO GET THAT ARTIFACT.
YOU WERE NOT SUPPOSED TO BE SUMMONING.
AND *YOU* WEREN'T SUPPOSED TO BE FOLLOWING ME, AND YET HERE WE ARE.
WELL, I DO LIKE A PUZZLE.
MR. VOSS, SIR, YOU DON'T KNOW WHAT THAT DOES.
I KNOW IT WAS WORTH PAYING ME A LOT OF MONEY TO GET, WHICH MEANS I VERY MUCH WANT TO KNOW WHAT IT DOES.
RRRRP
YES, I *DID* TELL THEM TO STAY WITH ME, BERNARD. THEY LISTENED ABOUT AS WELL AS COULD BE EXPECTED.
WE'LL NEVER MAKE IT TO HIM IN TIME.
NO, WE WON'T, BUT THAT DOESN'T MEAN WE CANNOT STOP HIM.
WAIT, YOU--

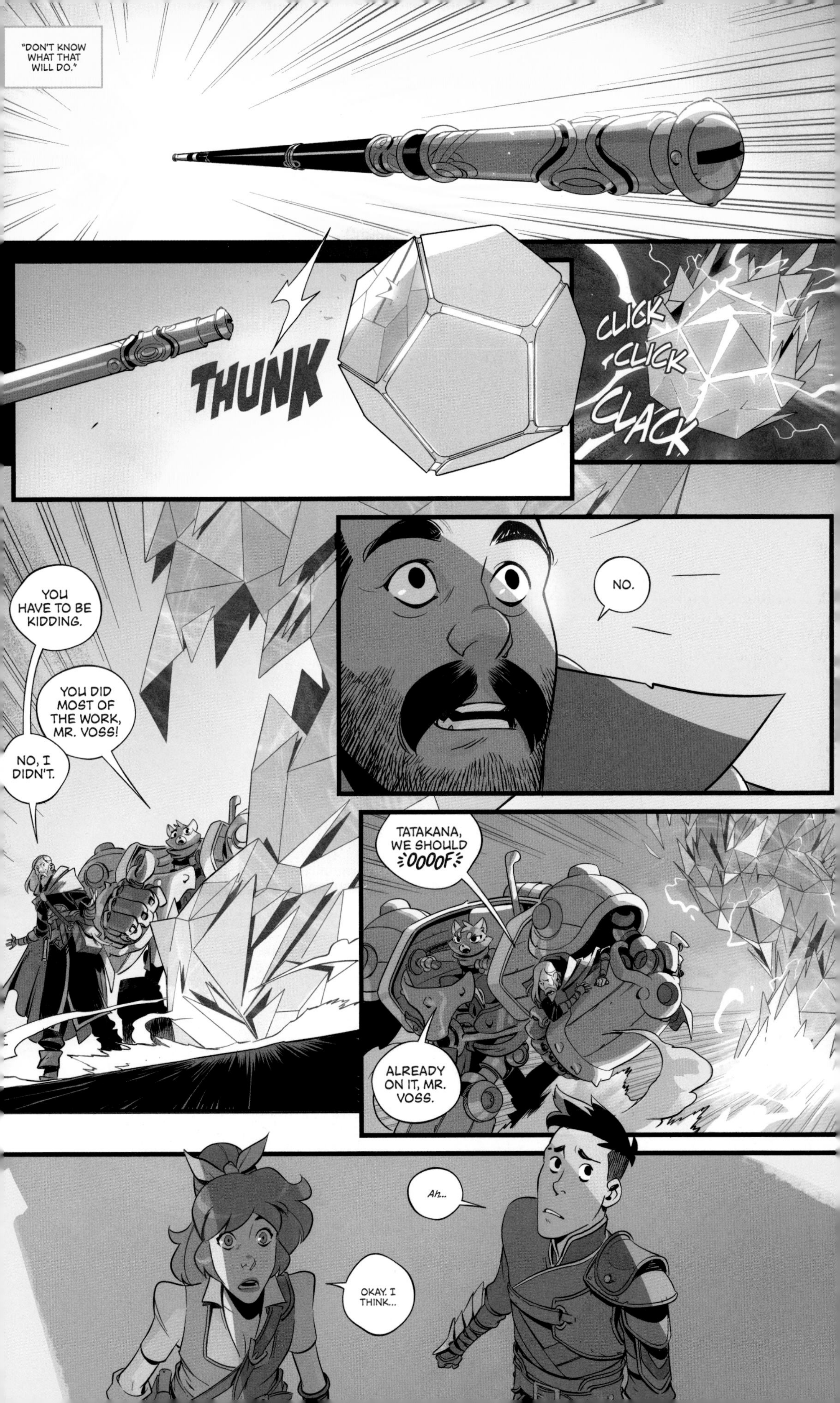
"DON'T KNOW WHAT THAT WILL DO."
THUNK
CLICK
CLICK
CLACK
YOU HAVE TO BE KIDDING.
NO.
YOU DID MOST OF THE WORK, MR. VOSS!
NO, I DIDN'T.
TATAKANA, WE SHOULD OOOOF
ALREADY ON IT, MR. VOSS.
Ah...
OKAY. I THINK...

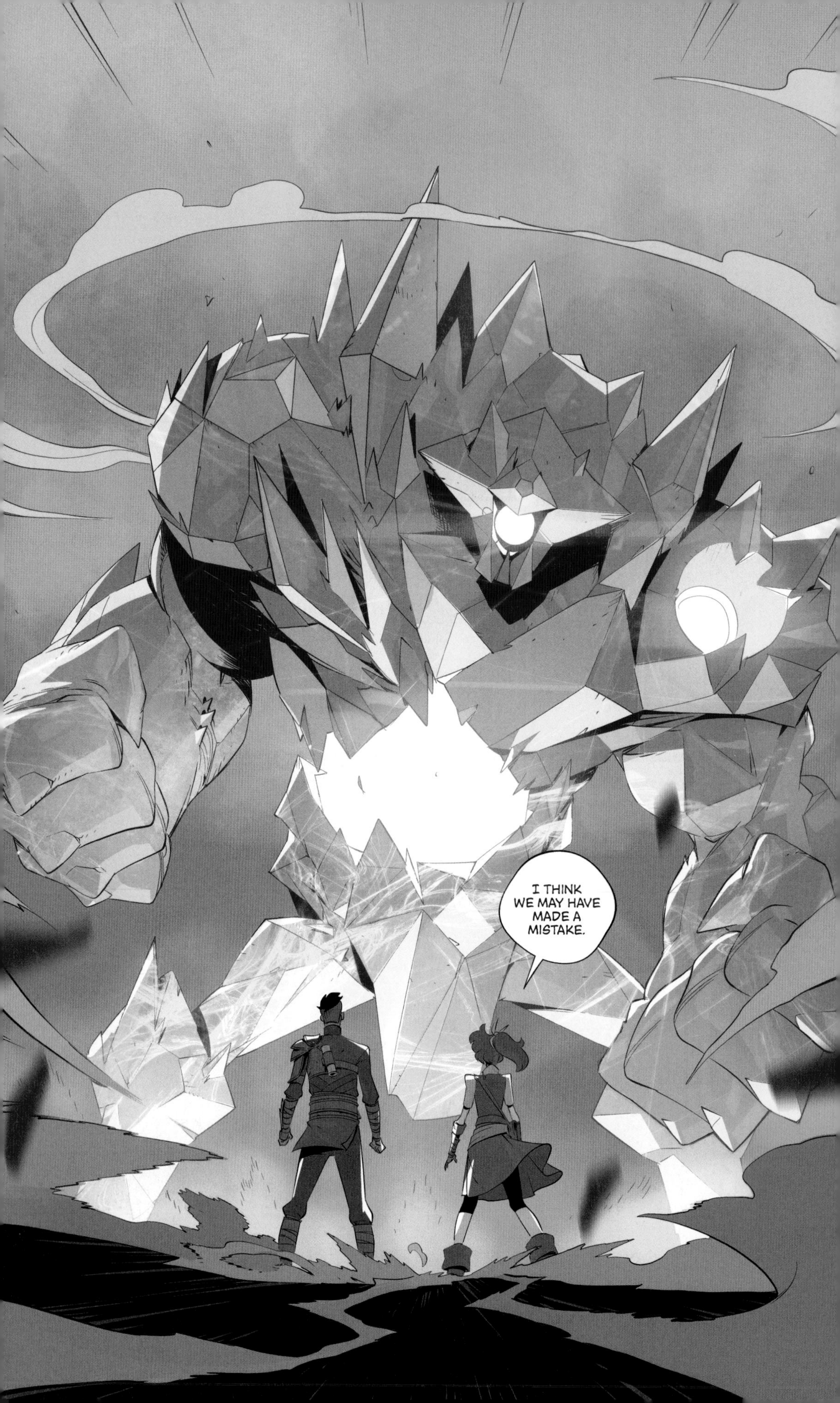
I THINK WE MAY HAVE MADE A MISTAKE.

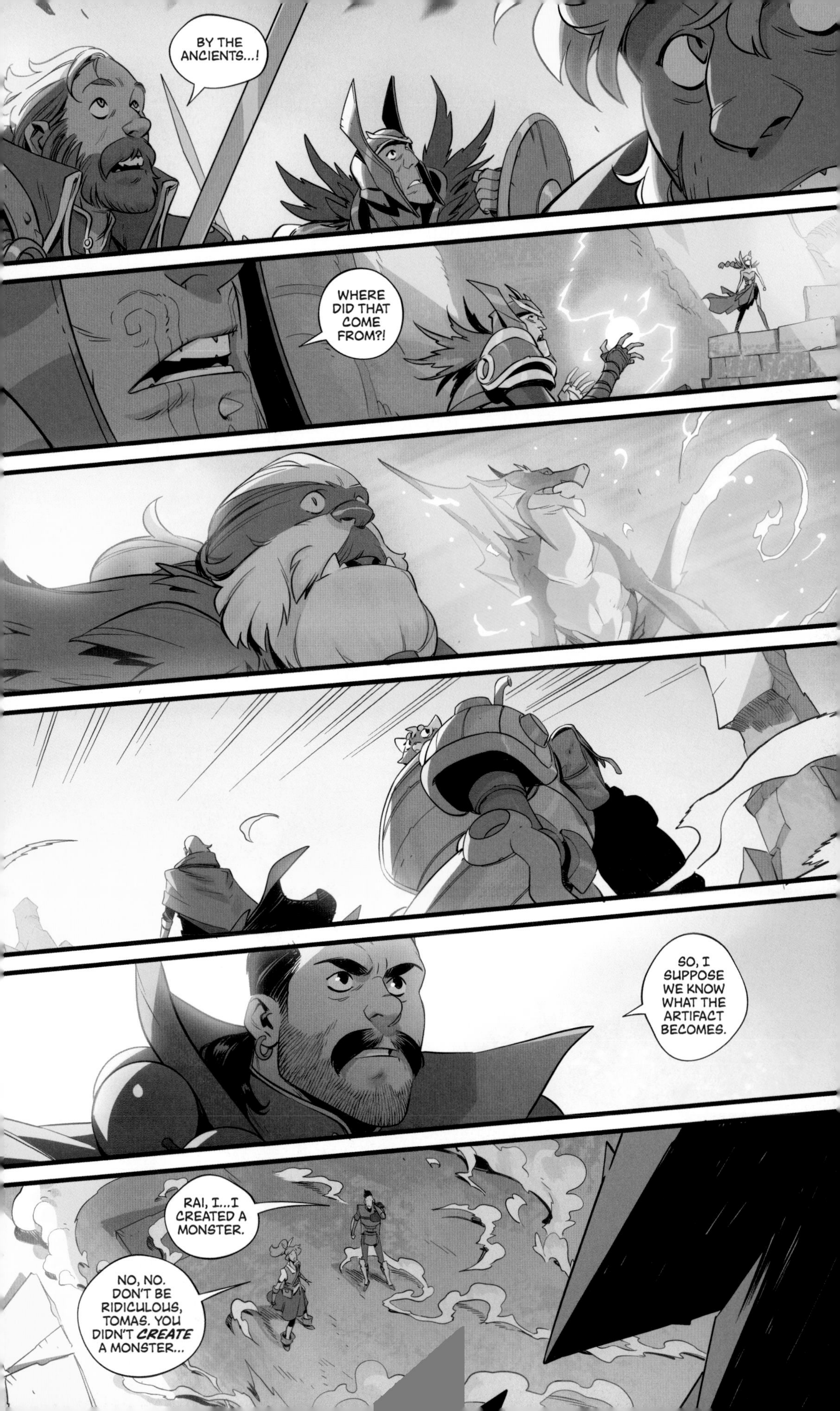
BY THE ANCIENTS...!
WHERE DID THAT COME FROM?!
SO, I SUPPOSE WE KNOW WHAT THE ARTIFACT BECOMES.
RAI, I...I CREATED A MONSTER.
NO, NO. DON'T BE RIDICULOUS, TOMAS. YOU DIDN'T *CREATE* A MONSTER...

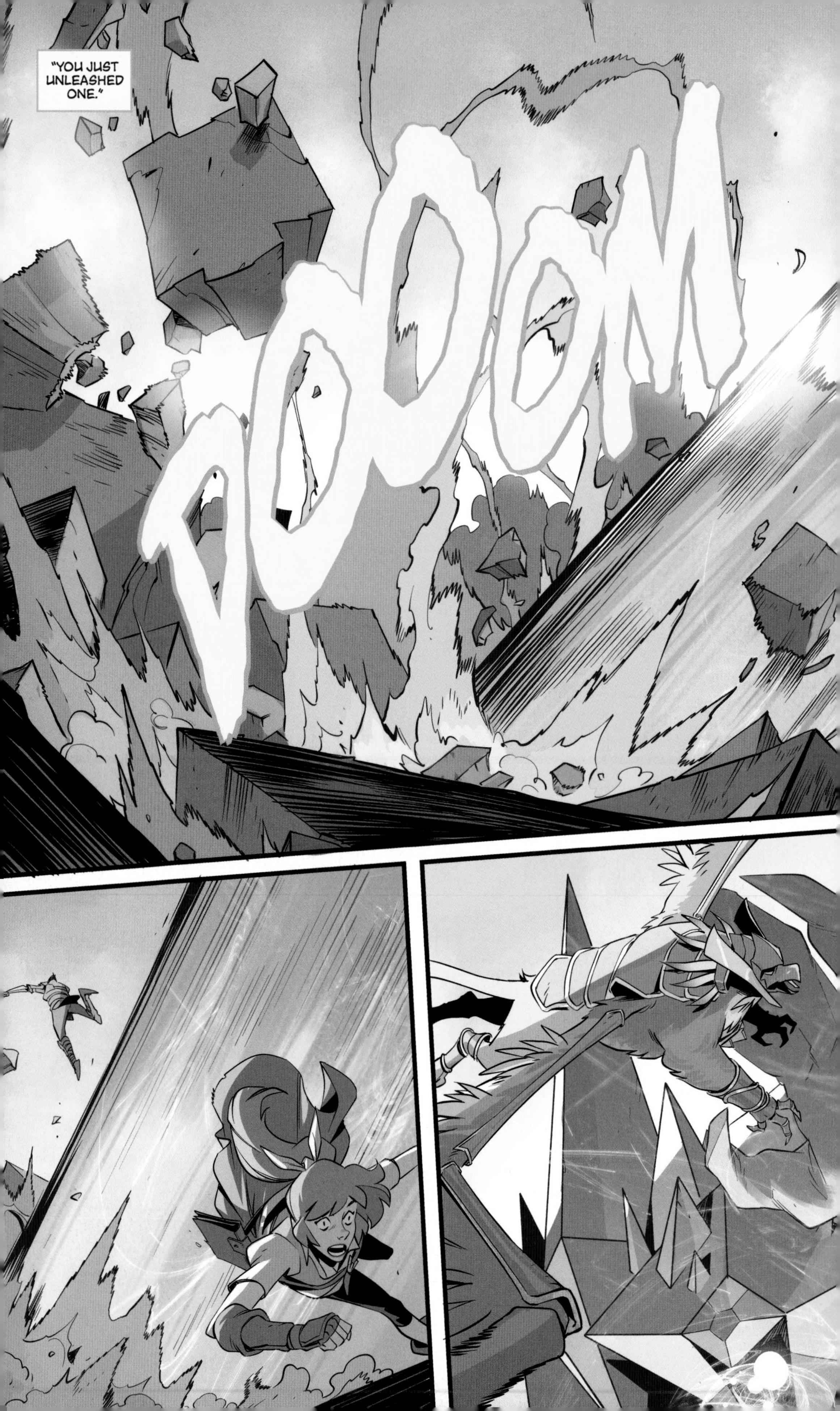
"YOU JUST UNLEASHED ONE."
DOOOM

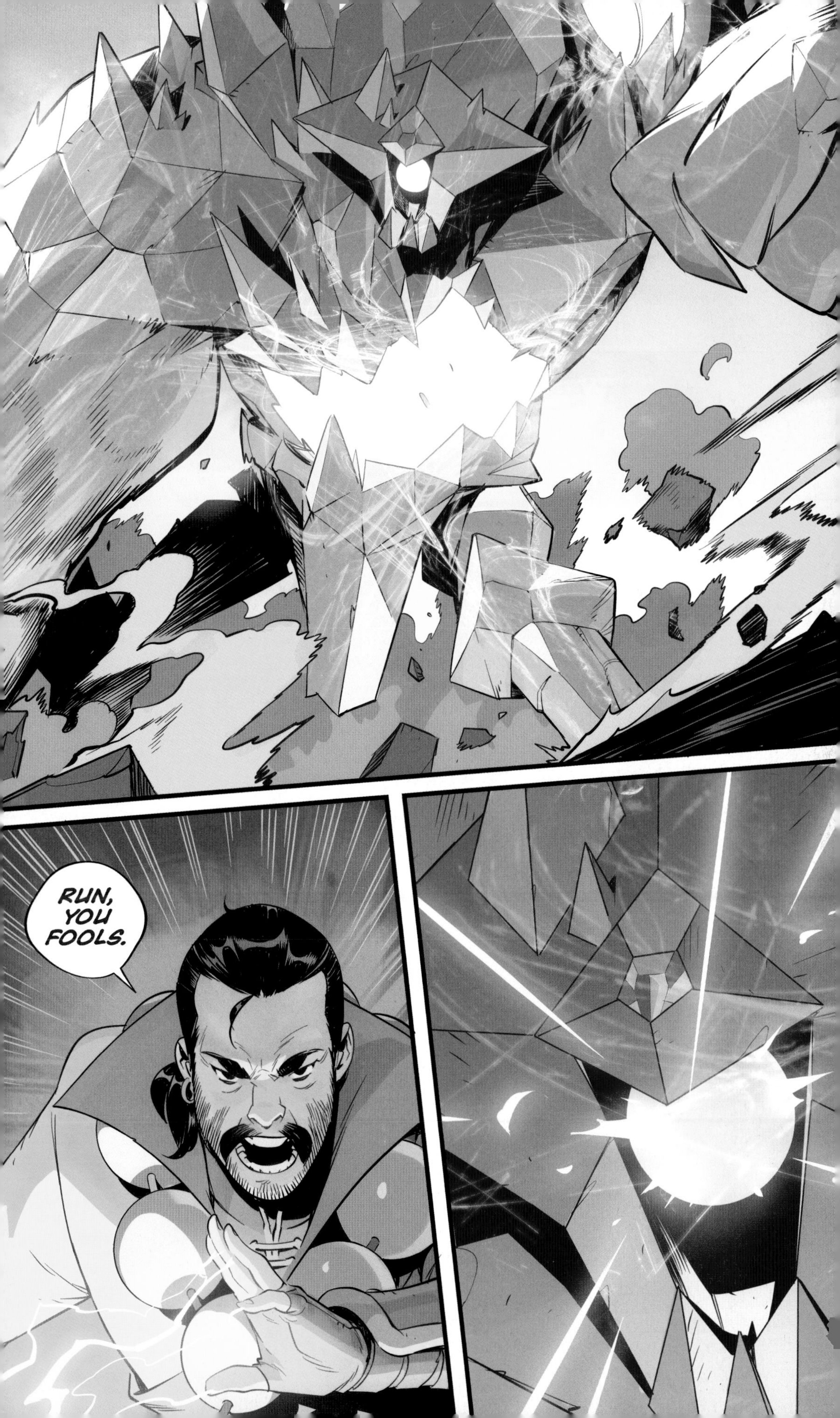
RUN, YOU FOOLS.

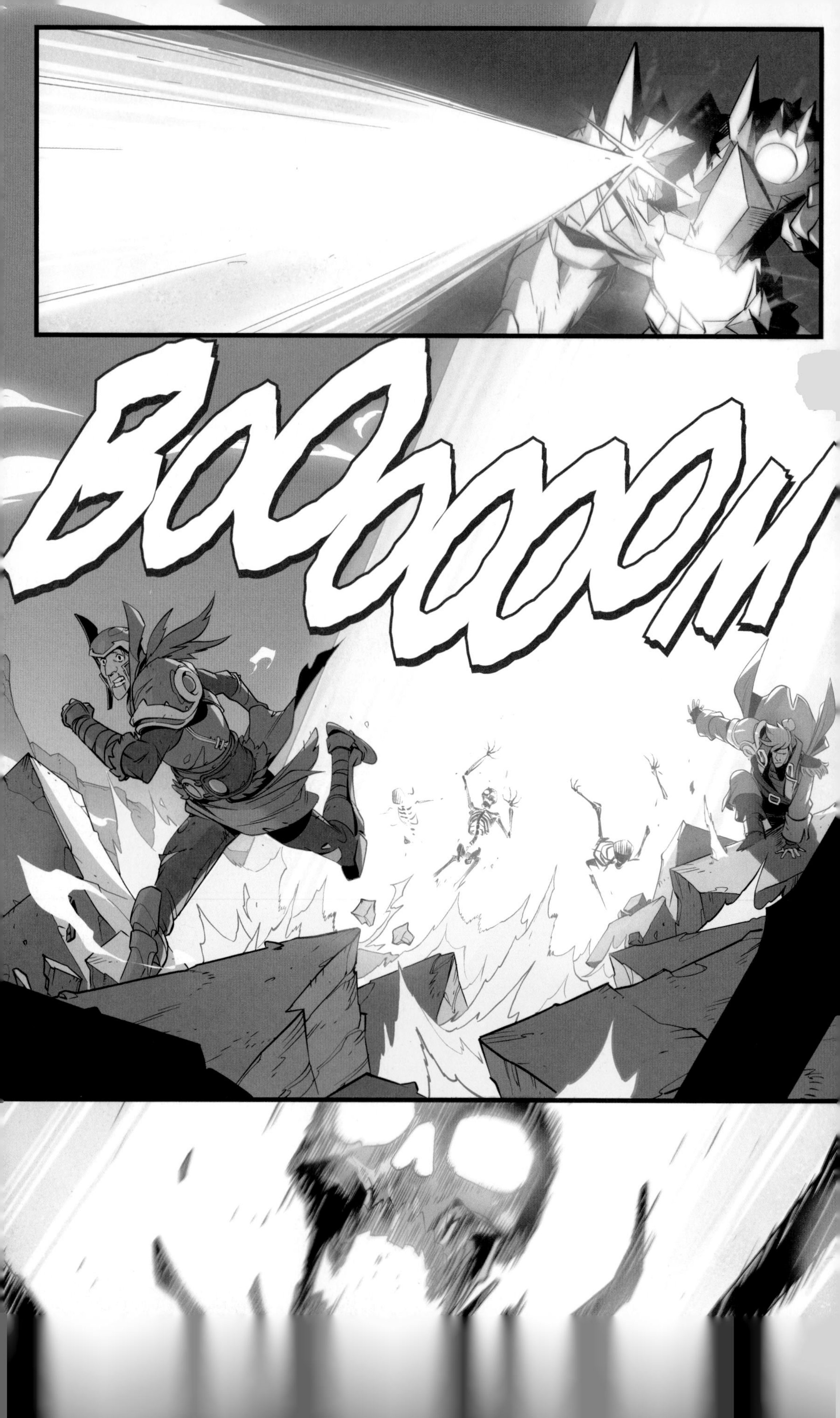
BOOOOOM

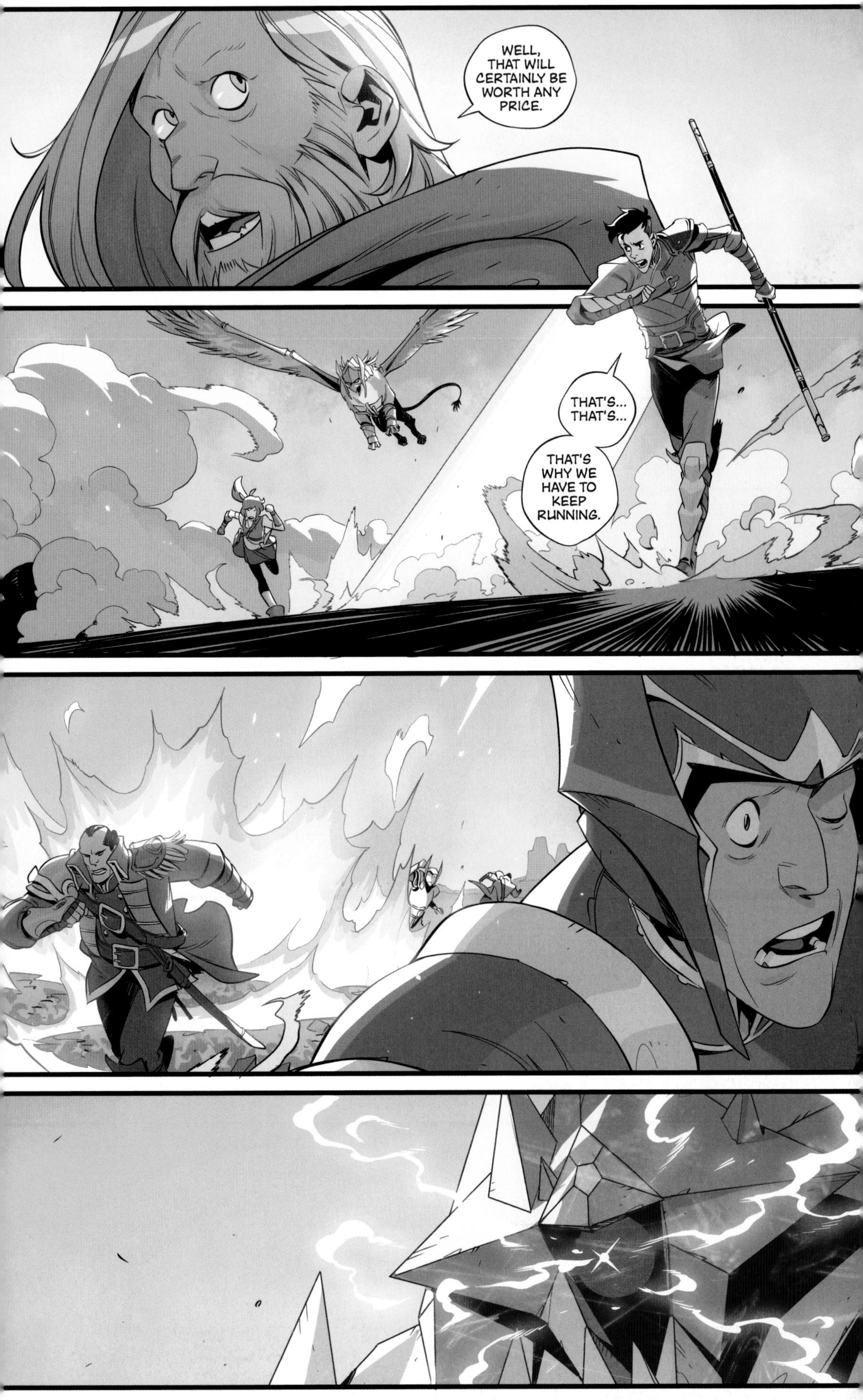
WELL, THAT WILL CERTAINLY BE WORTH ANY PRICE.
THAT'S... THAT'S...
THAT'S WHY WE HAVE TO KEEP RUNNING.

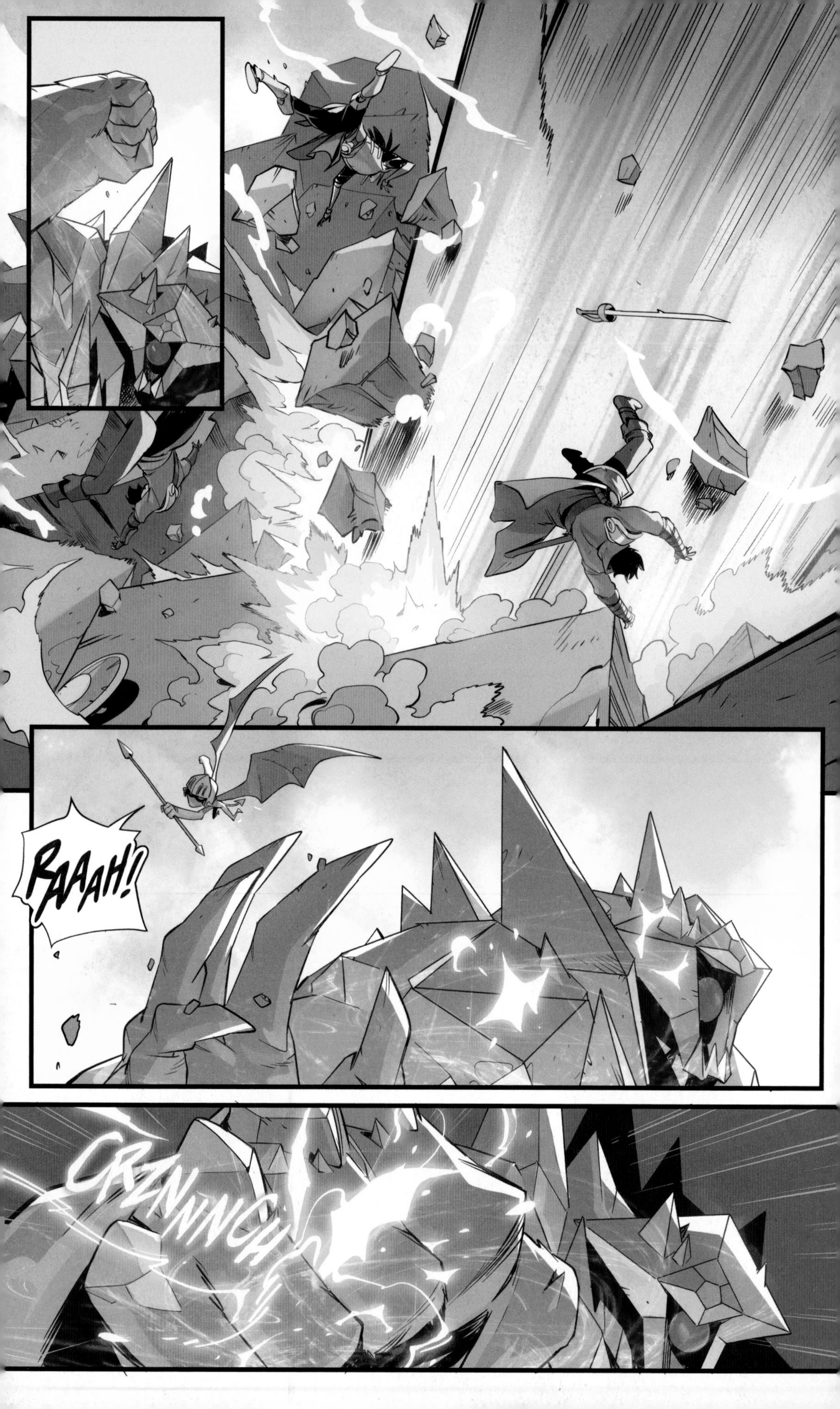
RAAAH!
CRZNNNCH!

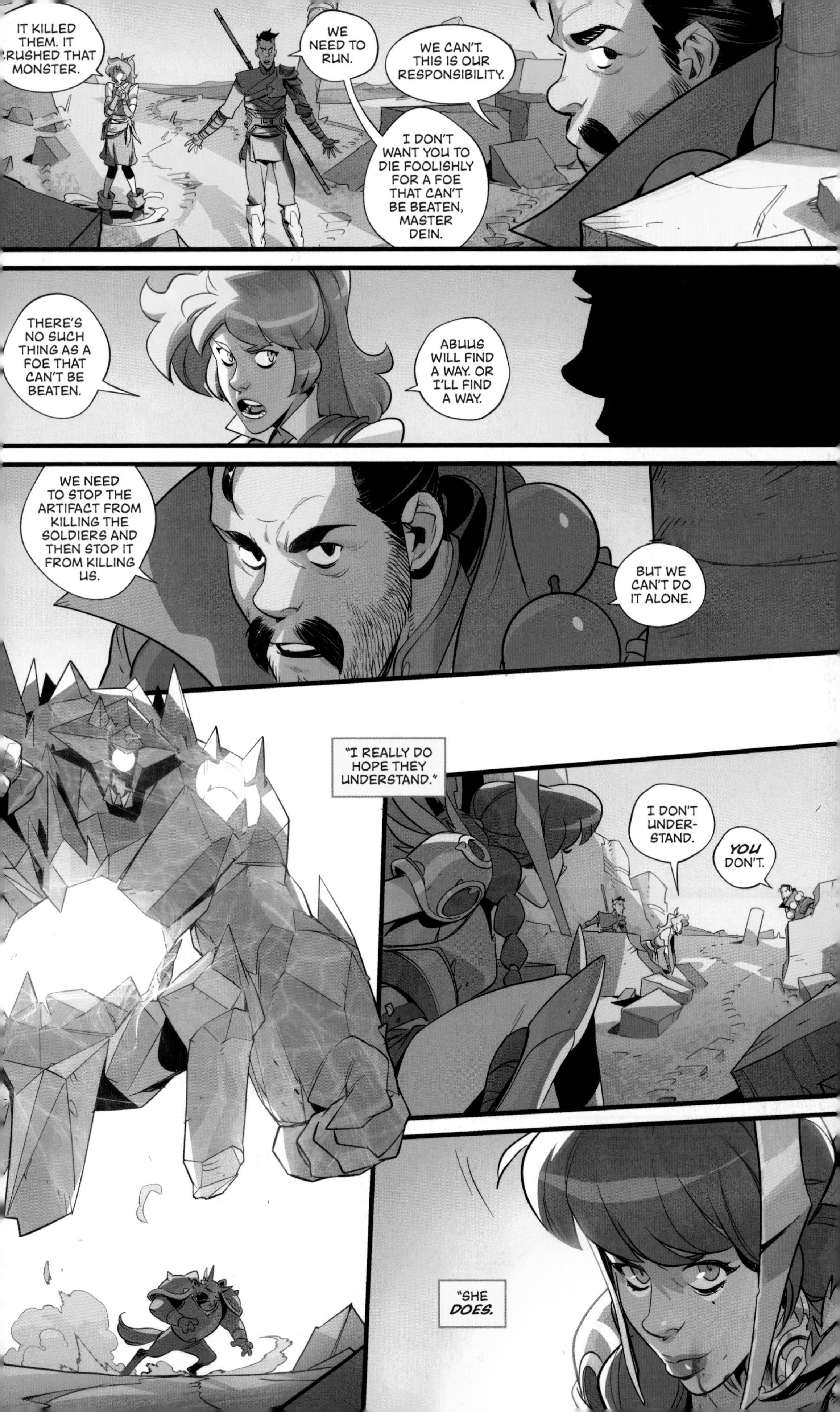
IT KILLED THEM. IT CRUSHED THAT MONSTER.
WE NEED TO RUN.
WE CAN'T. THIS IS OUR RESPONSIBILITY.
I DON'T WANT YOU TO DIE FOOLISHLY FOR A FOE THAT CAN'T BE BEATEN, MASTER DEIN.
THERE'S NO SUCH THING AS A FOE THAT CAN'T BE BEATEN.
ABUUS WILL FIND A WAY. OR I'LL FIND A WAY.
WE NEED TO STOP THE ARTIFACT FROM KILLING THE SOLDIERS AND THEN STOP IT FROM KILLING US.
BUT WE CAN'T DO IT ALONE.
"I REALLY DO HOPE THEY UNDERSTAND."
I DON'T UNDER-STAND.
YOU DON'T.
"SHE *DOES.*

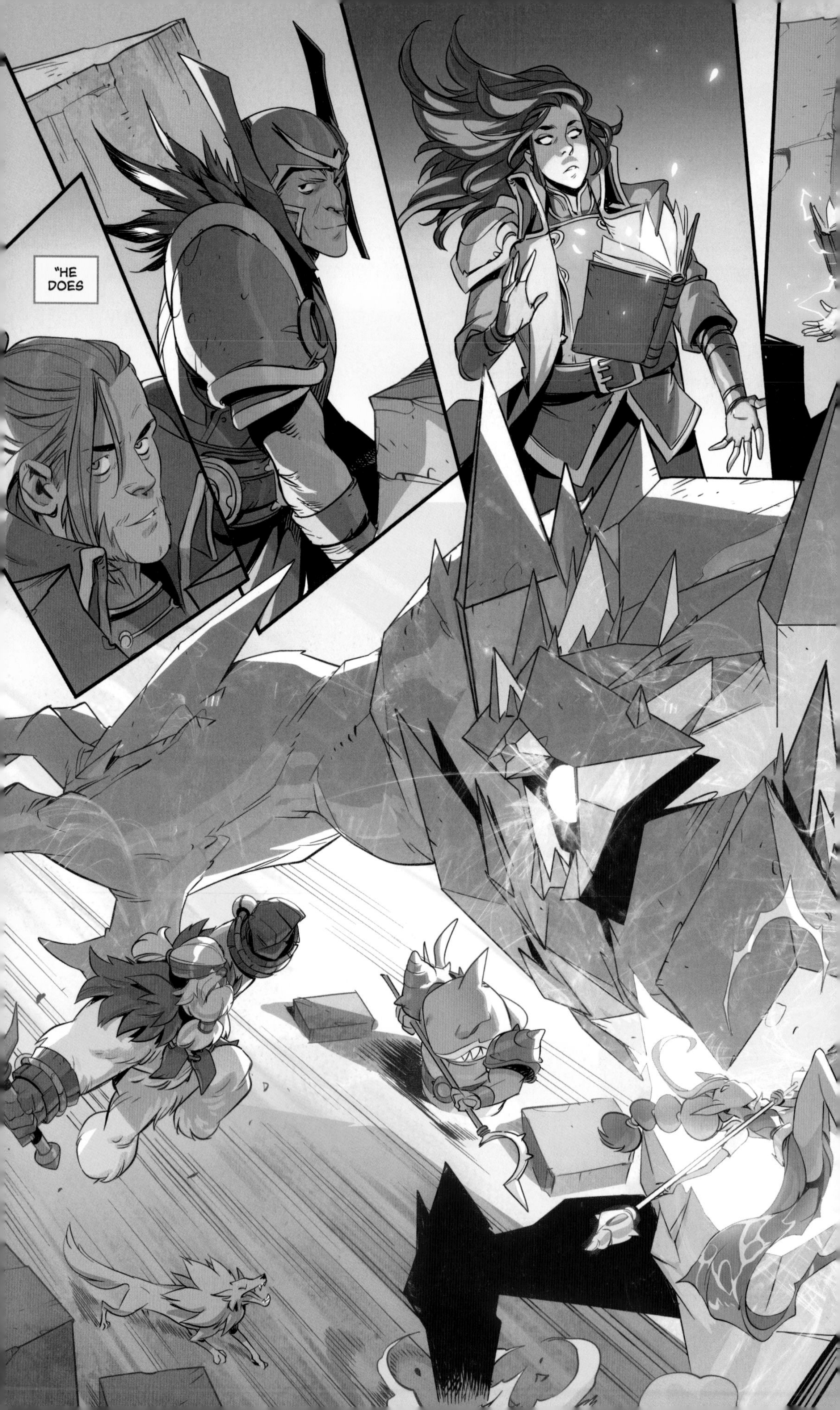
"HE DOES

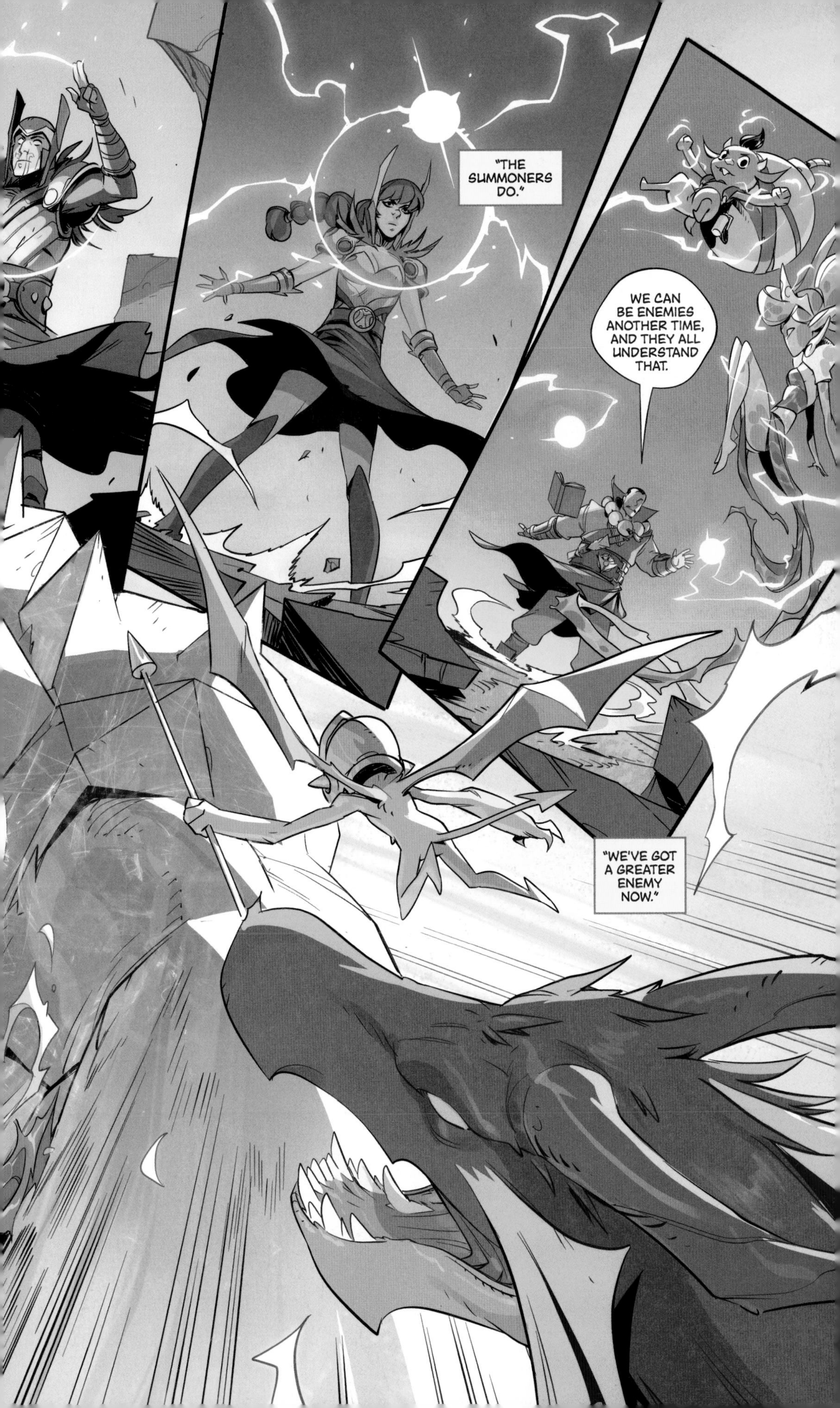
"THE SUMMONERS DO."
WE CAN BE ENEMIES ANOTHER TIME, AND THEY ALL UNDERSTAND THAT.
"WE'VE GOT A GREATER ENEMY NOW."

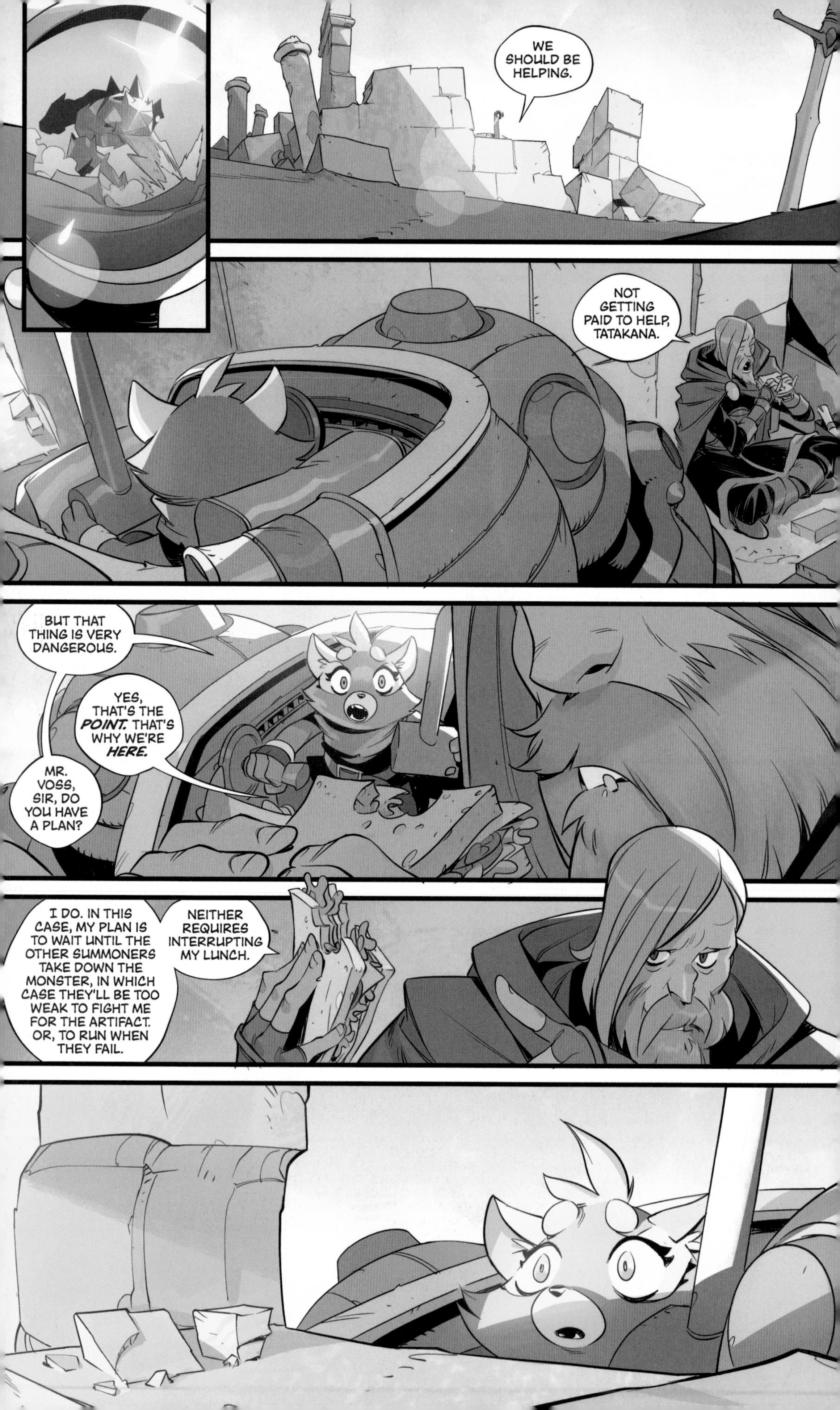
WE SHOULD BE HELPING.
NOT GETTING PAID TO HELP, TATAKANA.
BUT THAT THING IS VERY DANGEROUS.
YES, THAT'S THE *POINT.* THAT'S WHY WE'RE *HERE.*
MR. VOSS, SIR, DO YOU HAVE A PLAN?
I DO. IN THIS CASE, MY PLAN IS TO WAIT UNTIL THE OTHER SUMMONERS TAKE DOWN THE MONSTER, IN WHICH CASE THEY'LL BE TOO WEAK TO FIGHT ME FOR THE ARTIFACT. OR, TO RUN WHEN THEY FAIL.
NEITHER REQUIRES INTERRUPTING MY LUNCH.

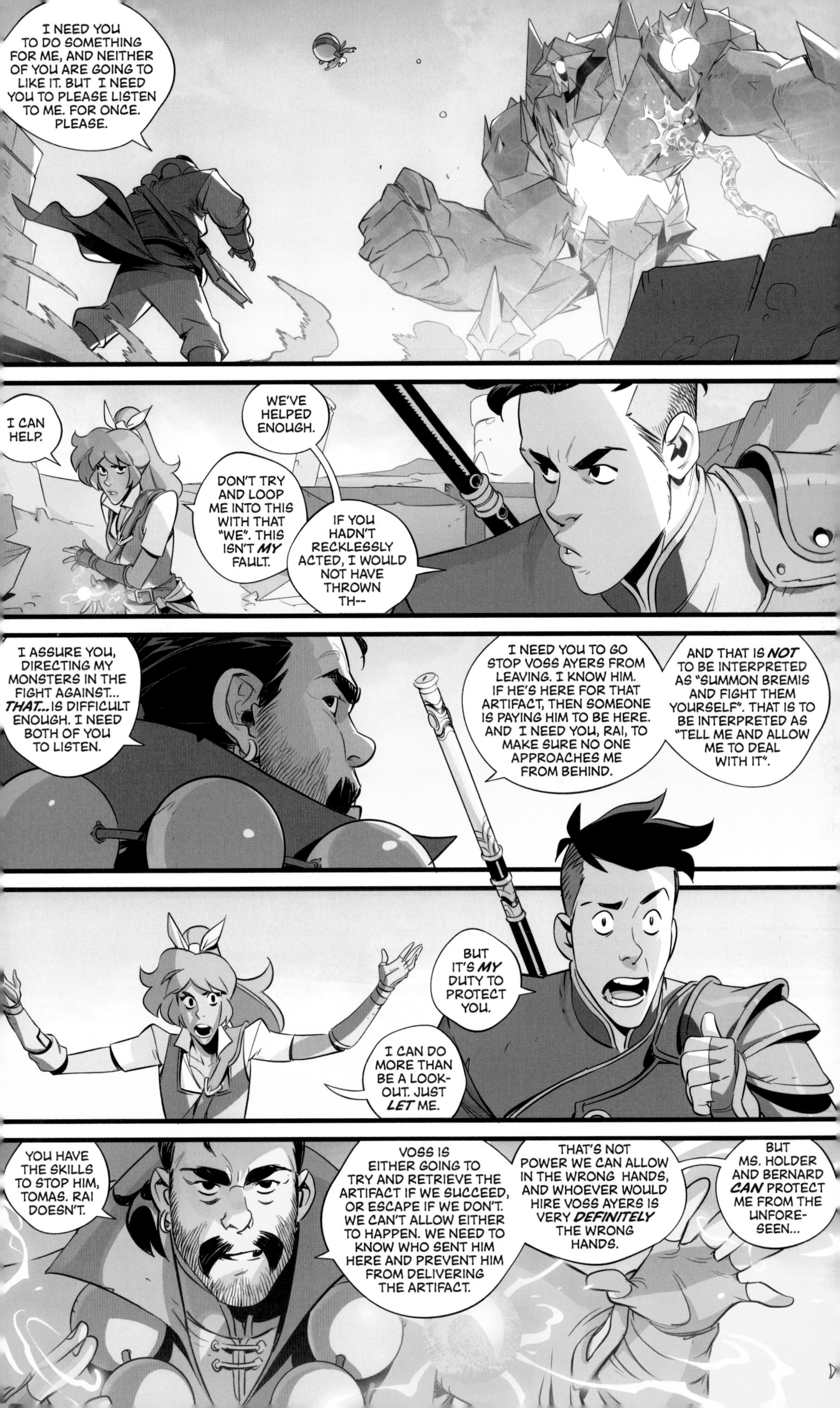
I NEED YOU TO DO SOMETHING FOR ME, AND NEITHER OF YOU ARE GOING TO LIKE IT. BUT I NEED YOU TO PLEASE LISTEN TO ME. FOR ONCE. PLEASE.
I CAN HELP.
WE'VE HELPED ENOUGH.
DON'T TRY AND LOOP ME INTO THIS WITH THAT "WE". THIS ISN'T *MY* FAULT.
IF YOU HADN'T RECKLESSLY ACTED, I WOULD NOT HAVE THROWN TH--
I ASSURE YOU, DIRECTING MY MONSTERS IN THE FIGHT AGAINST... *THAT...* IS DIFFICULT ENOUGH. I NEED BOTH OF YOU TO LISTEN.
I NEED YOU TO GO STOP VOSS AYERS FROM LEAVING. I KNOW HIM. IF HE'S HERE FOR THAT ARTIFACT, THEN SOMEONE IS PAYING HIM TO BE HERE. AND I NEED YOU, RAI, TO MAKE SURE NO ONE APPROACHES ME FROM BEHIND.
AND THAT IS *NOT* TO BE INTERPRETED AS "SUMMON BREMIS AND FIGHT THEM YOURSELF". THAT IS TO BE INTERPRETED AS "TELL ME AND ALLOW ME TO DEAL WITH IT".
BUT IT'S *MY* DUTY TO PROTECT YOU.
I CAN DO MORE THAN BE A LOOK-OUT. JUST *LET* ME.
YOU HAVE THE SKILLS TO STOP HIM, TOMAS. RAI DOESN'T.
VOSS IS EITHER GOING TO TRY AND RETRIEVE THE ARTIFACT IF WE SUCCEED, OR ESCAPE IF WE DON'T. WE CAN'T ALLOW EITHER TO HAPPEN. WE NEED TO KNOW WHO SENT HIM HERE AND PREVENT HIM FROM DELIVERING THE ARTIFACT.
THAT'S NOT POWER WE CAN ALLOW IN THE WRONG HANDS, AND WHOEVER WOULD HIRE VOSS AYERS IS VERY *DEFINITELY* THE WRONG HANDS.
BUT MS. HOLDER AND BERNARD *CAN* PROTECT ME FROM THE UNFORE-SEEN...

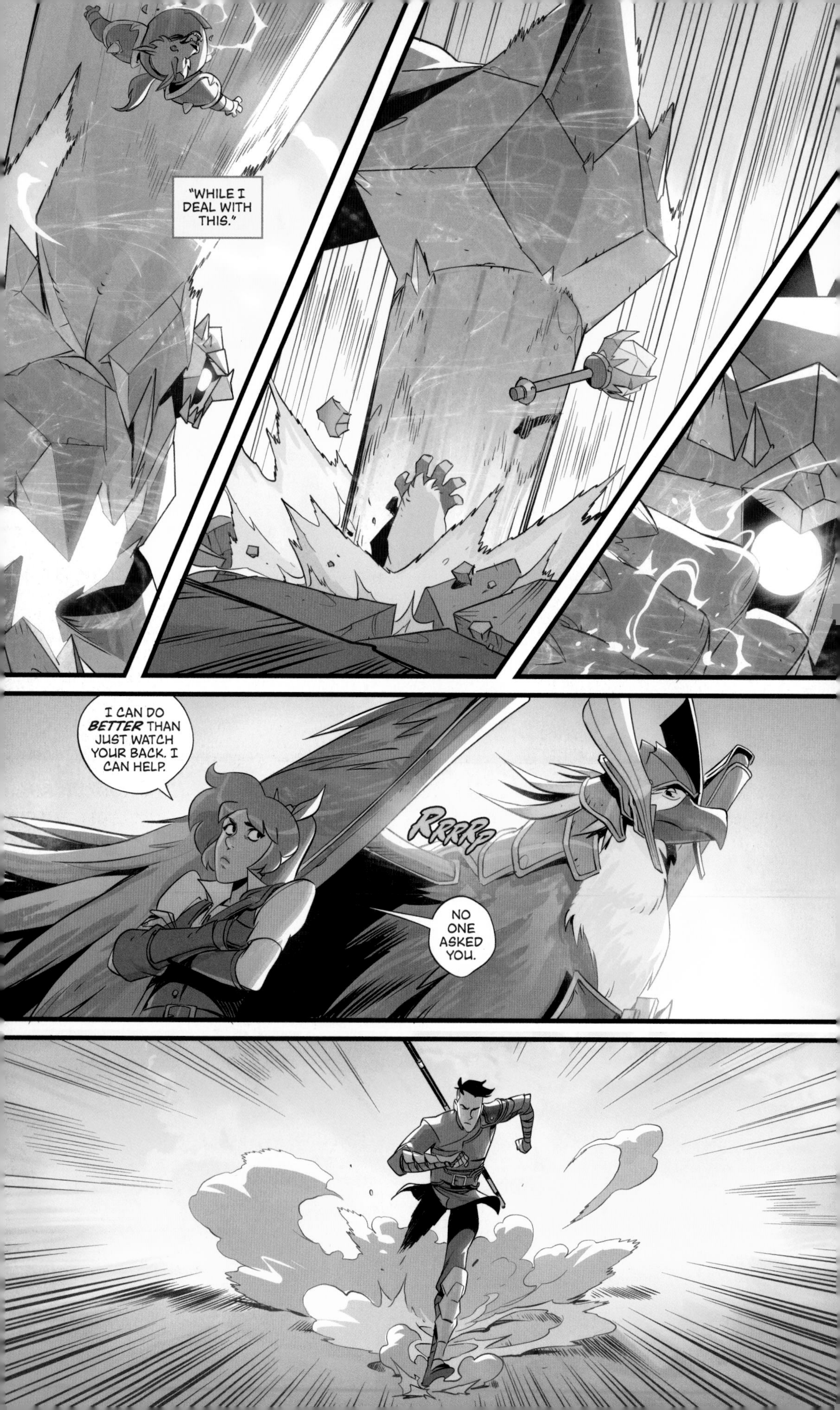
"WHILE I DEAL WITH THIS."
I CAN DO BETTER THAN JUST WATCH YOUR BACK. I CAN HELP.
RRRRP
NO ONE ASKED YOU.

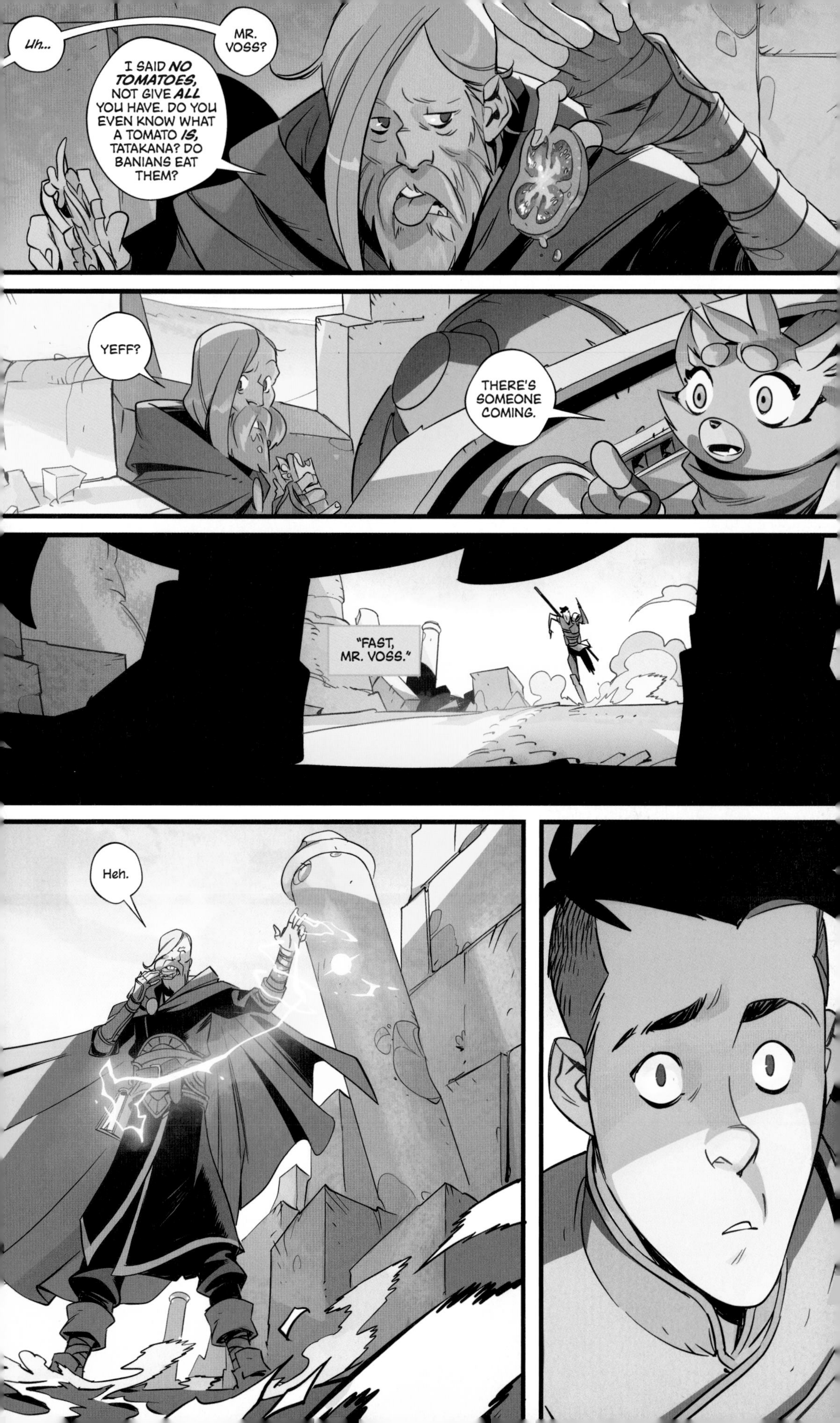
Uh...
Mr. Voss?
I said *no tomatoes,* not give *all* you have. Do you even know what a tomato *is,* Tatakana? Do Banians eat them?
Yeff?
There's someone coming.
"Fast, Mr. Voss."
Heh.

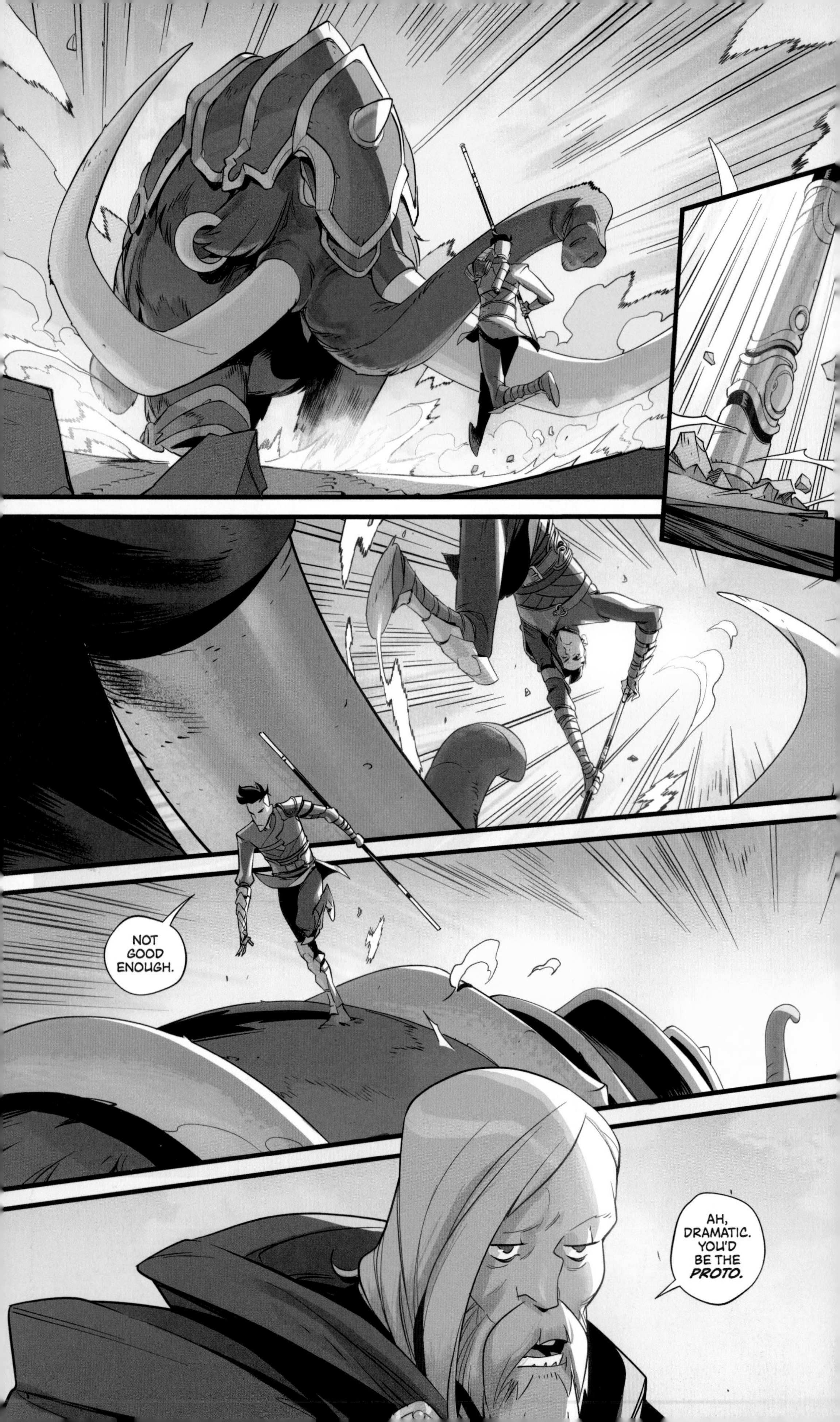
NOT GOOD ENOUGH.
AH, DRAMATIC. YOU'D BE THE *PROTO.*

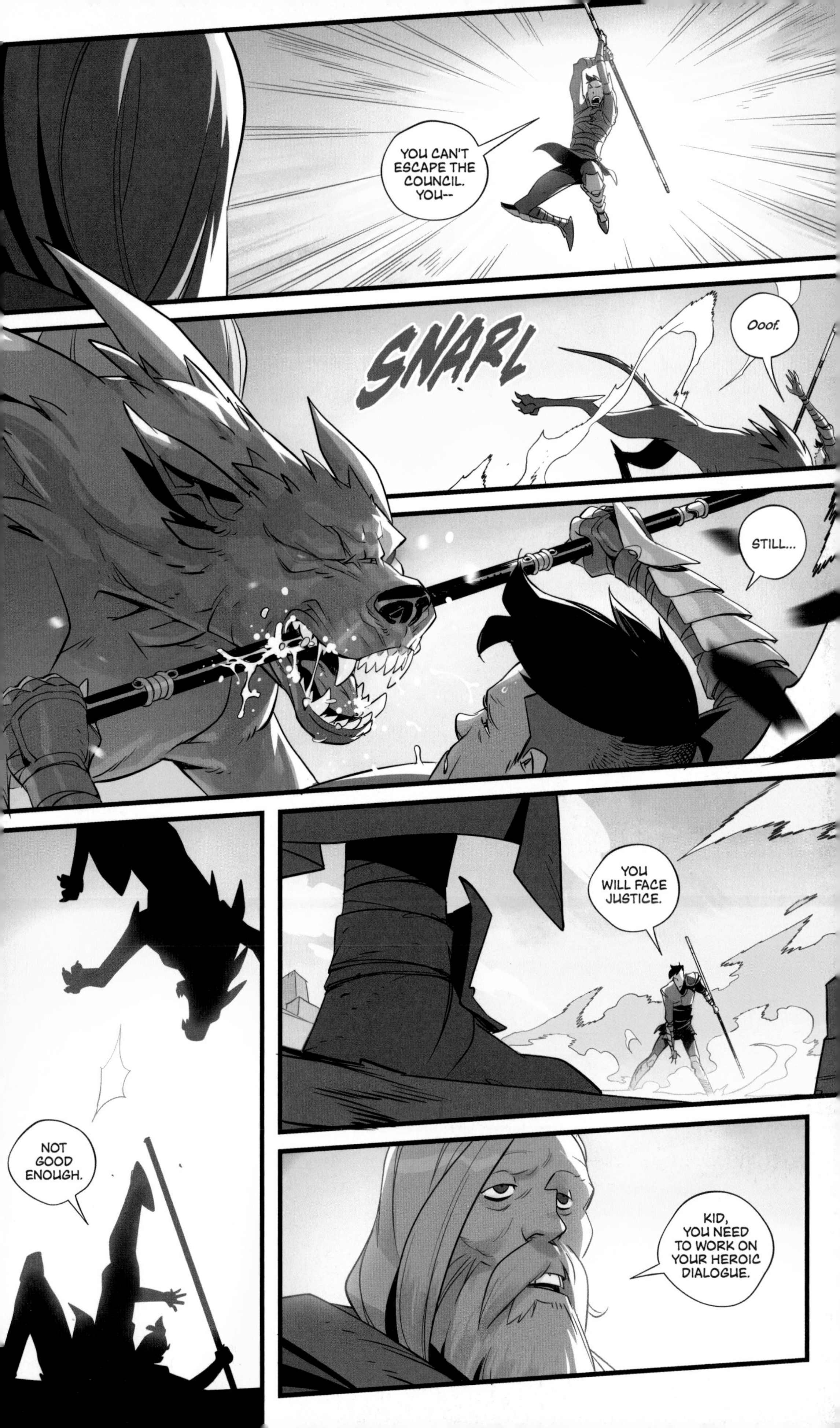
YOU CAN'T ESCAPE THE COUNCIL. YOU--
SNARL
Ooof.
STILL...
YOU WILL FACE JUSTICE.
NOT GOOD ENOUGH.
KID, YOU NEED TO WORK ON YOUR HEROIC DIALOGUE.

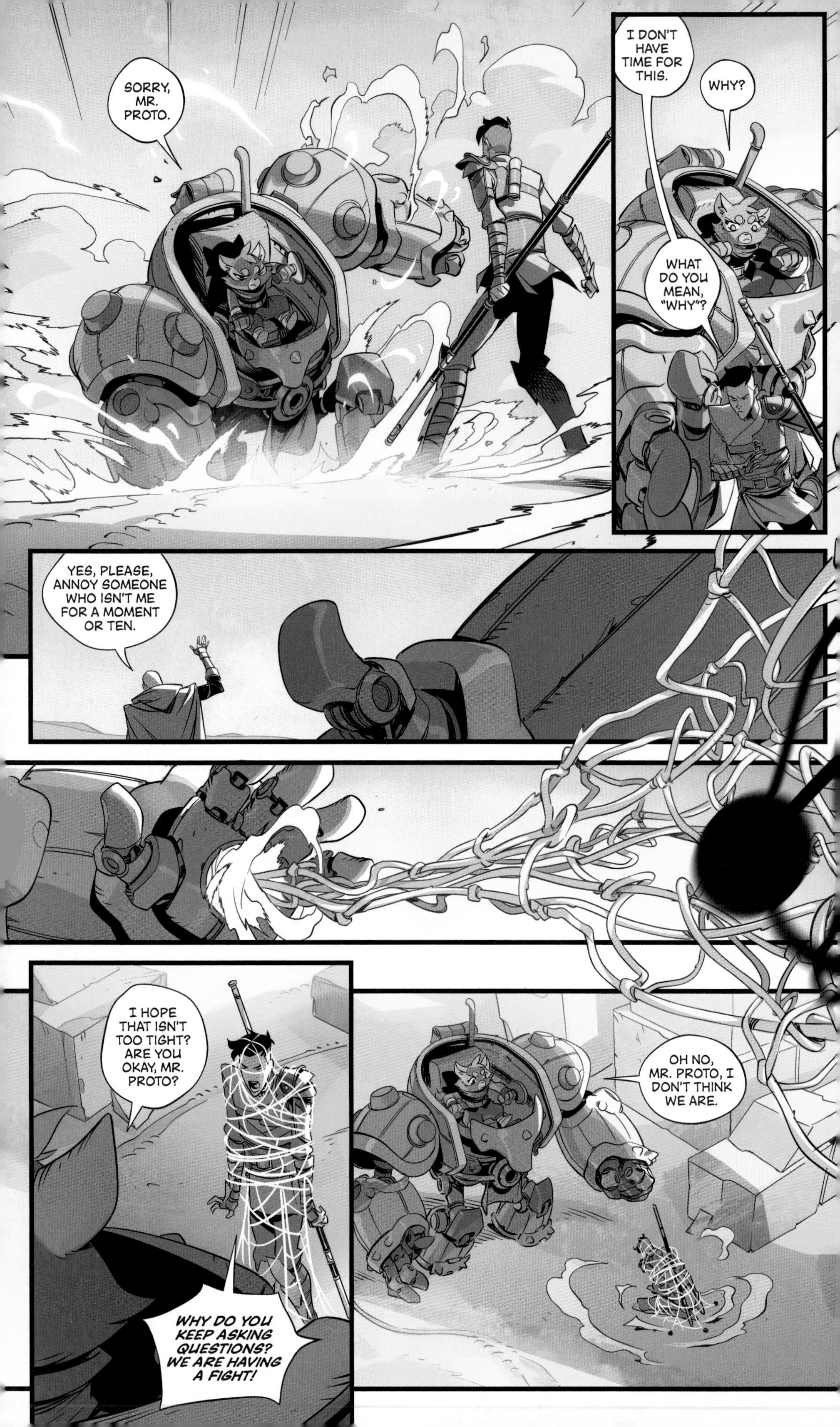
SORRY, MR. PROTO.
I DON'T HAVE TIME FOR THIS.
WHY?
WHAT DO YOU MEAN, "WHY"?
YES, PLEASE, ANNOY SOMEONE WHO ISN'T ME FOR A MOMENT OR TEN.
I HOPE THAT ISN'T TOO TIGHT? ARE YOU OKAY, MR. PROTO?
WHY DO YOU KEEP ASKING QUESTIONS? WE ARE HAVING A FIGHT!
OH NO, MR. PROTO, I DON'T THINK WE ARE.

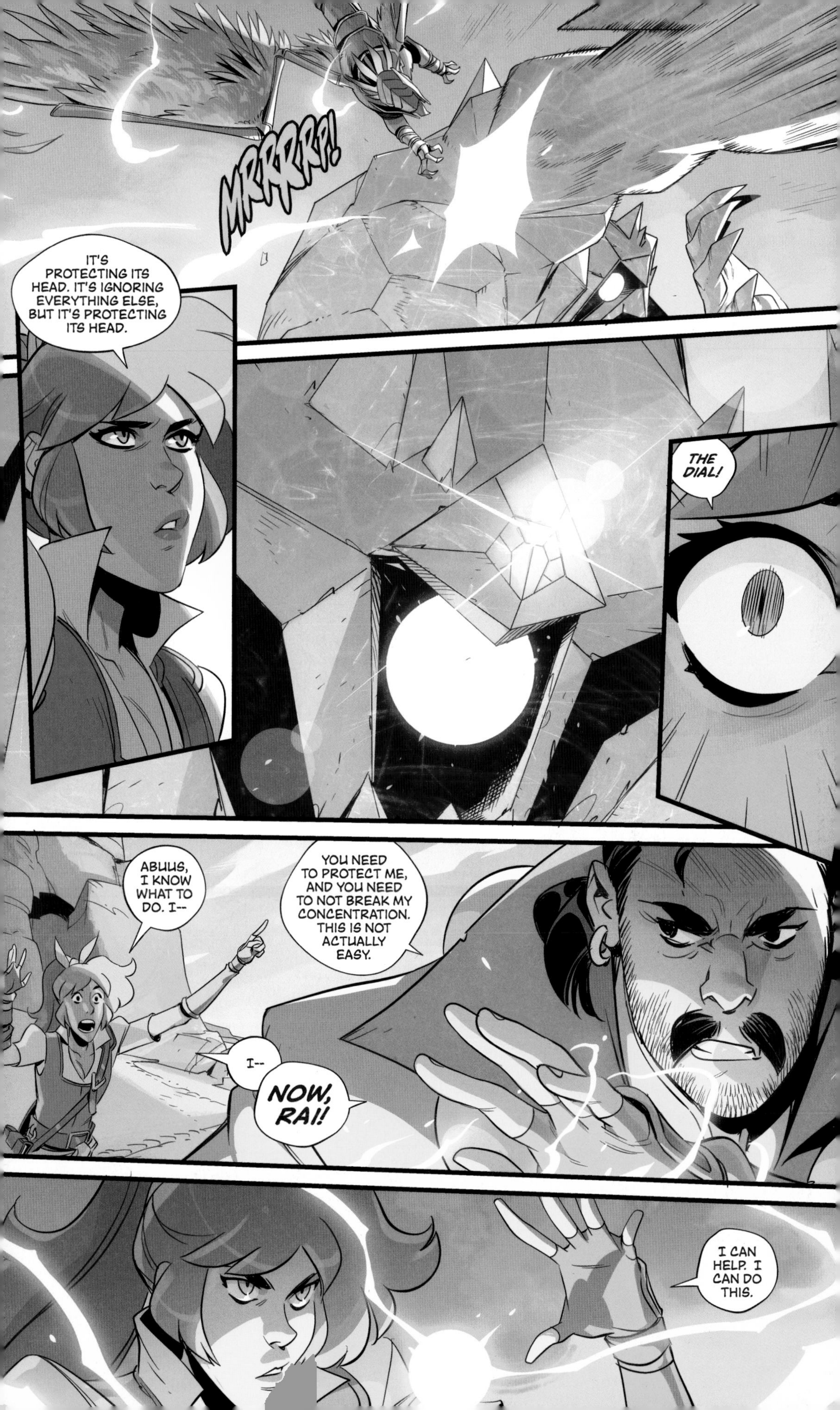
MRRRRP!
IT'S PROTECTING ITS HEAD. IT'S IGNORING EVERYTHING ELSE, BUT IT'S PROTECTING ITS HEAD.
THE DIAL!
ABULIS, I KNOW WHAT TO DO. I--
YOU NEED TO PROTECT ME, AND YOU NEED TO NOT BREAK MY CONCENTRATION. THIS IS NOT ACTUALLY EASY.
I--
NOW, RAI!
I CAN HELP. I CAN DO THIS.

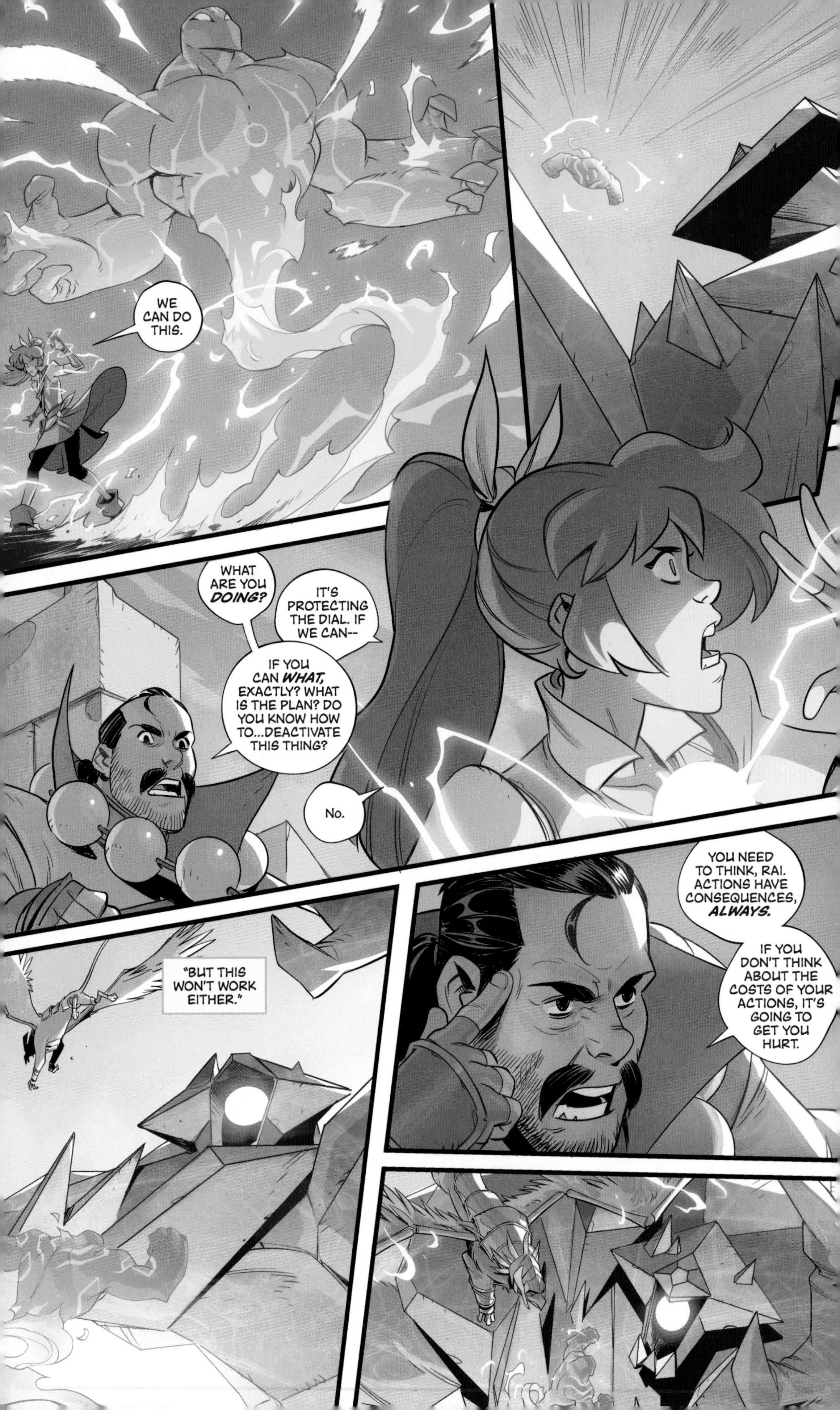
WE CAN DO THIS.
WHAT ARE YOU DOING?
IT'S PROTECTING THE DIAL. IF WE CAN--
IF YOU CAN WHAT, EXACTLY? WHAT IS THE PLAN? DO YOU KNOW HOW TO...DEACTIVATE THIS THING?
No.
"BUT THIS WON'T WORK EITHER."
YOU NEED TO THINK, RAI. ACTIONS HAVE CONSEQUENCES, ALWAYS.
IF YOU DON'T THINK ABOUT THE COSTS OF YOUR ACTIONS, IT'S GOING TO GET YOU HURT.

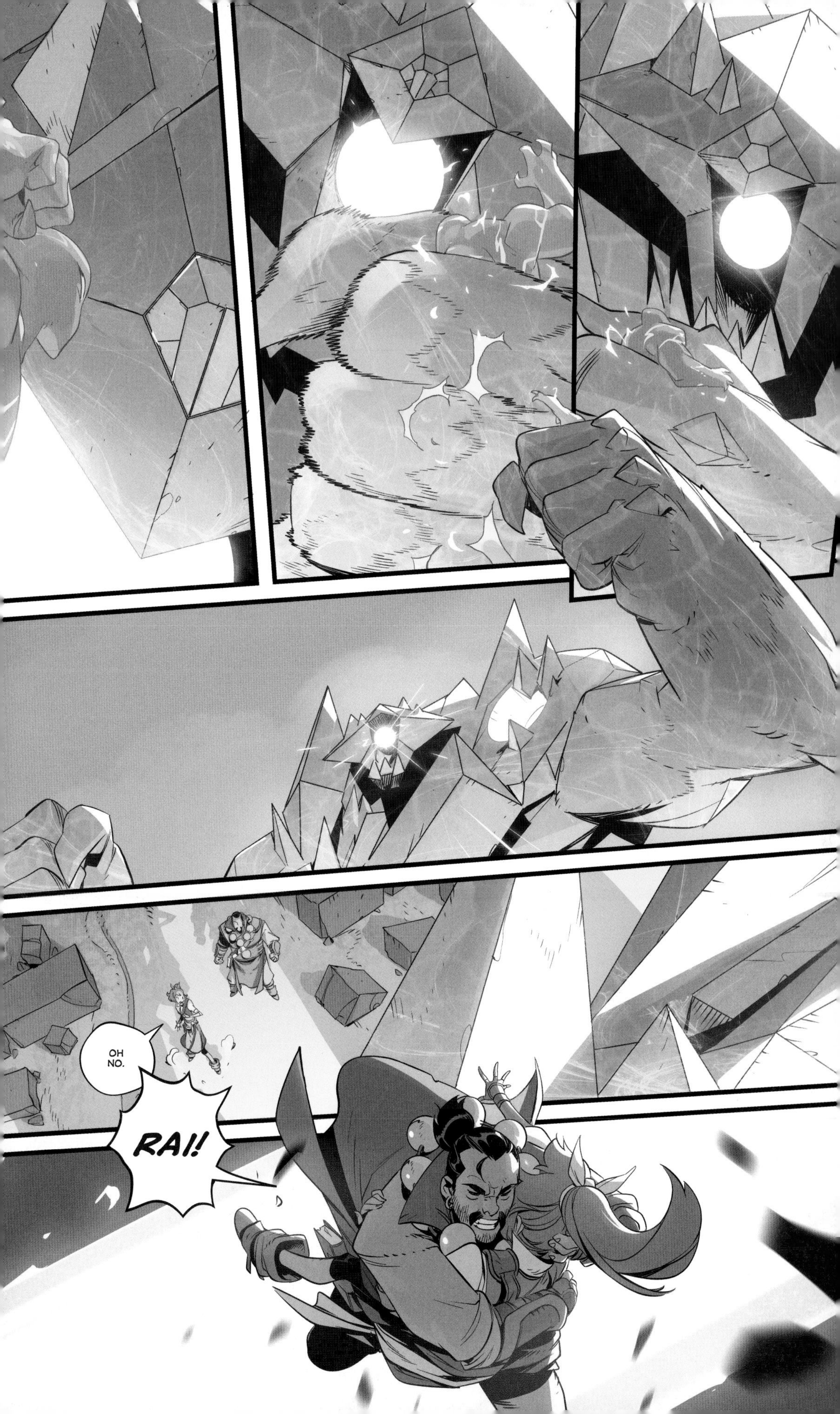
OH NO.
RAI!

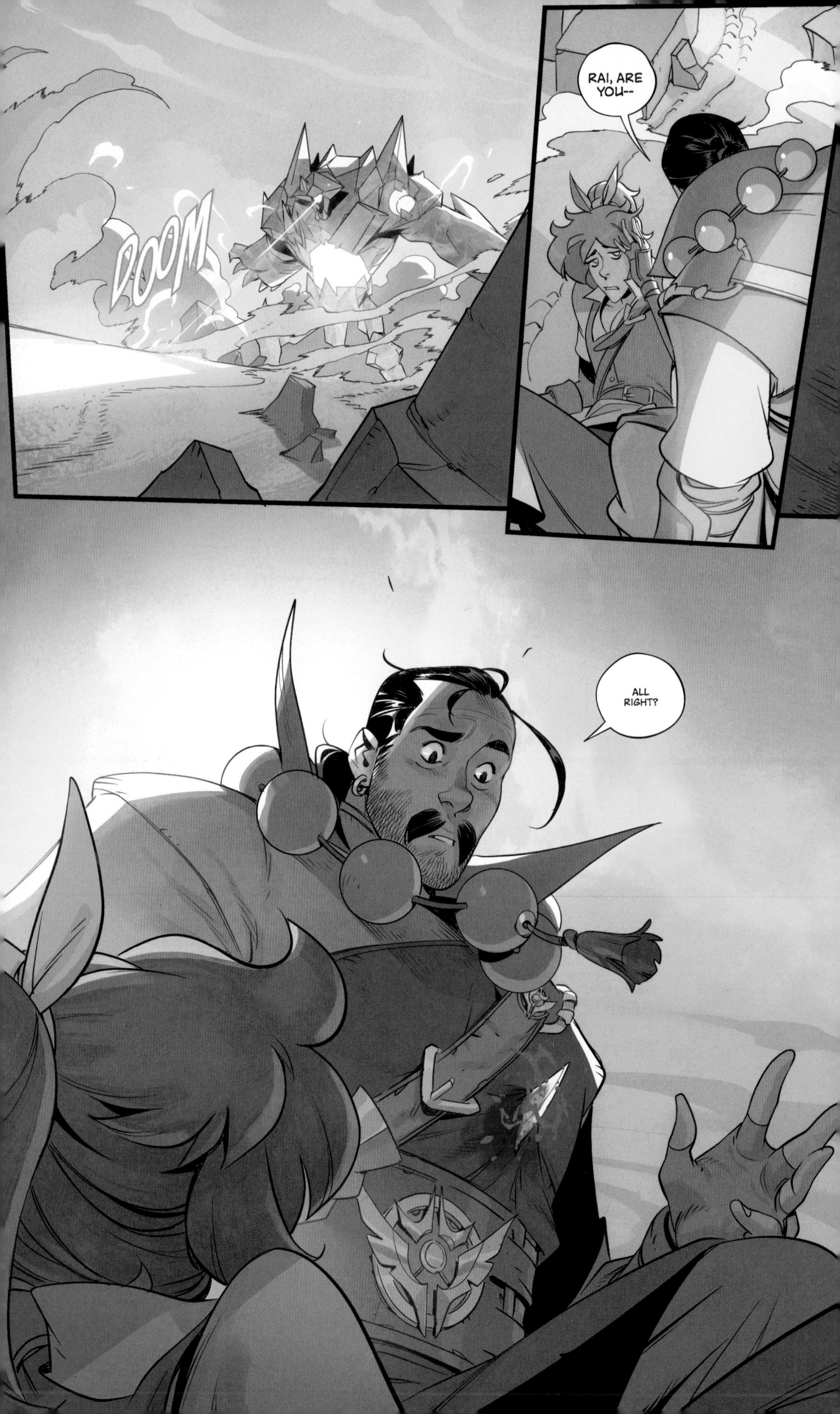
DOOM
RAI, ARE YOU--
ALL RIGHT?

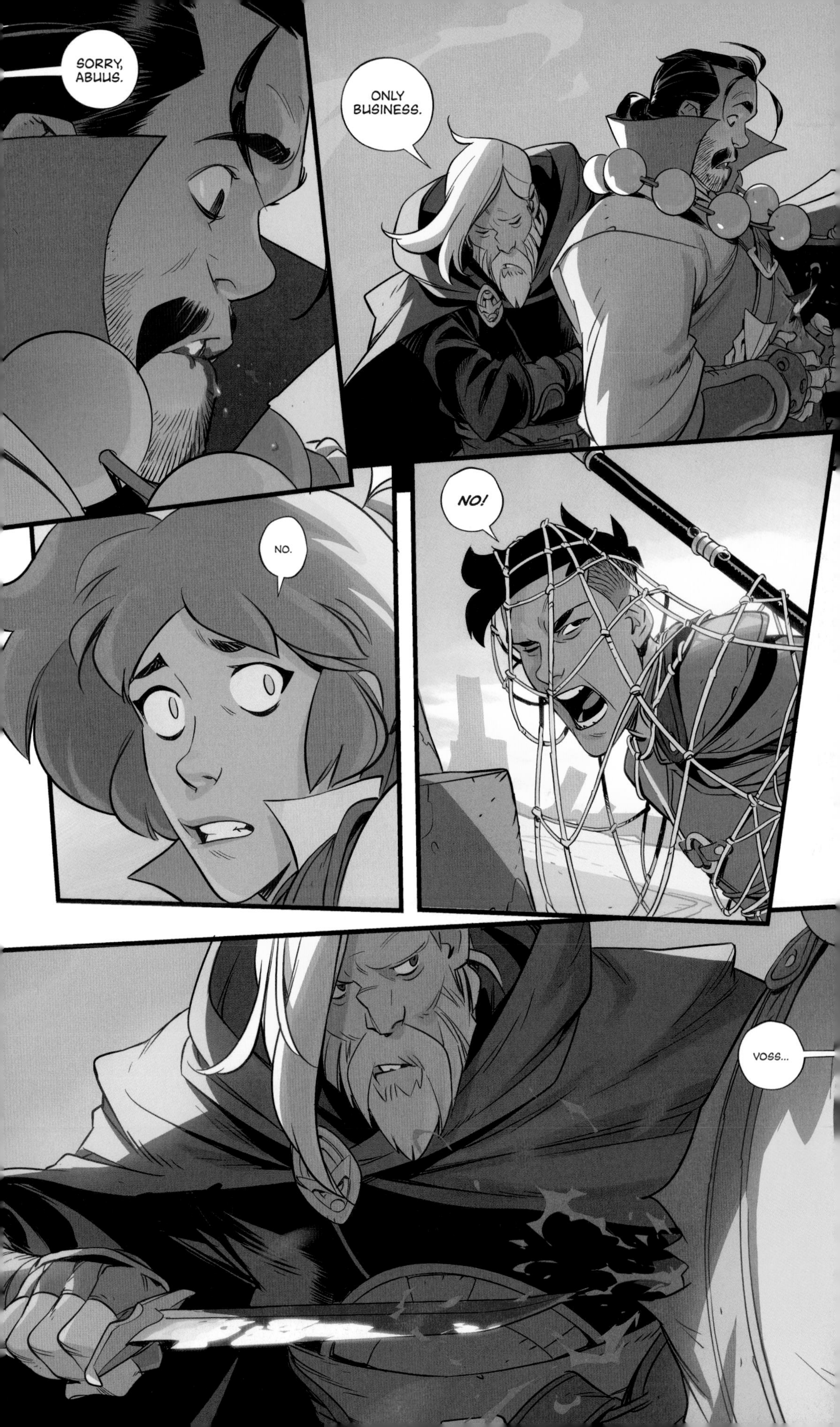
SORRY, ABUUS.
ONLY BUSINESS.
NO.
NO!
VOSS...

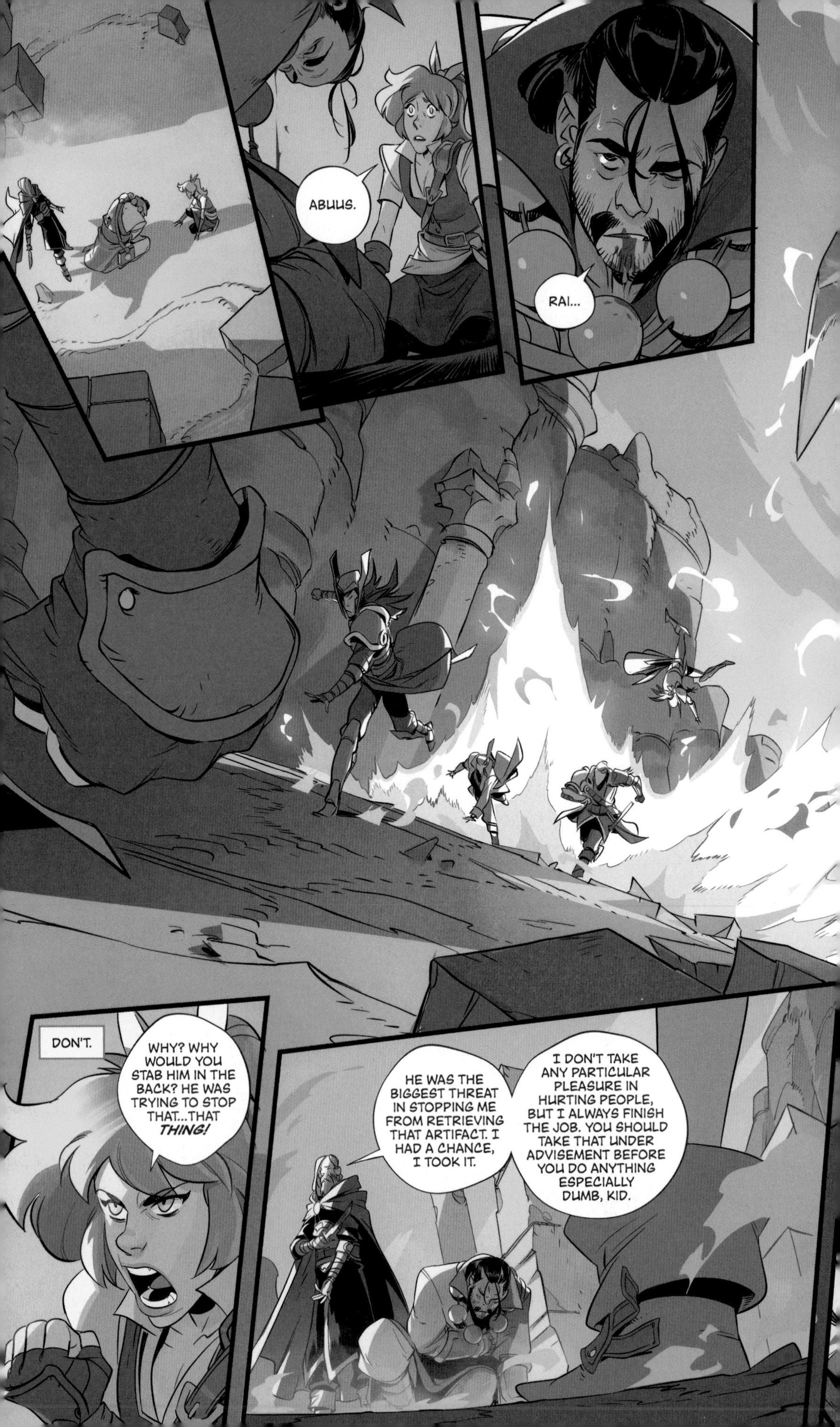
ABUUS.
RAI...
DON'T.
WHY? WHY WOULD YOU STAB HIM IN THE BACK? HE WAS TRYING TO STOP THAT...THAT *THING!*
HE WAS THE BIGGEST THREAT IN STOPPING ME FROM RETRIEVING THAT ARTIFACT. I HAD A CHANCE, I TOOK IT.
I DON'T TAKE ANY PARTICULAR PLEASURE IN HURTING PEOPLE, BUT I ALWAYS FINISH THE JOB. YOU SHOULD TAKE THAT UNDER ADVISEMENT BEFORE YOU DO ANYTHING ESPECIALLY DUMB, KID.

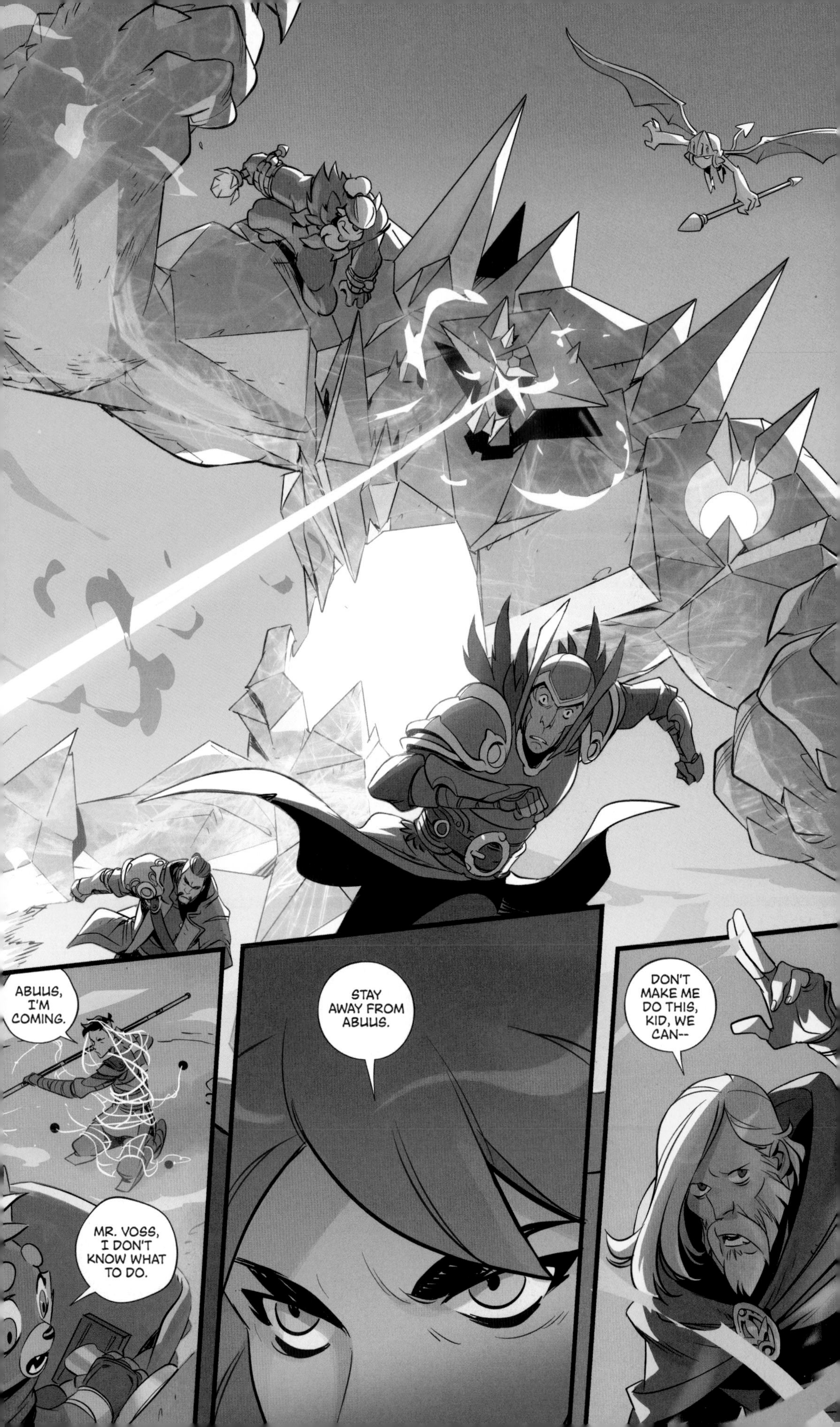
ABUUS, I'M COMING.
MR. VOSS, I DON'T KNOW WHAT TO DO.
STAY AWAY FROM ABUUS.
DON'T MAKE ME DO THIS, KID, WE CAN--

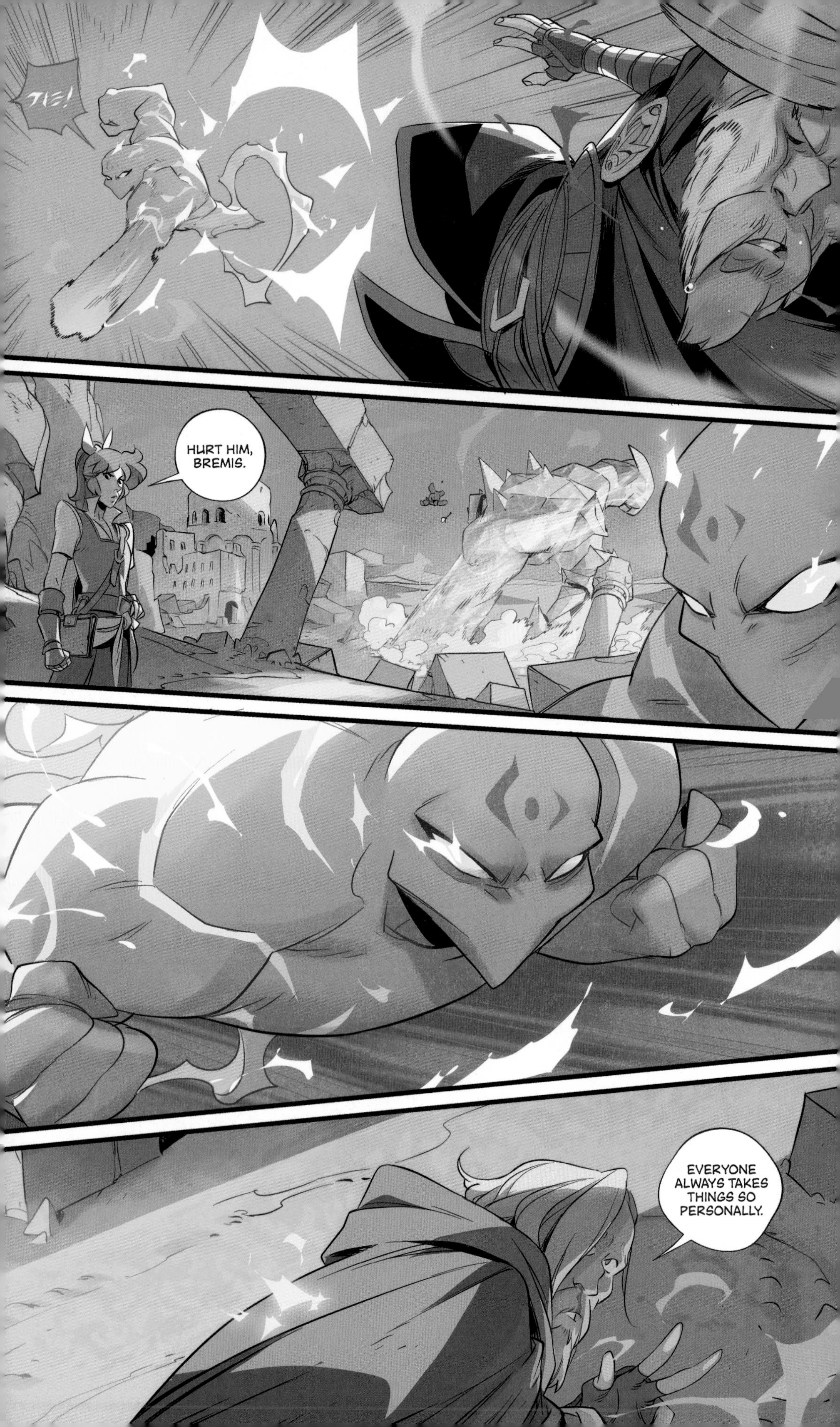
HURT HIM, BREMIS.
EVERYONE ALWAYS TAKES THINGS SO PERSONALLY.

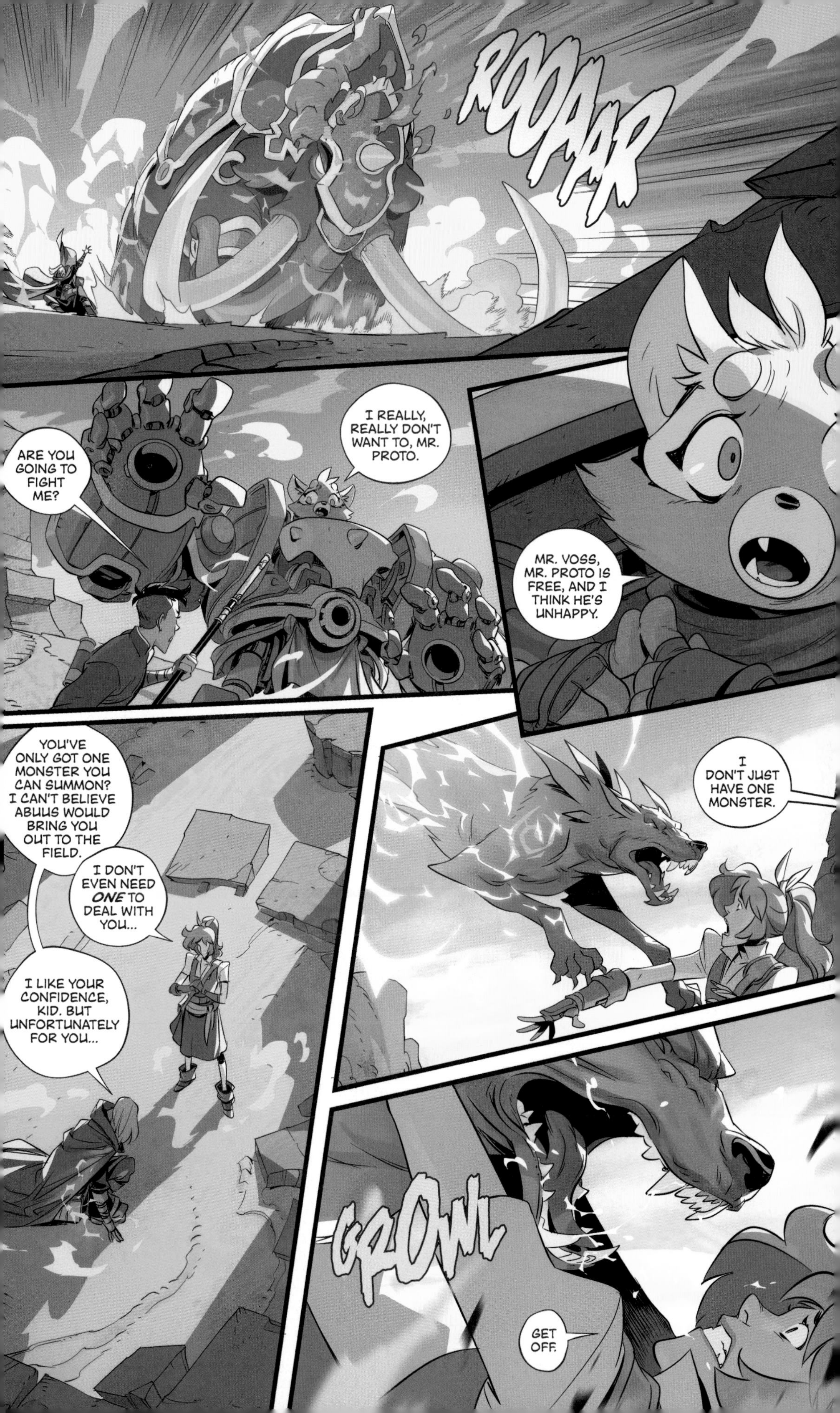
ROOAAR
ARE YOU GOING TO FIGHT ME?
I REALLY, REALLY DON'T WANT TO, MR. PROTO.
MR. VOSS, MR. PROTO IS FREE, AND I THINK HE'S UNHAPPY.
YOU'VE ONLY GOT ONE MONSTER YOU CAN SUMMON? I CAN'T BELIEVE ABUUS WOULD BRING YOU OUT TO THE FIELD.
I DON'T EVEN NEED *ONE* TO DEAL WITH YOU...
I LIKE YOUR CONFIDENCE, KID. BUT UNFORTUNATELY FOR YOU...
I DON'T JUST HAVE ONE MONSTER.
GROWL
GET OFF.

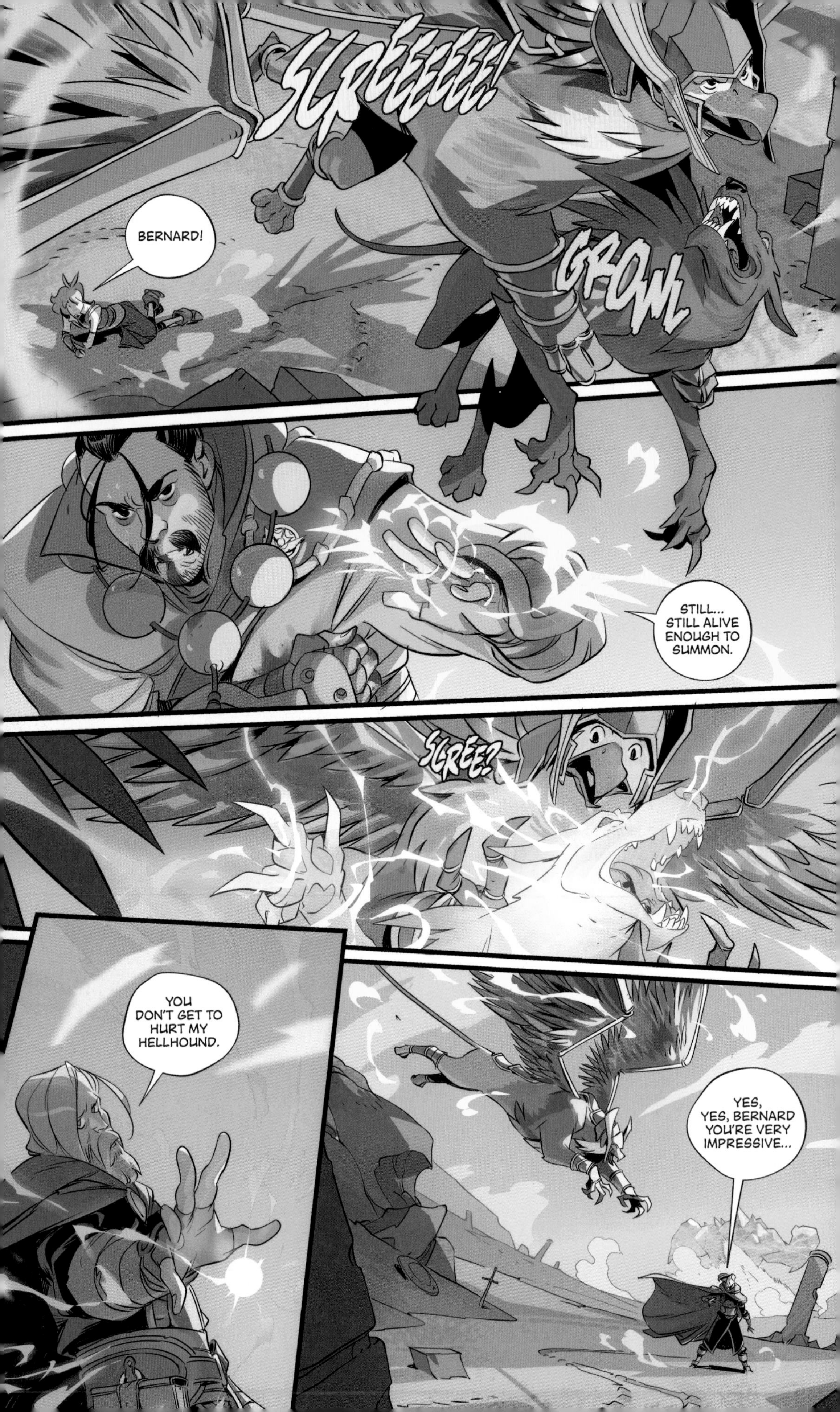
SCREEEEEEE!
BERNARD!
GROWL
STILL... STILL ALIVE ENOUGH TO SUMMON.
SCREE?
YOU DON'T GET TO HURT MY HELLHOUND.
YES, YES, BERNARD YOU'RE VERY IMPRESSIVE...

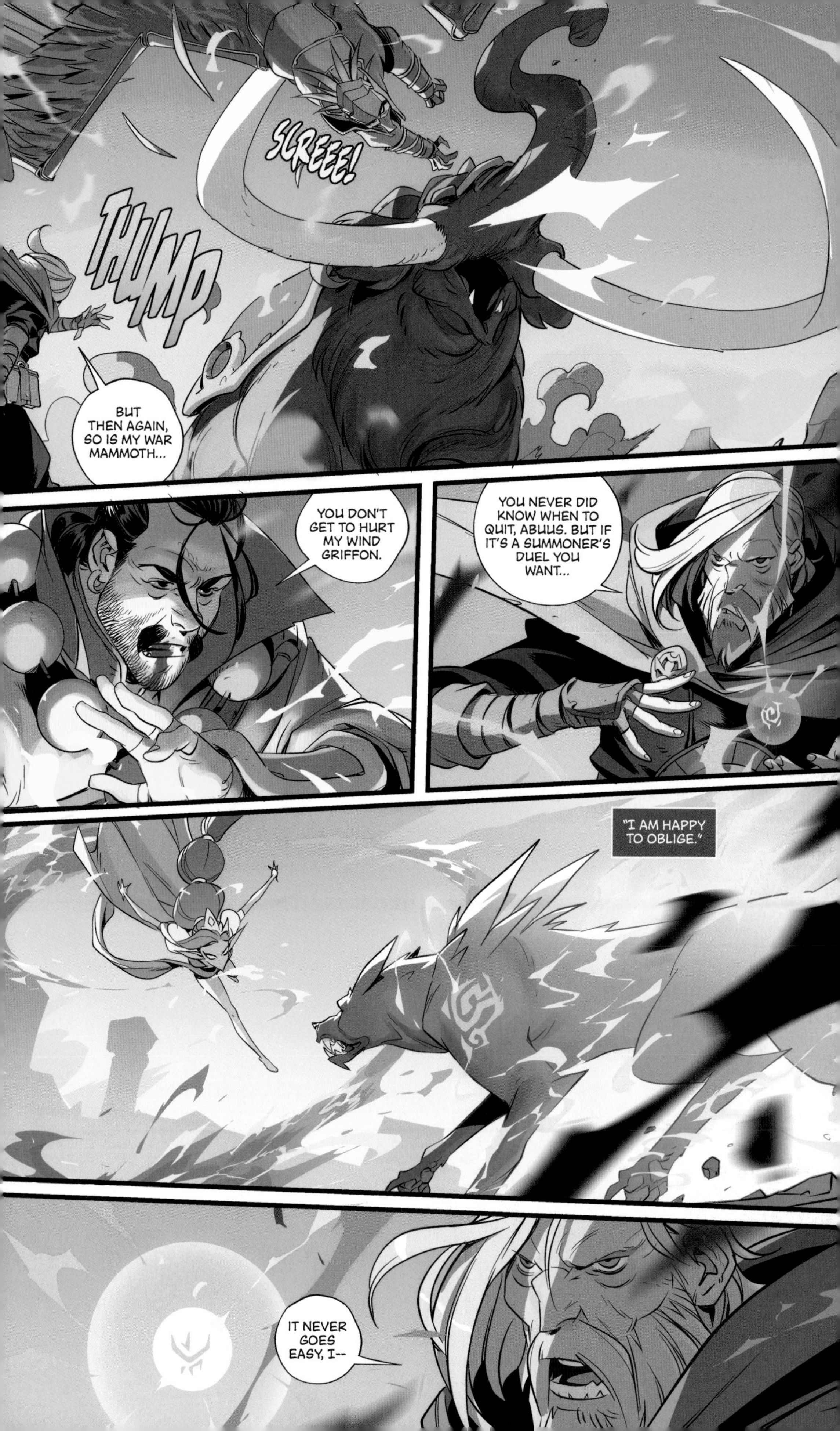
SCREEE!
THUMP
BUT THEN AGAIN, SO IS MY WAR MAMMOTH...
YOU DON'T GET TO HURT MY WIND GRIFFON.
YOU NEVER DID KNOW WHEN TO QUIT, ABUUS. BUT IF IT'S A SUMMONER'S DUEL YOU WANT...
"I AM HAPPY TO OBLIGE."
IT NEVER GOES EASY, I--

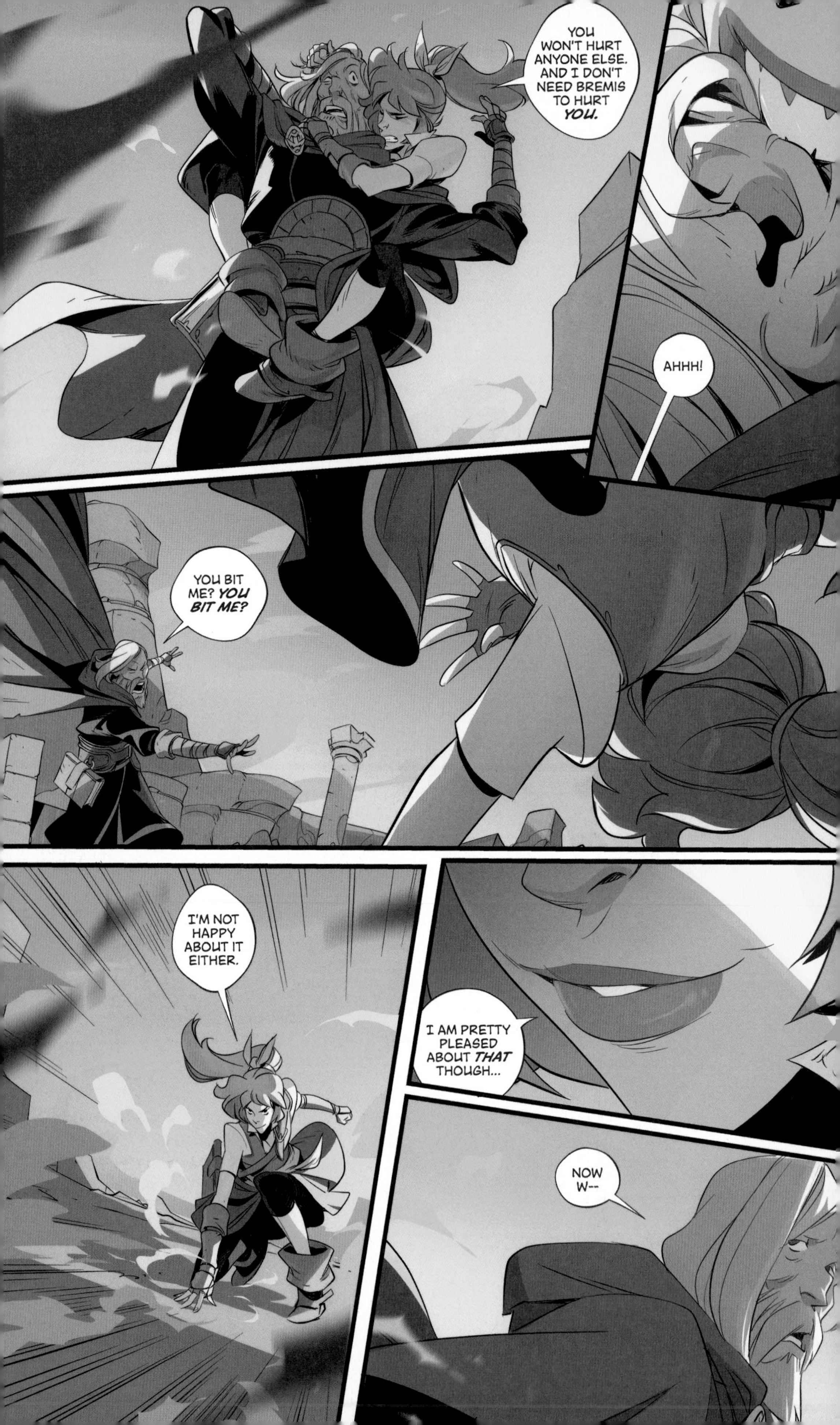
YOU WON'T HURT ANYONE ELSE. AND I DON'T NEED BREMIS TO HURT *YOU.*
AHHH!
YOU BIT ME? *YOU BIT ME?*
I'M NOT HAPPY ABOUT IT EITHER.
I AM PRETTY PLEASED ABOUT *THAT* THOUGH...
NOW W--

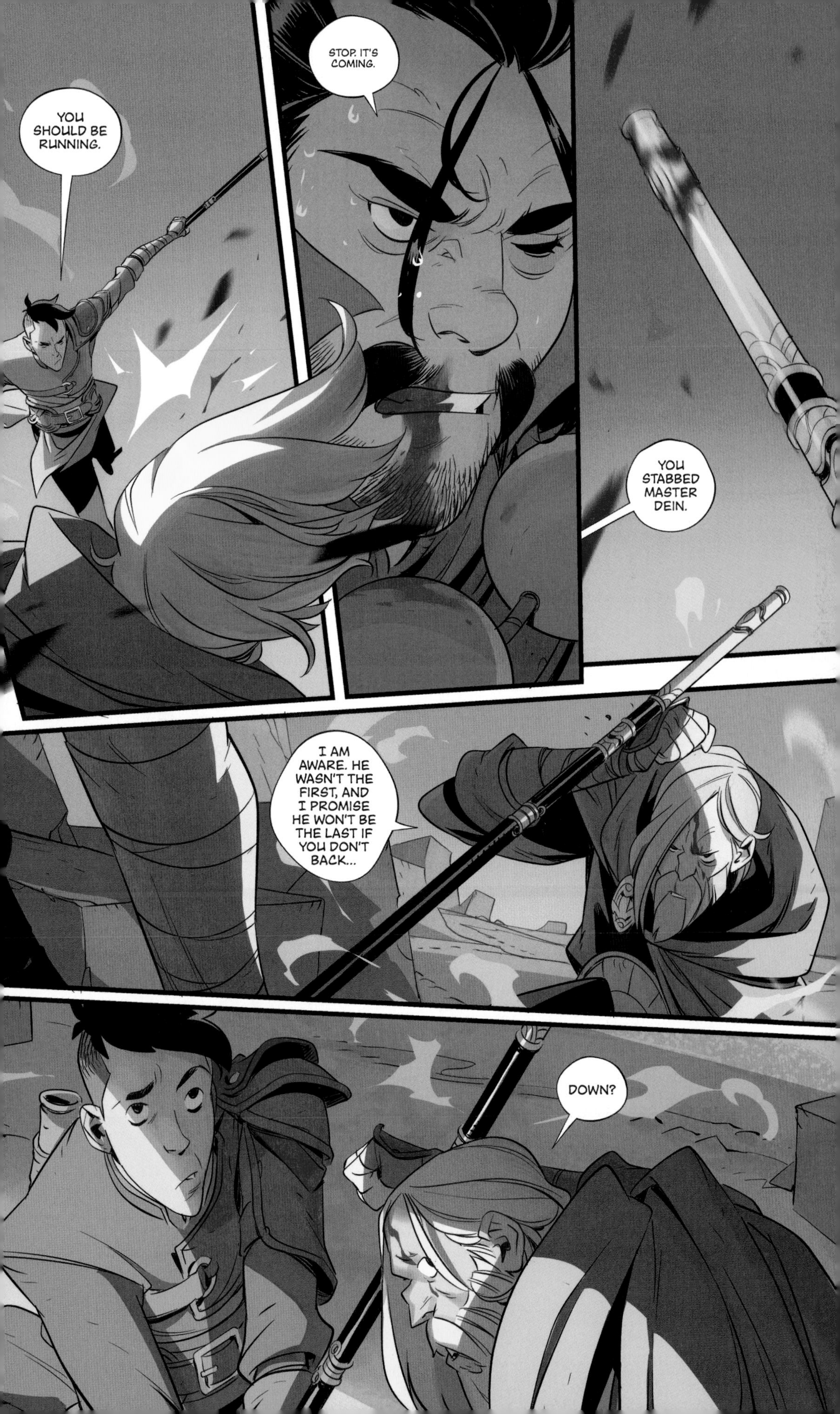
YOU SHOULD BE RUNNING.
STOP. IT'S COMING.
YOU STABBED MASTER DEIN.
I AM AWARE. HE WASN'T THE FIRST, AND I PROMISE HE WON'T BE THE LAST IF YOU DON'T BACK...
DOWN?

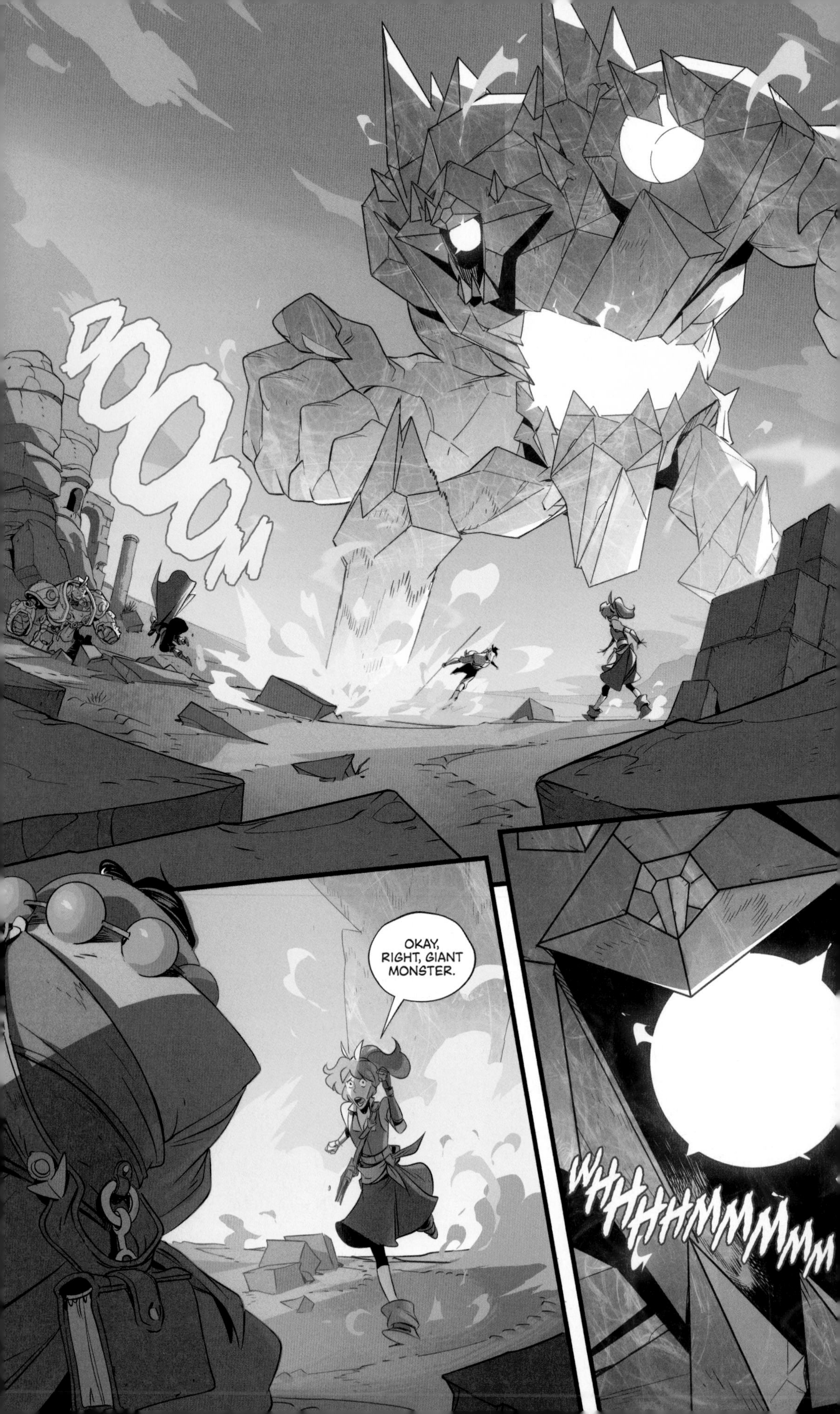

DOOOOM
OKAY, RIGHT, GIANT MONSTER.
WHHHHMMMMMM

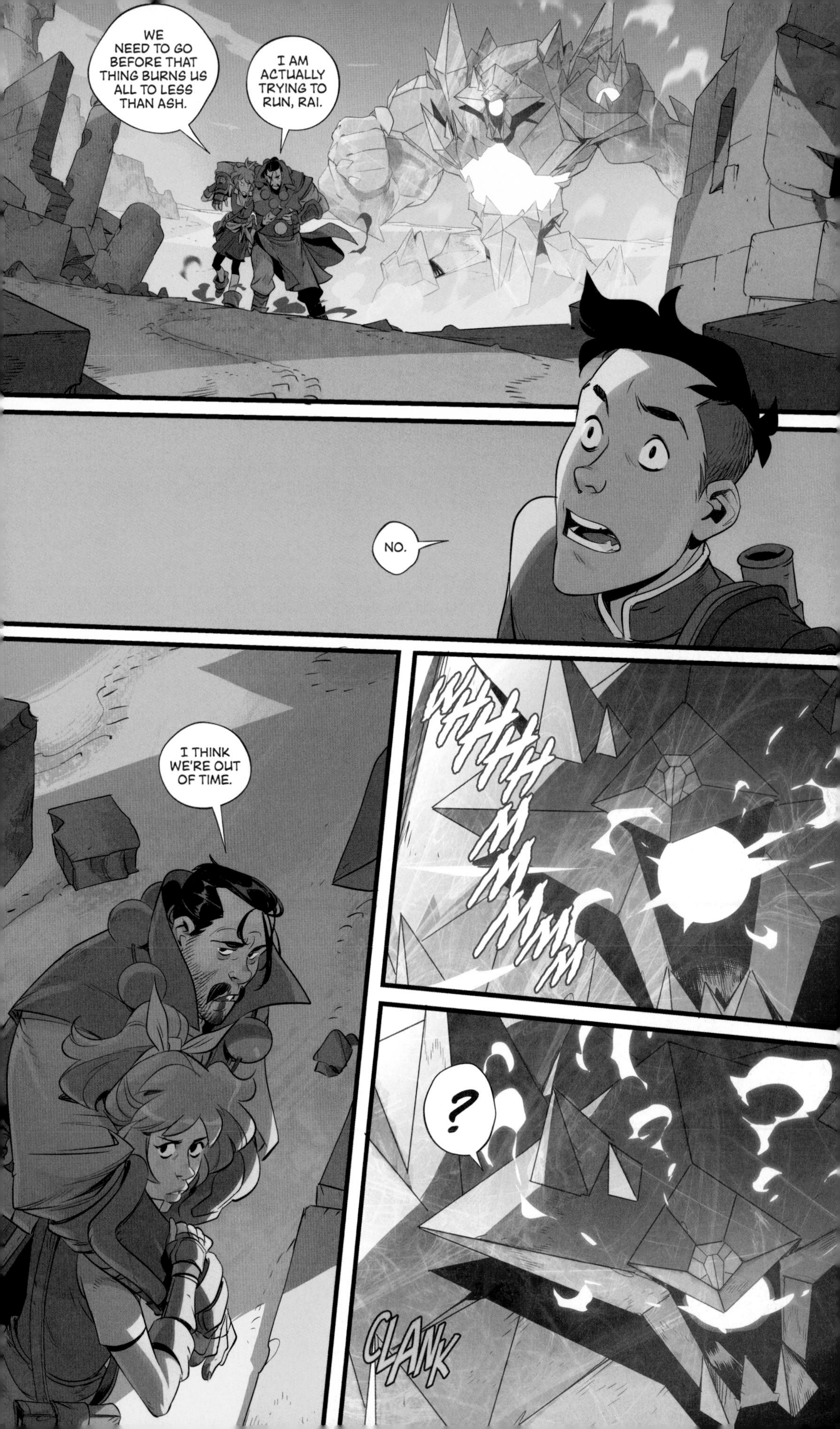

WE NEED TO GO BEFORE THAT THING BURNS US ALL TO LESS THAN ASH.
I AM ACTUALLY TRYING TO RUN, RAI.
NO.
I THINK WE'RE OUT OF TIME.
WHHHMMMMMM
?
CLANK

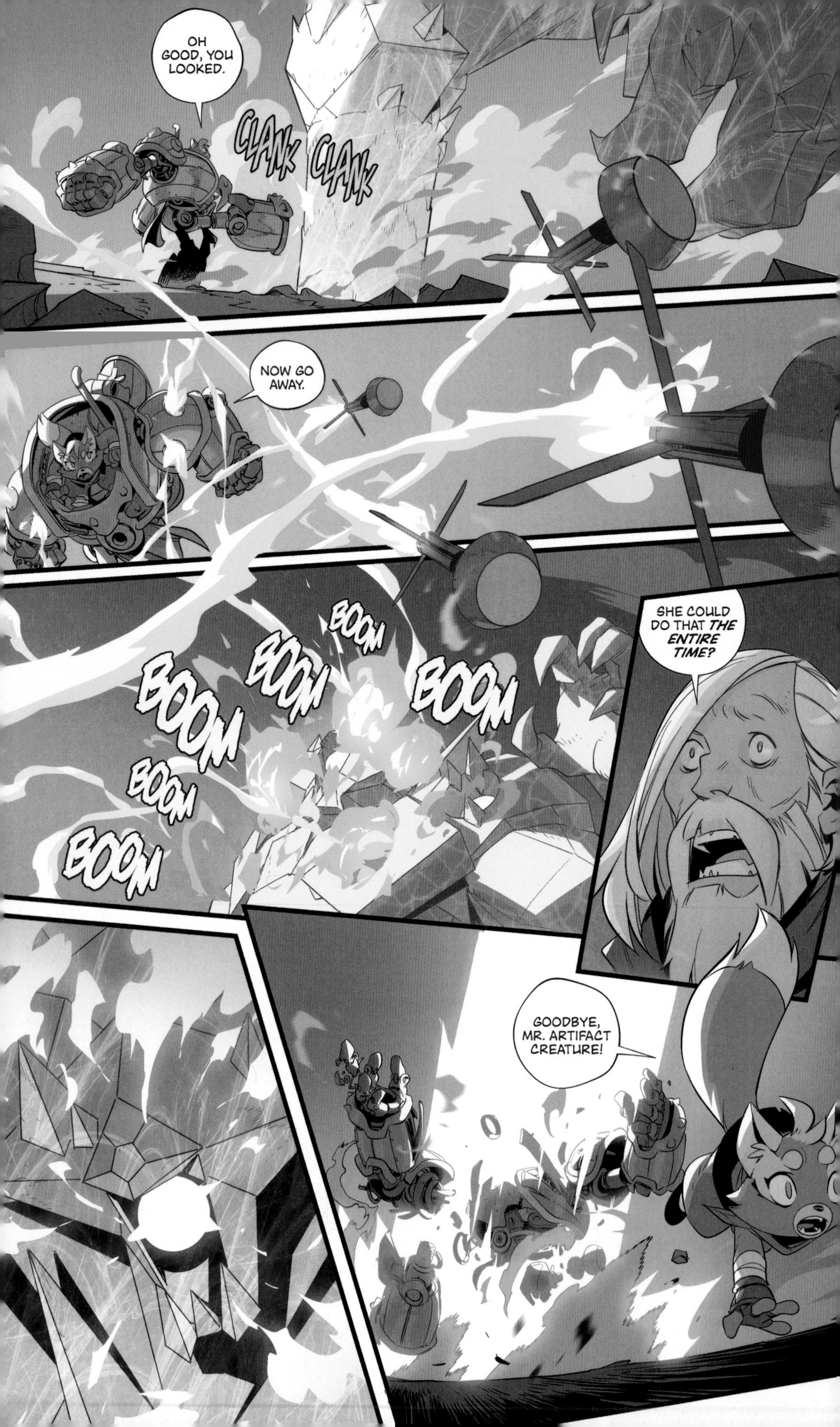
OH GOOD, YOU LOOKED.
CLANK CLANK
NOW GO AWAY.
BOOM
BOOM
BOOM
BOOM
BOOM
BOOM
SHE COULD DO THAT *THE ENTIRE TIME?*
GOODBYE, MR. ARTIFACT CREATURE!

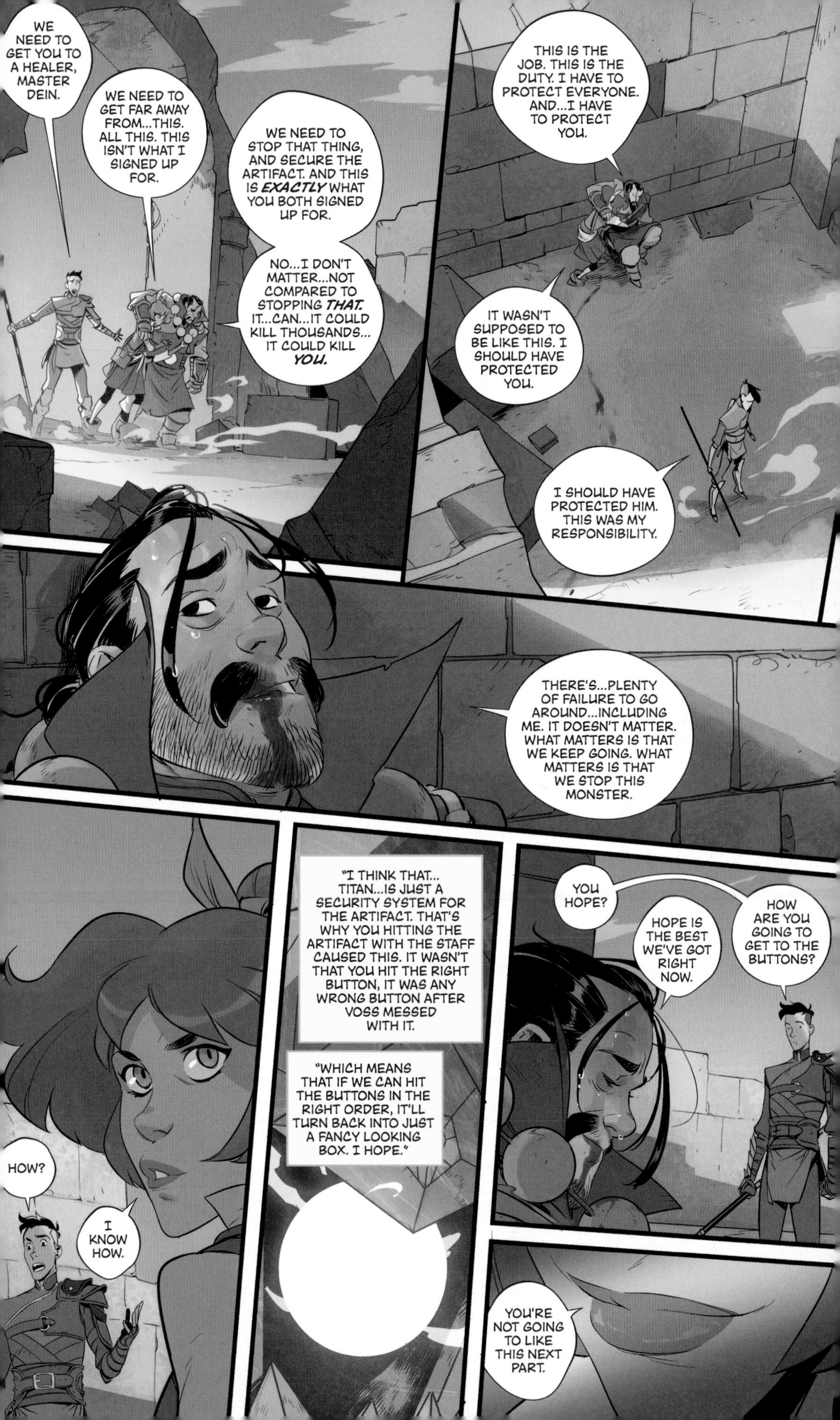

WE NEED TO GET YOU TO A HEALER, MASTER DEIN.
WE NEED TO GET FAR AWAY FROM...THIS. ALL THIS. THIS ISN'T WHAT I SIGNED UP FOR.
WE NEED TO STOP THAT THING, AND SECURE THE ARTIFACT. AND THIS IS *EXACTLY* WHAT YOU BOTH SIGNED UP FOR.
NO...I DON'T MATTER...NOT COMPARED TO STOPPING *THAT.* IT...CAN...IT COULD KILL THOUSANDS... IT COULD KILL *YOU.*
THIS IS THE JOB. THIS IS THE DUTY. I HAVE TO PROTECT EVERYONE. AND...I HAVE TO PROTECT YOU.
IT WASN'T SUPPOSED TO BE LIKE THIS. I SHOULD HAVE PROTECTED YOU.
I SHOULD HAVE PROTECTED HIM. THIS WAS MY RESPONSIBILITY.
THERE'S...PLENTY OF FAILURE TO GO AROUND...INCLUDING ME. IT DOESN'T MATTER. WHAT MATTERS IS THAT WE KEEP GOING. WHAT MATTERS IS THAT WE STOP THIS MONSTER.
HOW?
I KNOW HOW.
"I THINK THAT... TITAN...IS JUST A SECURITY SYSTEM FOR THE ARTIFACT. THAT'S WHY YOU HITTING THE ARTIFACT WITH THE STAFF CAUSED THIS. IT WASN'T THAT YOU HIT THE RIGHT BUTTON, IT WAS ANY WRONG BUTTON AFTER VOSS MESSED WITH IT.
"WHICH MEANS THAT IF WE CAN HIT THE BUTTONS IN THE RIGHT ORDER, IT'LL TURN BACK INTO JUST A FANCY LOOKING BOX. I HOPE."
YOU HOPE?
HOPE IS THE BEST WE'VE GOT RIGHT NOW.
HOW ARE YOU GOING TO GET TO THE BUTTONS?
YOU'RE NOT GOING TO LIKE THIS NEXT PART.

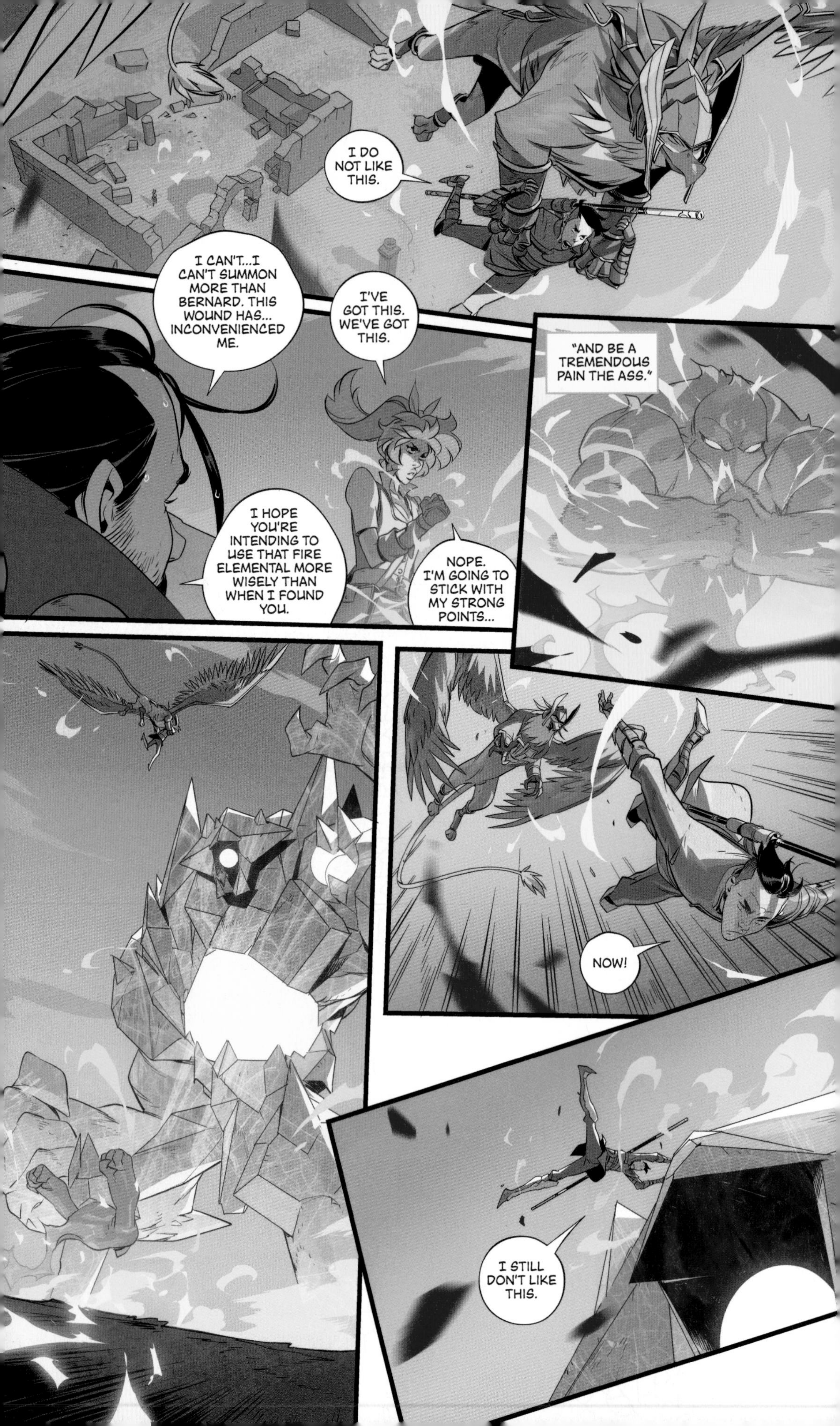
I DO NOT LIKE THIS.
I CAN'T...I CAN'T SUMMON MORE THAN BERNARD. THIS WOUND HAS... INCONVENIENCED ME.
I'VE GOT THIS. WE'VE GOT THIS.
I HOPE YOU'RE INTENDING TO USE THAT FIRE ELEMENTAL MORE WISELY THAN WHEN I FOUND YOU.
NOPE. I'M GOING TO STICK WITH MY STRONG POINTS...
"AND BE A TREMENDOUS PAIN THE ASS."
NOW!
I STILL DON'T LIKE THIS.

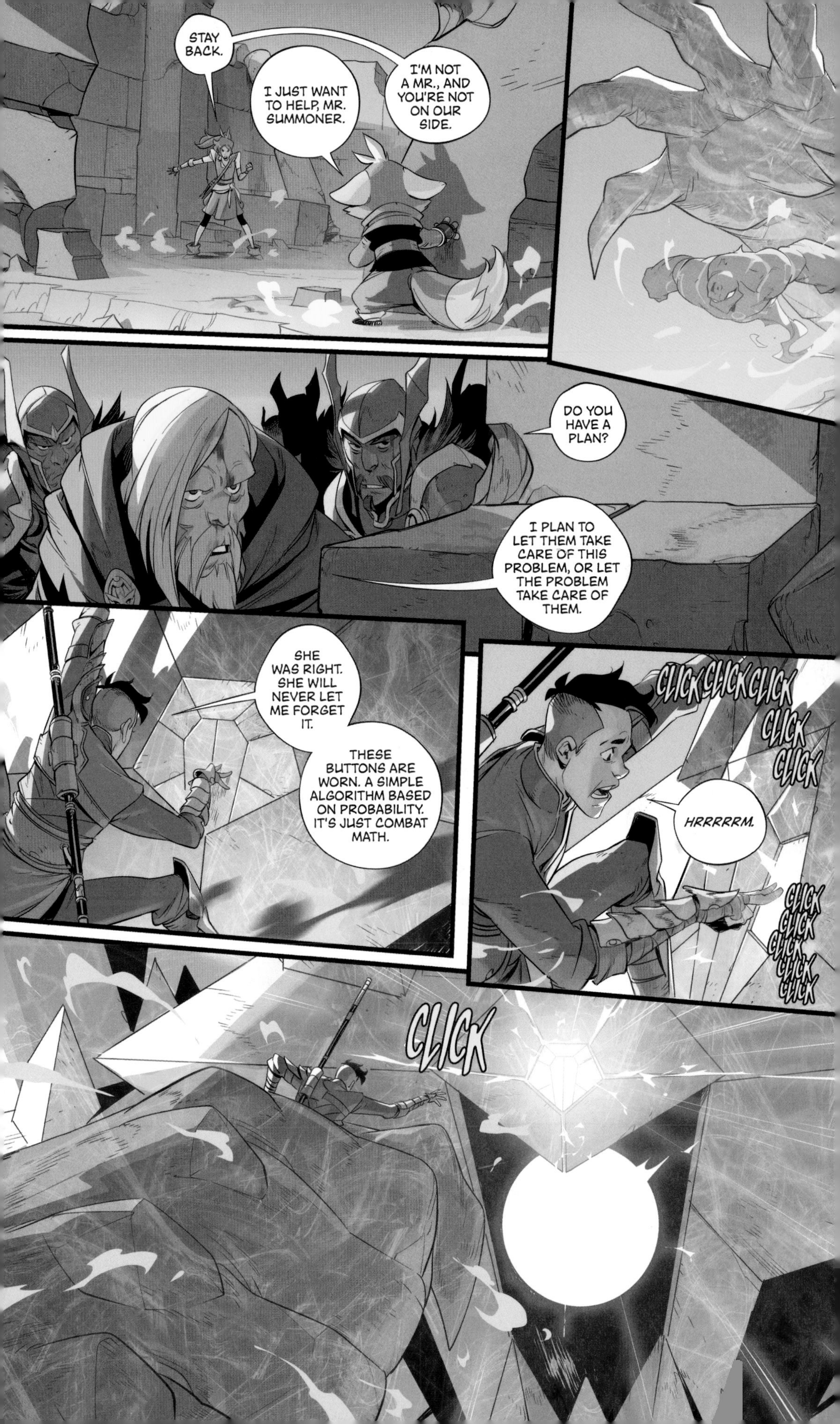
STAY BACK.
I JUST WANT TO HELP, MR. SUMMONER.
I'M NOT A MR., AND YOU'RE NOT ON OUR SIDE.
DO YOU HAVE A PLAN?
I PLAN TO LET THEM TAKE CARE OF THIS PROBLEM, OR LET THE PROBLEM TAKE CARE OF THEM.
SHE WAS RIGHT. SHE WILL NEVER LET ME FORGET IT.
THESE BUTTONS ARE WORN. A SIMPLE ALGORITHM BASED ON PROBABILITY. IT'S JUST COMBAT MATH.
CLICK CLICK CLICK CLICK CLICK
HRRRRRM.
CLICK CLICK CLICK CLICK CLICK
CLICK

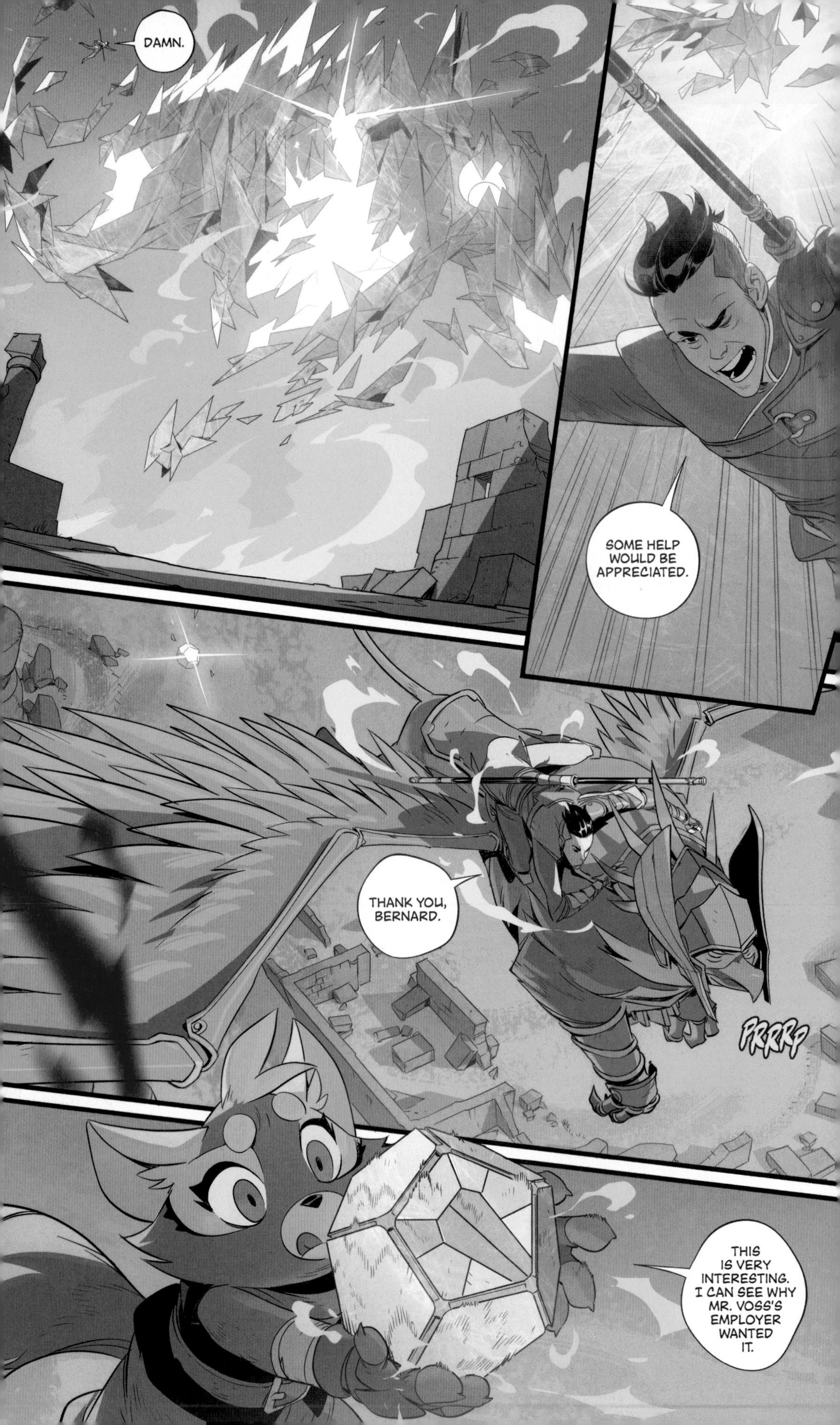
DAMN.
SOME HELP WOULD BE APPRECIATED.
THANK YOU, BERNARD.
PRRRP
THIS IS VERY INTERESTING. I CAN SEE WHY MR. VOSS'S EMPLOYER WANTED IT.

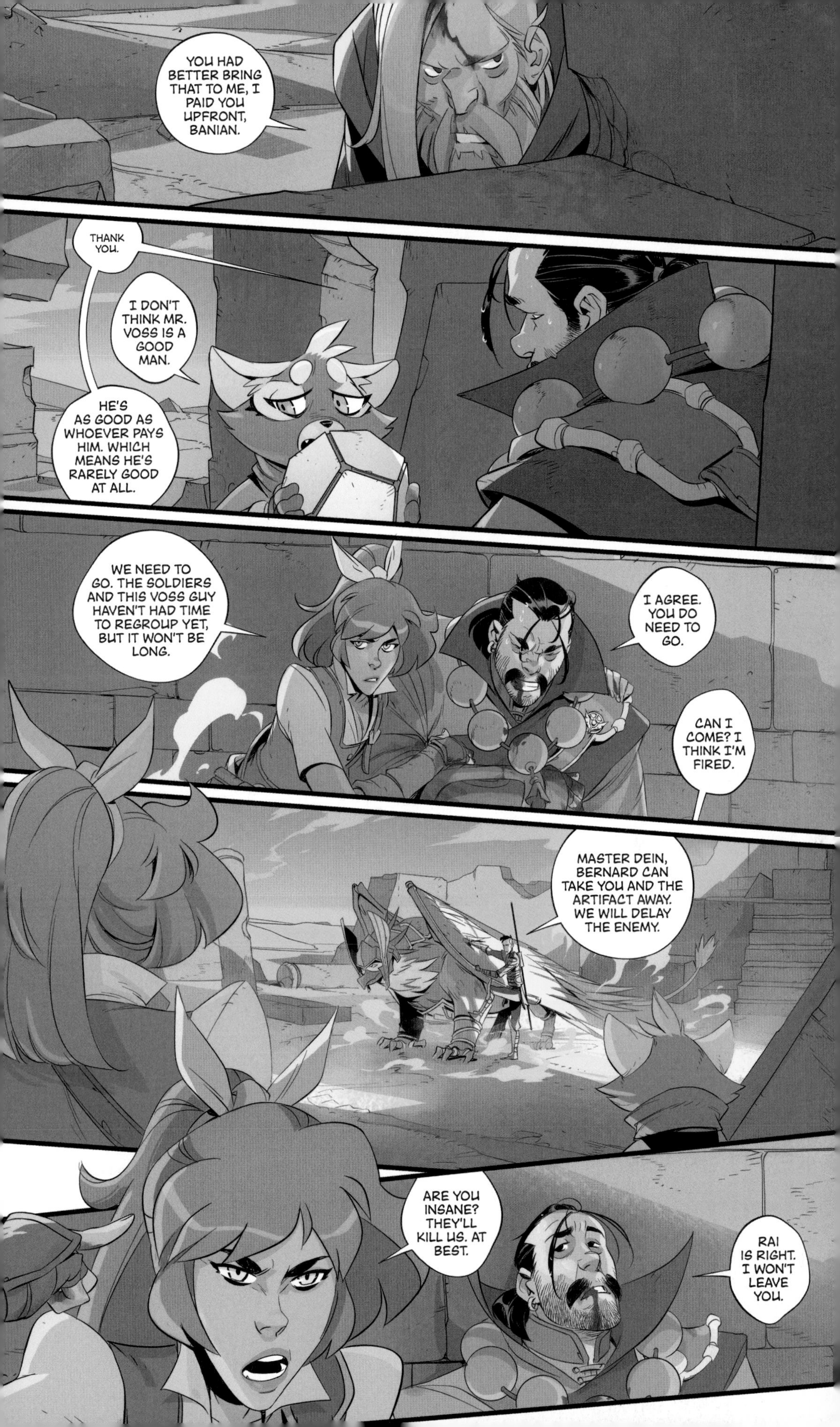
YOU HAD BETTER BRING THAT TO ME, I PAID YOU UPFRONT, BANIAN.
THANK YOU.
I DON'T THINK MR. VOSS IS A GOOD MAN.
HE'S AS GOOD AS WHOEVER PAYS HIM. WHICH MEANS HE'S RARELY GOOD AT ALL.
WE NEED TO GO. THE SOLDIERS AND THIS VOSS GUY HAVEN'T HAD TIME TO REGROUP YET, BUT IT WON'T BE LONG.
I AGREE. YOU DO NEED TO GO.
CAN I COME? I THINK I'M FIRED.
MASTER DEIN, BERNARD CAN TAKE YOU AND THE ARTIFACT AWAY. WE WILL DELAY THE ENEMY.
ARE YOU INSANE? THEY'LL KILL US. AT BEST.
RAI IS RIGHT. I WON'T LEAVE YOU.

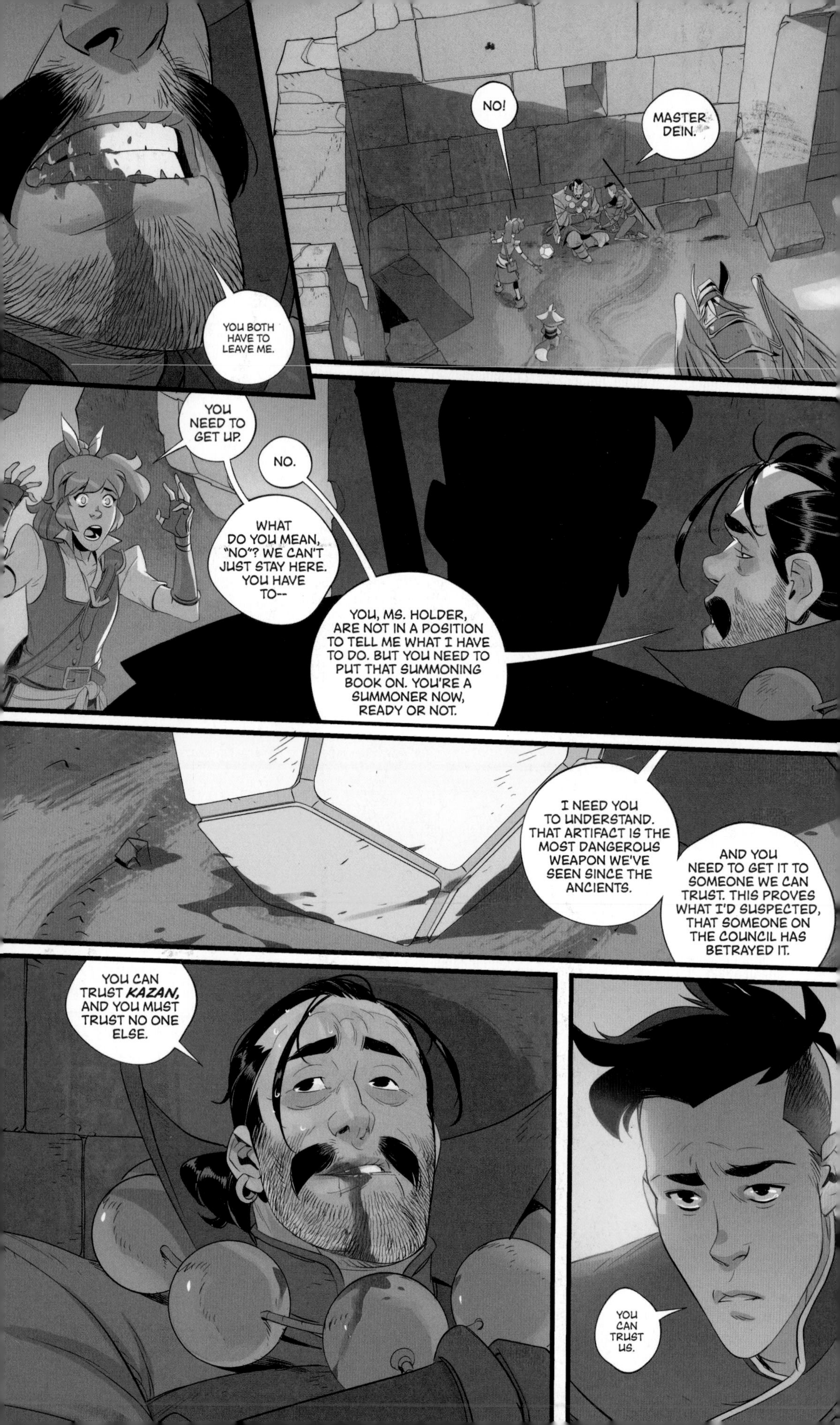
YOU BOTH HAVE TO LEAVE ME.
NO!
MASTER DEIN.
YOU NEED TO GET UP.
NO.
WHAT DO YOU MEAN, "NO"? WE CAN'T JUST STAY HERE. YOU HAVE TO--
YOU, MS. HOLDER, ARE NOT IN A POSITION TO TELL ME WHAT I HAVE TO DO. BUT YOU NEED TO PUT THAT SUMMONING BOOK ON. YOU'RE A SUMMONER NOW, READY OR NOT.
I NEED YOU TO UNDERSTAND. THAT ARTIFACT IS THE MOST DANGEROUS WEAPON WE'VE SEEN SINCE THE ANCIENTS.
AND YOU NEED TO GET IT TO SOMEONE WE CAN TRUST. THIS PROVES WHAT I'D SUSPECTED, THAT SOMEONE ON THE COUNCIL HAS BETRAYED IT.
YOU CAN TRUST *KAZAN,* AND YOU MUST TRUST NO ONE ELSE.
YOU CAN TRUST US.

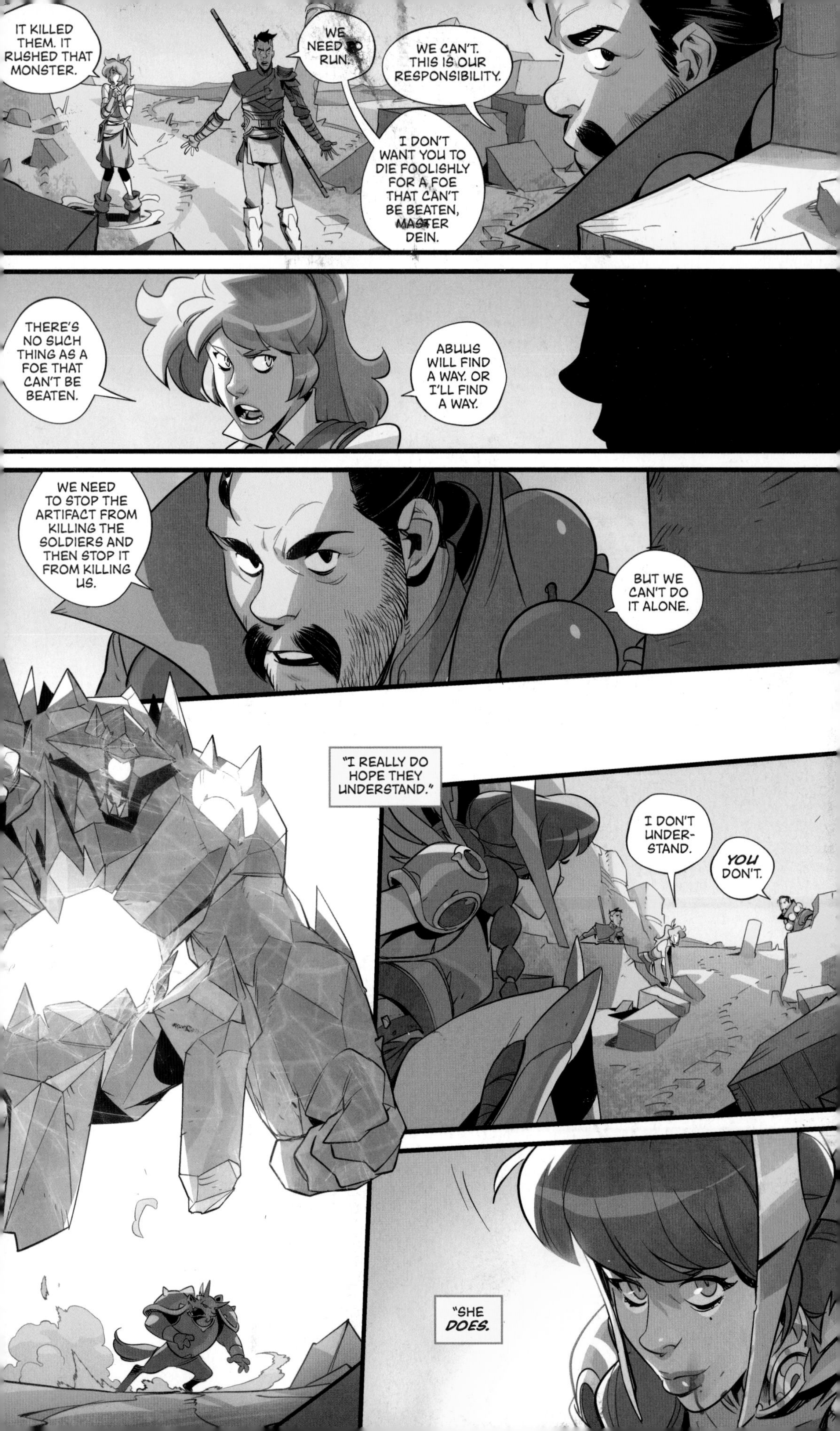

IT KILLED THEM. IT RUSHED THAT MONSTER.
WE NEED TO RUN.
WE CAN'T. THIS IS OUR RESPONSIBILITY.
I DON'T WANT YOU TO DIE FOOLISHLY FOR A FOE THAT CAN'T BE BEATEN, MASTER DEIN.
THERE'S NO SUCH THING AS A FOE THAT CAN'T BE BEATEN.
ABUUS WILL FIND A WAY. OR I'LL FIND A WAY.
WE NEED TO STOP THE ARTIFACT FROM KILLING THE SOLDIERS AND THEN STOP IT FROM KILLING US.
BUT WE CAN'T DO IT ALONE.
"I REALLY DO HOPE THEY UNDERSTAND."
I DON'T UNDER-STAND.
YOU DON'T.
"SHE *DOES.*

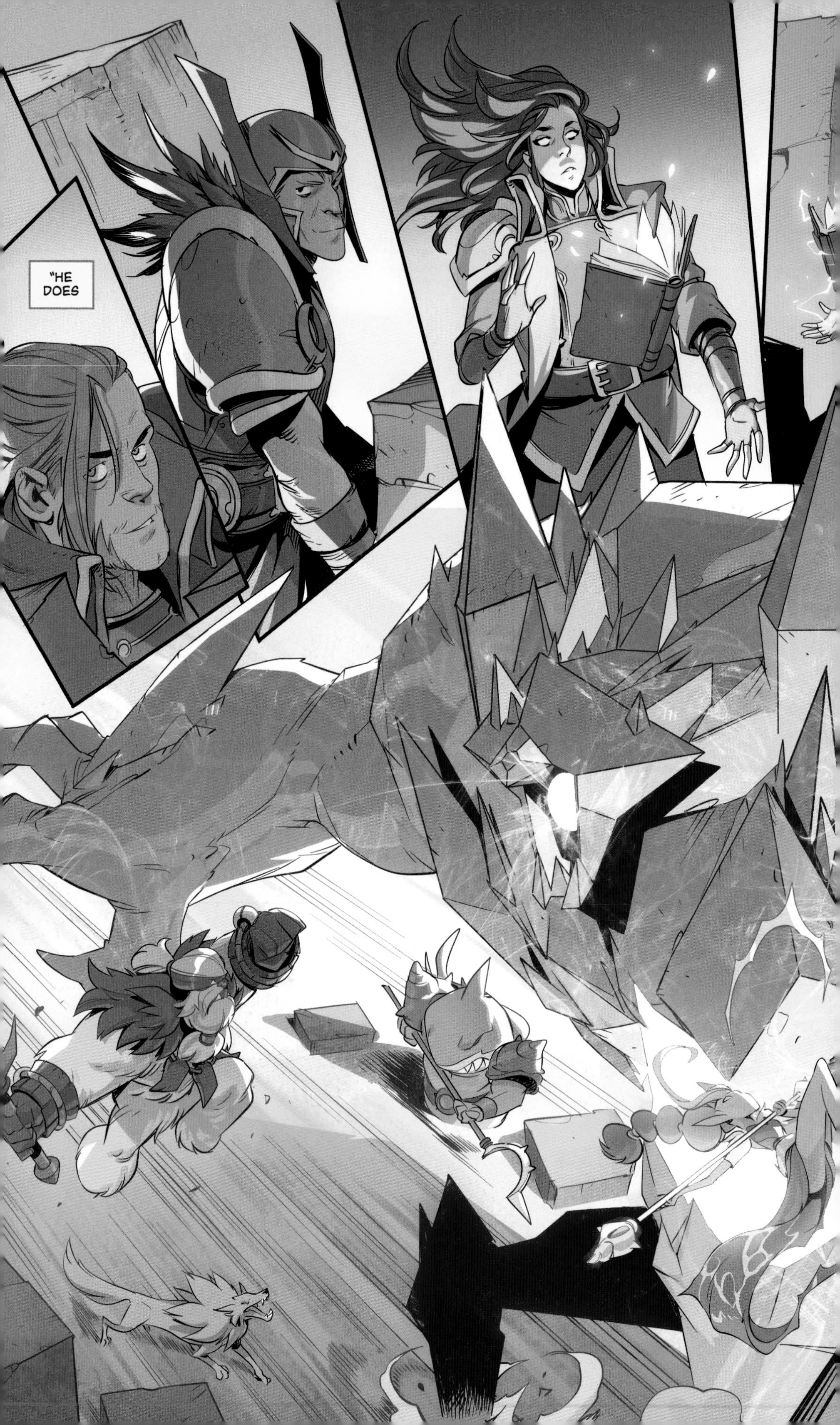
"HE
DOES

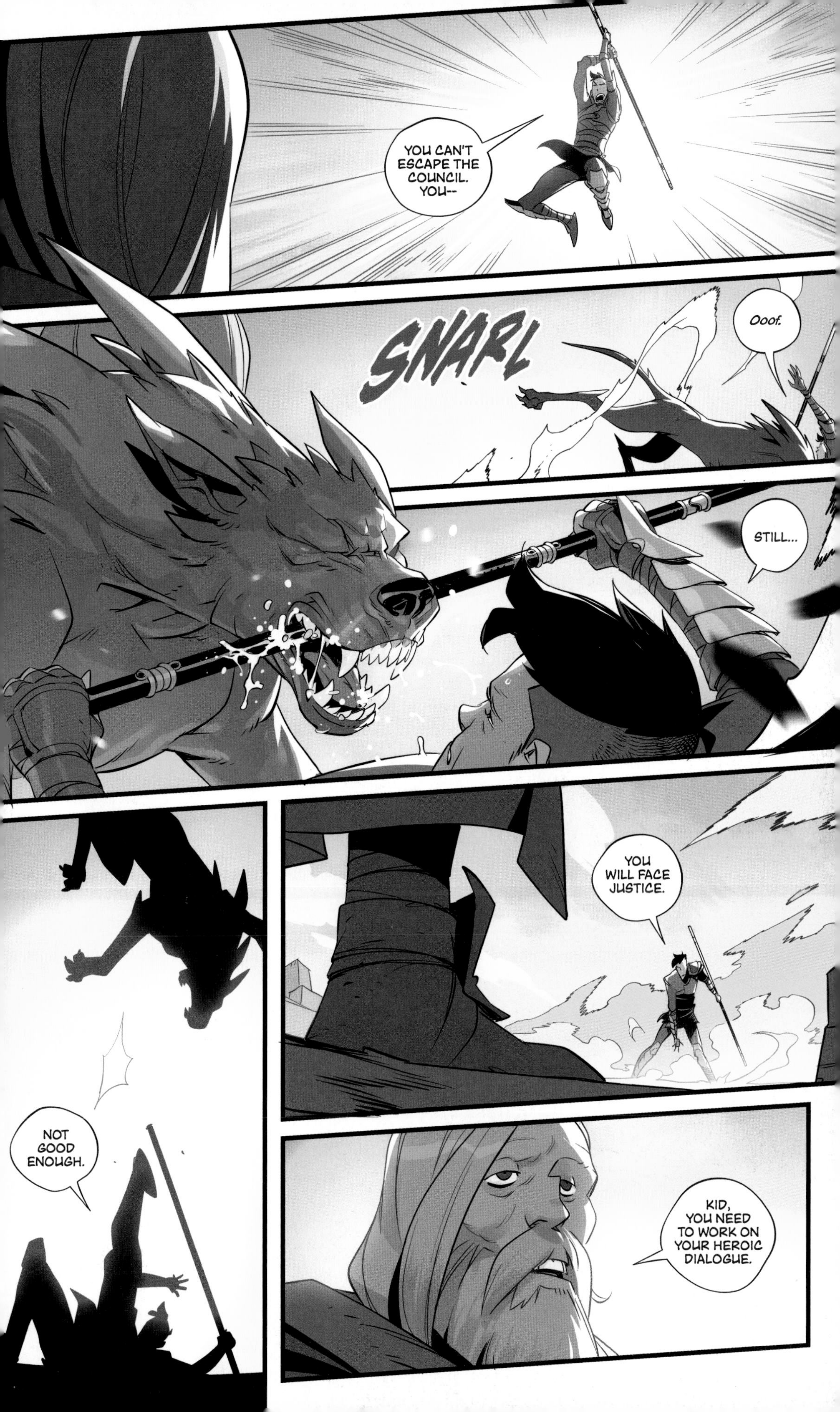
YOU CAN'T ESCAPE THE COUNCIL. YOU--
SNARL
Ooof.
STILL...
NOT GOOD ENOUGH.
YOU WILL FACE JUSTICE.
KID, YOU NEED TO WORK ON YOUR HEROIC DIALOGUE.

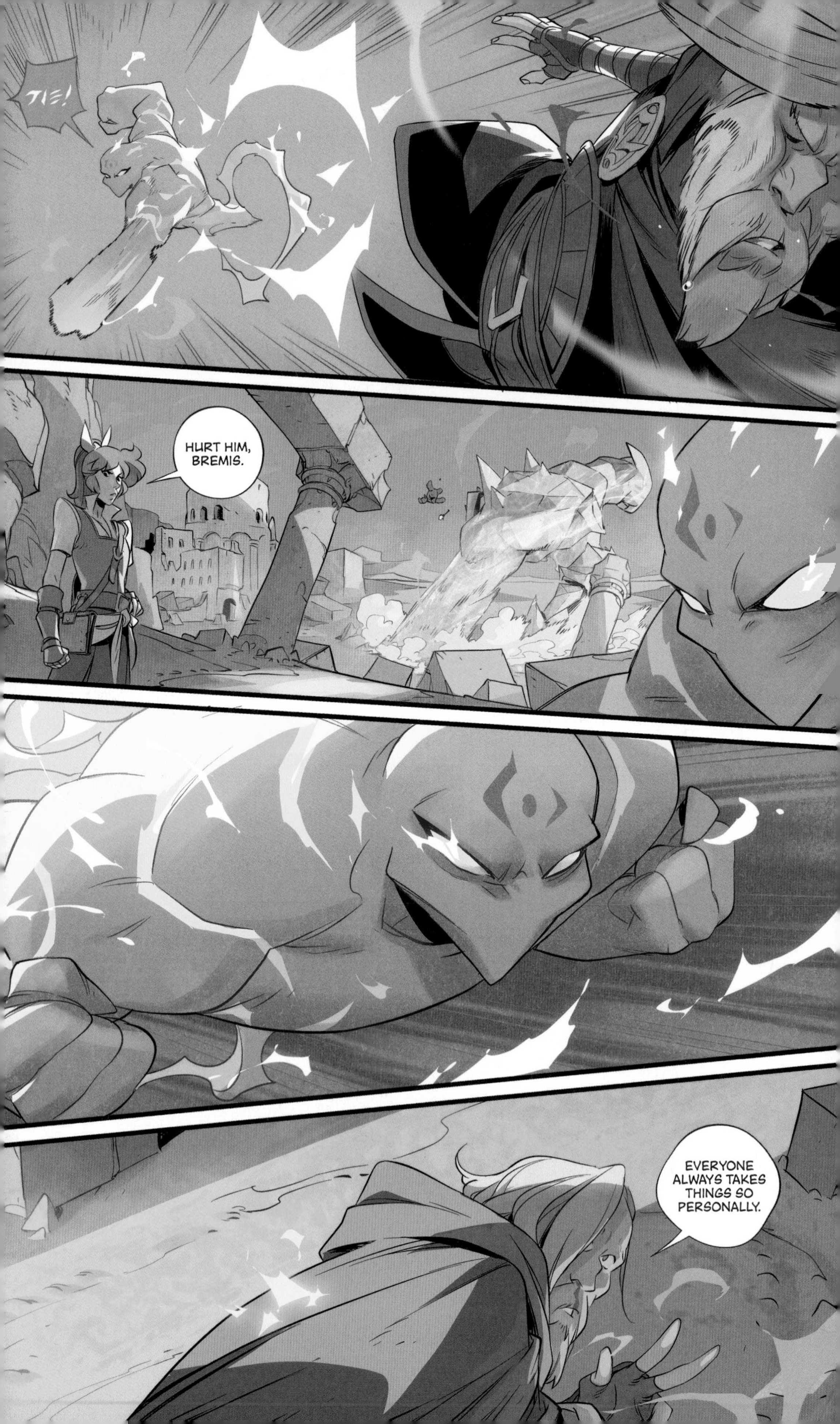
TIE!
HURT HIM, BREMIS.
EVERYONE ALWAYS TAKES THINGS SO PERSONALLY.

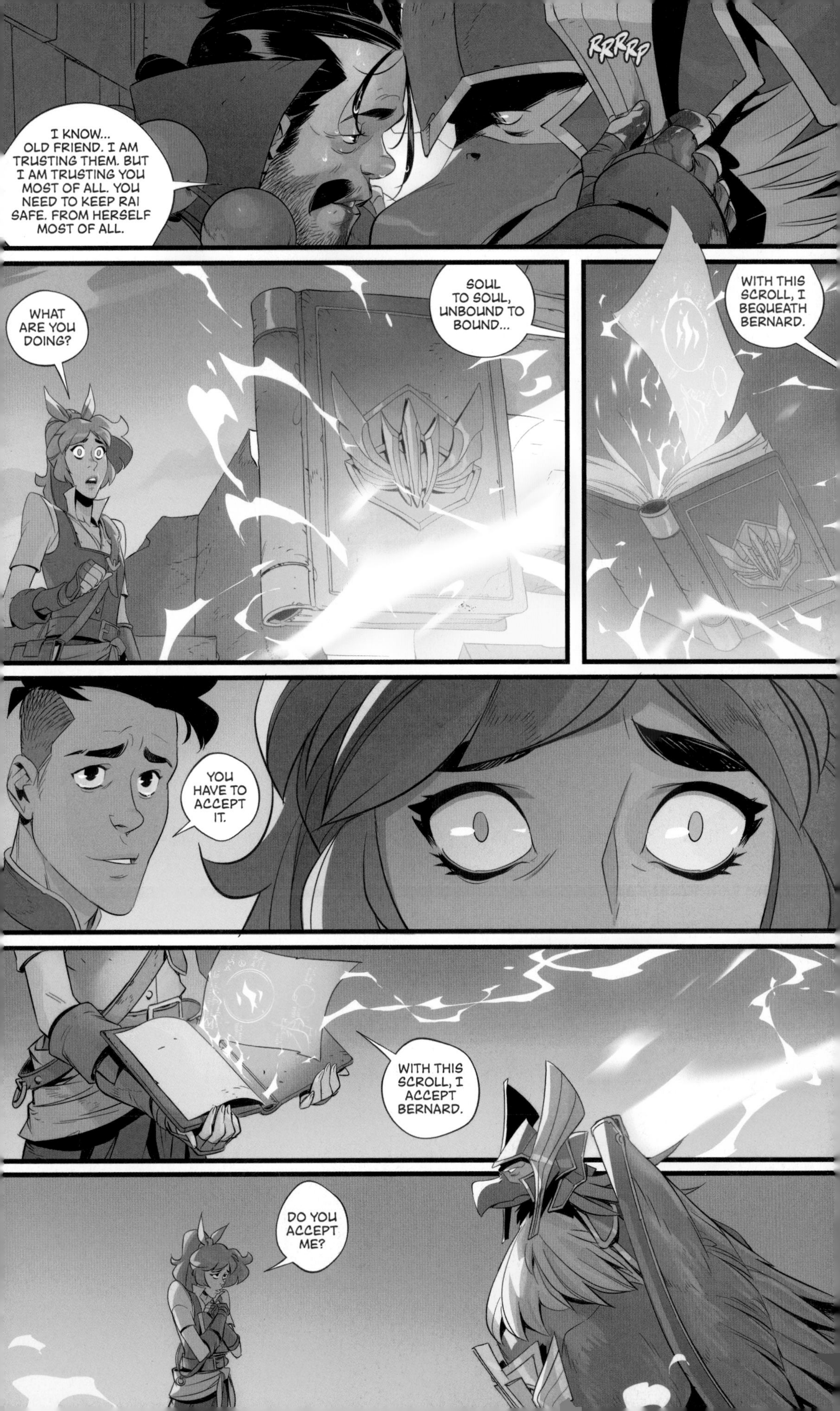
RRRRP
I KNOW... OLD FRIEND. I AM TRUSTING THEM. BUT I AM TRUSTING YOU MOST OF ALL. YOU NEED TO KEEP RAI SAFE. FROM HERSELF MOST OF ALL.
WHAT ARE YOU DOING?
SOUL TO SOUL, UNBOUND TO BOUND...
WITH THIS SCROLL, I BEQUEATH BERNARD.
YOU HAVE TO ACCEPT IT.
WITH THIS SCROLL, I ACCEPT BERNARD.
DO YOU ACCEPT ME?

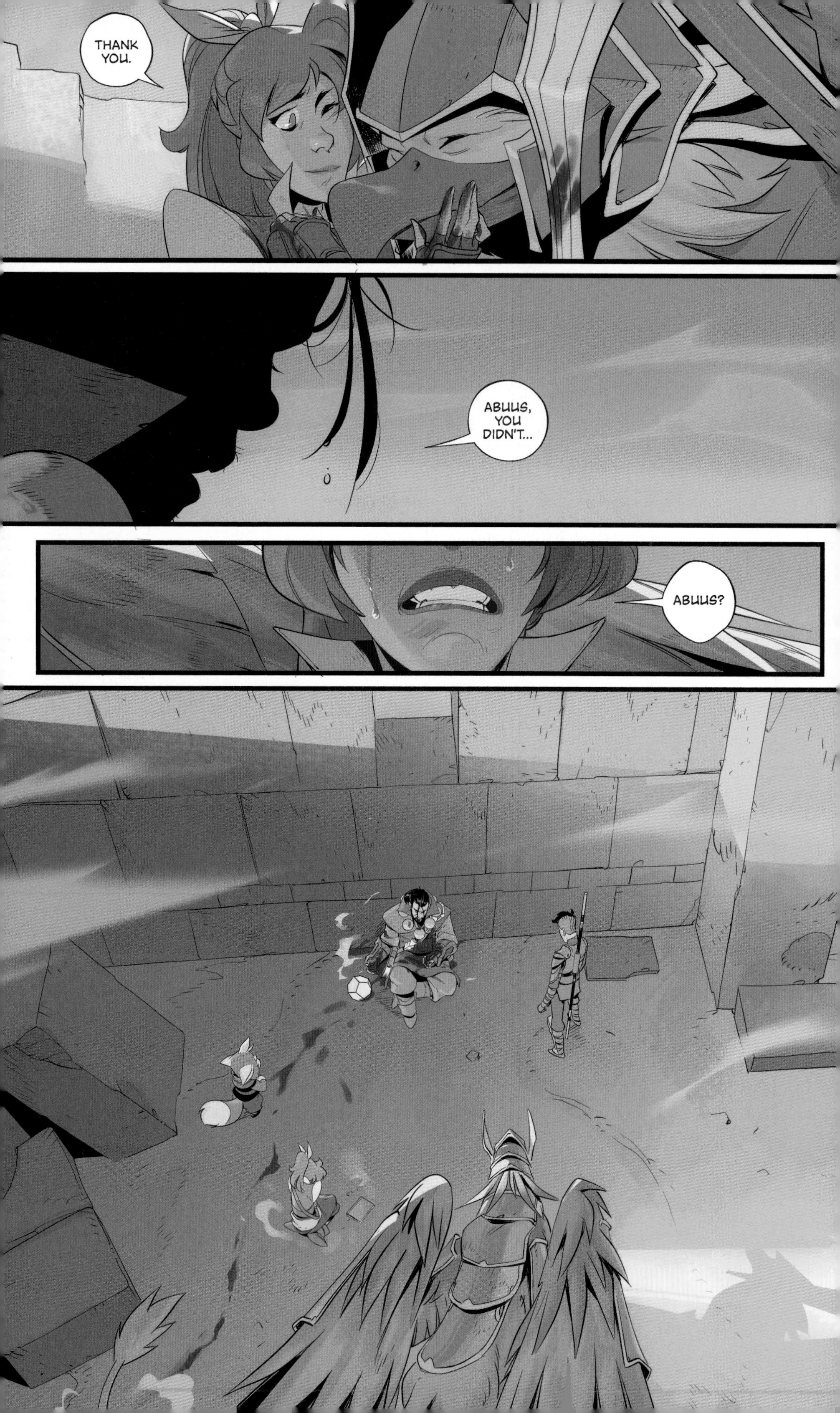
THANK YOU.
ABUUS, YOU DIDN'T...
ABUUS?

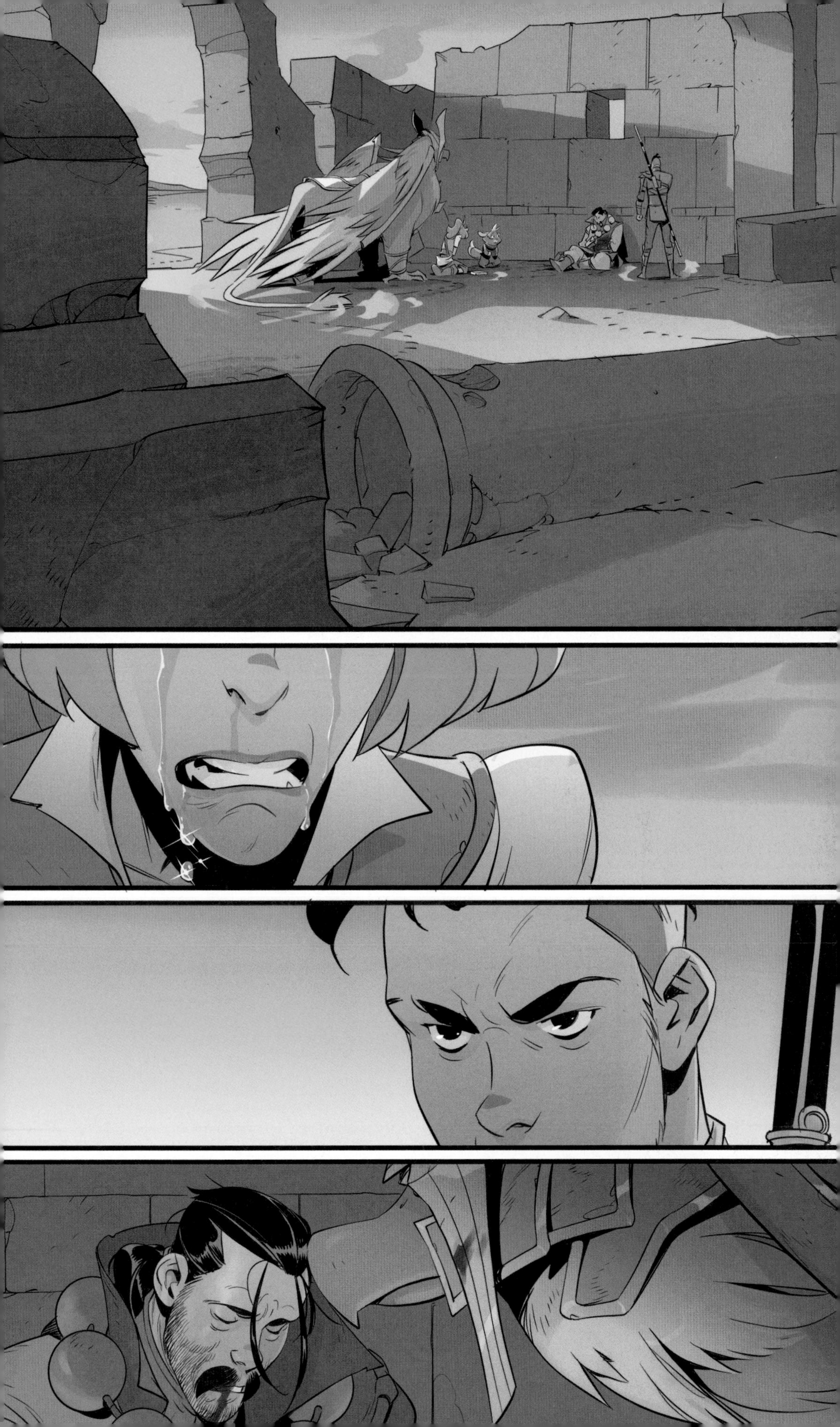

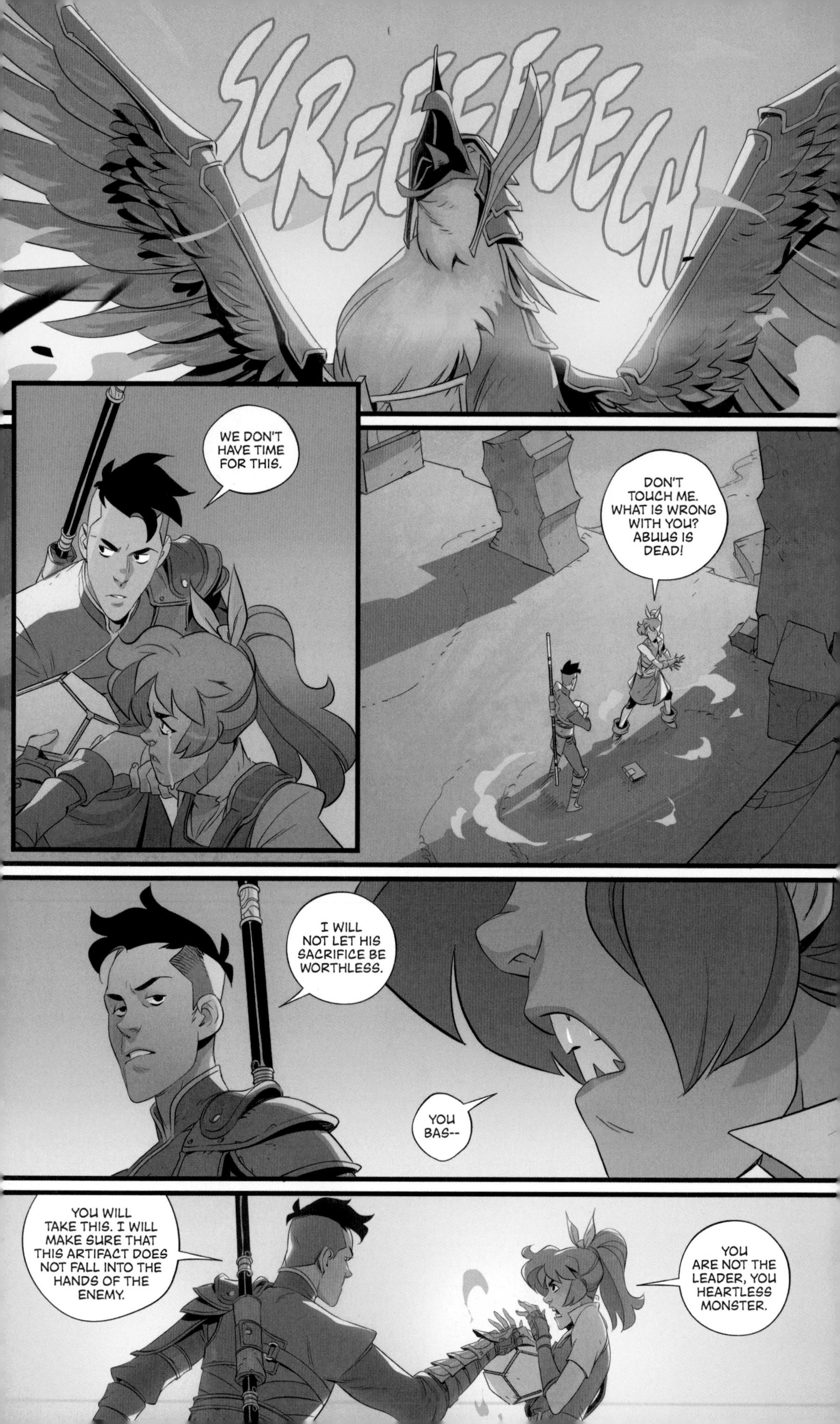
SCREEEEEEECH
WE DON'T HAVE TIME FOR THIS.
DON'T TOUCH ME. WHAT IS WRONG WITH YOU? ABUUS IS DEAD!
I WILL NOT LET HIS SACRIFICE BE WORTHLESS.
YOU BAS--
YOU WILL TAKE THIS. I WILL MAKE SURE THAT THIS ARTIFACT DOES NOT FALL INTO THE HANDS OF THE ENEMY.
YOU ARE NOT THE LEADER, YOU HEARTLESS MONSTER.

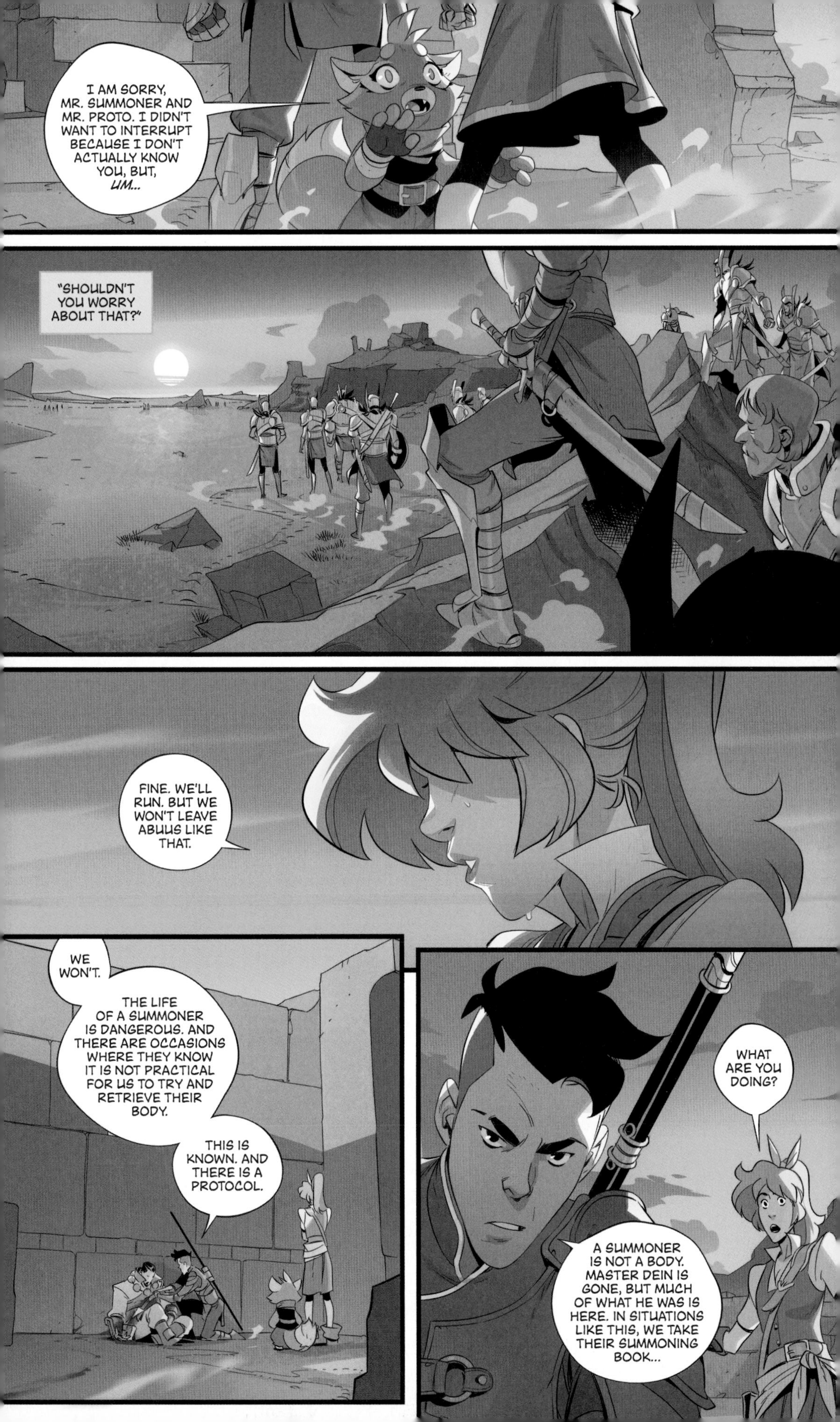
I AM SORRY, MR. SUMMONER AND MR. PROTO. I DIDN'T WANT TO INTERRUPT BECAUSE I DON'T ACTUALLY KNOW YOU, BUT, *UM...*
"SHOULDN'T YOU WORRY ABOUT THAT?"
FINE. WE'LL RUN. BUT WE WON'T LEAVE ABUUS LIKE THAT.
WE WON'T.
THE LIFE OF A SUMMONER IS DANGEROUS. AND THERE ARE OCCASIONS WHERE THEY KNOW IT IS NOT PRACTICAL FOR US TO TRY AND RETRIEVE THEIR BODY.
THIS IS KNOWN. AND THERE IS A PROTOCOL.
WHAT ARE YOU DOING?
A SUMMONER IS NOT A BODY. MASTER DEIN IS GONE, BUT MUCH OF WHAT HE WAS IS HERE. IN SITUATIONS LIKE THIS, WE TAKE THEIR SUMMONING BOOK...

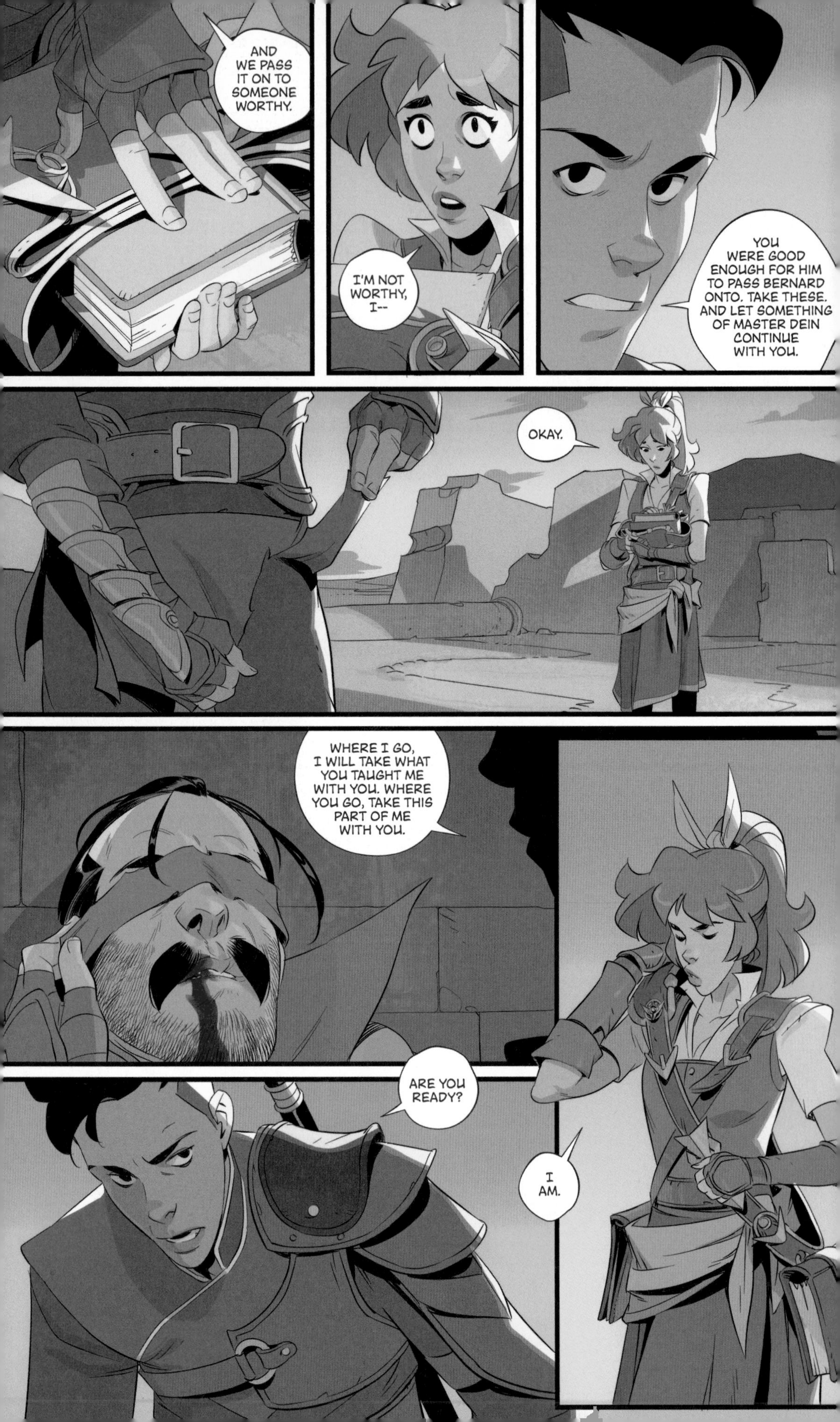
AND WE PASS IT ON TO SOMEONE WORTHY.
I'M NOT WORTHY, I--
YOU WERE GOOD ENOUGH FOR HIM TO PASS BERNARD ONTO. TAKE THESE. AND LET SOMETHING OF MASTER DEIN CONTINUE WITH YOU.
OKAY.
WHERE I GO, I WILL TAKE WHAT YOU TAUGHT ME WITH YOU. WHERE YOU GO, TAKE THIS PART OF ME WITH YOU.
ARE YOU READY?
I AM.

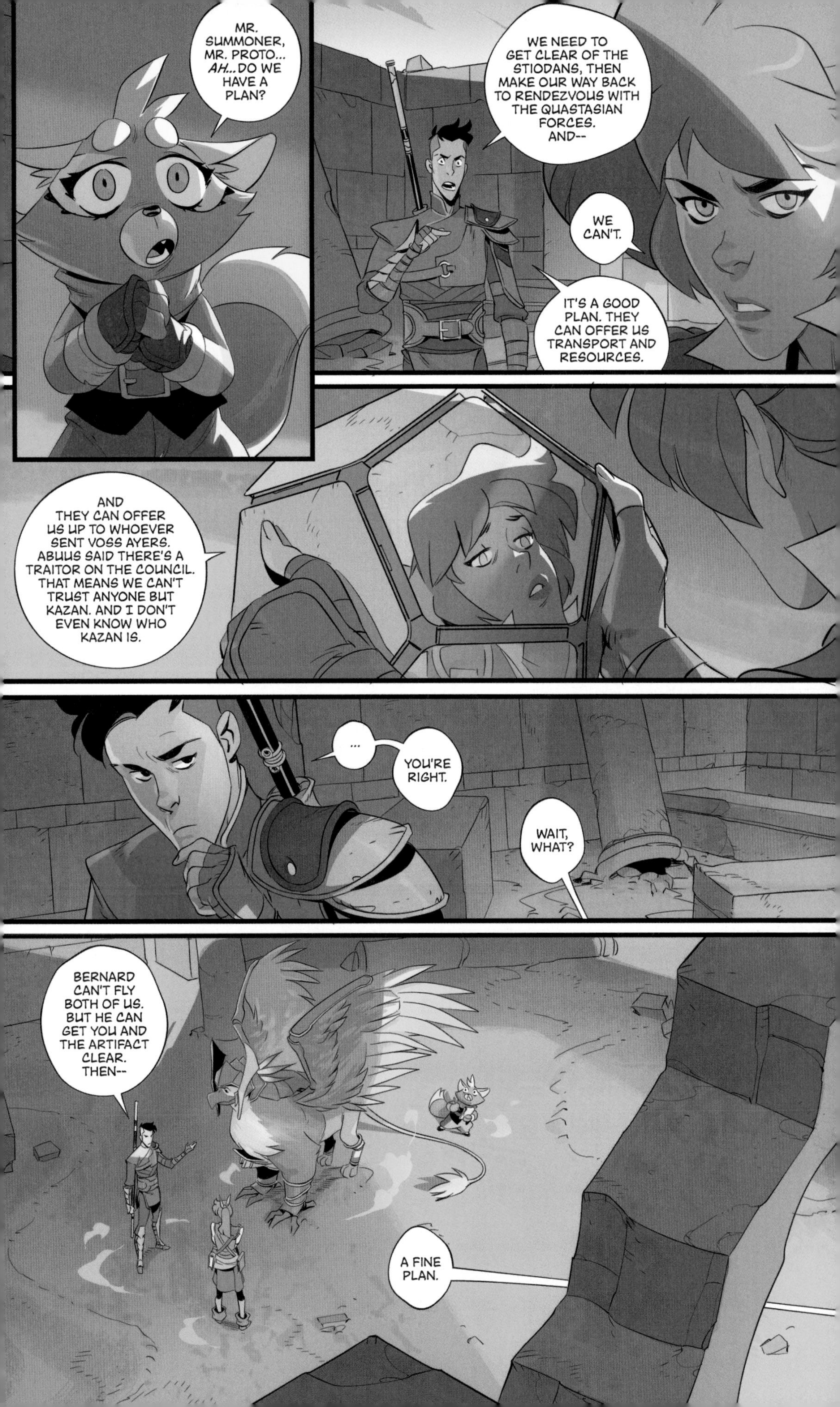

MR. SUMMONER, MR. PROTO... *AH...* DO WE HAVE A PLAN?
WE NEED TO GET CLEAR OF THE STIODANS, THEN MAKE OUR WAY BACK TO RENDEZVOUS WITH THE QUASTASIAN FORCES. AND--
WE CAN'T.
IT'S A GOOD PLAN. THEY CAN OFFER US TRANSPORT AND RESOURCES.
AND THEY CAN OFFER US UP TO WHOEVER SENT VOSS AYERS. ABUUS SAID THERE'S A TRAITOR ON THE COUNCIL. THAT MEANS WE CAN'T TRUST ANYONE BUT KAZAN. AND I DON'T EVEN KNOW WHO KAZAN IS.
...
YOU'RE RIGHT.
WAIT, WHAT?
BERNARD CAN'T FLY BOTH OF US. BUT HE CAN GET YOU AND THE ARTIFACT CLEAR. THEN--
A FINE PLAN.

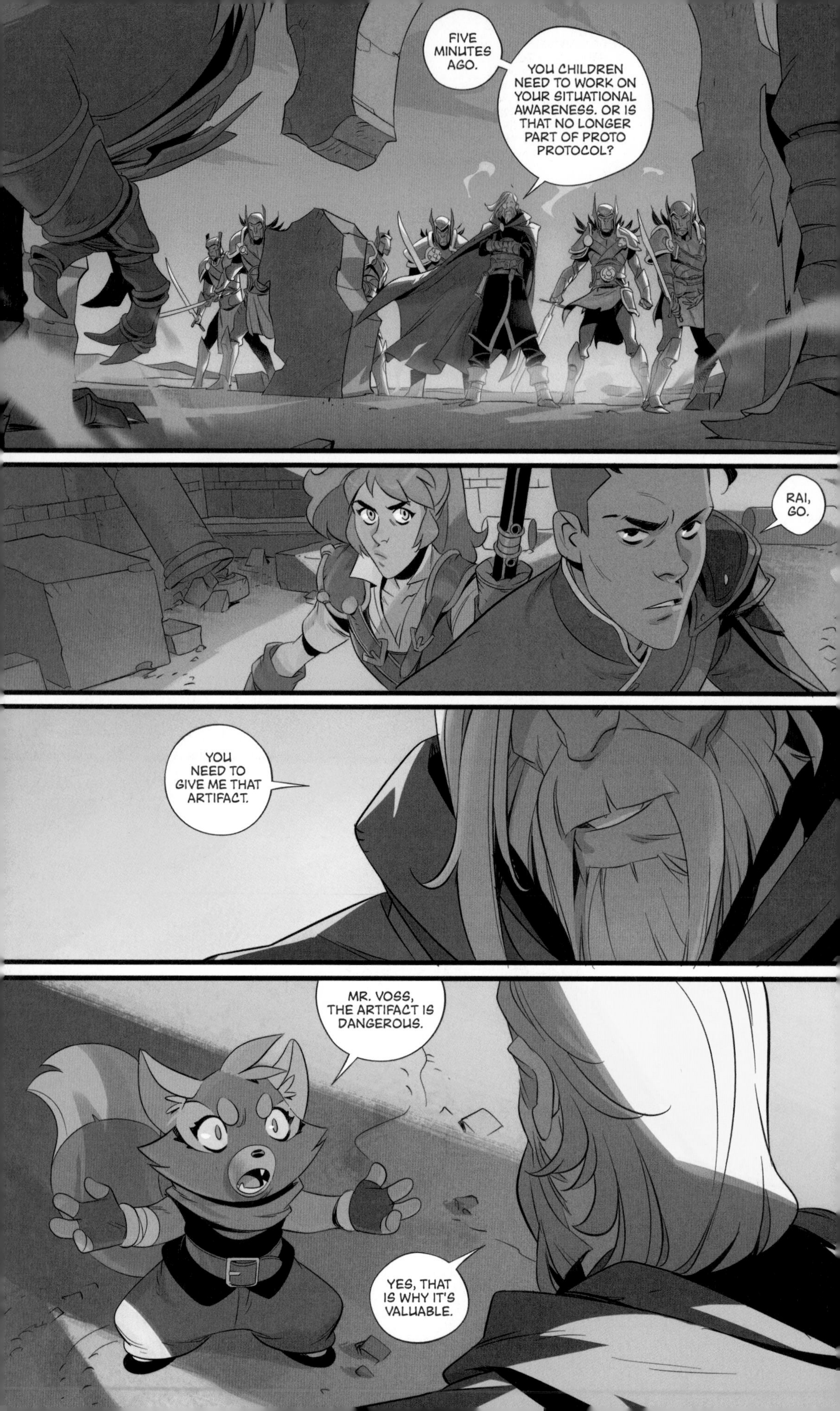
FIVE MINUTES AGO.
YOU CHILDREN NEED TO WORK ON YOUR SITUATIONAL AWARENESS. OR IS THAT NO LONGER PART OF PROTO PROTOCOL?
RAI, GO.
YOU NEED TO GIVE ME THAT ARTIFACT.
MR. VOSS, THE ARTIFACT IS DANGEROUS.
YES, THAT IS WHY IT'S VALUABLE.

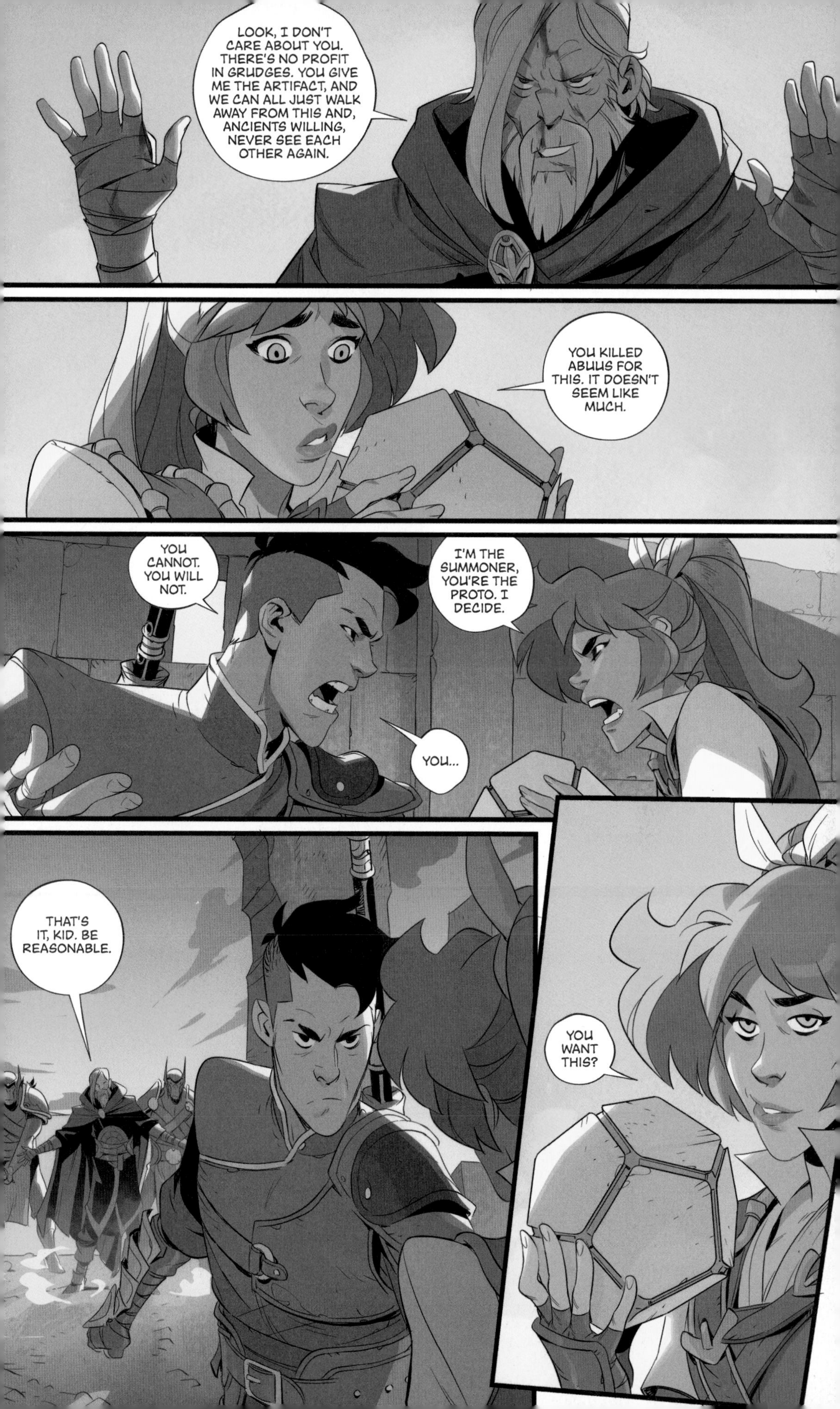
LOOK, I DON'T CARE ABOUT YOU. THERE'S NO PROFIT IN GRUDGES. YOU GIVE ME THE ARTIFACT, AND WE CAN ALL JUST WALK AWAY FROM THIS AND, ANCIENTS WILLING, NEVER SEE EACH OTHER AGAIN.
YOU KILLED ABUUS FOR THIS. IT DOESN'T SEEM LIKE MUCH.
YOU CANNOT. YOU WILL NOT.
I'M THE SUMMONER, YOU'RE THE PROTO. I DECIDE.
YOU...
THAT'S IT, KID. BE REASONABLE.
YOU WANT THIS?

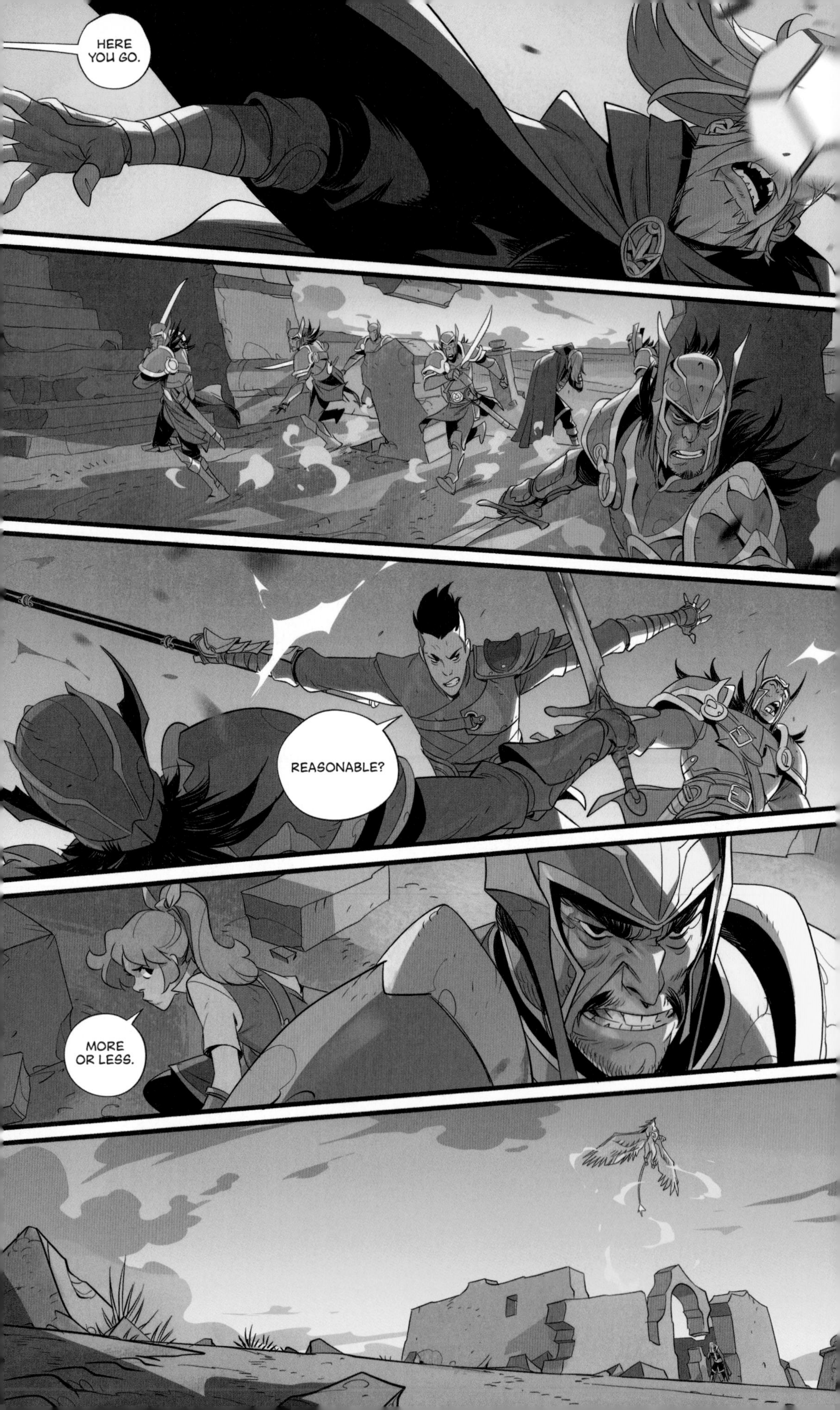
HERE YOU GO.
REASONABLE?
MORE OR LESS.

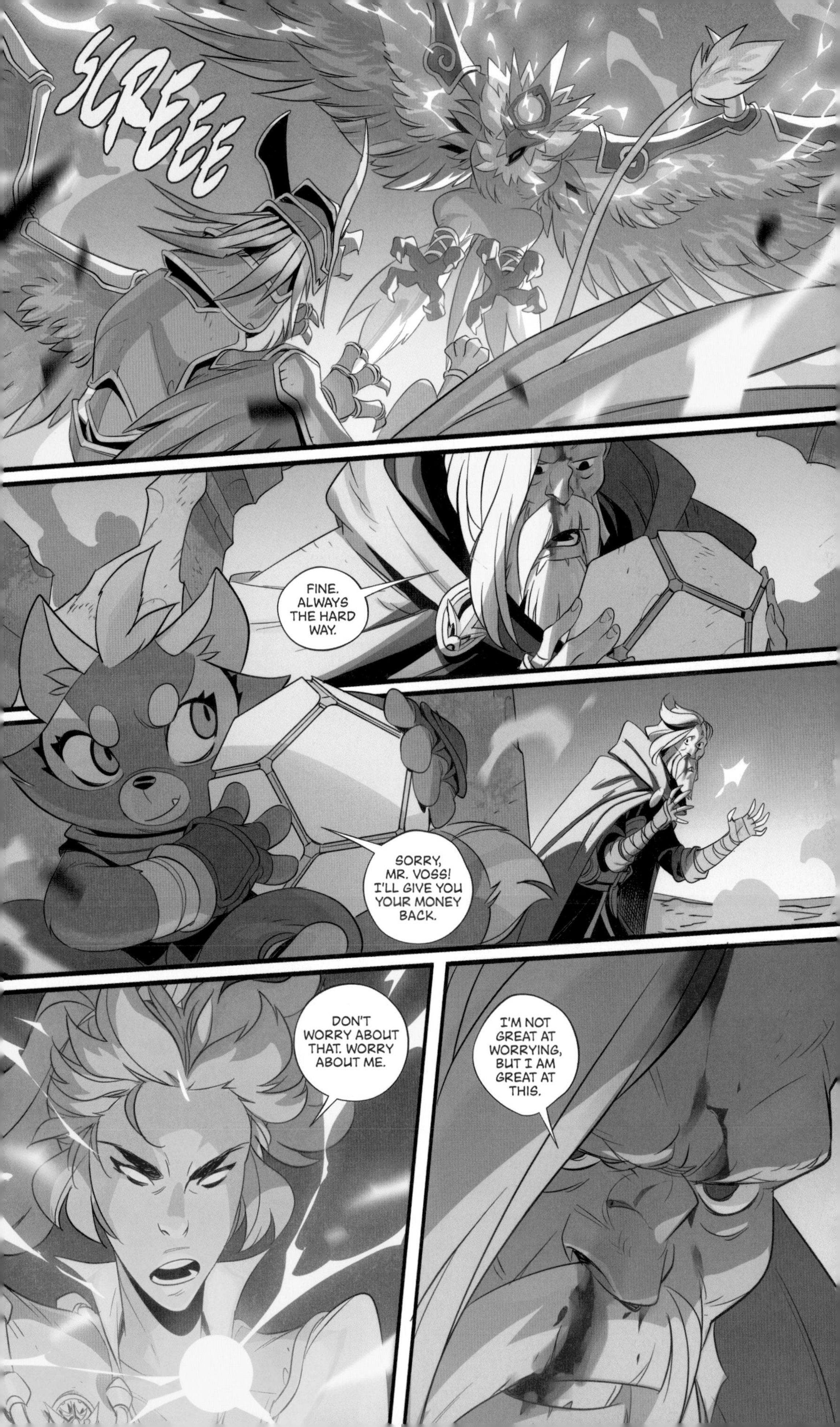
SCREEEE
FINE. ALWAYS THE HARD WAY.
SORRY, MR. VOSS! I'LL GIVE YOU YOUR MONEY BACK.
DON'T WORRY ABOUT THAT. WORRY ABOUT ME.
I'M NOT GREAT AT WORRYING, BUT I AM GREAT AT THIS.

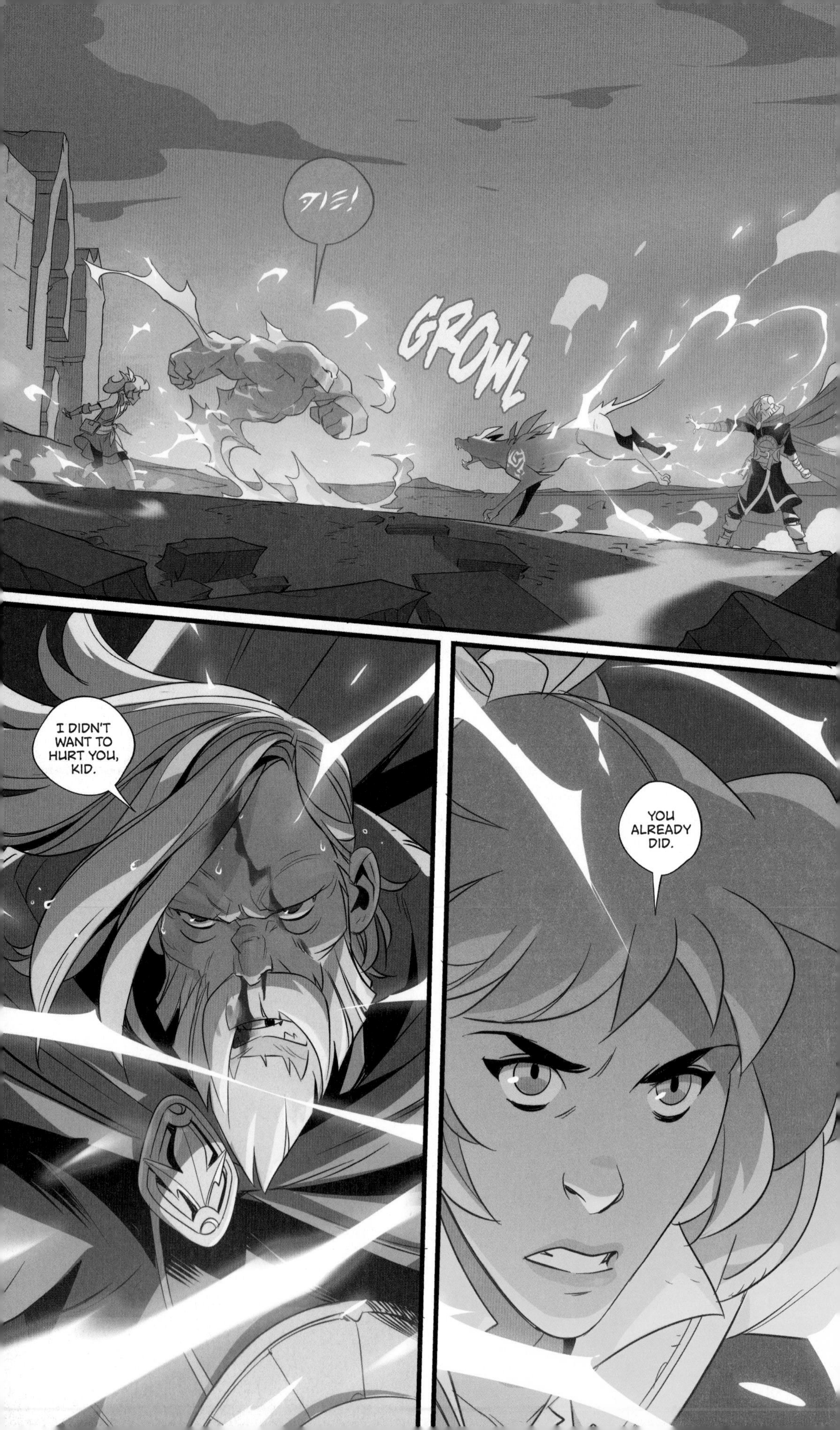
GROWL
I DIDN'T WANT TO HURT YOU, KID.
YOU ALREADY DID.

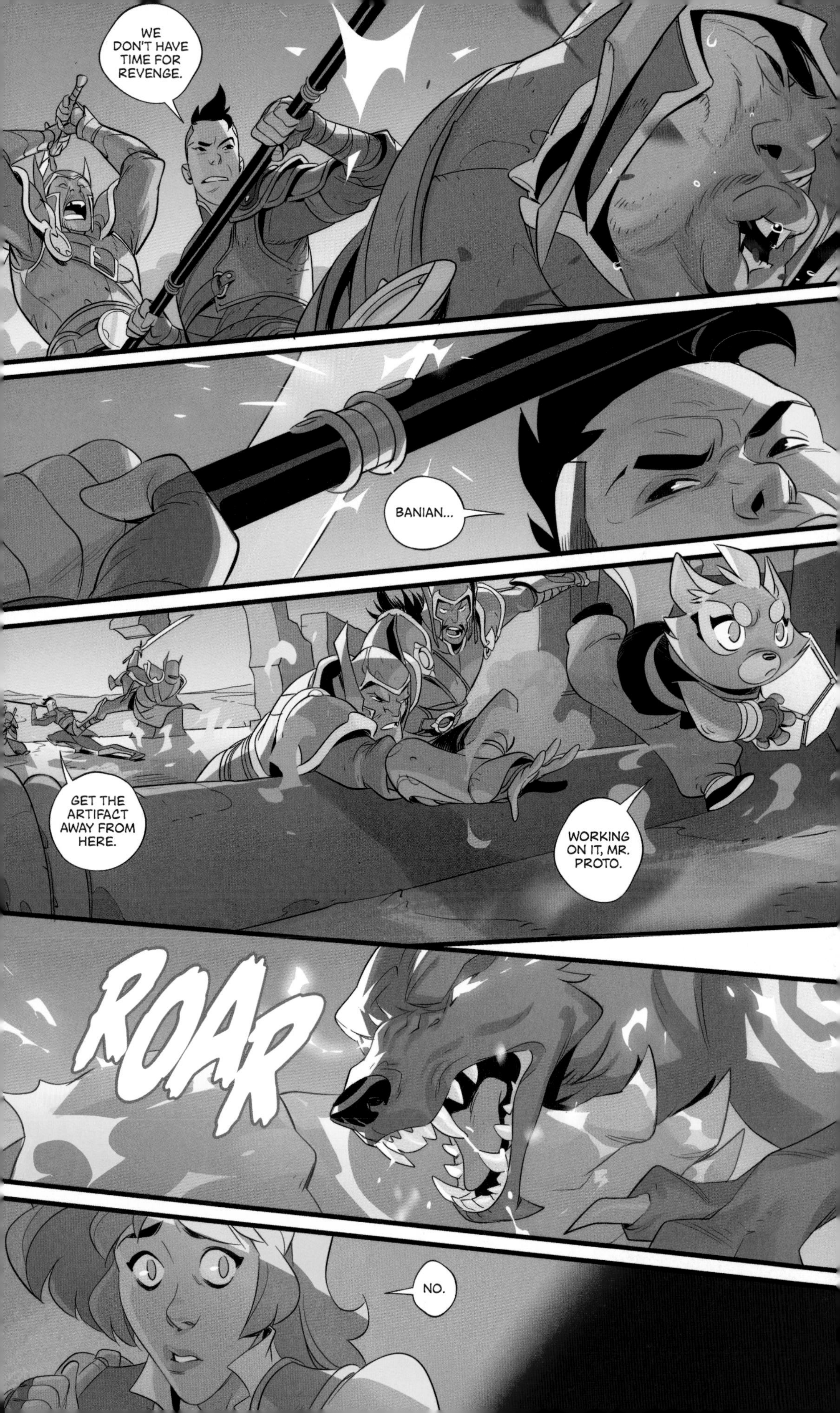
WE DON'T HAVE TIME FOR REVENGE.
BANIAN...
GET THE ARTIFACT AWAY FROM HERE.
WORKING ON IT, MR. PROTO.
ROAR
NO.

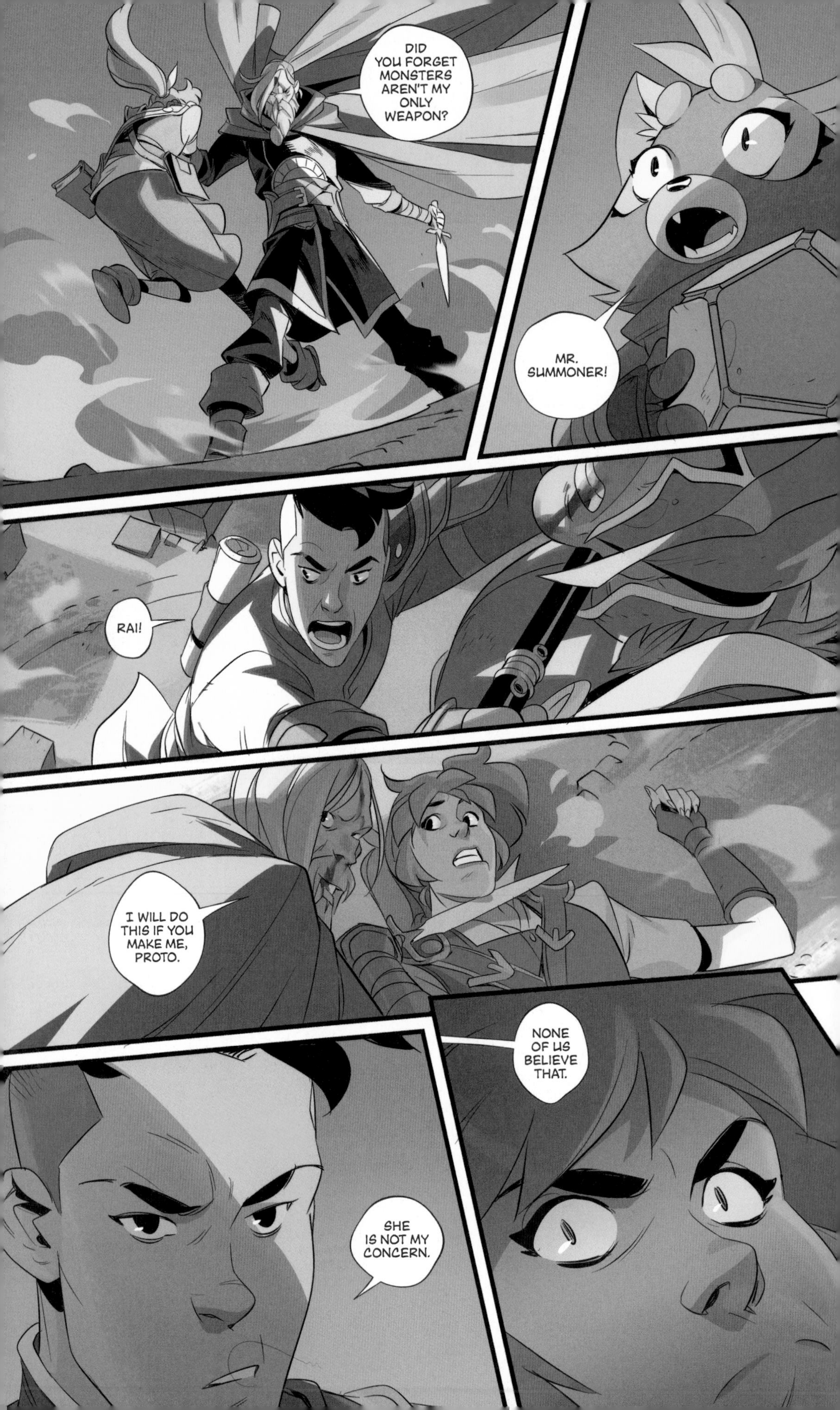
DID YOU FORGET MONSTERS AREN'T MY ONLY WEAPON?
MR. SUMMONER!
RAI!
I WILL DO THIS IF YOU MAKE ME, PROTO.
NONE OF US BELIEVE THAT.
SHE IS NOT MY CONCERN.

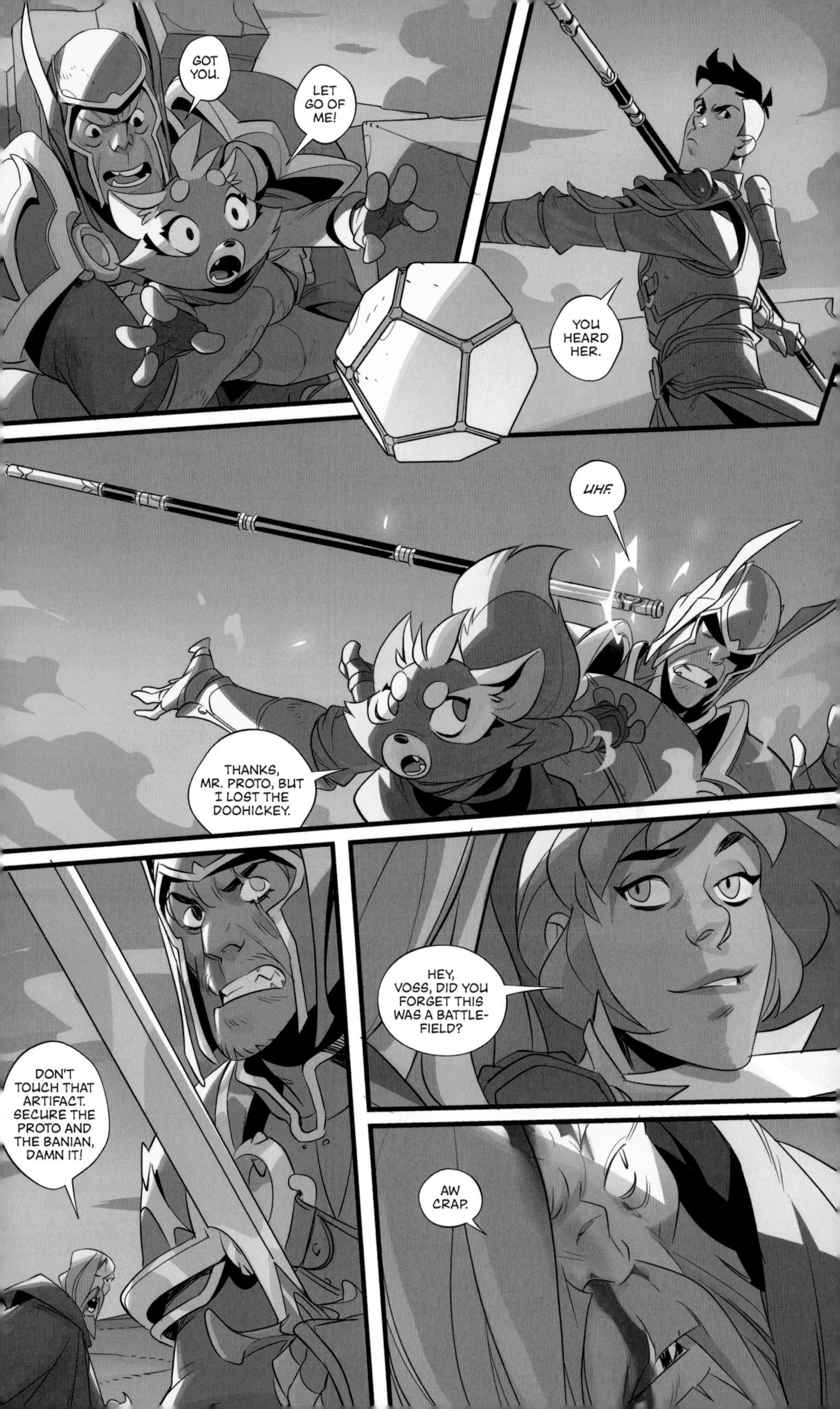
GOT YOU.
LET GO OF ME!
YOU HEARD HER.
UHF.
THANKS, MR. PROTO, BUT I LOST THE DOOHICKEY.
HEY, VOSS, DID YOU FORGET THIS WAS A BATTLE-FIELD?
DON'T TOUCH THAT ARTIFACT. SECURE THE PROTO AND THE BANIAN, DAMN IT!
AW CRAP.

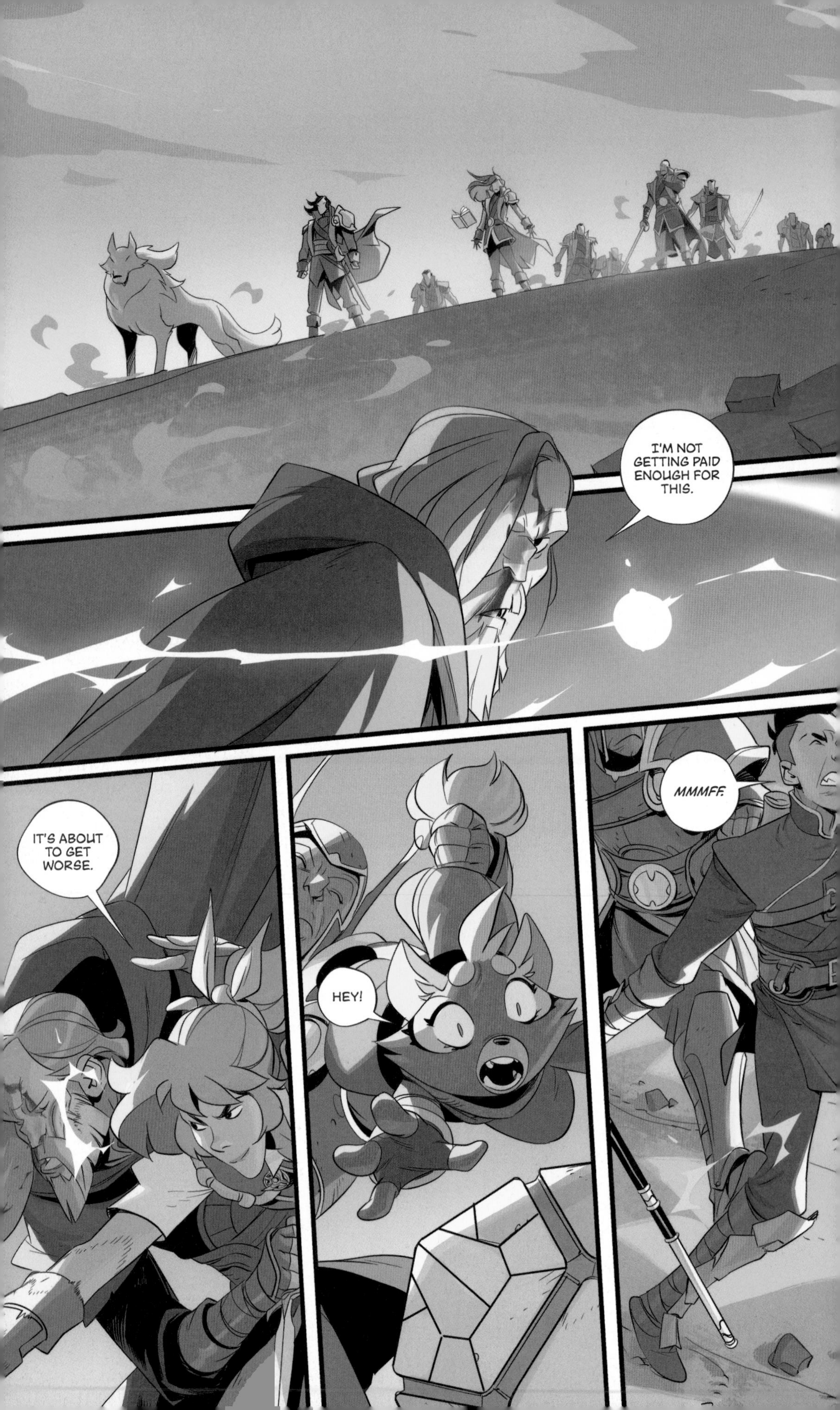
I'M NOT GETTING PAID ENOUGH FOR THIS.
IT'S ABOUT TO GET WORSE.
HEY!
MMMFF.

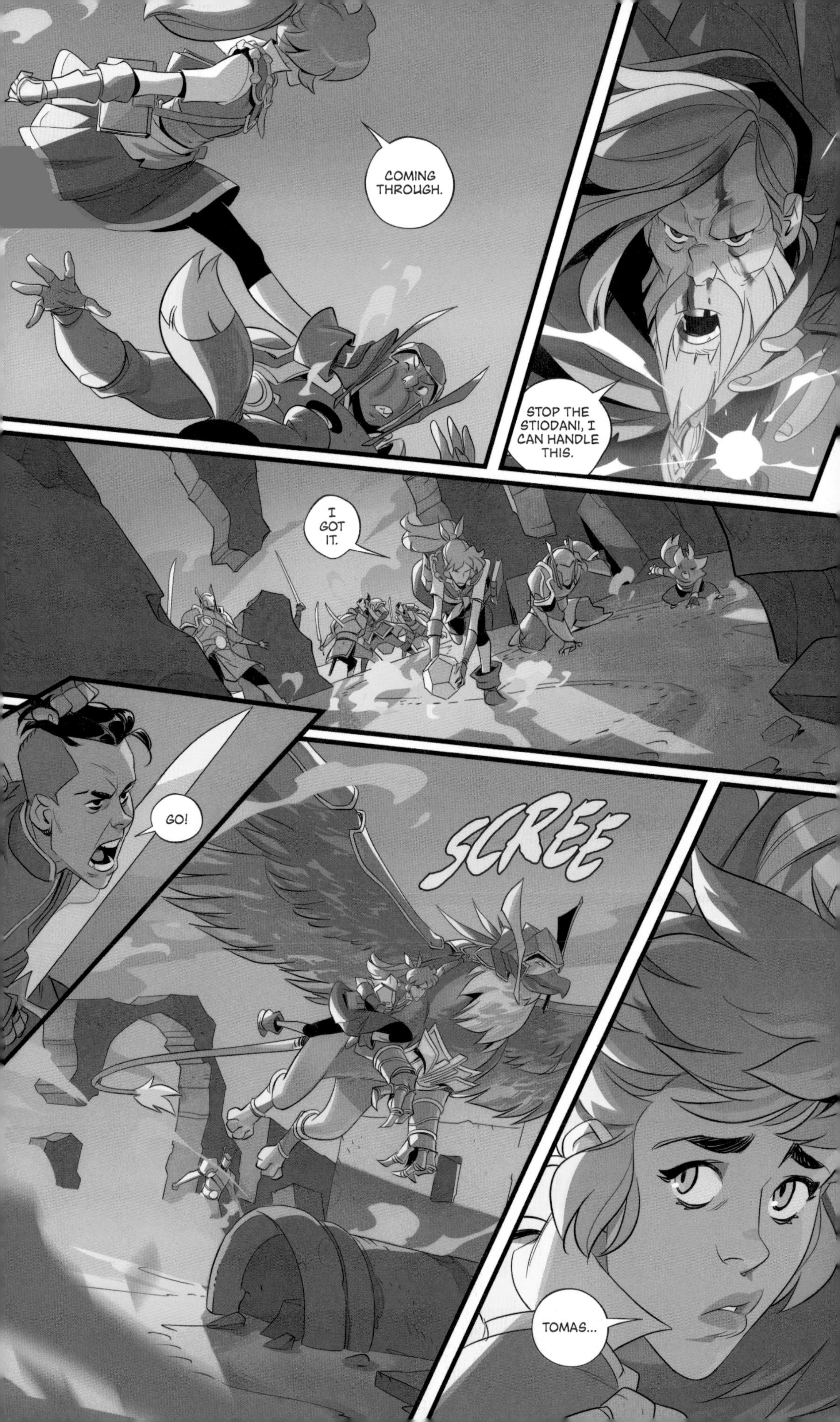
COMING THROUGH.
STOP THE STIODANI, I CAN HANDLE THIS.
I GOT IT.
GO!
SCREE
TOMAS...

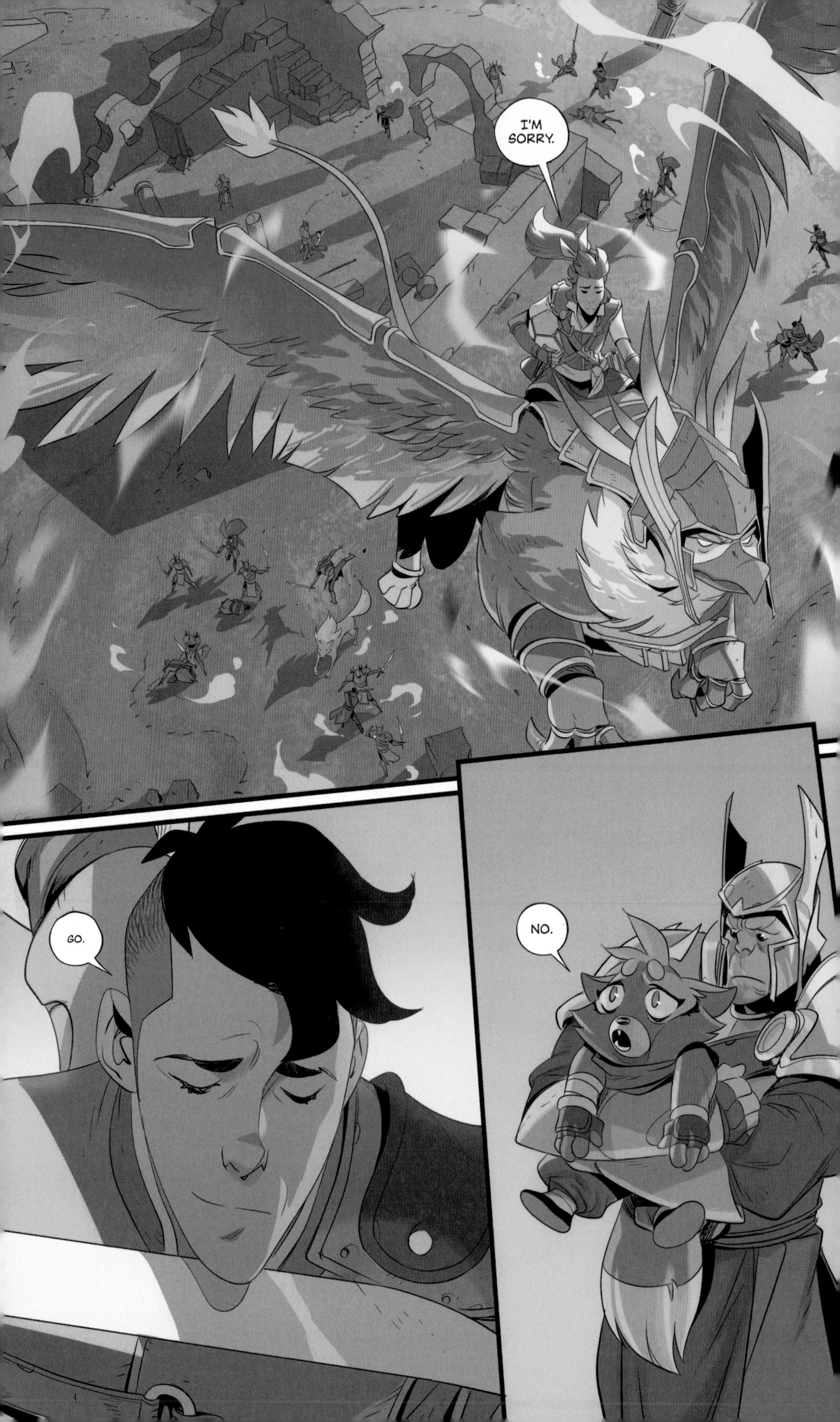
I'M SORRY.
GO.
NO.

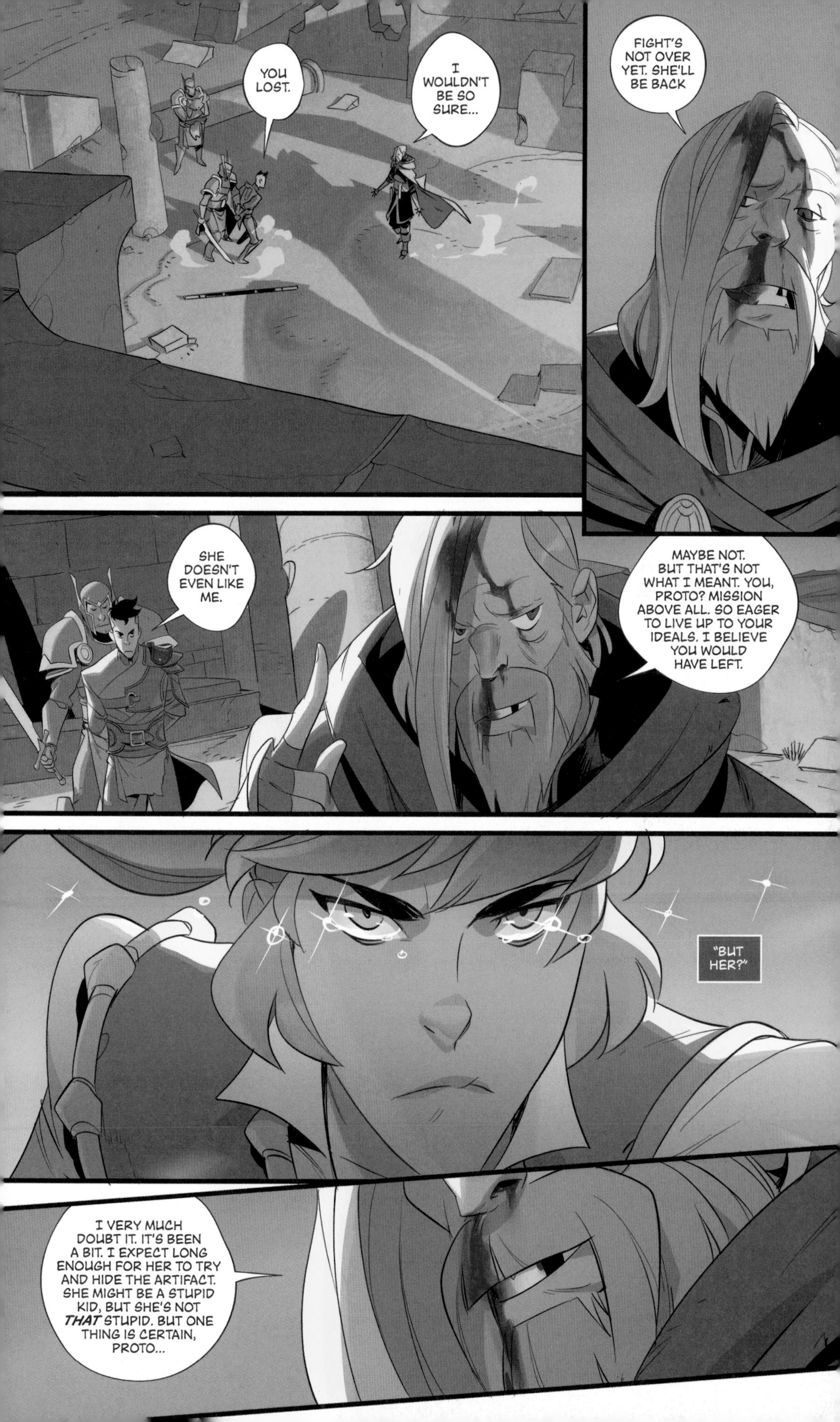
YOU LOST.
I WOULDN'T BE SO SURE...
FIGHT'S NOT OVER YET. SHE'LL BE BACK
SHE DOESN'T EVEN LIKE ME.
MAYBE NOT. BUT THAT'S NOT WHAT I MEANT. YOU, PROTO? MISSION ABOVE ALL. SO EAGER TO LIVE UP TO YOUR IDEALS. I BELIEVE YOU WOULD HAVE LEFT.
"BUT HER?"
I VERY MUCH DOUBT IT. IT'S BEEN A BIT. I EXPECT LONG ENOUGH FOR HER TO TRY AND HIDE THE ARTIFACT. SHE MIGHT BE A STUPID KID, BUT SHE'S NOT *THAT* STUPID. BUT ONE THING IS CERTAIN, PROTO...

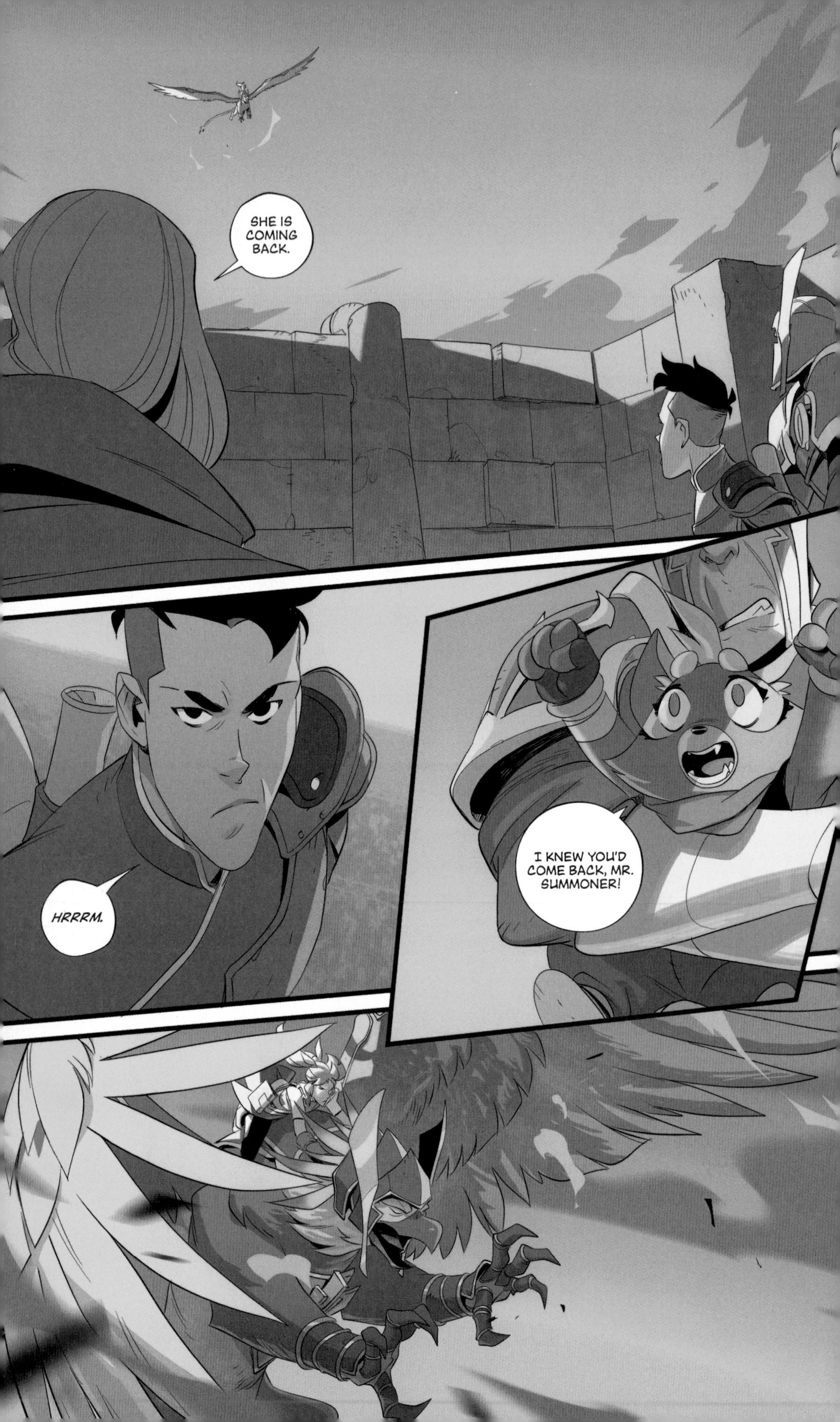
SHE IS COMING BACK.
HRRRM.
I KNEW YOU'D COME BACK, MR. SUMMONER!

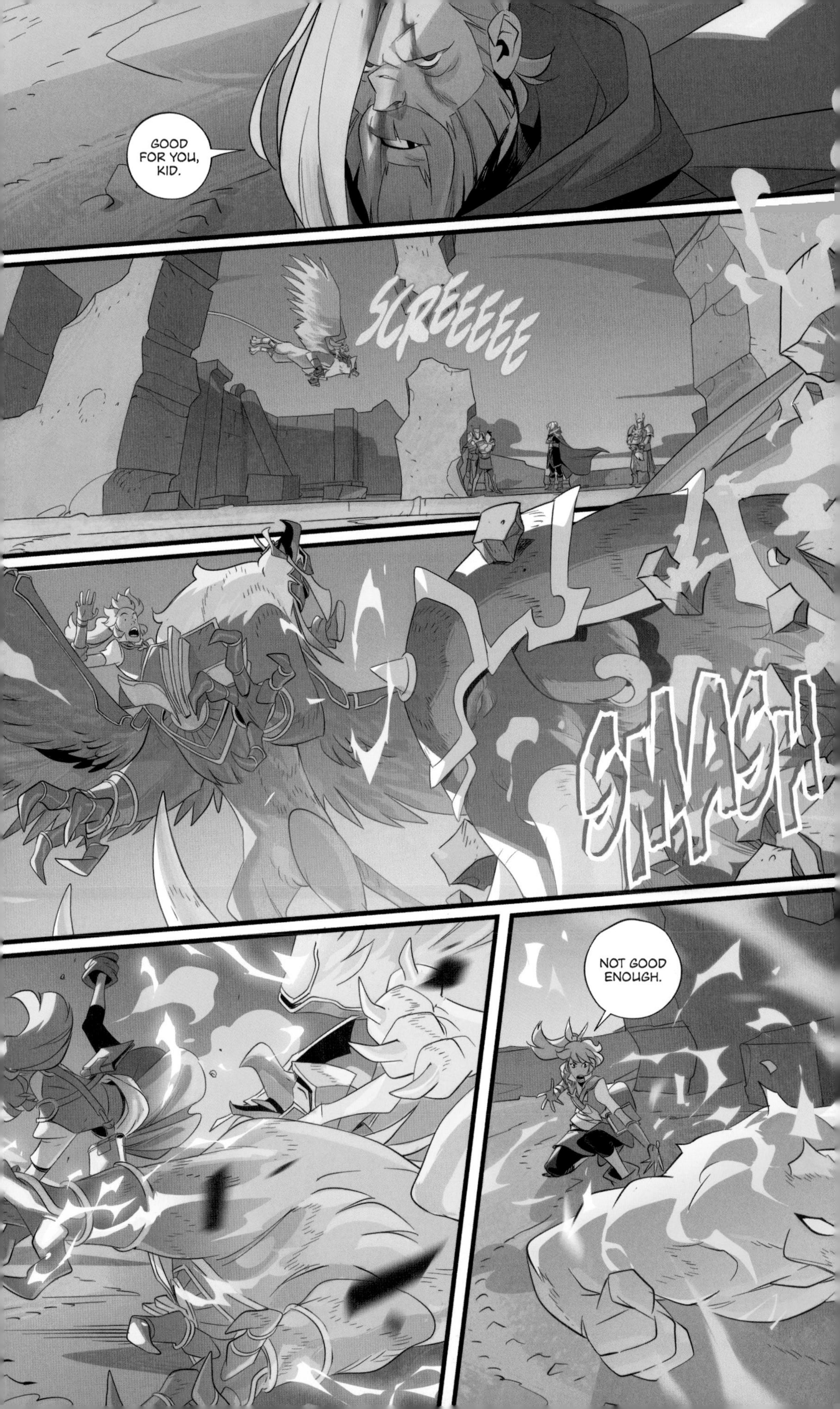
GOOD FOR YOU, KID.
SCREEEEEE
SMASH
NOT GOOD ENOUGH.

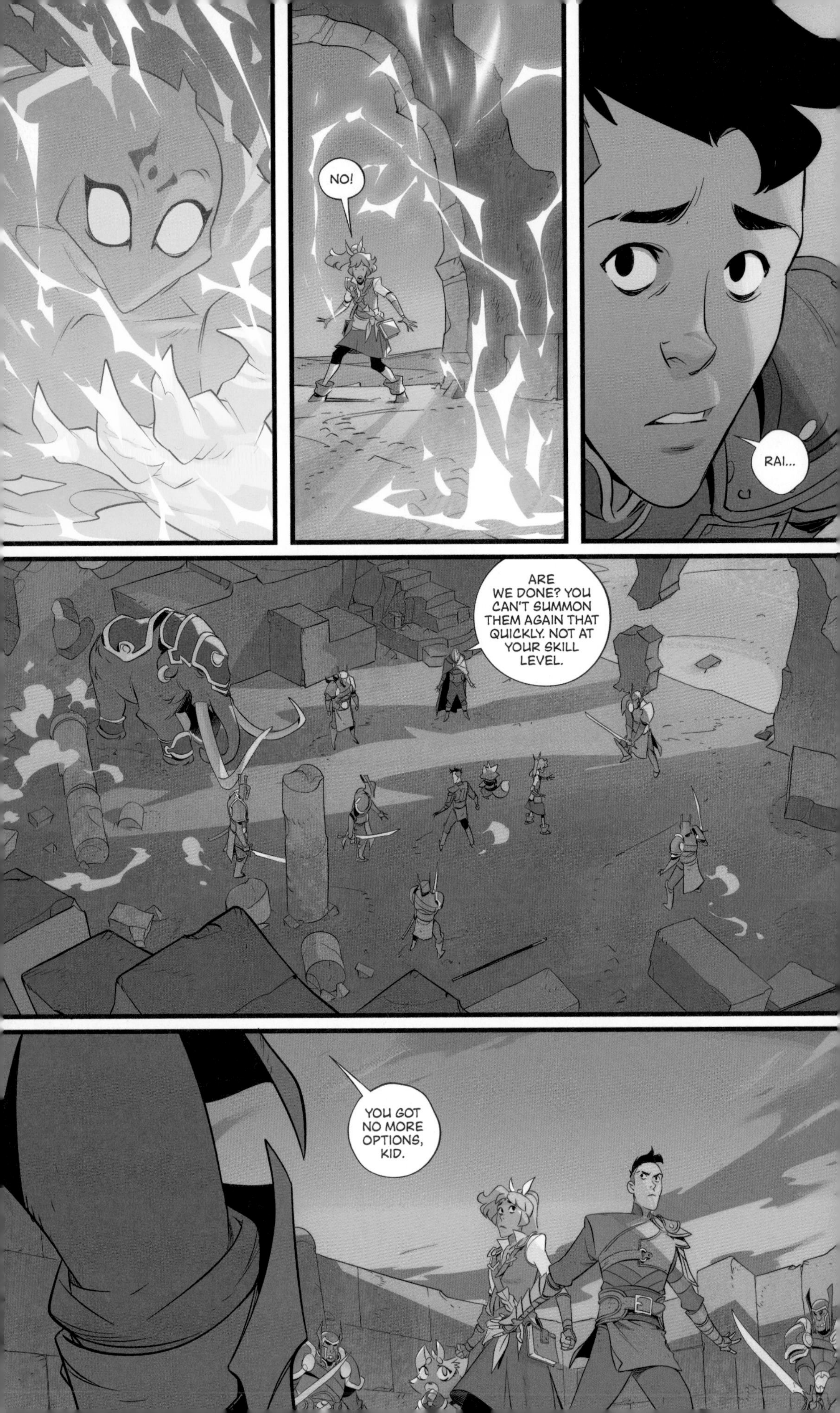
NO!
RAI...
ARE WE DONE? YOU CAN'T SUMMON THEM AGAIN THAT QUICKLY. NOT AT YOUR SKILL LEVEL.
YOU GOT NO MORE OPTIONS, KID.

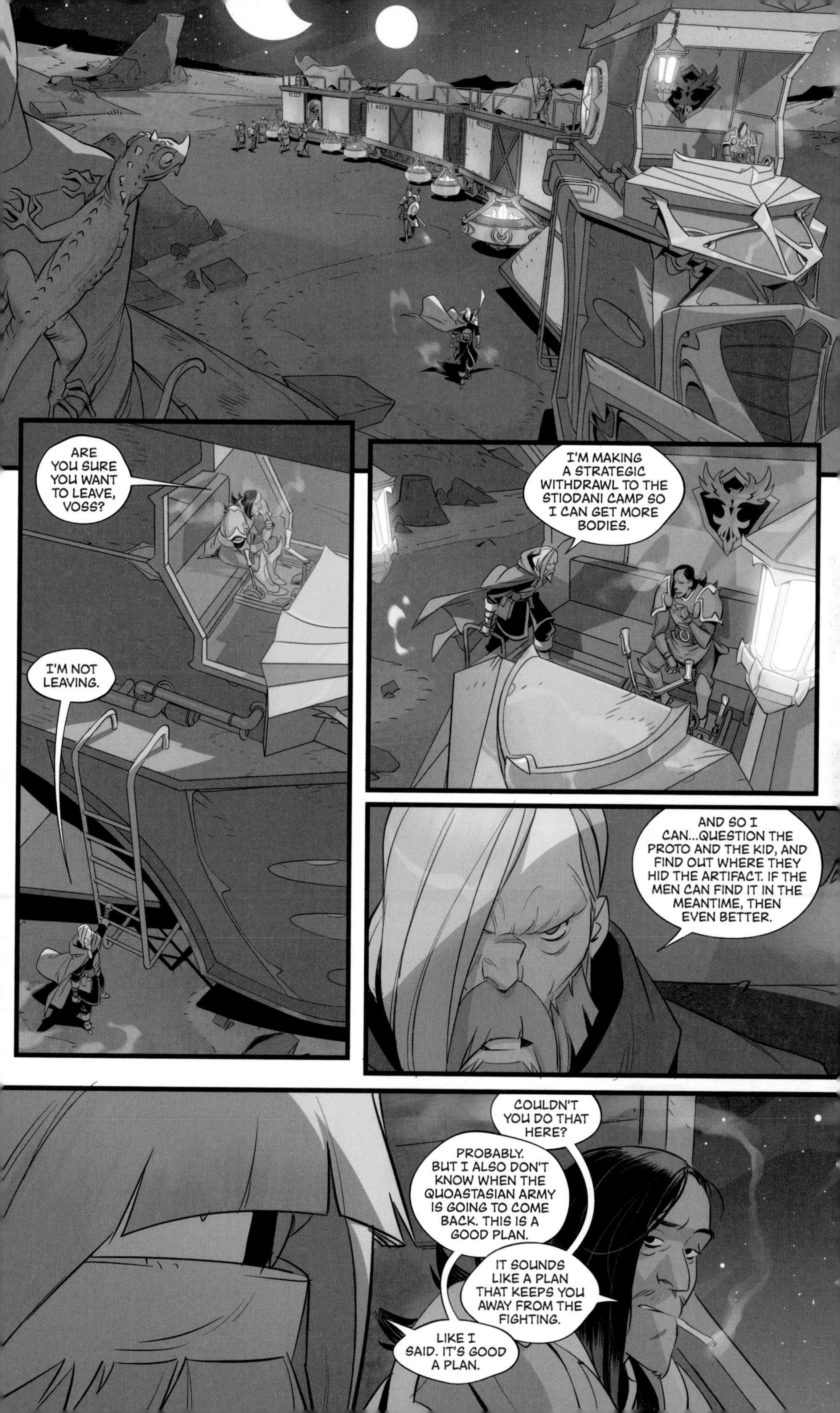
ARE YOU SURE YOU WANT TO LEAVE, VOSS?
I'M NOT LEAVING.
I'M MAKING A STRATEGIC WITHDRAWL TO THE STIODANI CAMP SO I CAN GET MORE BODIES.
AND SO I CAN...QUESTION THE PROTO AND THE KID, AND FIND OUT WHERE THEY HID THE ARTIFACT. IF THE MEN CAN FIND IT IN THE MEANTIME, THEN EVEN BETTER.
COULDN'T YOU DO THAT HERE?
PROBABLY. BUT I ALSO DON'T KNOW WHEN THE QUOASTASIAN ARMY IS GOING TO COME BACK. THIS IS A GOOD PLAN.
IT SOUNDS LIKE A PLAN THAT KEEPS YOU AWAY FROM THE FIGHTING.
LIKE I SAID. IT'S GOOD A PLAN.

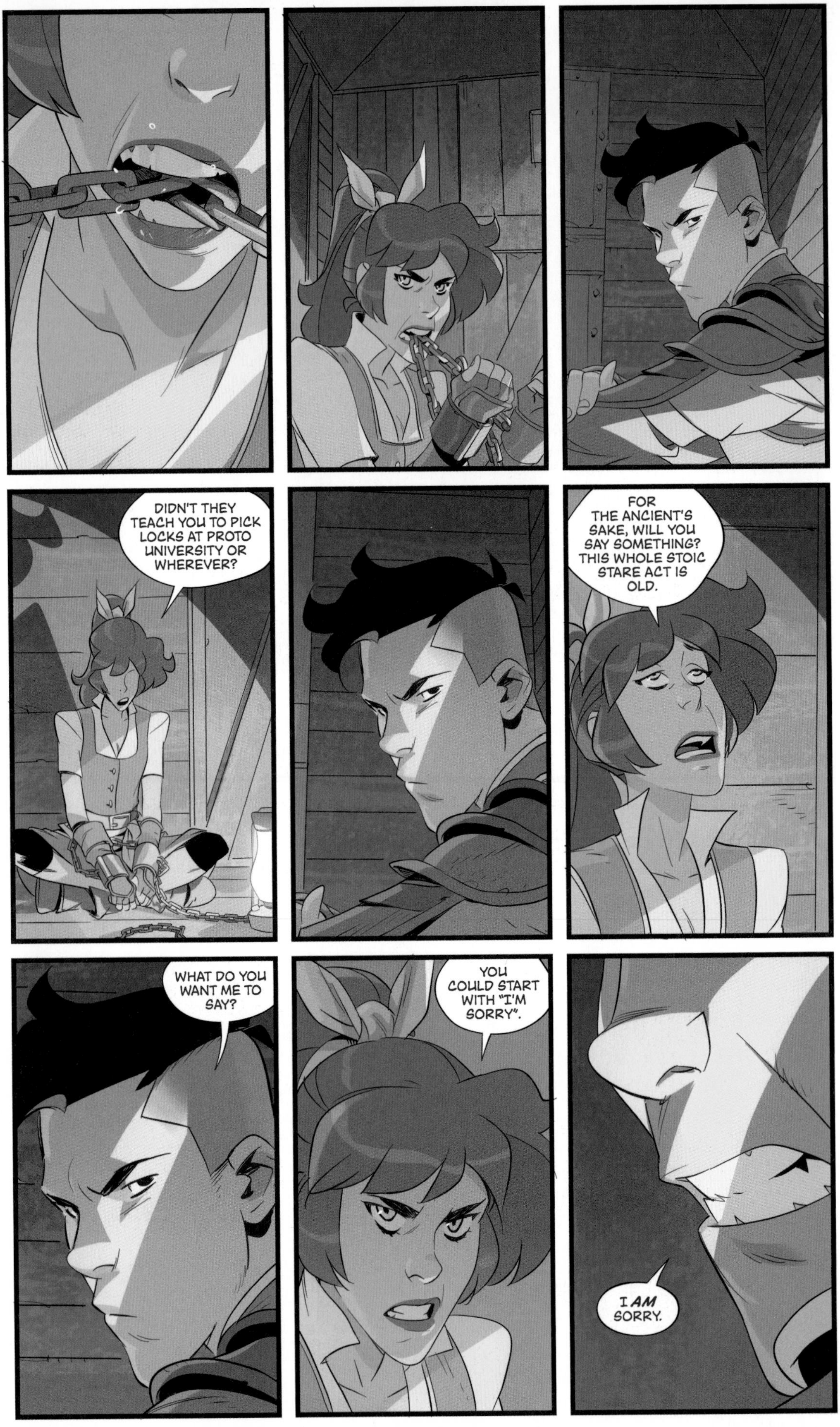
DIDN'T THEY TEACH YOU TO PICK LOCKS AT PROTO UNIVERSITY OR WHEREVER?
FOR THE ANCIENT'S SAKE, WILL YOU SAY SOMETHING? THIS WHOLE STOIC STARE ACT IS OLD.
WHAT DO YOU WANT ME TO SAY?
YOU COULD START WITH "I'M SORRY".
I *AM* SORRY.

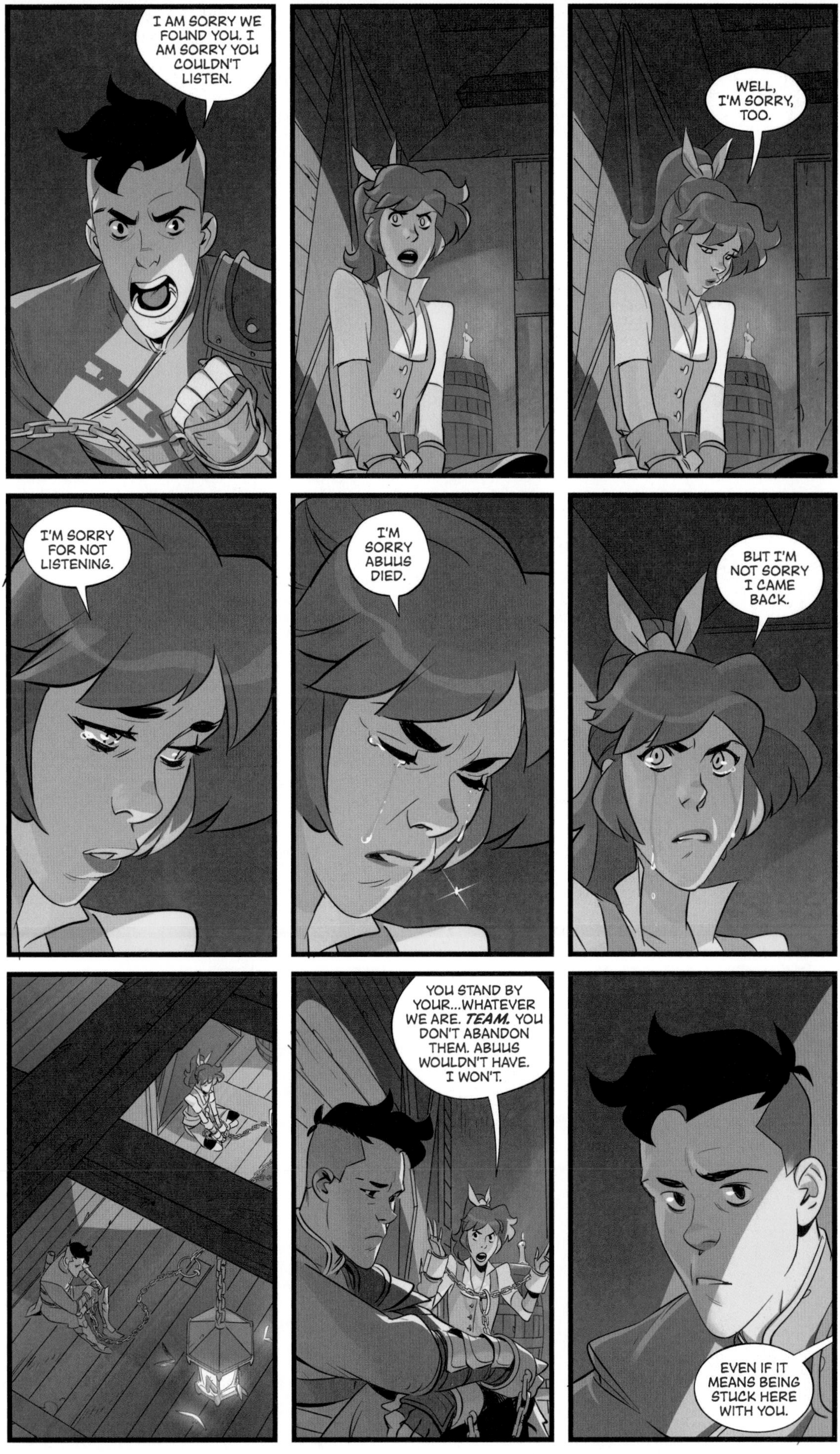
I AM SORRY WE FOUND YOU. I AM SORRY YOU COULDN'T LISTEN.
WELL, I'M SORRY, TOO.
I'M SORRY FOR NOT LISTENING.
I'M SORRY ABUUS DIED.
BUT I'M NOT SORRY I CAME BACK.
YOU STAND BY YOUR...WHATEVER WE ARE. ***TEAM.*** YOU DON'T ABANDON THEM. ABUUS WOULDN'T HAVE. I WON'T.
EVEN IF IT MEANS BEING STUCK HERE WITH YOU.

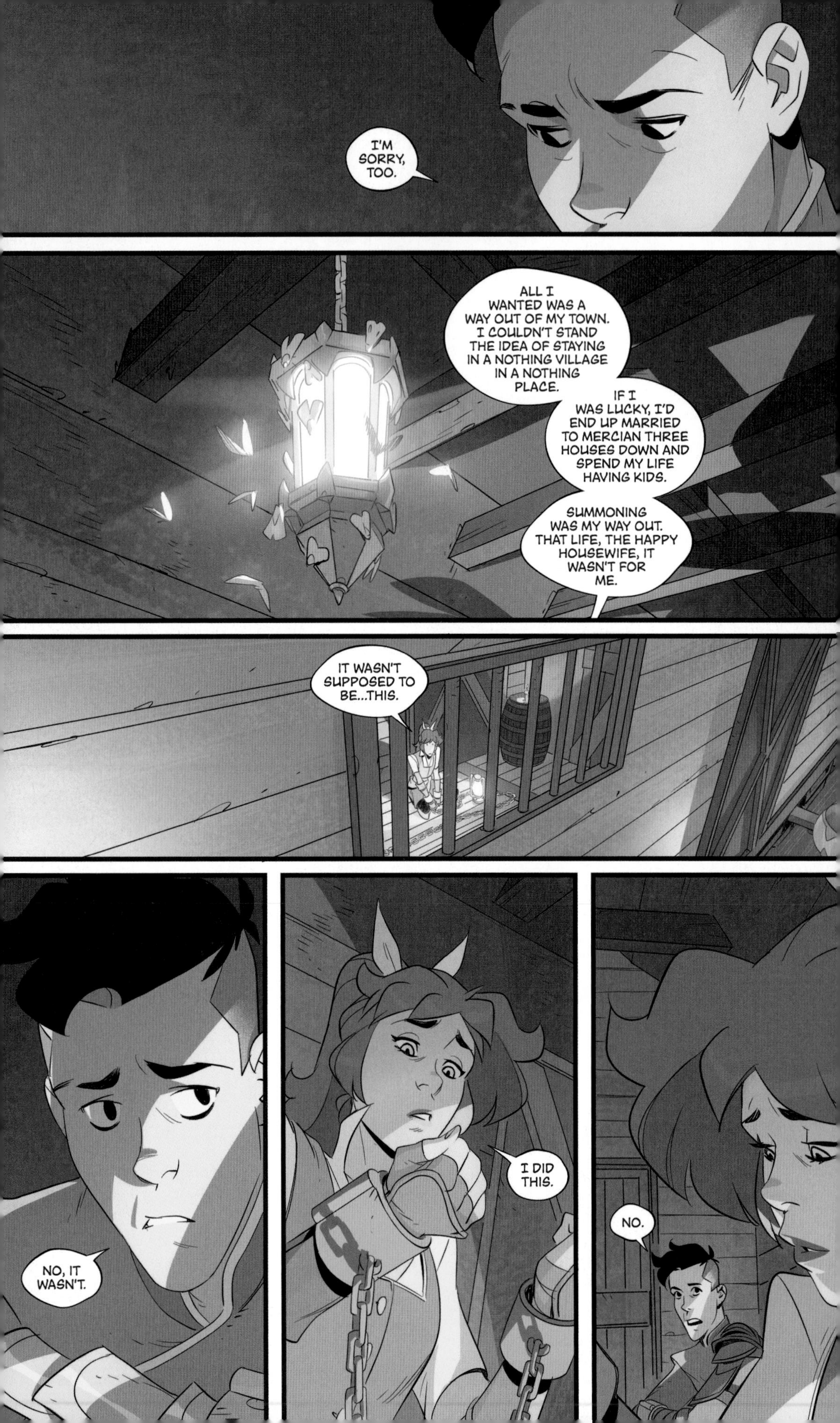

I'M SORRY, TOO.
ALL I WANTED WAS A WAY OUT OF MY TOWN. I COULDN'T STAND THE IDEA OF STAYING IN A NOTHING VILLAGE IN A NOTHING PLACE.
IF I WAS LUCKY, I'D END UP MARRIED TO MERCIAN THREE HOUSES DOWN AND SPEND MY LIFE HAVING KIDS.
SUMMONING WAS MY WAY OUT. THAT LIFE, THE HAPPY HOUSEWIFE, IT WASN'T FOR ME.
IT WASN'T SUPPOSED TO BE...THIS.
NO, IT WASN'T.
I DID THIS.
NO.

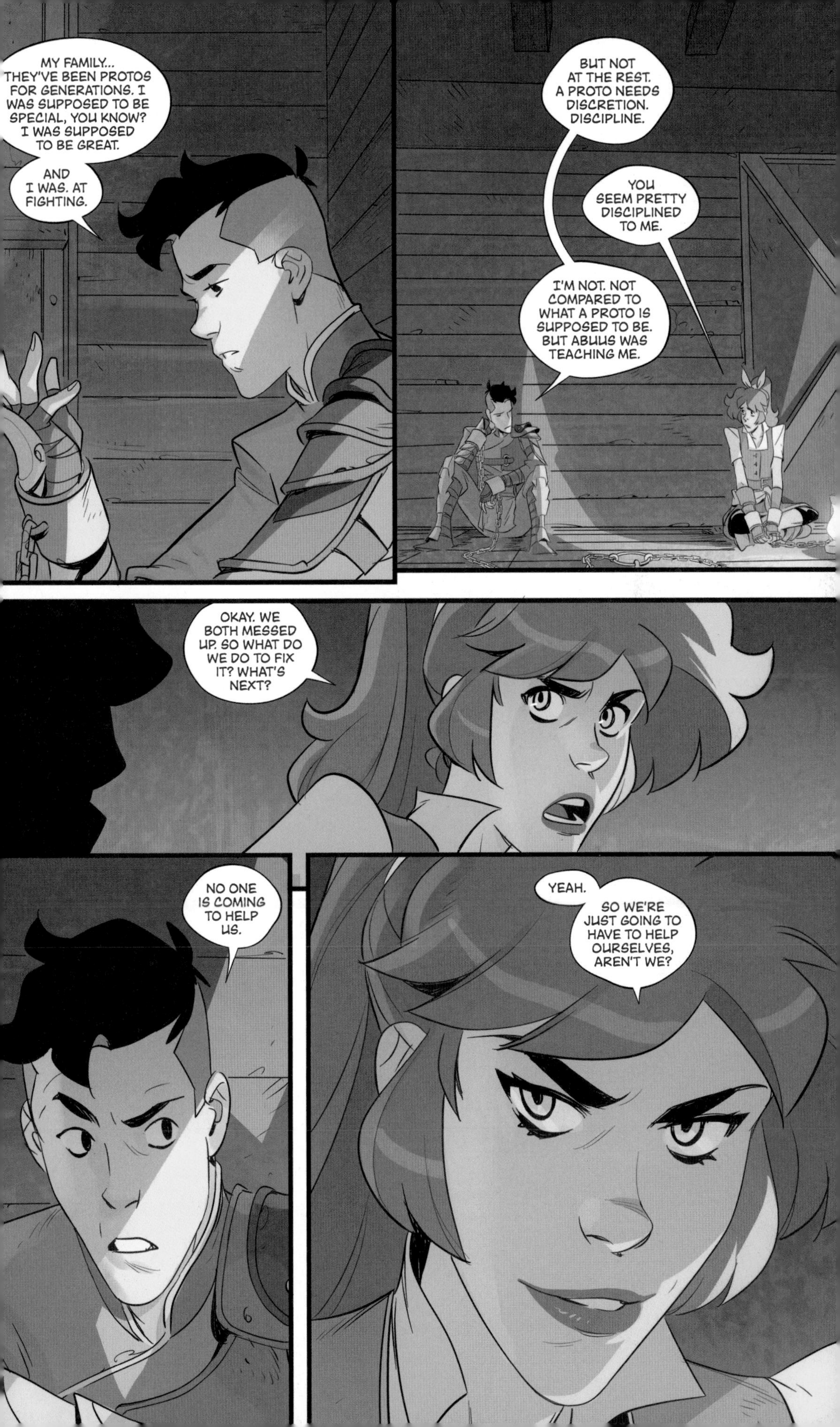
MY FAMILY... THEY'VE BEEN PROTOS FOR GENERATIONS. I WAS SUPPOSED TO BE SPECIAL, YOU KNOW? I WAS SUPPOSED TO BE GREAT.
AND I WAS. AT FIGHTING.
BUT NOT AT THE REST. A PROTO NEEDS DISCRETION. DISCIPLINE.
YOU SEEM PRETTY DISCIPLINED TO ME.
I'M NOT. NOT COMPARED TO WHAT A PROTO IS SUPPOSED TO BE. BUT ABUUS WAS TEACHING ME.
OKAY. WE BOTH MESSED UP. SO WHAT DO WE DO TO FIX IT? WHAT'S NEXT?
NO ONE IS COMING TO HELP US.
YEAH.
SO WE'RE JUST GOING TO HAVE TO HELP OURSELVES, AREN'T WE?

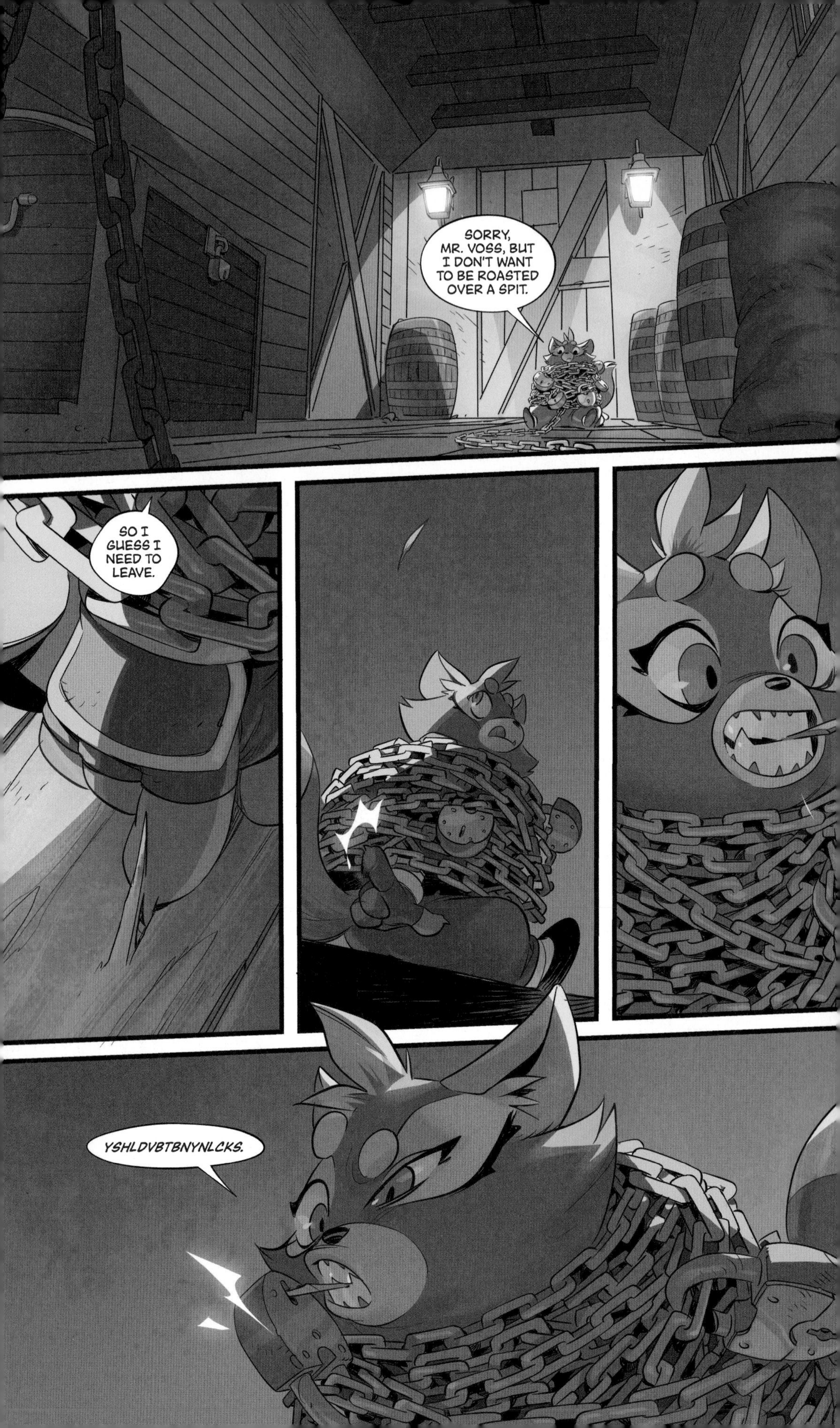
SORRY, MR. VOSS, BUT I DON'T WANT TO BE ROASTED OVER A SPIT.
SO I GUESS I NEED TO LEAVE.
YSHLDVBTBNYNLCKS.

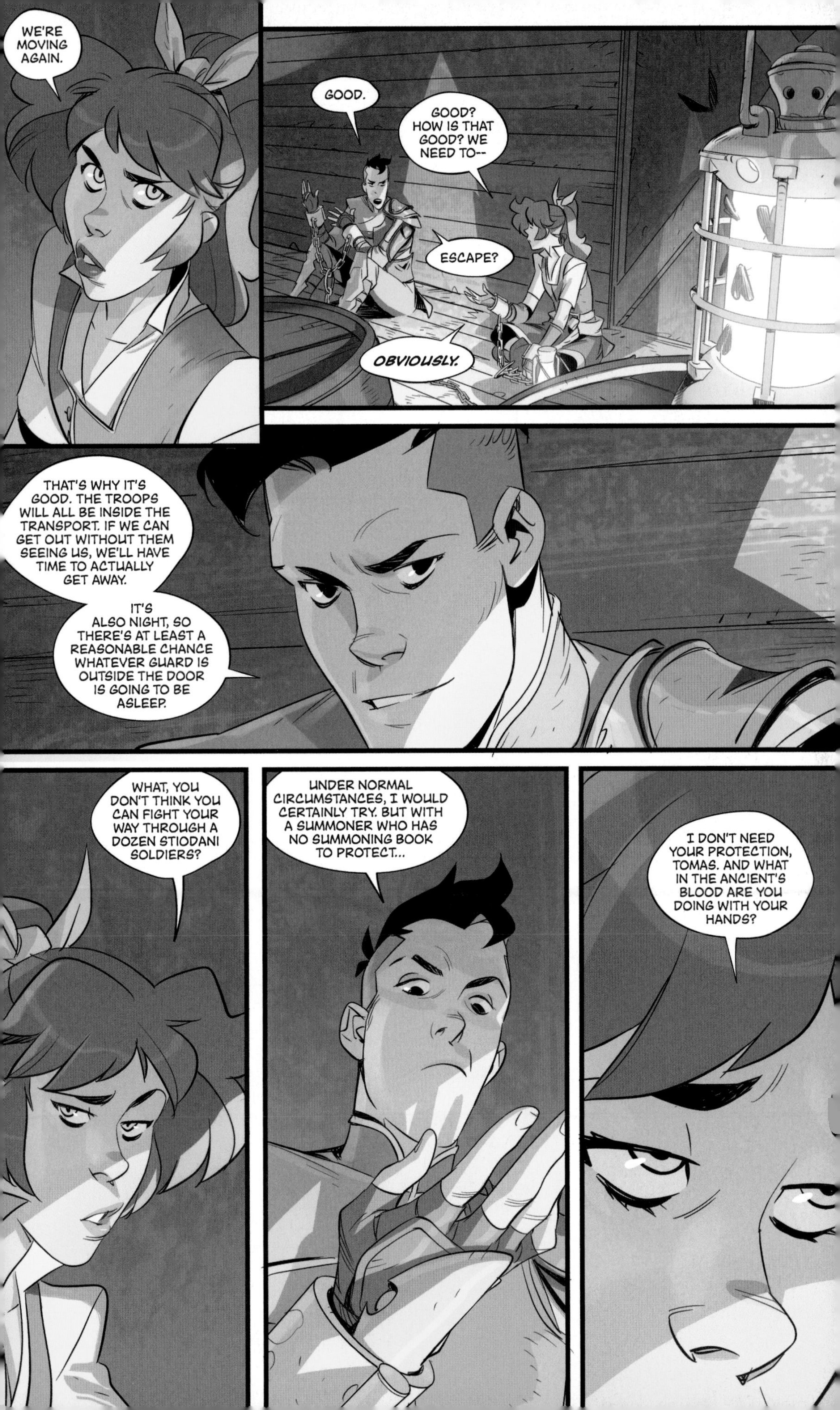
WE'RE MOVING AGAIN.
GOOD.
GOOD? HOW IS THAT GOOD? WE NEED TO--
ESCAPE?
OBVIOUSLY.
THAT'S WHY IT'S GOOD. THE TROOPS WILL ALL BE INSIDE THE TRANSPORT. IF WE CAN GET OUT WITHOUT THEM SEEING US, WE'LL HAVE TIME TO ACTUALLY GET AWAY.
IT'S ALSO NIGHT, SO THERE'S AT LEAST A REASONABLE CHANCE WHATEVER GUARD IS OUTSIDE THE DOOR IS GOING TO BE ASLEEP.
WHAT, YOU DON'T THINK YOU CAN FIGHT YOUR WAY THROUGH A DOZEN STIODANI SOLDIERS?
UNDER NORMAL CIRCUMSTANCES, I WOULD CERTAINLY TRY. BUT WITH A SUMMONER WHO HAS NO SUMMONING BOOK TO PROTECT...
I DON'T NEED YOUR PROTECTION, TOMAS. AND WHAT IN THE ANCIENT'S BLOOD ARE YOU DOING WITH YOUR HANDS?

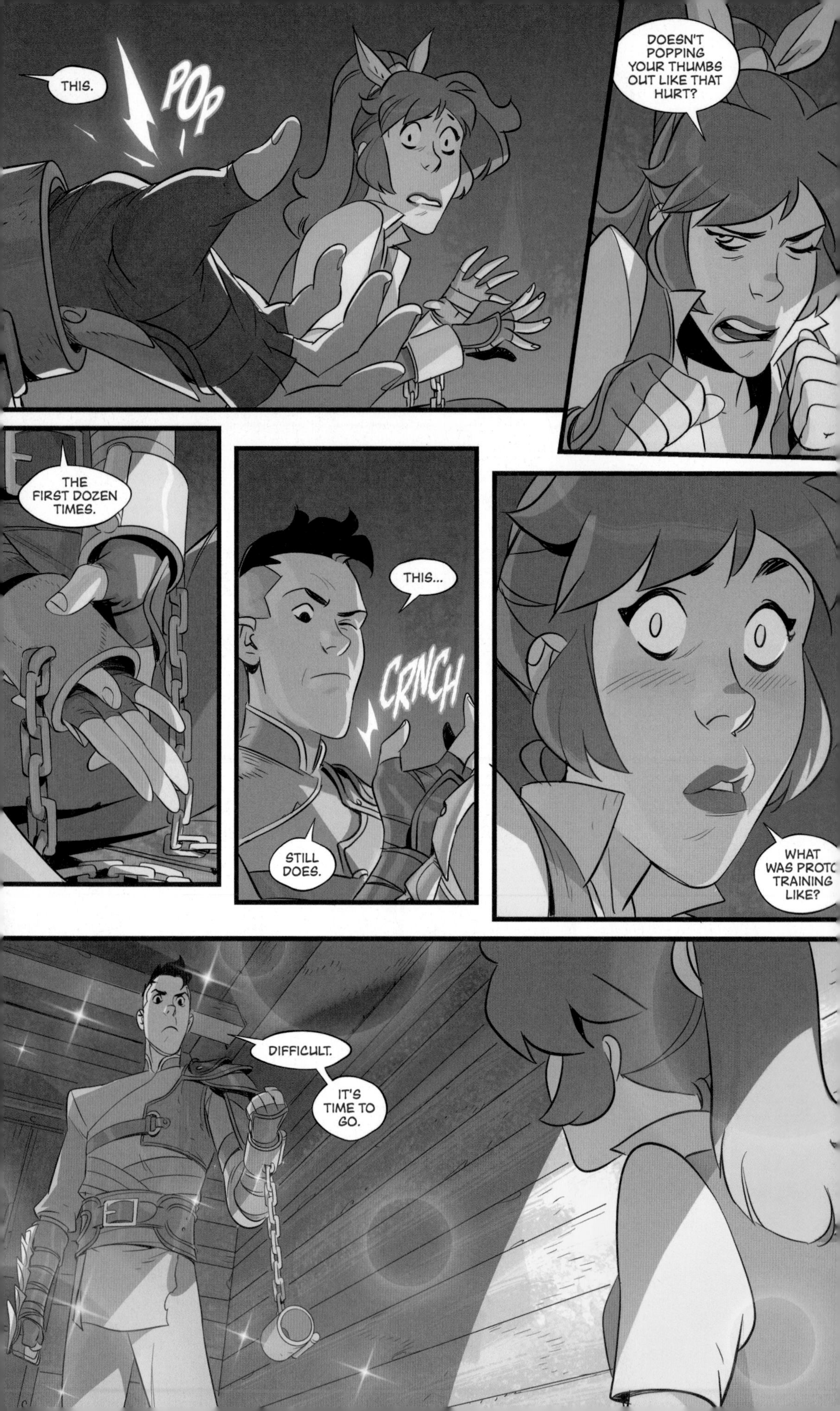
THIS.
POP
DOESN'T POPPING YOUR THUMBS OUT LIKE THAT HURT?
THE FIRST DOZEN TIMES.
THIS...
CRNCH
STILL DOES.
WHAT WAS PROTO TRAINING LIKE?
DIFFICULT.
IT'S TIME TO GO.

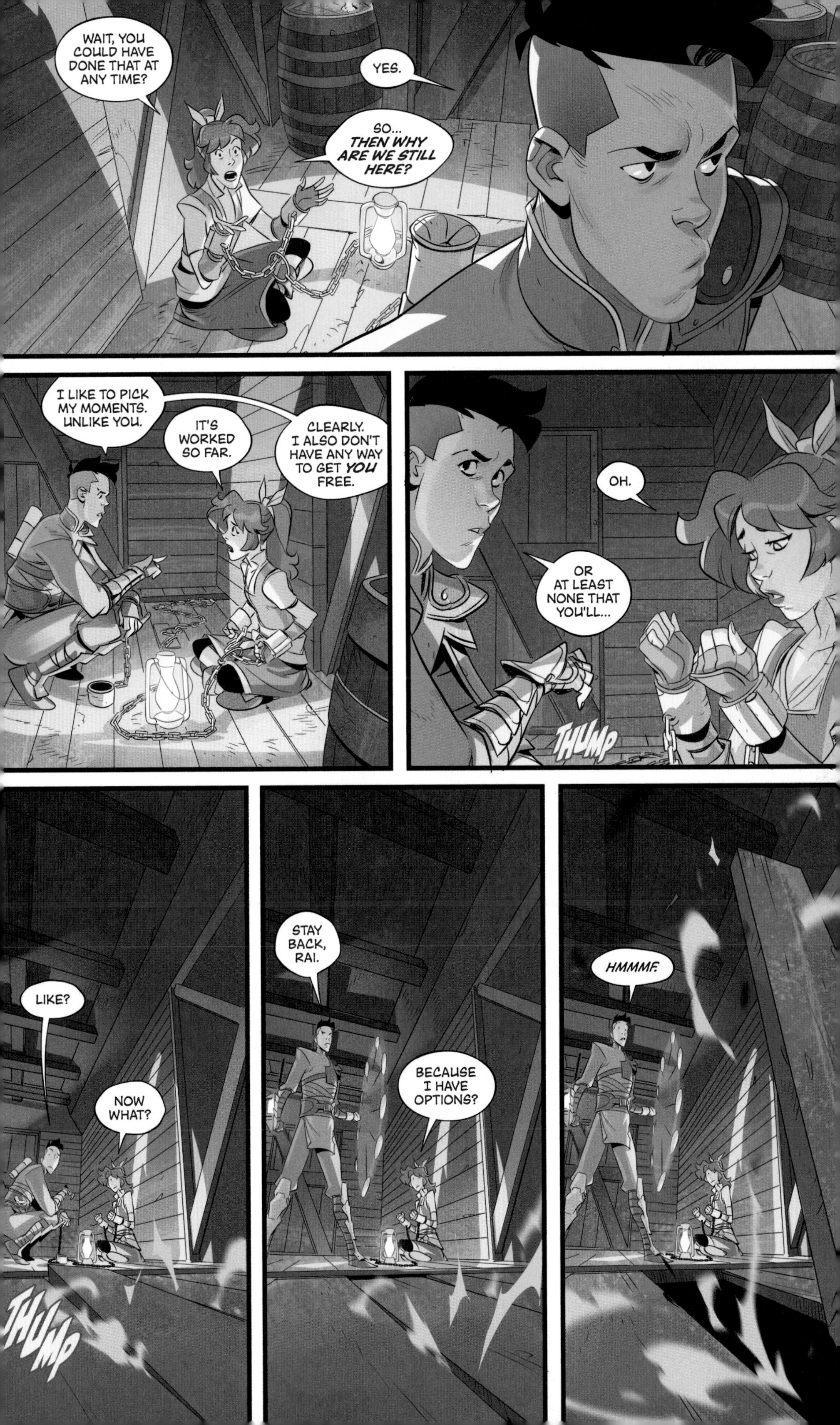
WAIT, YOU COULD HAVE DONE THAT AT ANY TIME?
YES.
SO... THEN WHY ARE WE STILL HERE?
I LIKE TO PICK MY MOMENTS. UNLIKE YOU.
IT'S WORKED SO FAR.
CLEARLY. I ALSO DON'T HAVE ANY WAY TO GET YOU FREE.
OH.
OR AT LEAST NONE THAT YOU'LL...
THUMP
LIKE?
NOW WHAT?
THUMP
STAY BACK, RAI.
BECAUSE I HAVE OPTIONS?
HMMMF.

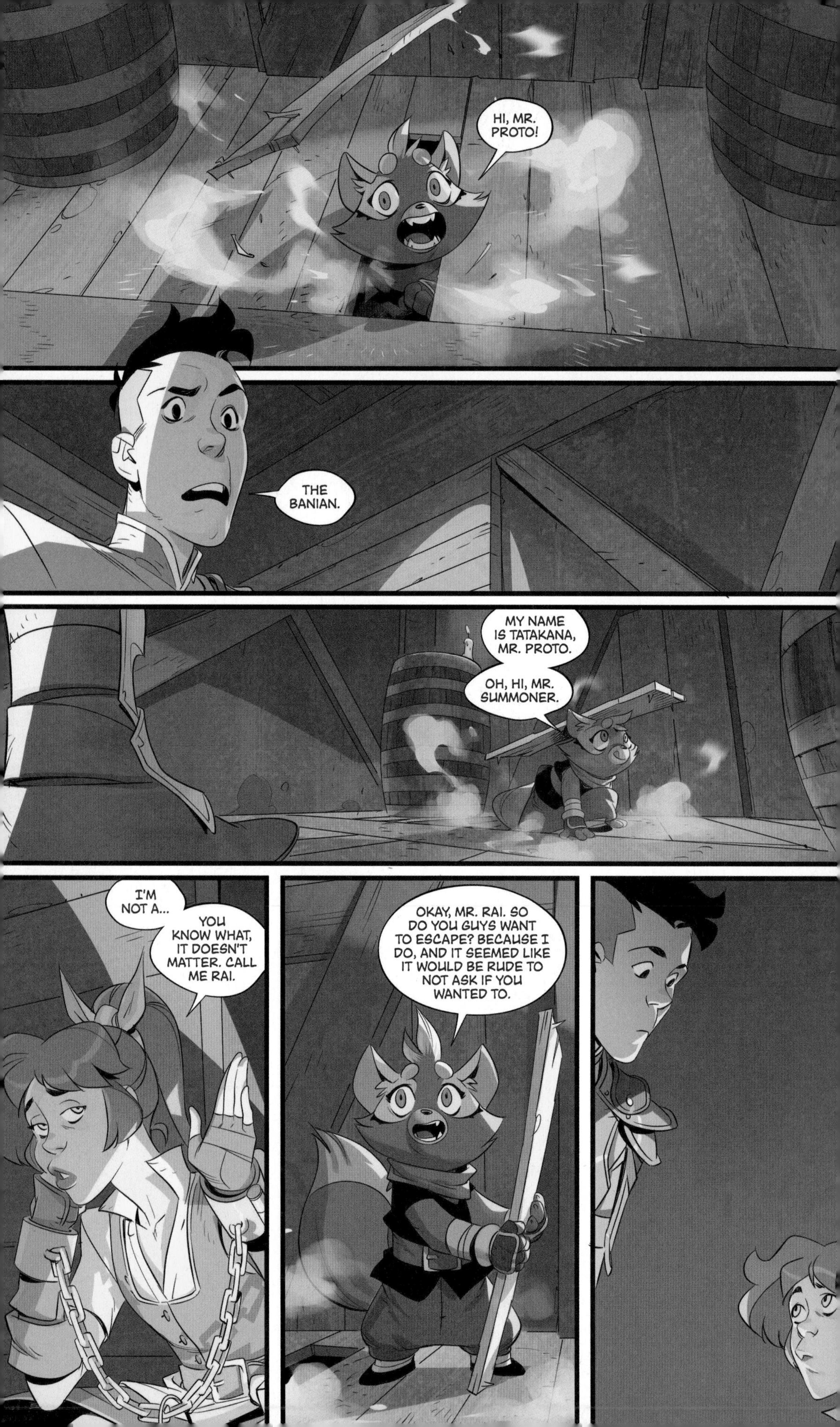
HI, MR. PROTO!
THE BANIAN.
MY NAME IS TATAKANA, MR. PROTO.
OH, HI, MR. SUMMONER.
I'M NOT A...
YOU KNOW WHAT, IT DOESN'T MATTER. CALL ME RAI.
OKAY, MR. RAI. SO DO YOU GUYS WANT TO ESCAPE? BECAUSE I DO, AND IT SEEMED LIKE IT WOULD BE RUDE TO NOT ASK IF YOU WANTED TO.

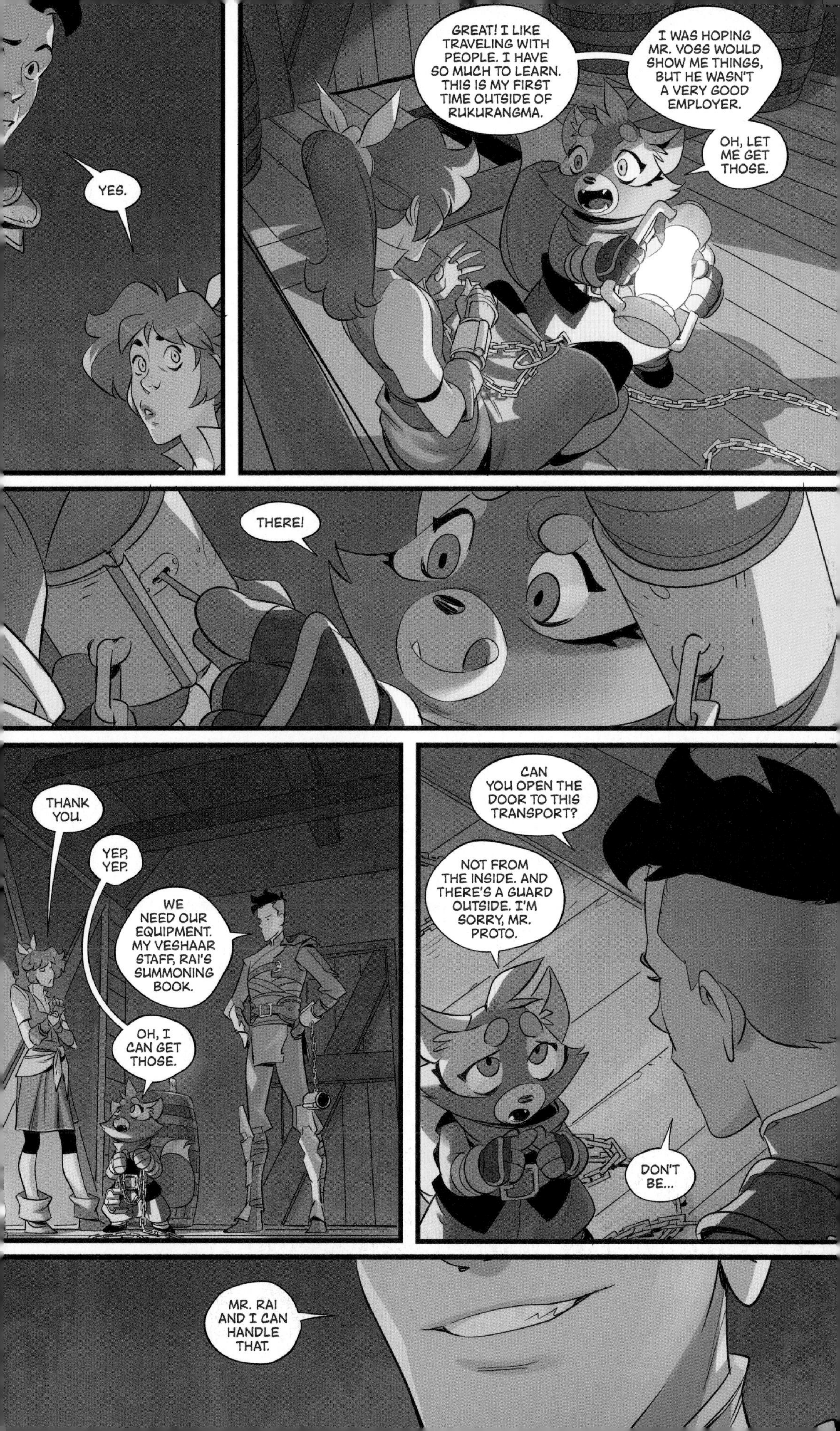
YES.
GREAT! I LIKE TRAVELING WITH PEOPLE. I HAVE SO MUCH TO LEARN. THIS IS MY FIRST TIME OUTSIDE OF RUKURANGMA.
I WAS HOPING MR. VOSS WOULD SHOW ME THINGS, BUT HE WASN'T A VERY GOOD EMPLOYER.
OH, LET ME GET THOSE.
THERE!
THANK YOU.
YEP, YEP.
WE NEED OUR EQUIPMENT. MY VESHAAR STAFF, RAI'S SUMMONING BOOK.
OH, I CAN GET THOSE.
CAN YOU OPEN THE DOOR TO THIS TRANSPORT?
NOT FROM THE INSIDE. AND THERE'S A GUARD OUTSIDE. I'M SORRY, MR. PROTO.
DON'T BE...
MR. RAI AND I CAN HANDLE THAT.

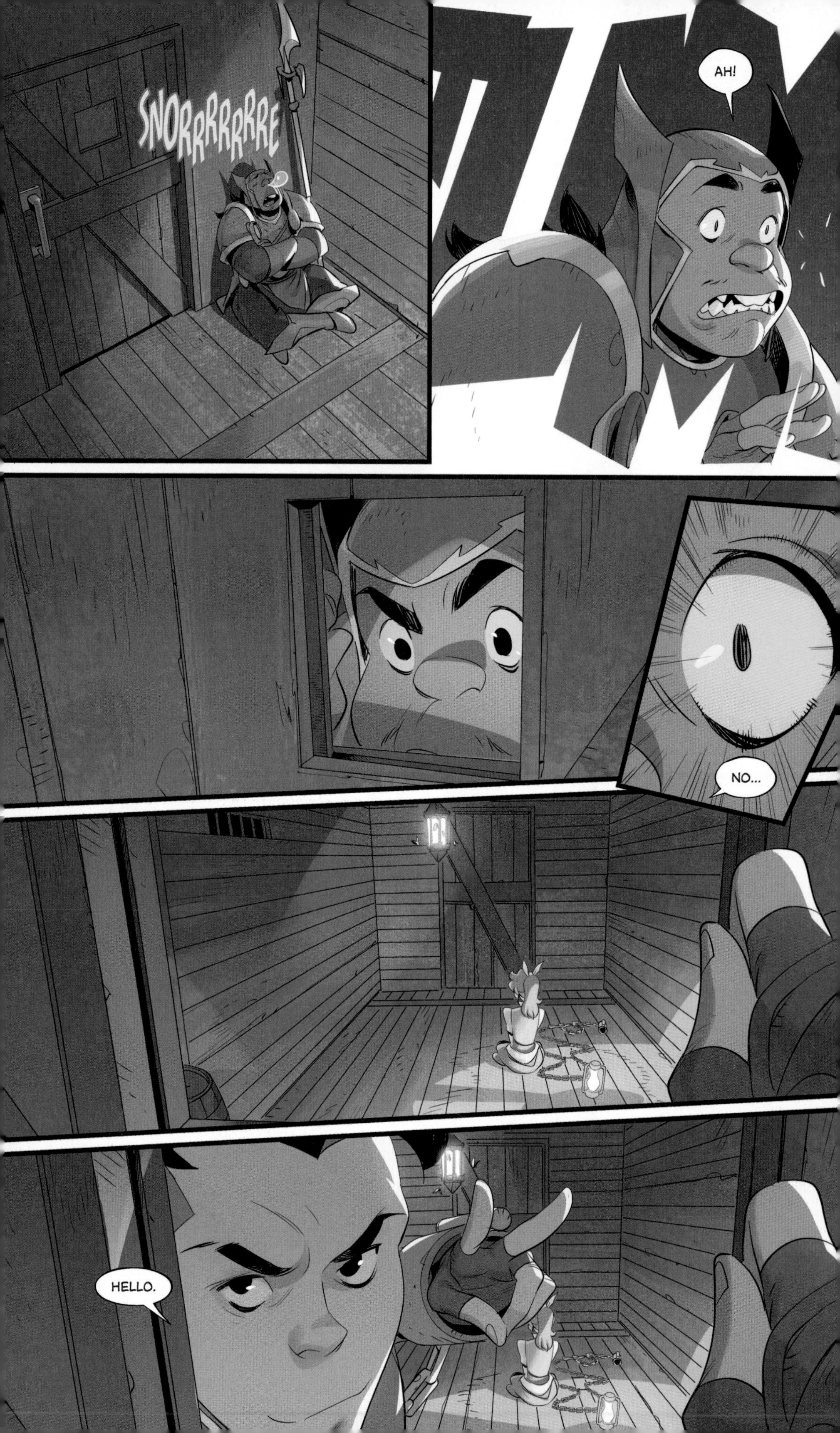
SNORRRRRRRE
AH!
NO...
HELLO.

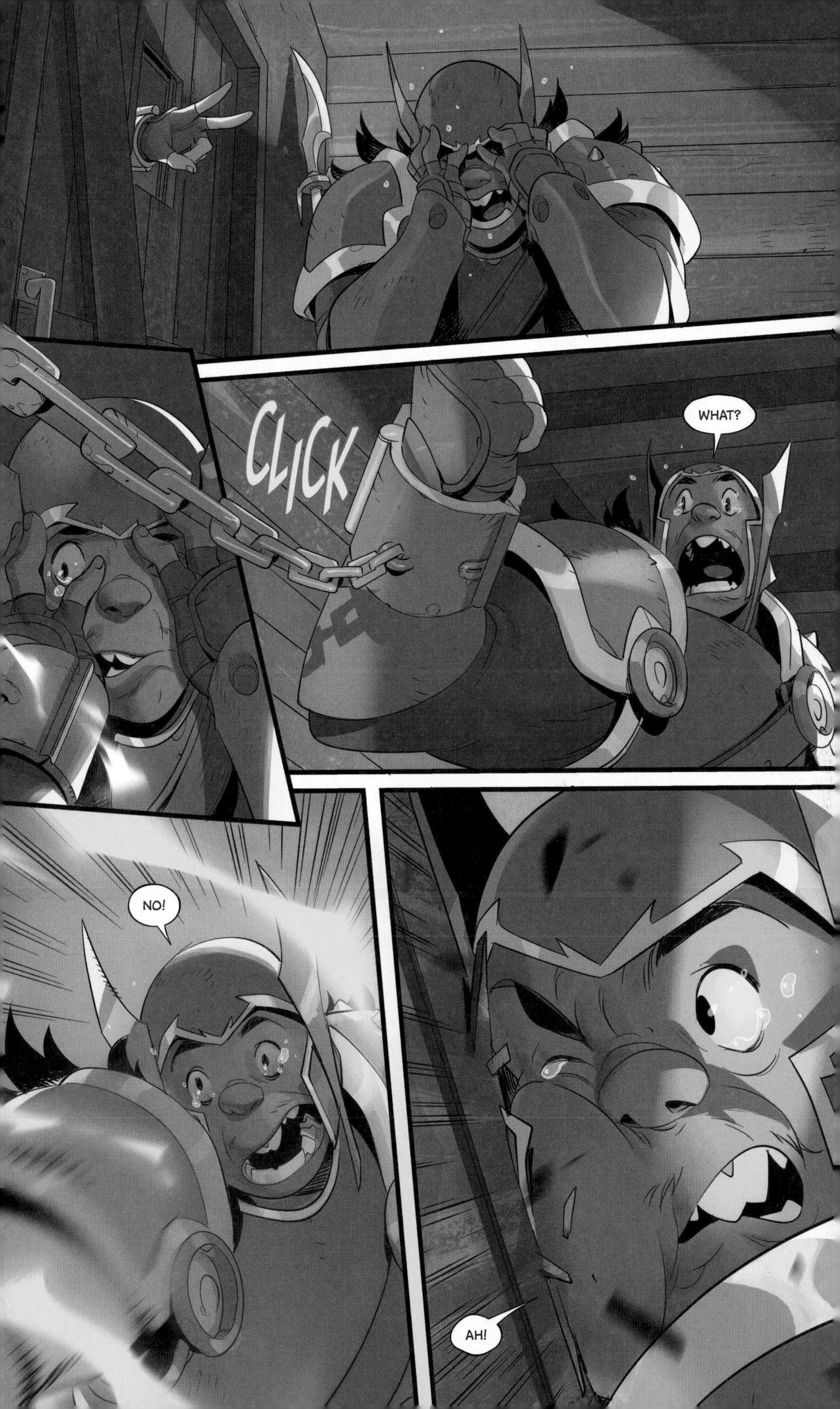
CLICK
WHAT?
NO!
AH!

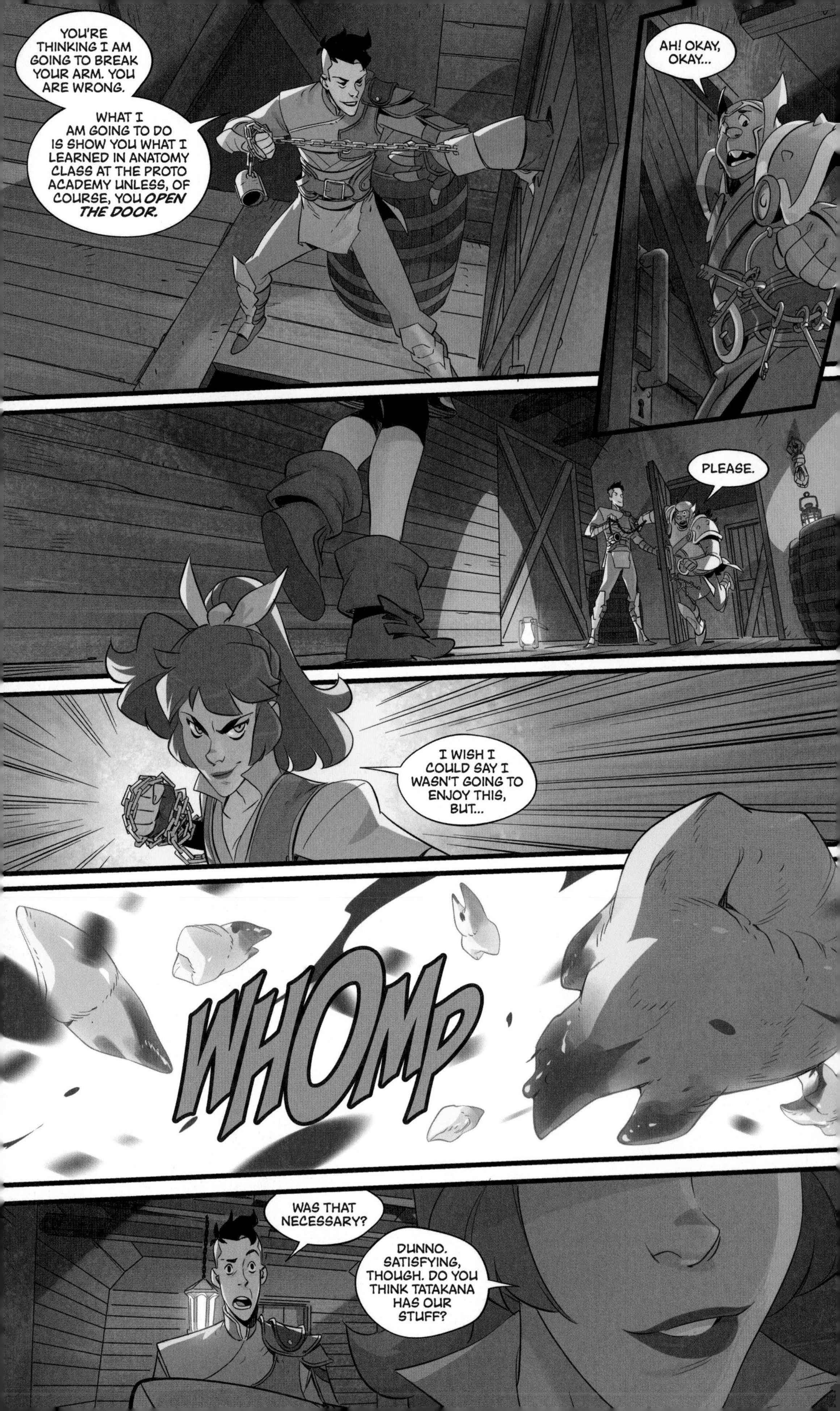
YOU'RE THINKING I AM GOING TO BREAK YOUR ARM. YOU ARE WRONG.
WHAT I AM GOING TO DO IS SHOW YOU WHAT I LEARNED IN ANATOMY CLASS AT THE PROTO ACADEMY UNLESS, OF COURSE, YOU *OPEN THE DOOR.*
AH! OKAY, OKAY...
PLEASE.
I WISH I COULD SAY I WASN'T GOING TO ENJOY THIS, BUT...
WHOMP
WAS THAT NECESSARY?
DUNNO. SATISFYING, THOUGH. DO YOU THINK TATAKANA HAS OUR STUFF?

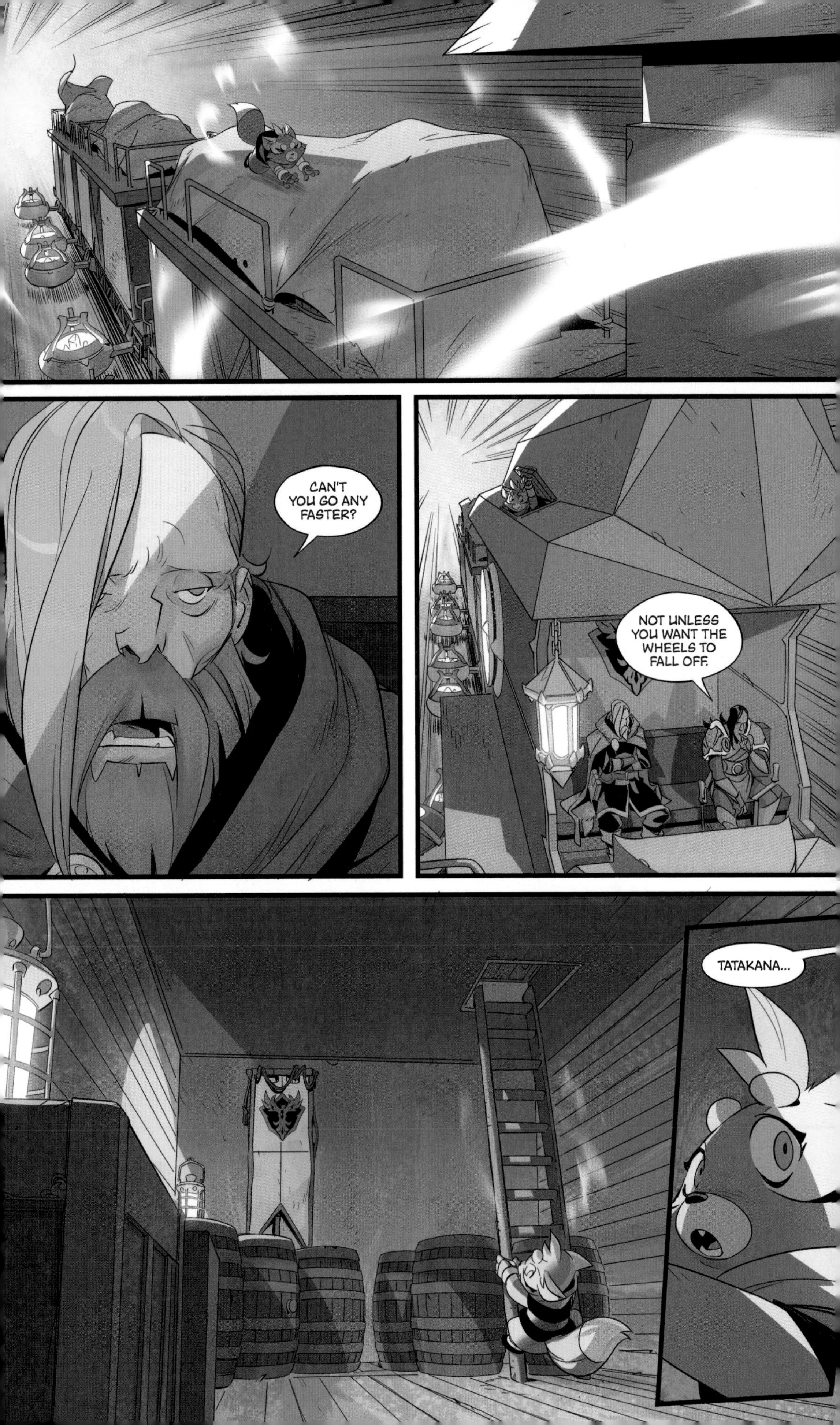
CAN'T YOU GO ANY FASTER?
NOT UNLESS YOU WANT THE WHEELS TO FALL OFF.
TATAKANA...

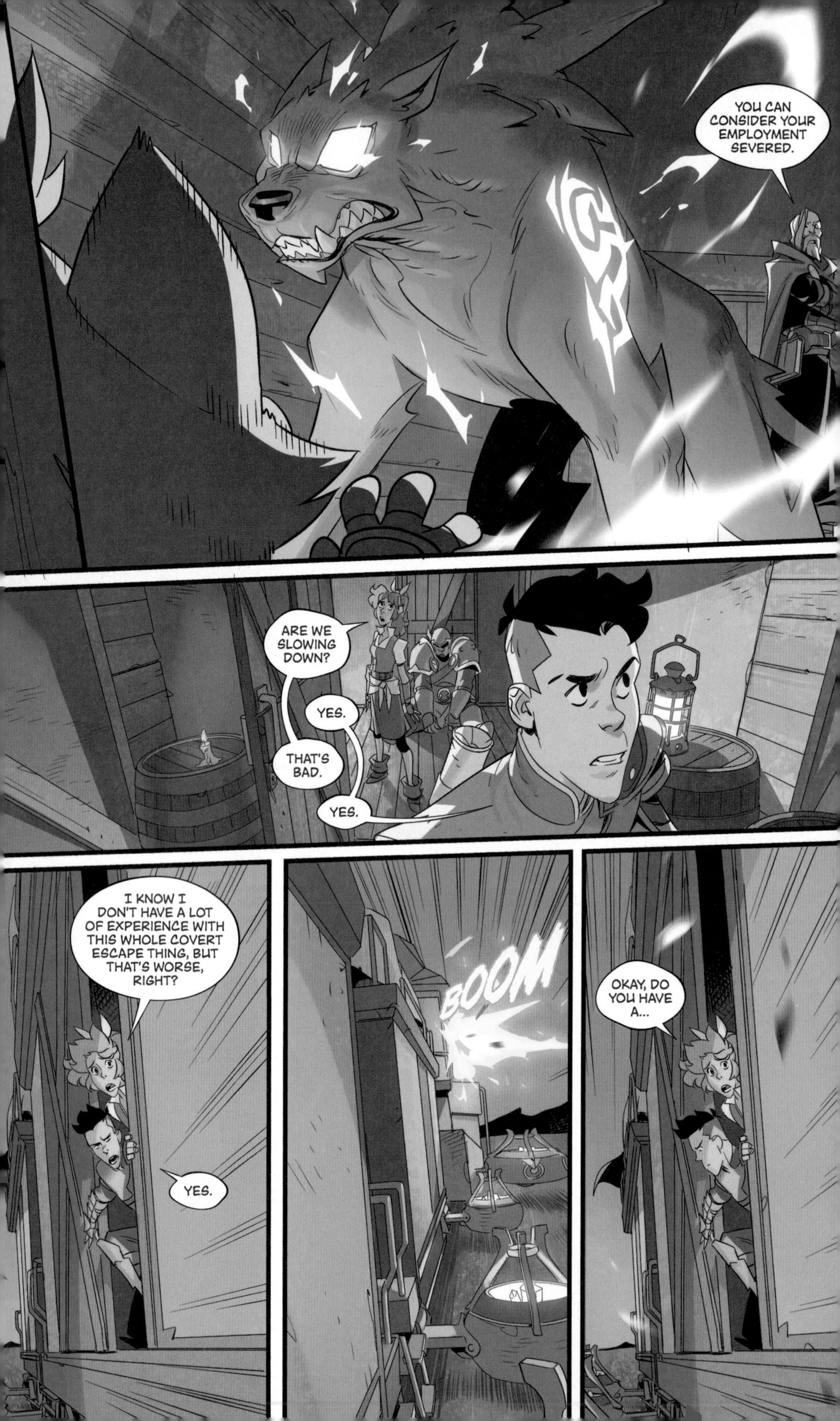
YOU CAN CONSIDER YOUR EMPLOYMENT SEVERED.
ARE WE SLOWING DOWN?
YES.
THAT'S BAD.
YES.
I KNOW I DON'T HAVE A LOT OF EXPERIENCE WITH THIS WHOLE COVERT ESCAPE THING, BUT THAT'S WORSE, RIGHT?
YES.
BOOM
OKAY, DO YOU HAVE A...

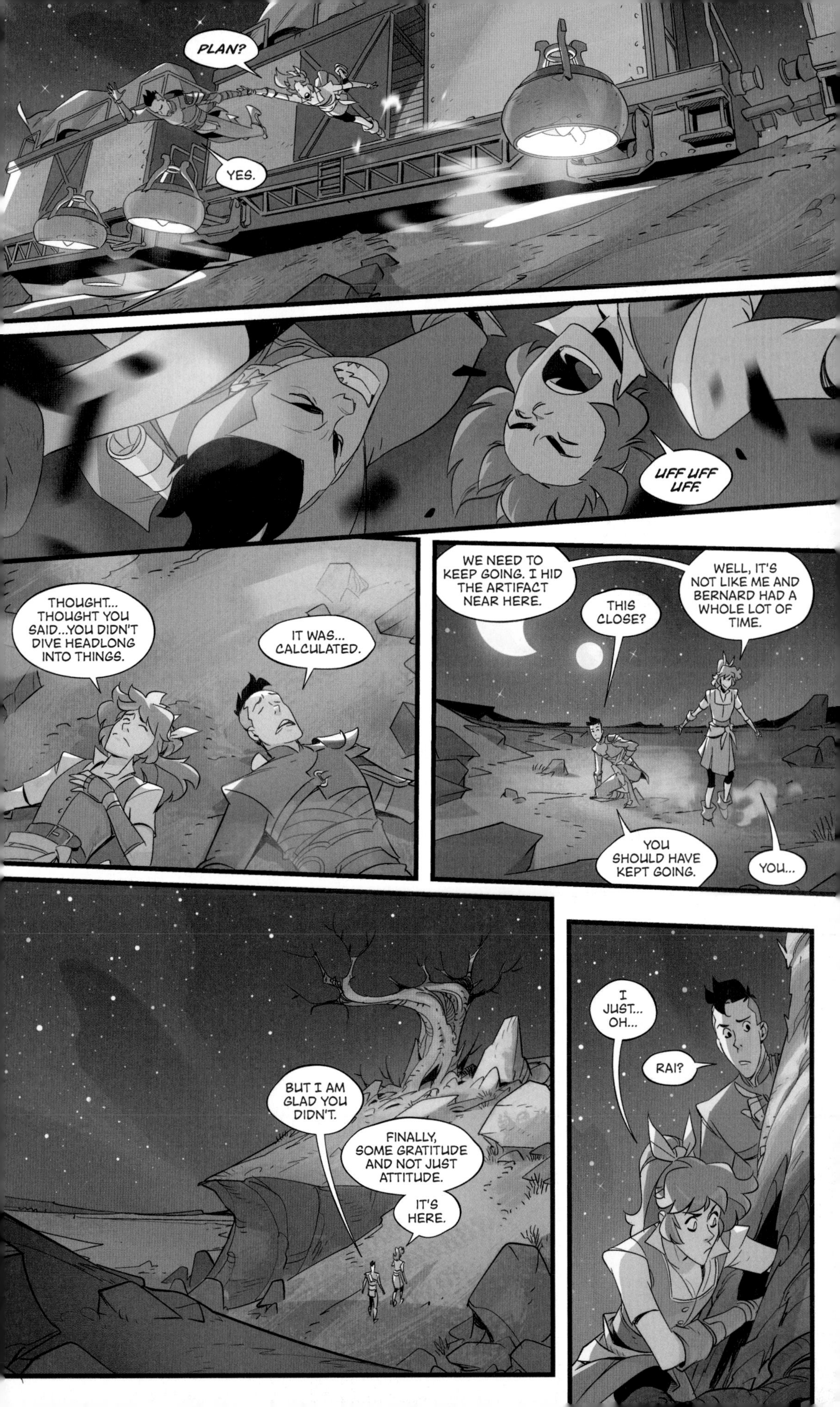
PLAN?
YES.
UFF UFF UFF.
THOUGHT... THOUGHT YOU SAID...YOU DIDN'T DIVE HEADLONG INTO THINGS.
IT WAS... CALCULATED.
WE NEED TO KEEP GOING. I HID THE ARTIFACT NEAR HERE.
THIS CLOSE?
WELL, IT'S NOT LIKE ME AND BERNARD HAD A WHOLE LOT OF TIME.
YOU SHOULD HAVE KEPT GOING.
YOU...
BUT I AM GLAD YOU DIDN'T.
FINALLY, SOME GRATITUDE AND NOT JUST ATTITUDE.
IT'S HERE.
I JUST... OH...
RAI?

"IT'S GONE."

AT LEAST YOU WERE ABLE TO FIND WHERE THE GIRL HID THIS. SHE'S NOT NEARLY AS CLEVER AS SHE'D LIKE TO BE.

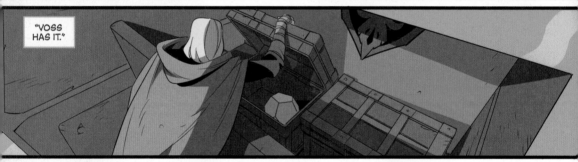

ARE YOU SURE?

THAT IT'S GONE? YES.

I MEANT--

I KNOW WHAT YOU MEANT. AM I SURE THIS IS THE PLACE I HID IT. I AM. AND IT'S GONE.

"VOSS HAS IT."

THEY FOUND IT.

THEY MUST HAVE. HOW DID WE MISS THEM WHEN WE CAME THROUGH?

I THINK YOU WERE PROBABLY COMING FROM A DIFFERENT VECTOR AND--

TATAKANA?

I GOT THE BOOKS AND THE STAFF THINGER.

(EXCELLENT CRAFTSMANSHIP ON THE STAFF. THAT LOCKING MECHANISM IS BEAUTIFUL.)

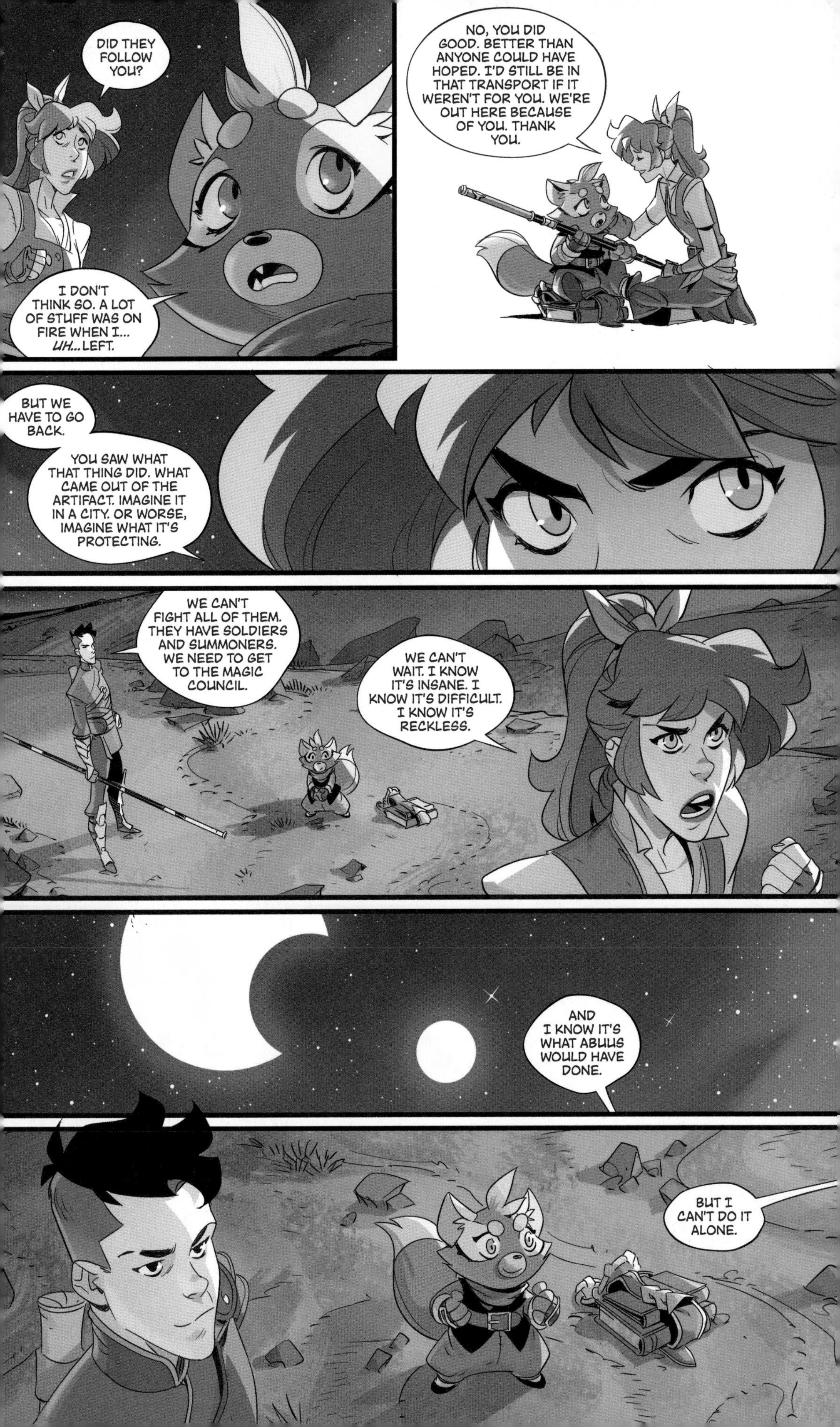

DID THEY FOLLOW YOU?
I DON'T THINK SO. A LOT OF STUFF WAS ON FIRE WHEN I... *UH...* LEFT.
NO, YOU DID GOOD. BETTER THAN ANYONE COULD HAVE HOPED. I'D STILL BE IN THAT TRANSPORT IF IT WEREN'T FOR YOU. WE'RE OUT HERE BECAUSE OF YOU. THANK YOU.
BUT WE HAVE TO GO BACK.
YOU SAW WHAT THAT THING DID. WHAT CAME OUT OF THE ARTIFACT. IMAGINE IT IN A CITY. OR WORSE, IMAGINE WHAT IT'S PROTECTING.
WE CAN'T FIGHT ALL OF THEM. THEY HAVE SOLDIERS AND SUMMONERS. WE NEED TO GET TO THE MAGIC COUNCIL.
WE CAN'T WAIT. I KNOW IT'S INSANE. I KNOW IT'S DIFFICULT. I KNOW IT'S RECKLESS.
AND I KNOW IT'S WHAT ABUUS WOULD HAVE DONE.
BUT I CAN'T DO IT ALONE.

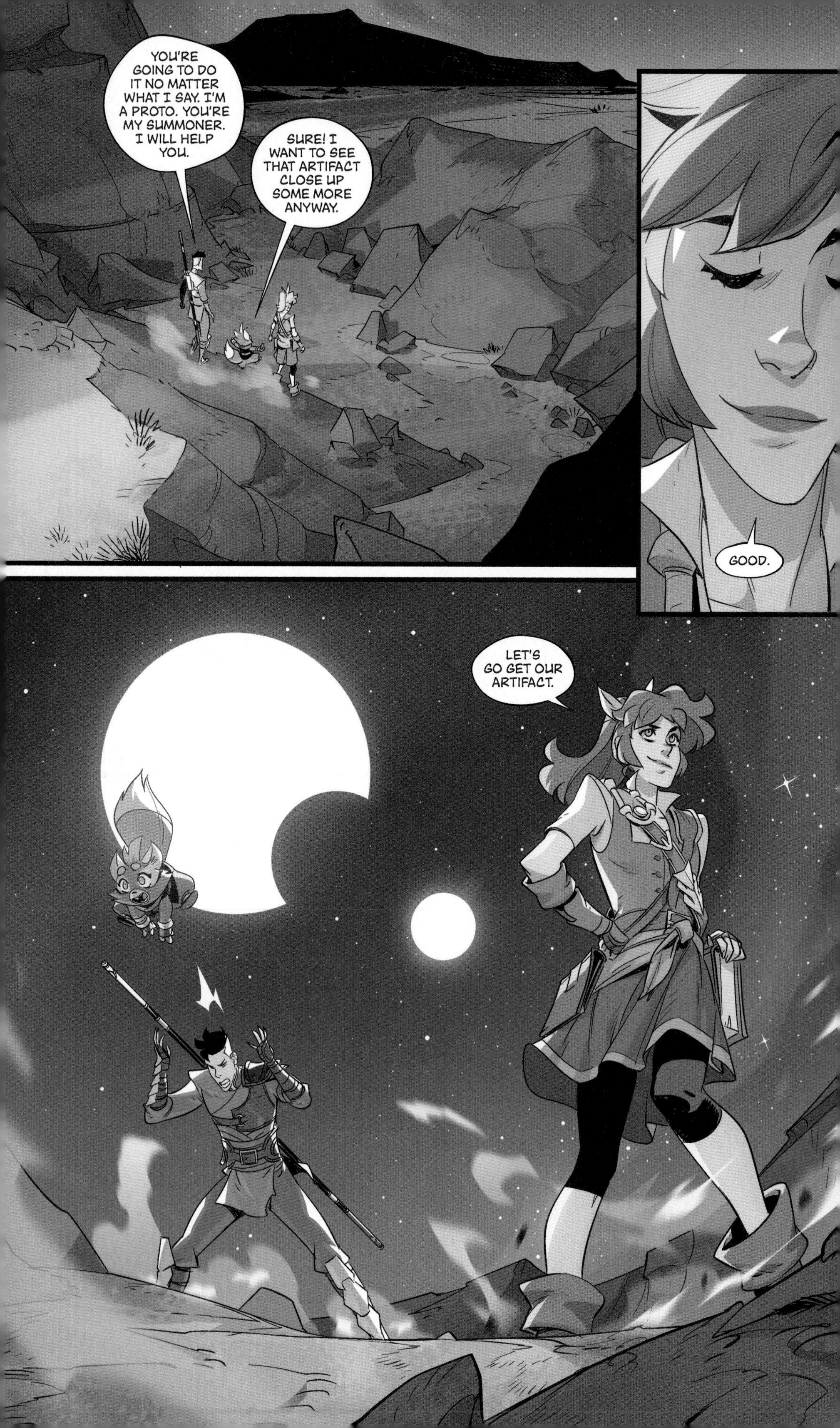
YOU'RE GOING TO DO IT NO MATTER WHAT I SAY. I'M A PROTO. YOU'RE MY SUMMONER. I WILL HELP YOU.
SURE! I WANT TO SEE THAT ARTIFACT CLOSE UP SOME MORE ANYWAY.
GOOD.
LET'S GO GET OUR ARTIFACT.

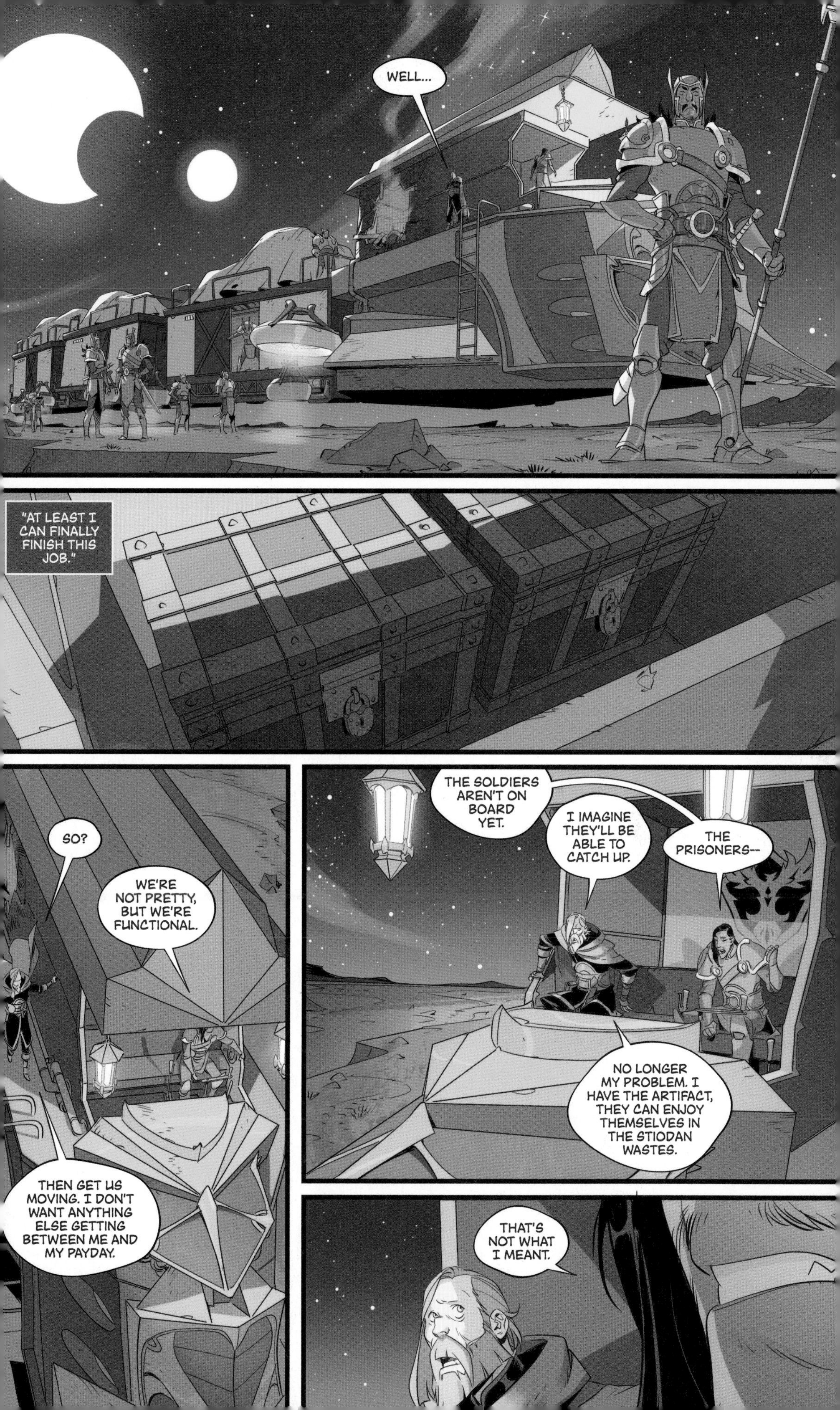

WELL...
"AT LEAST I CAN FINALLY FINISH THIS JOB."
SO?
WE'RE NOT PRETTY, BUT WE'RE FUNCTIONAL.
THEN GET US MOVING. I DON'T WANT ANYTHING ELSE GETTING BETWEEN ME AND MY PAYDAY.
THE SOLDIERS AREN'T ON BOARD YET.
I IMAGINE THEY'LL BE ABLE TO CATCH UP.
THE PRISONERS--
NO LONGER MY PROBLEM. I HAVE THE ARTIFACT, THEY CAN ENJOY THEMSELVES IN THE STIODAN WASTES.
THAT'S NOT WHAT I MEANT.

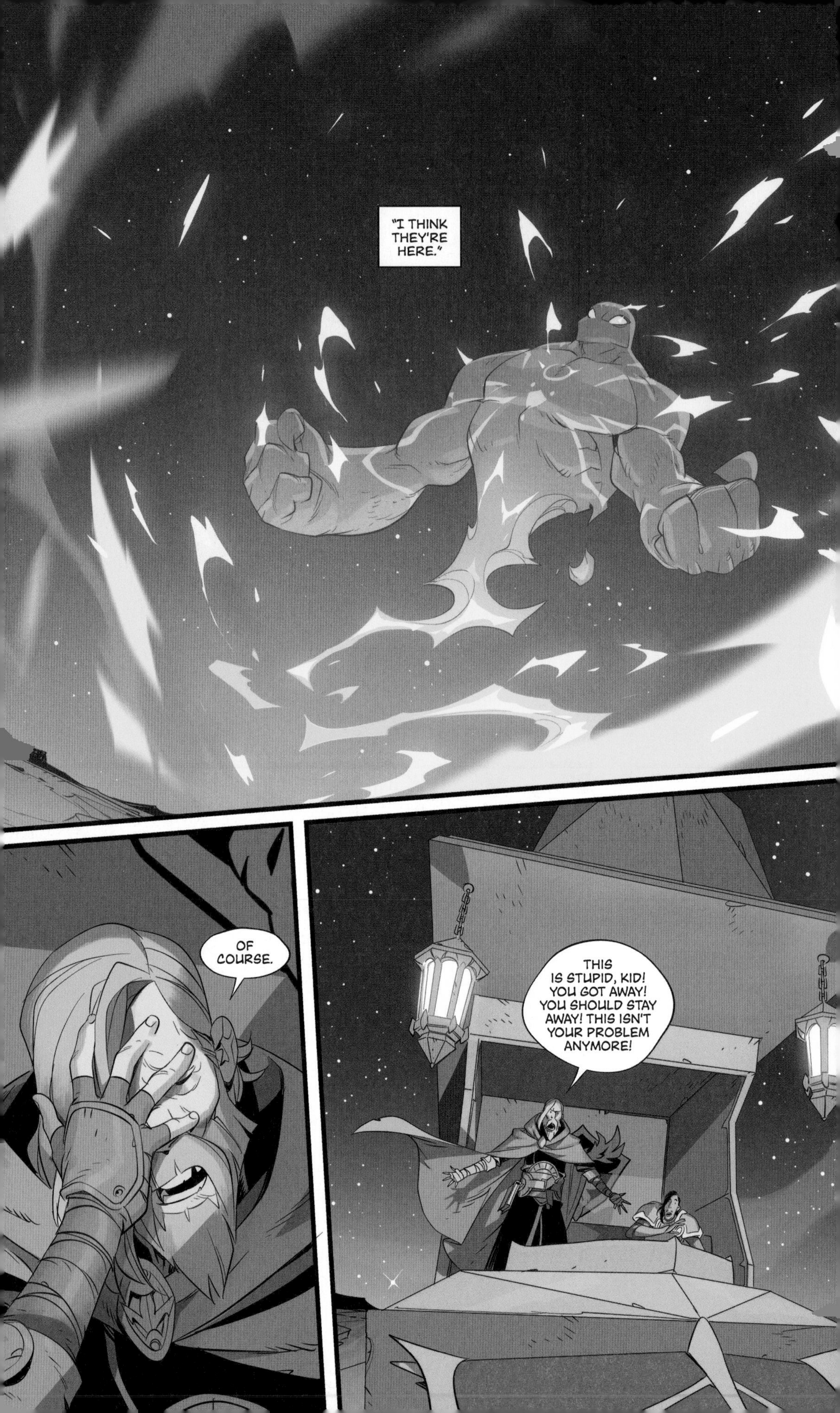
"I THINK THEY'RE HERE."
OF COURSE.
THIS IS STUPID, KID! YOU GOT AWAY! YOU SHOULD STAY AWAY! THIS ISN'T YOUR PROBLEM ANYMORE!

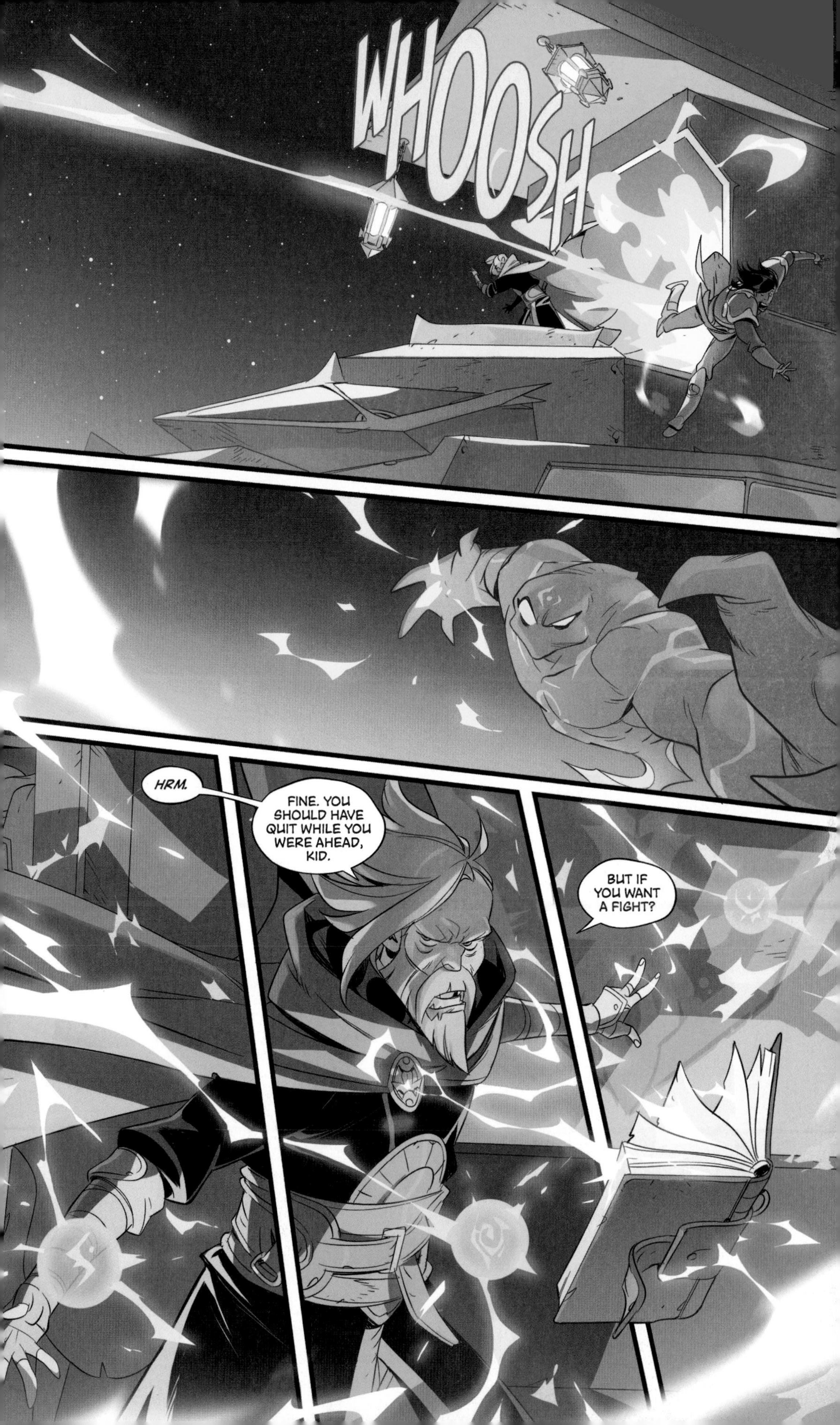
WHOOSH
HRM.
FINE. YOU SHOULD HAVE QUIT WHILE YOU WERE AHEAD, KID.
BUT IF YOU WANT A FIGHT?

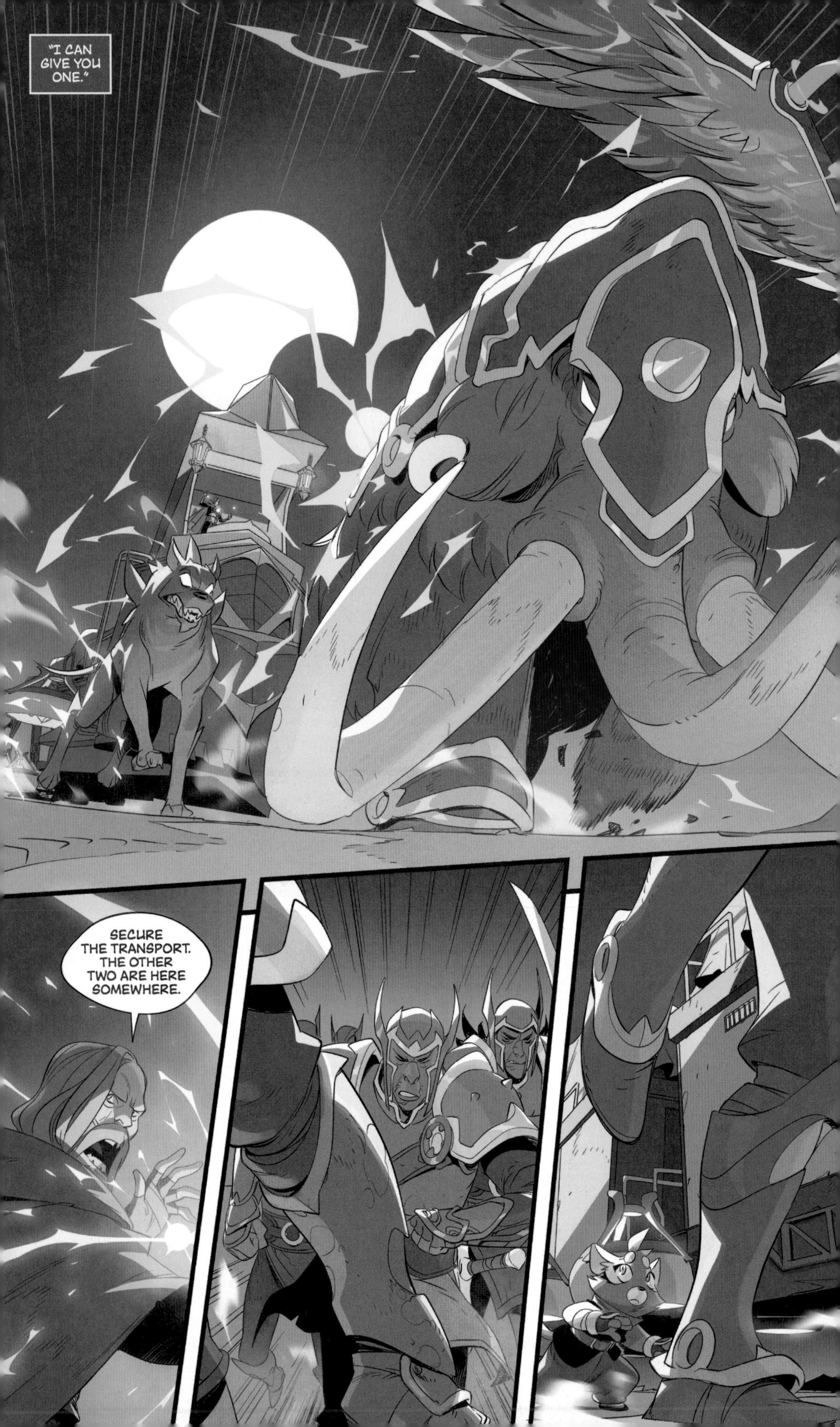
"I CAN GIVE YOU ONE."
SECURE THE TRANSPORT. THE OTHER TWO ARE HERE SOMEWHERE.

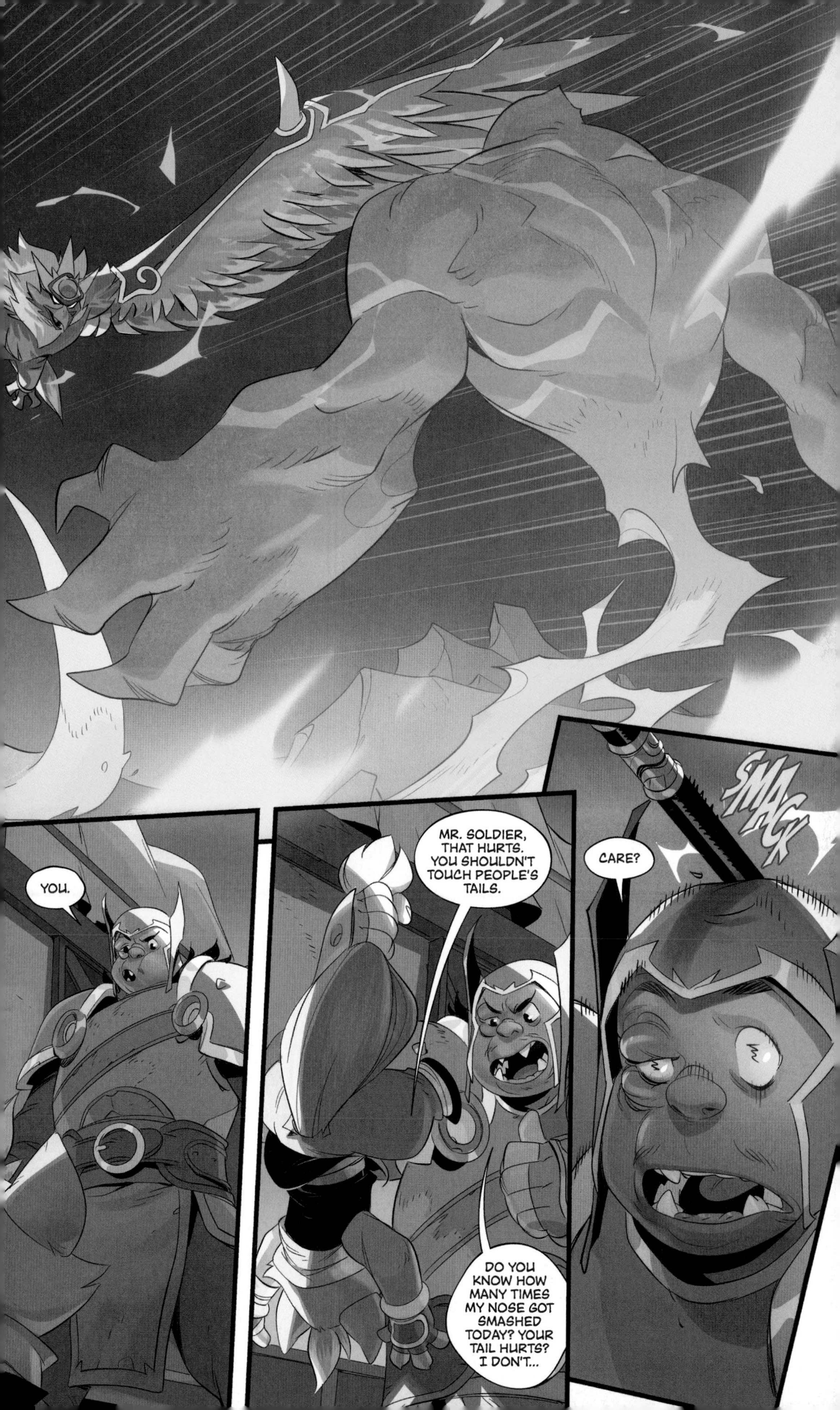
YOU.
MR. SOLDIER, THAT HURTS. YOU SHOULDN'T TOUCH PEOPLE'S TAILS.
DO YOU KNOW HOW MANY TIMES MY NOSE GOT SMASHED TODAY? YOUR TAIL HURTS? I DON'T...
CARE?
SMACK

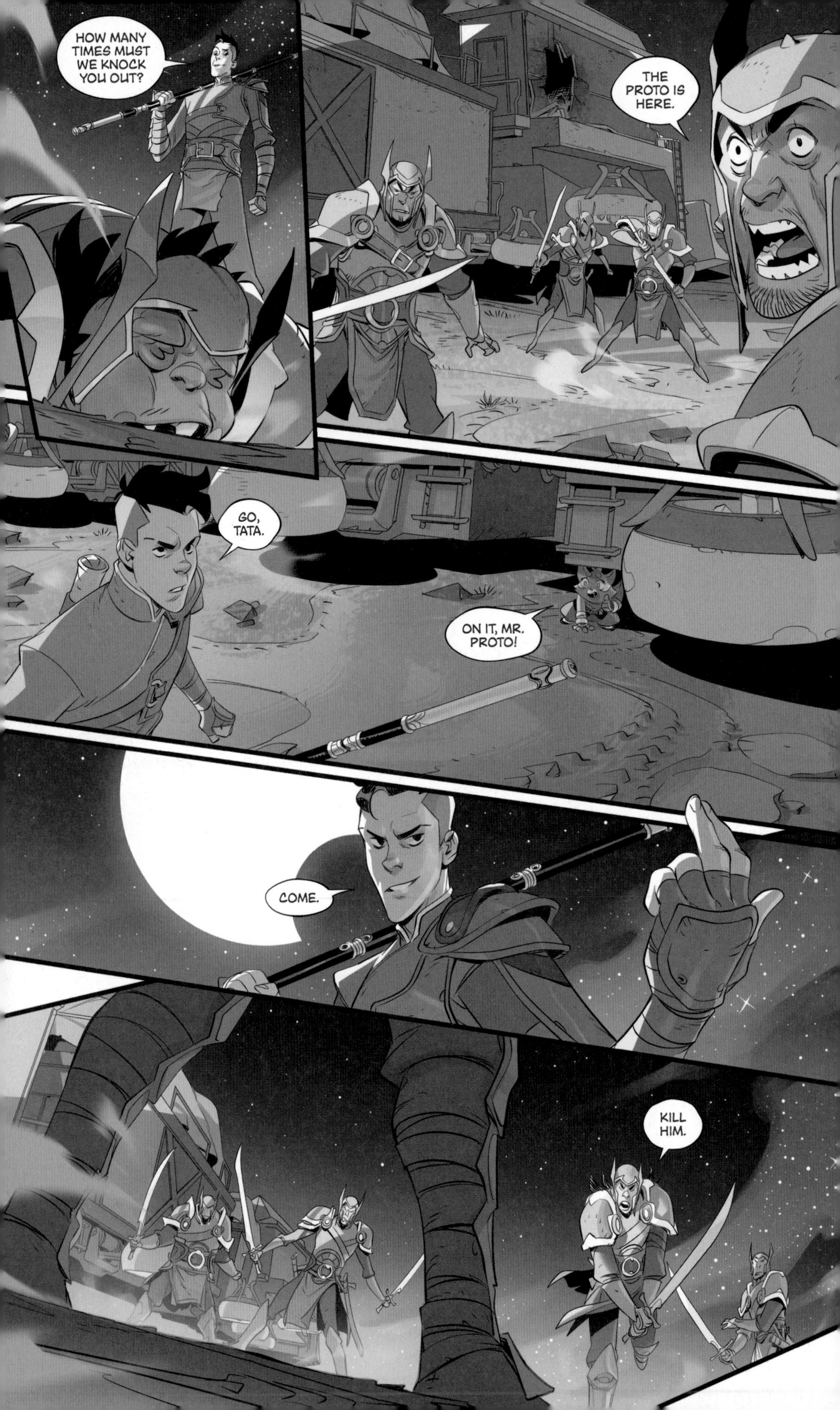
HOW MANY TIMES MUST WE KNOCK YOU OUT?
THE PROTO IS HERE.
GO, TATA.
ON IT, MR. PROTO!
COME.
KILL HIM.

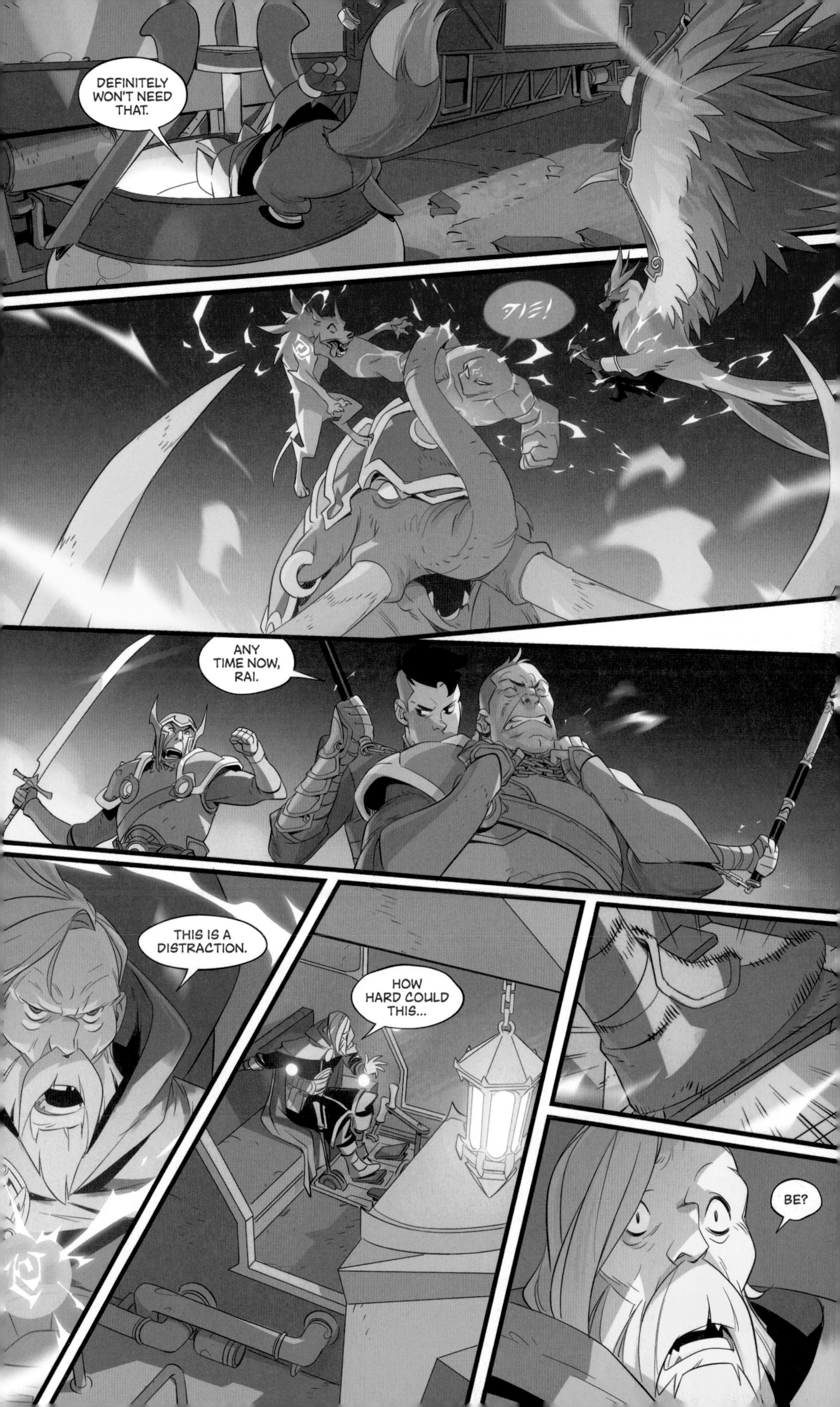

DEFINITELY WON'T NEED THAT.
ANY TIME NOW, RAI.
THIS IS A DISTRACTION.
HOW HARD COULD THIS...
BE?

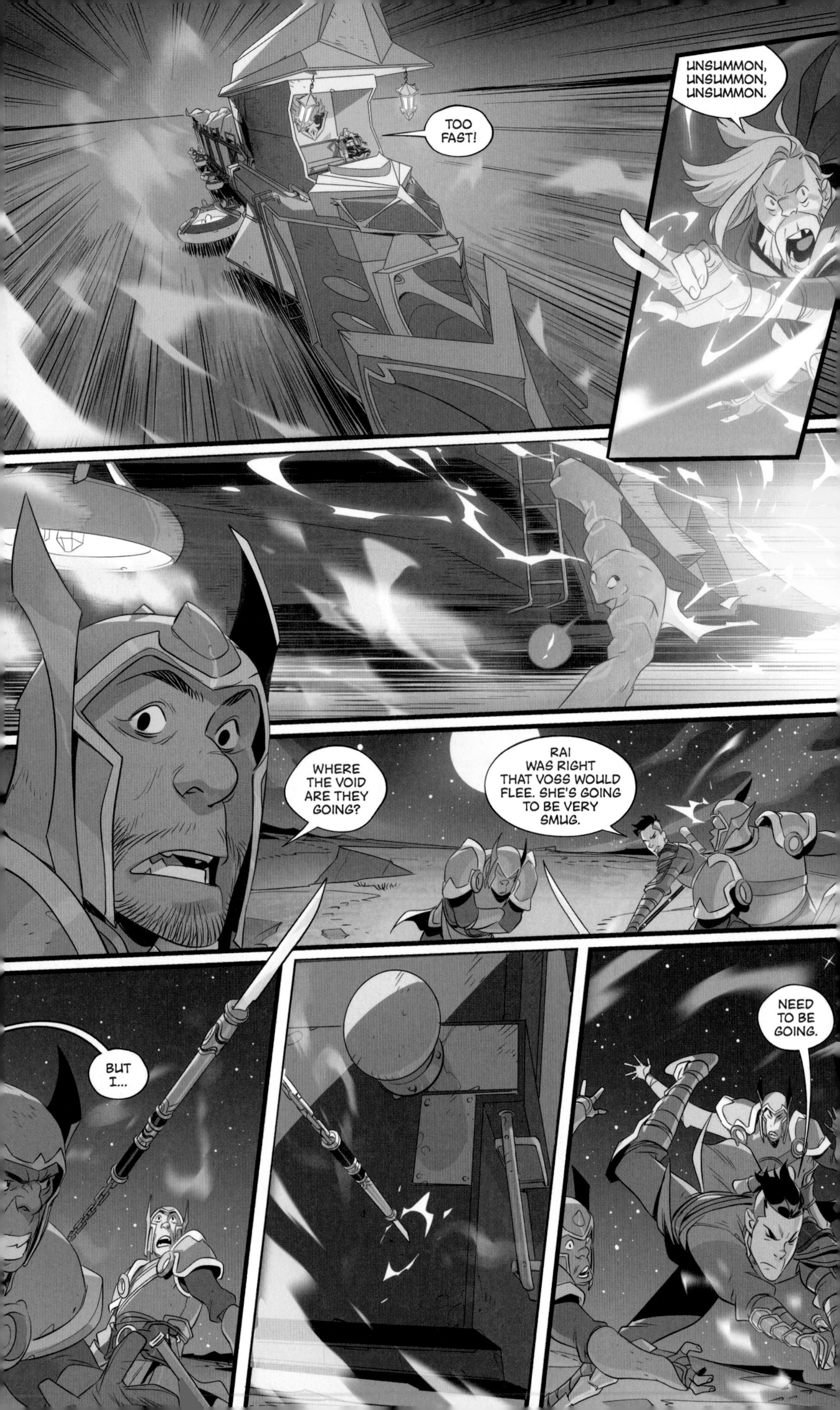
TOO FAST!
UNSUMMON, UNSUMMON, UNSUMMON.
WHERE THE VOID ARE THEY GOING?
RAI WAS RIGHT THAT VOSS WOULD FLEE. SHE'S GOING TO BE VERY SMUG.
BUT I...
NEED TO BE GOING.

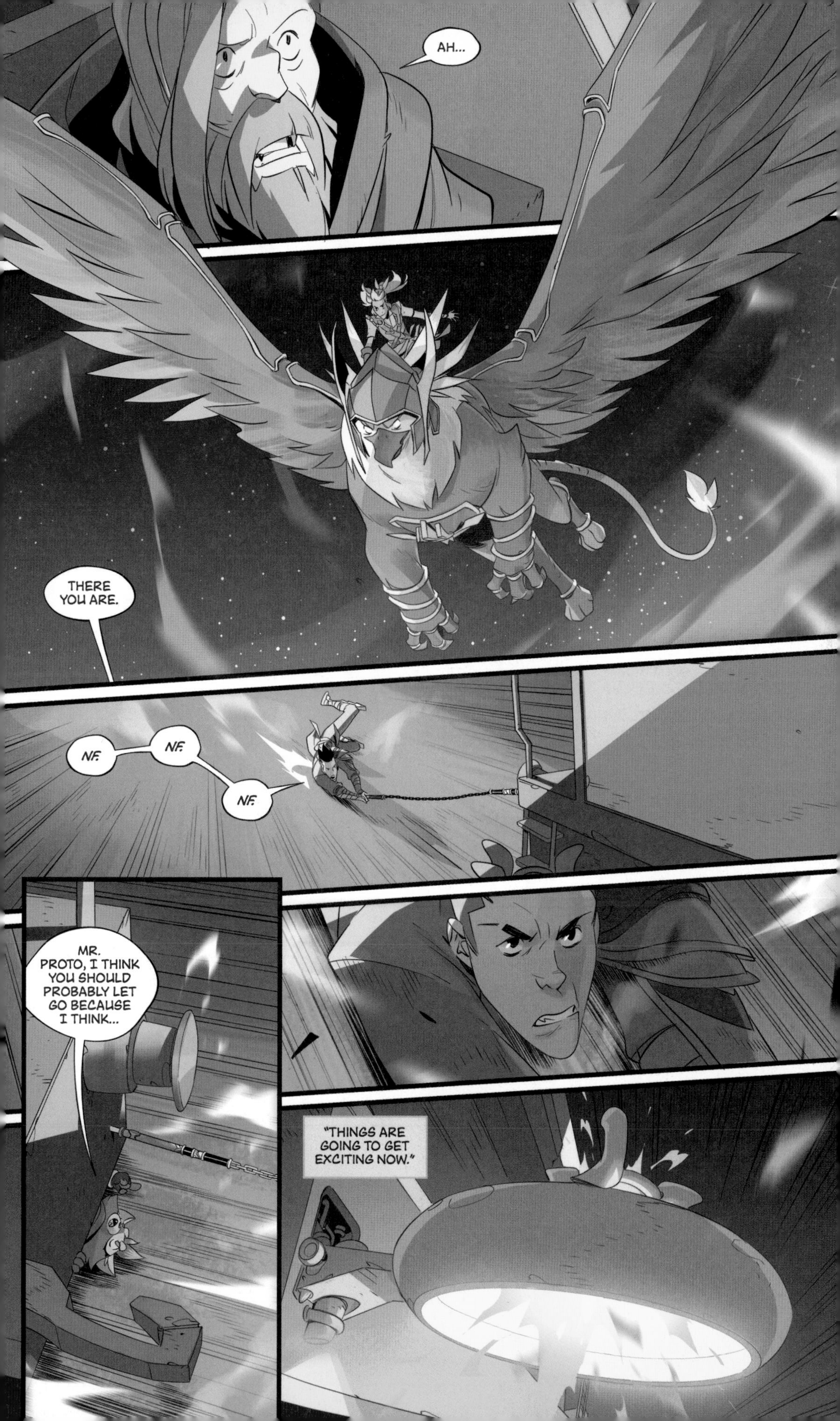
AH...
THERE YOU ARE.
NF.
NF.
NF.
MR. PROTO, I THINK YOU SHOULD PROBABLY LET GO BECAUSE I THINK...
"THINGS ARE GOING TO GET EXCITING NOW."

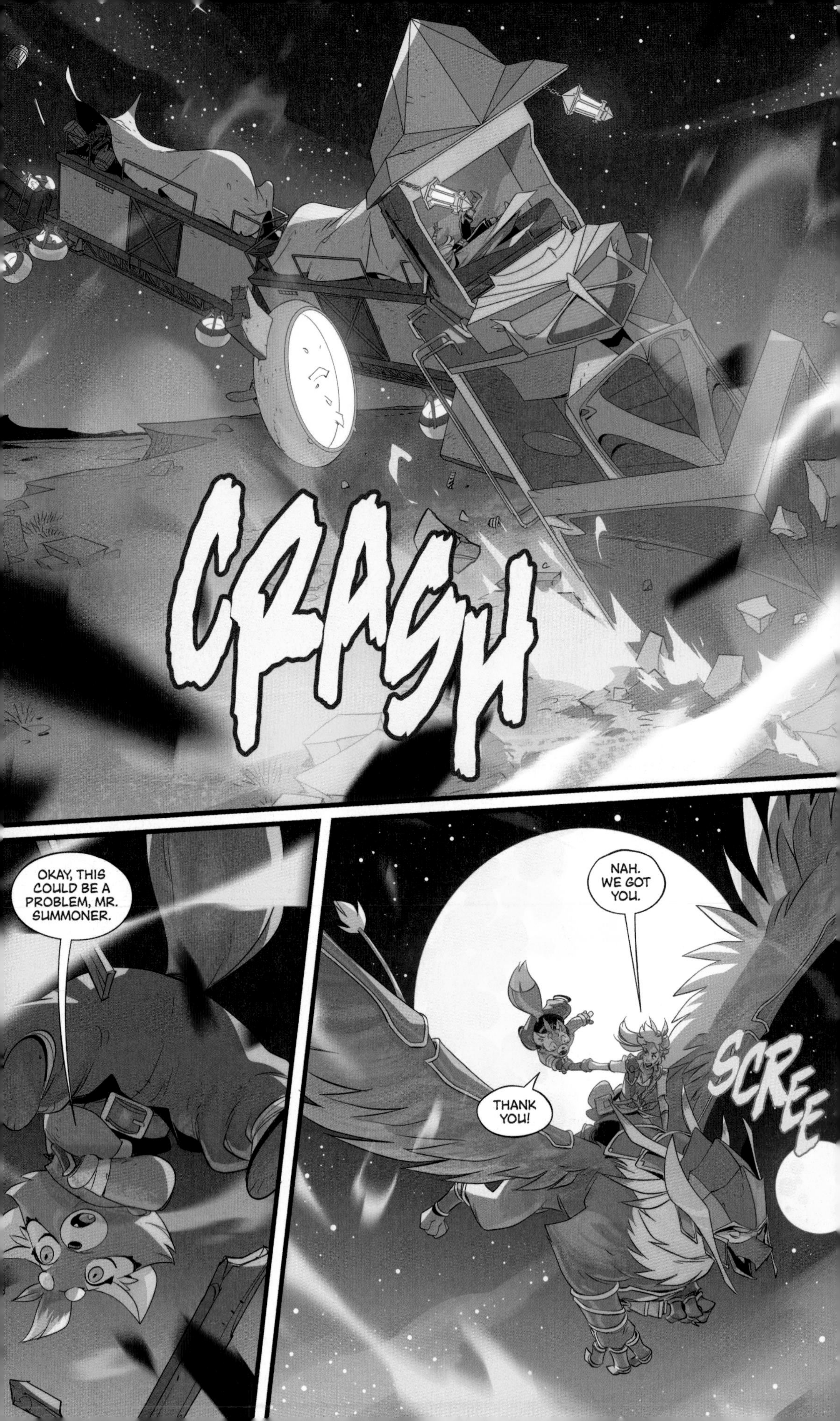
CRASH
OKAY, THIS COULD BE A PROBLEM, MR. SUMMONER.
NAH. WE GOT YOU.
THANK YOU!
SCREEE

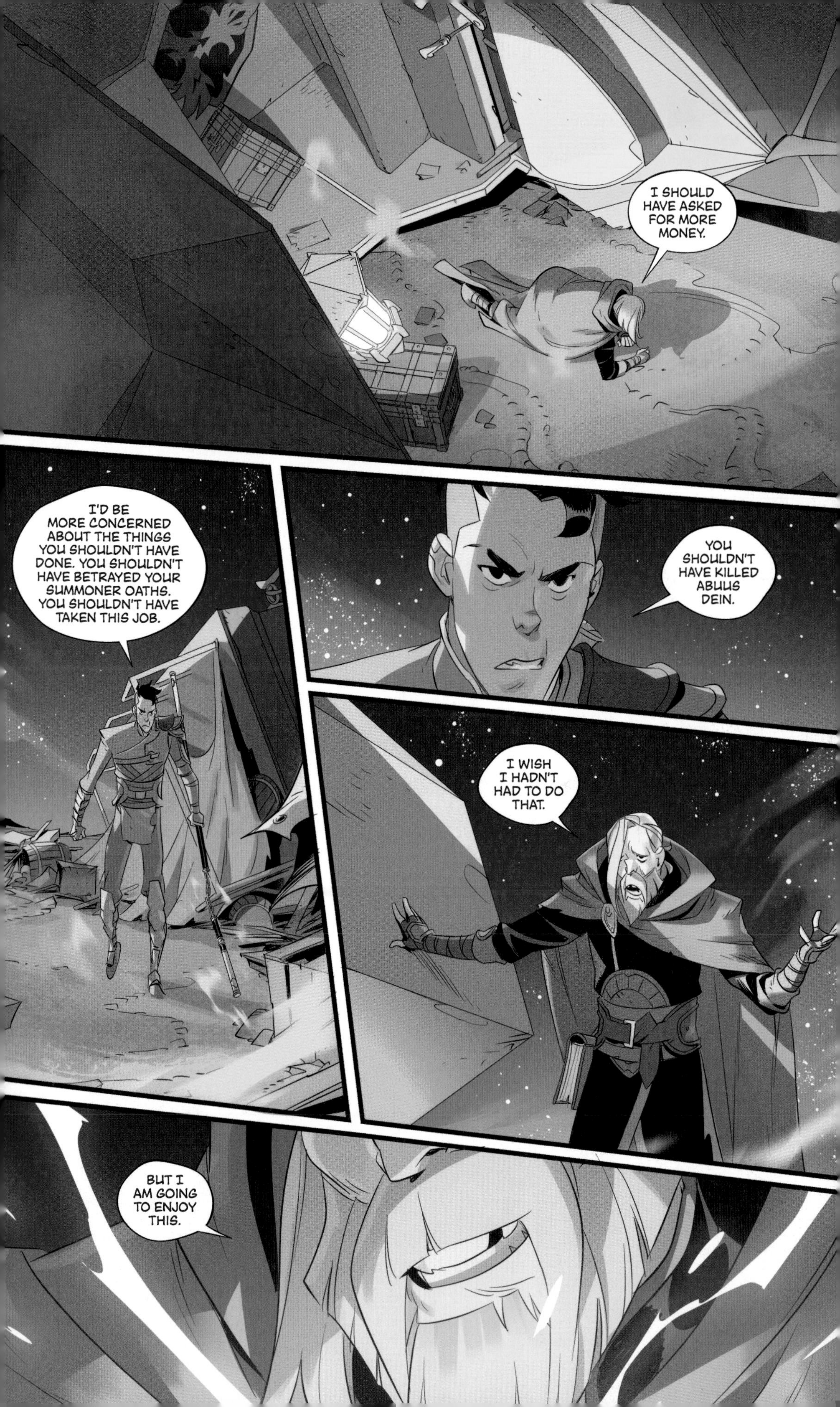
I SHOULD HAVE ASKED FOR MORE MONEY.
I'D BE MORE CONCERNED ABOUT THE THINGS YOU SHOULDN'T HAVE DONE. YOU SHOULDN'T HAVE BETRAYED YOUR SUMMONER OATHS. YOU SHOULDN'T HAVE TAKEN THIS JOB.
YOU SHOULDN'T HAVE KILLED ABUUS DEIN.
I WISH I HADN'T HAD TO DO THAT.
BUT I AM GOING TO ENJOY THIS.

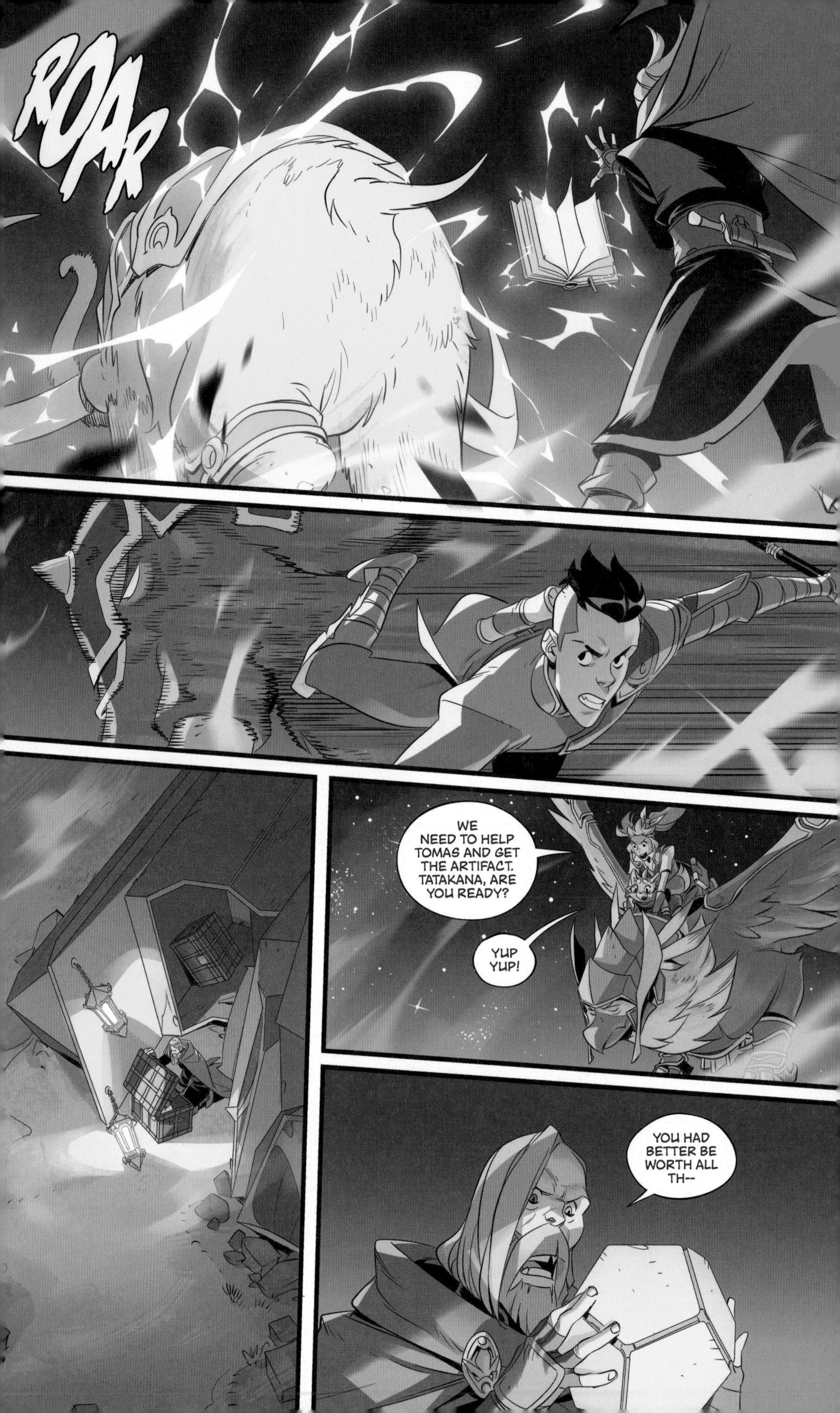
ROAR
WE NEED TO HELP TOMAS AND GET THE ARTIFACT. TATAKANA, ARE YOU READY?
YUP YUP!
YOU HAD BETTER BE WORTH ALL TH--

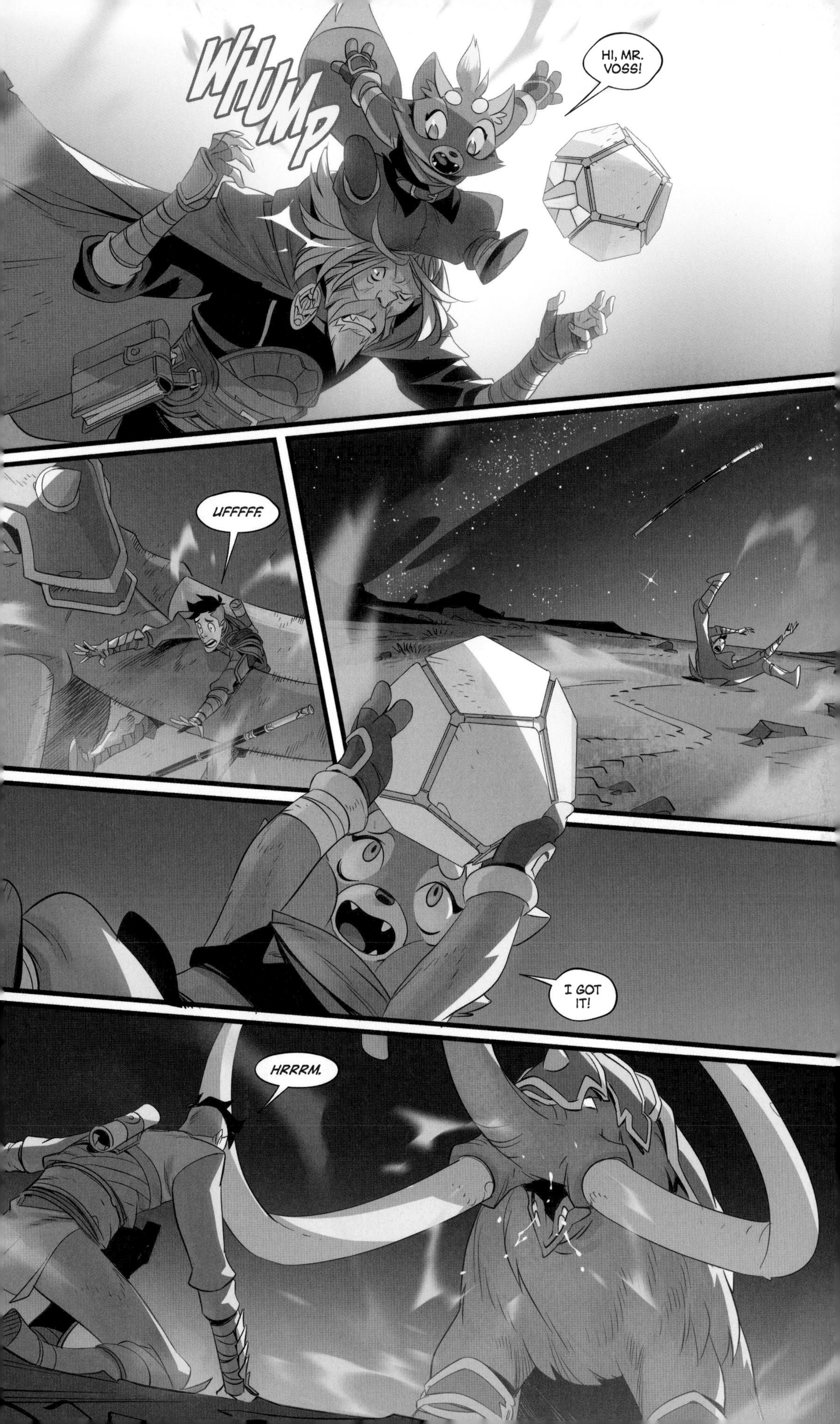
WHUMP
HI, MR. VOSS!
UFFFFF.
I GOT IT!
HRRRM.

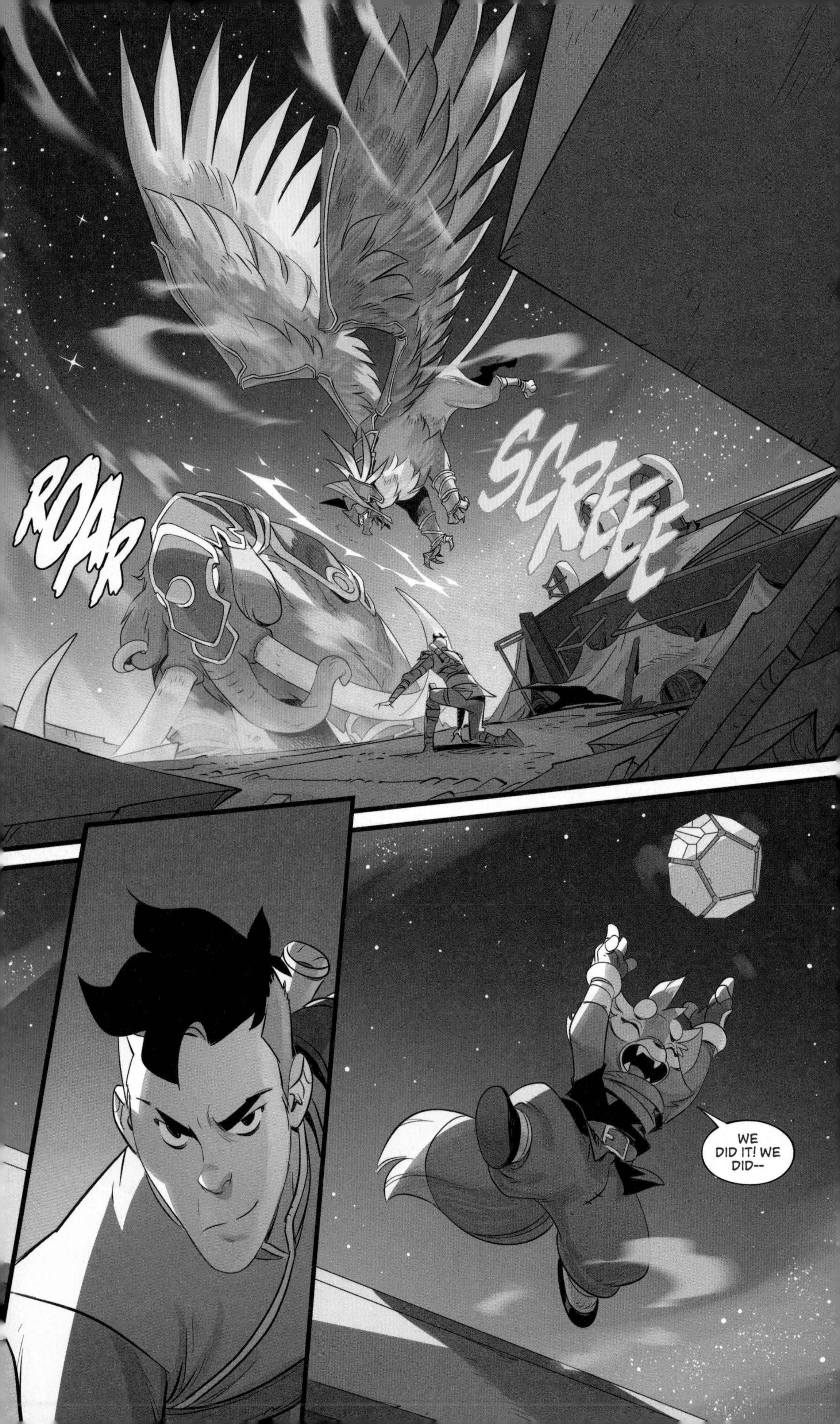
ROAR
SCREEE
WE DID IT! WE DID--

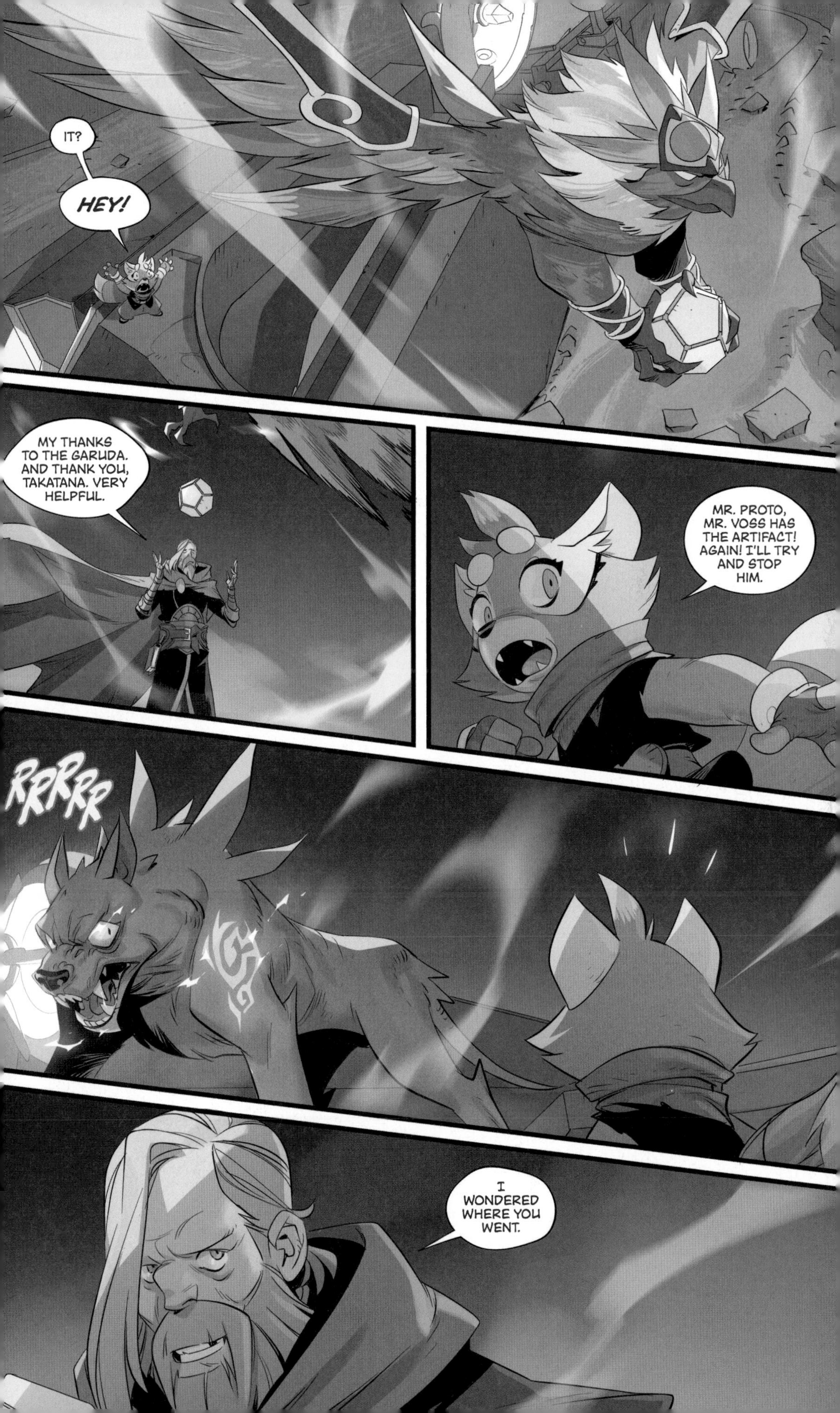
IT?
HEY!
MY THANKS TO THE GARUDA. AND THANK YOU, TAKATANA. VERY HELPFUL.
MR. PROTO, MR. VOSS HAS THE ARTIFACT! AGAIN! I'LL TRY AND STOP HIM.
RRRRR
I WONDERED WHERE YOU WENT.

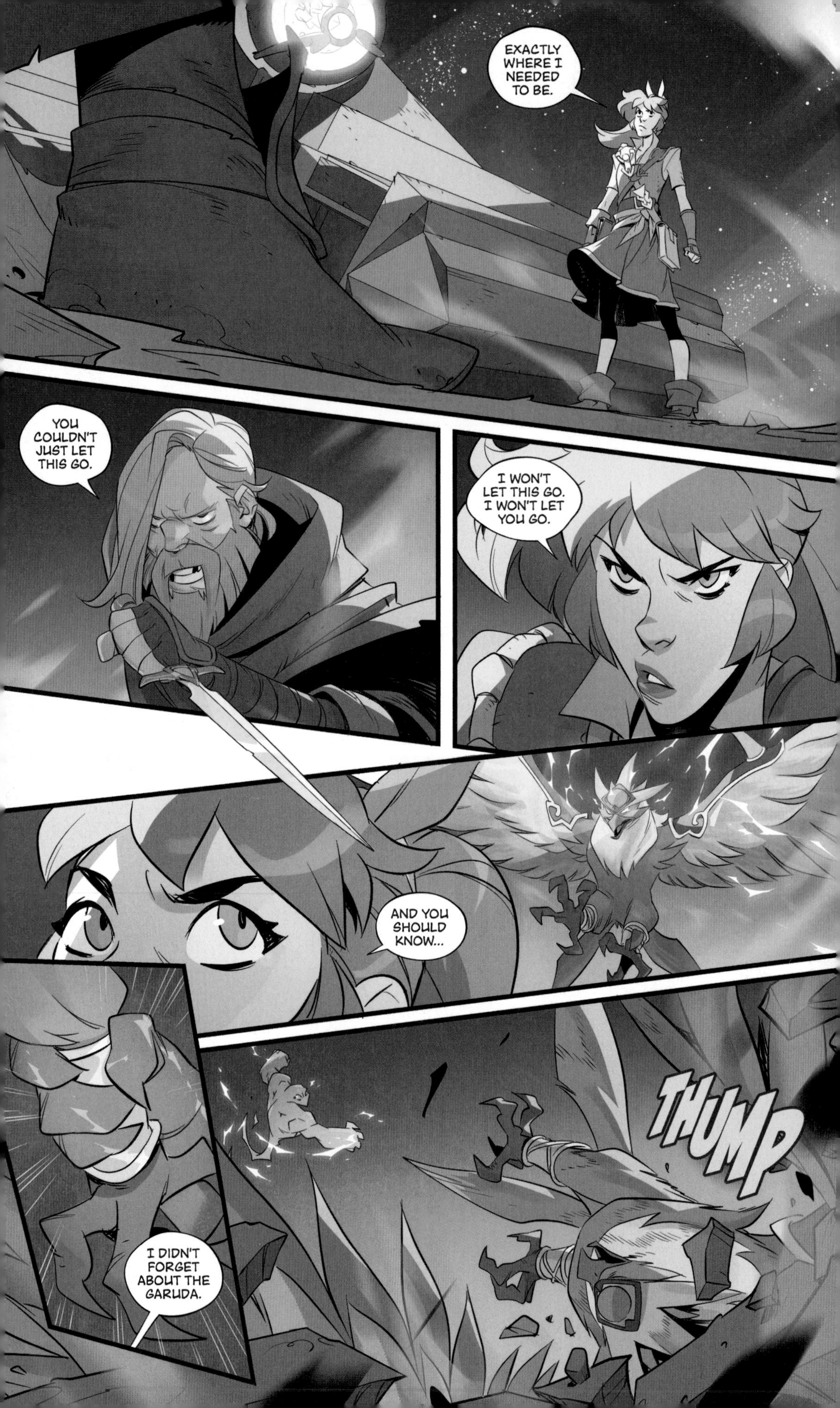
EXACTLY WHERE I NEEDED TO BE.
YOU COULDN'T JUST LET THIS GO.
I WON'T LET THIS GO. I WON'T LET YOU GO.
AND YOU SHOULD KNOW...
THUMP
I DIDN'T FORGET ABOUT THE GARUDA.

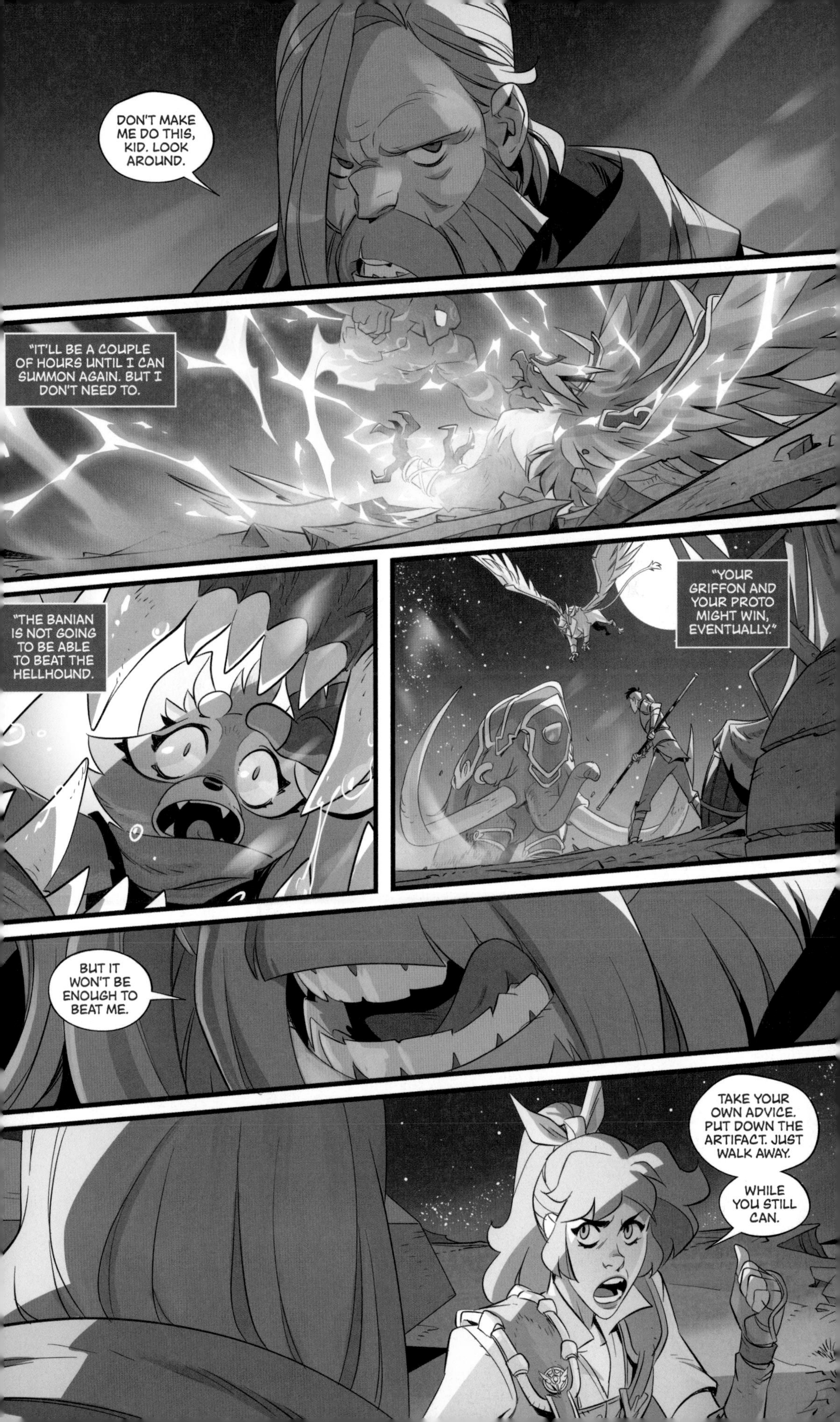
DON'T MAKE ME DO THIS, KID. LOOK AROUND.
"IT'LL BE A COUPLE OF HOURS UNTIL I CAN SUMMON AGAIN. BUT I DON'T NEED TO.
"THE BANIAN IS NOT GOING TO BE ABLE TO BEAT THE HELLHOUND.
"YOUR GRIFFON AND YOUR PROTO MIGHT WIN, EVENTUALLY."
BUT IT WON'T BE ENOUGH TO BEAT ME.
TAKE YOUR OWN ADVICE. PUT DOWN THE ARTIFACT. JUST WALK AWAY.
WHILE YOU STILL CAN.

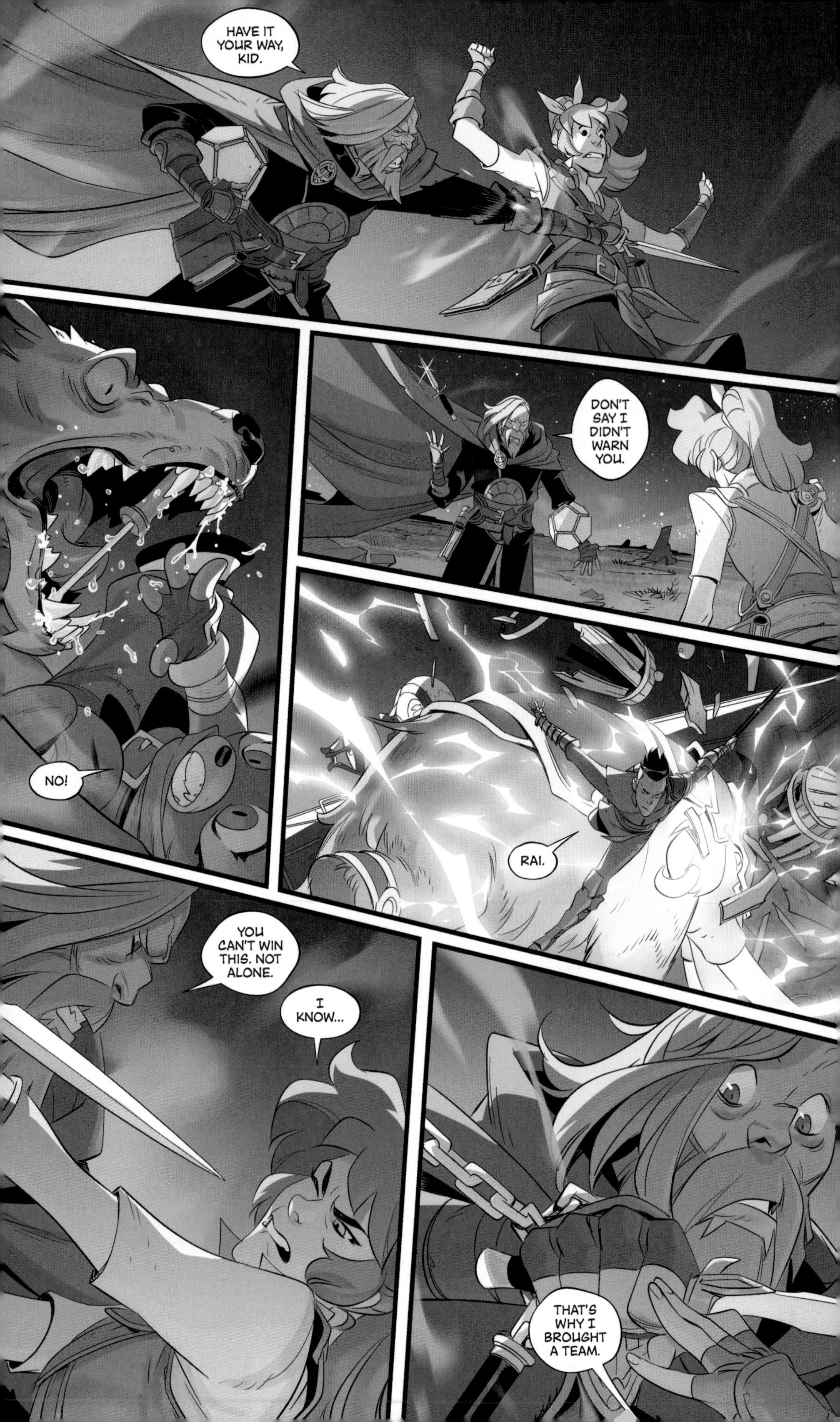
HAVE IT YOUR WAY, KID.
DON'T SAY I DIDN'T WARN YOU.
NO!
RAI.
YOU CAN'T WIN THIS. NOT ALONE.
I KNOW...
THAT'S WHY I BROUGHT A TEAM.

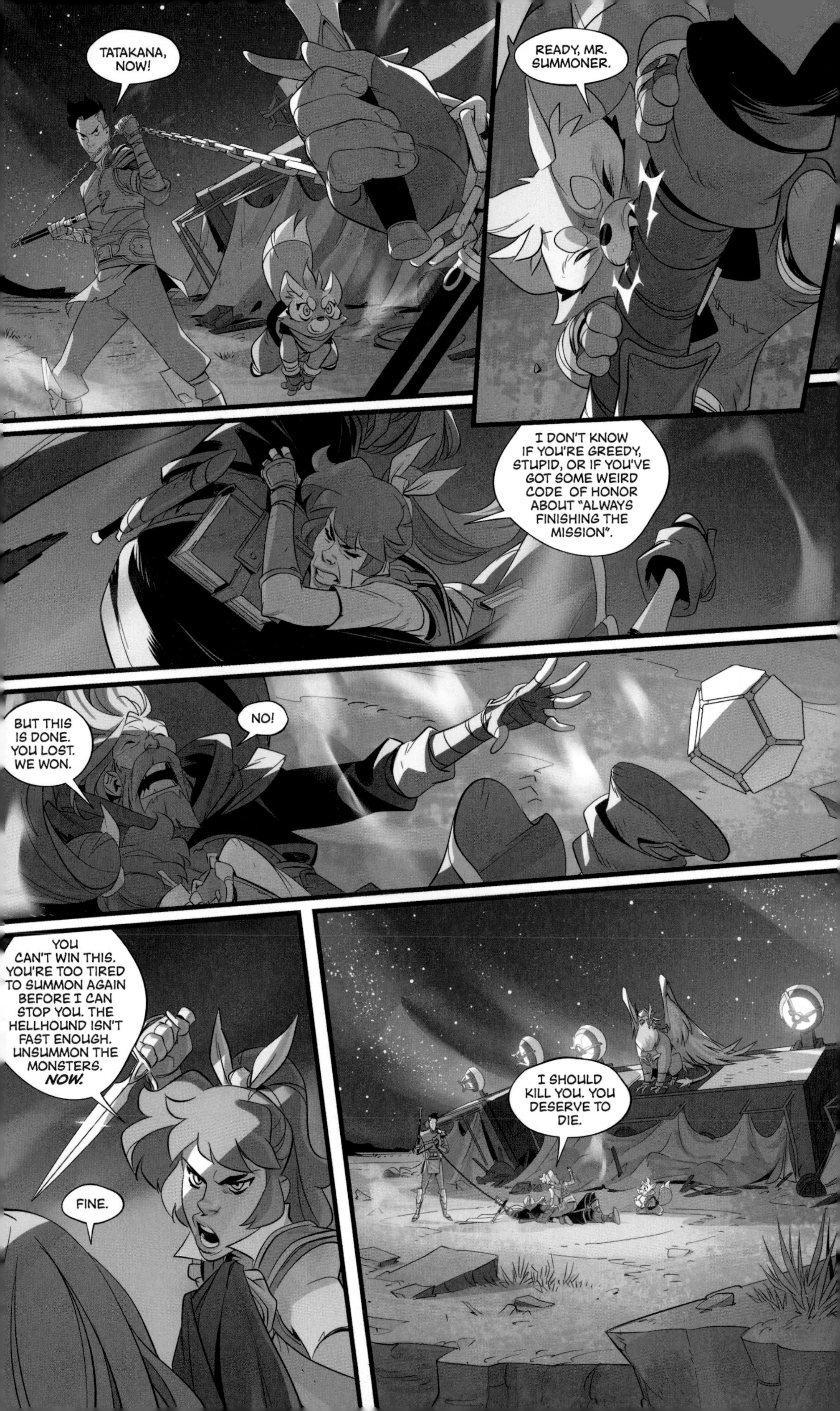
TATAKANA, NOW!
READY, MR. SUMMONER.
I DON'T KNOW IF YOU'RE GREEDY, STUPID, OR IF YOU'VE GOT SOME WEIRD CODE OF HONOR ABOUT "ALWAYS FINISHING THE MISSION".
BUT THIS IS DONE. YOU LOST. WE WON.
NO!
YOU CAN'T WIN THIS. YOU'RE TOO TIRED TO SUMMON AGAIN BEFORE I CAN STOP YOU. THE HELLHOUND ISN'T FAST ENOUGH. UNSUMMON THE MONSTERS. NOW.
FINE.
I SHOULD KILL YOU. YOU DESERVE TO DIE.

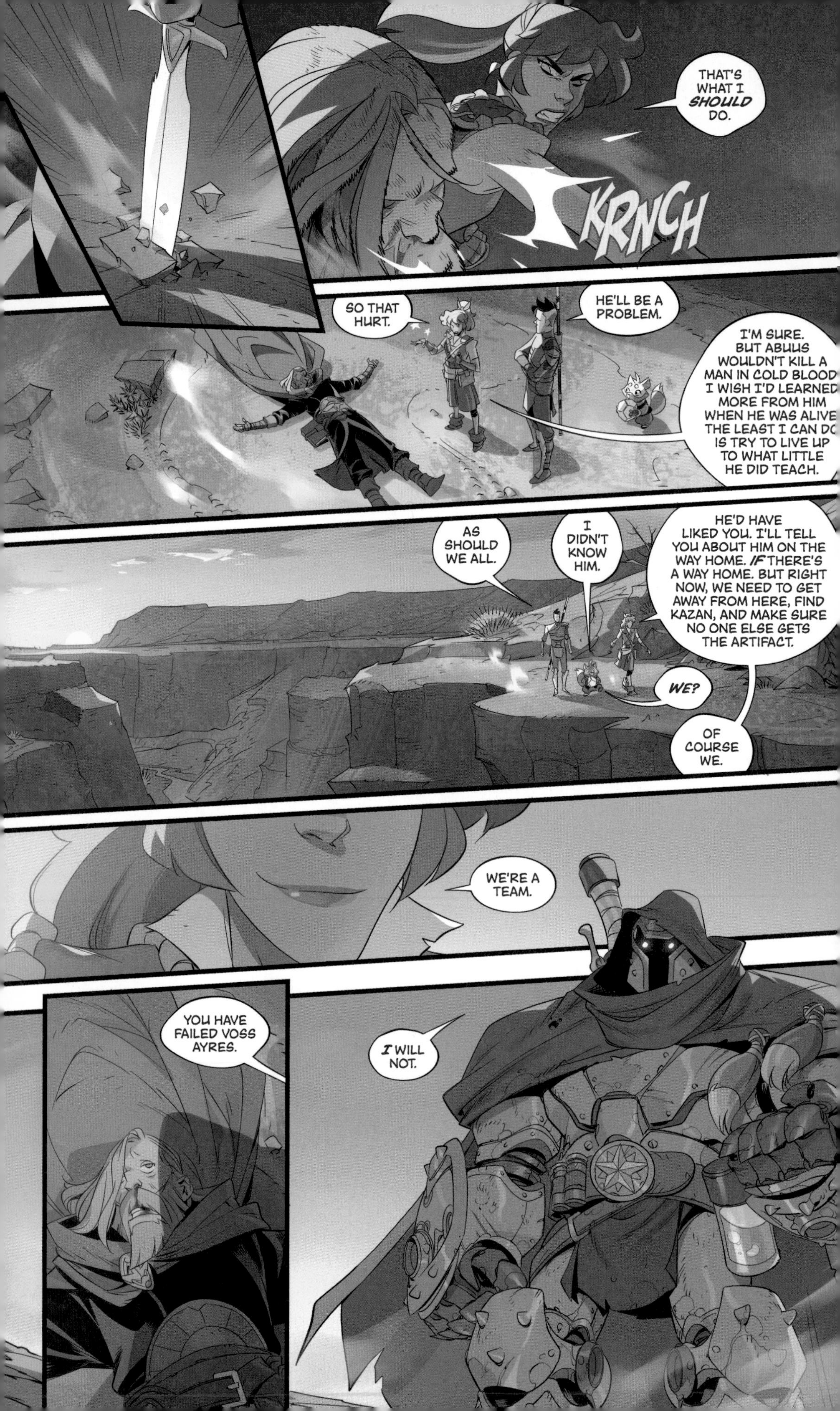
THAT'S WHAT I *SHOULD* DO.
KRNCH
SO THAT HURT.
HE'LL BE A PROBLEM.
I'M SURE. BUT ABUUS WOULDN'T KILL A MAN IN COLD BLOOD. I WISH I'D LEARNED MORE FROM HIM WHEN HE WAS ALIVE. THE LEAST I CAN DO IS TRY TO LIVE UP TO WHAT LITTLE HE DID TEACH.
AS SHOULD WE ALL.
I DIDN'T KNOW HIM.
HE'D HAVE LIKED YOU. I'LL TELL YOU ABOUT HIM ON THE WAY HOME. *IF* THERE'S A WAY HOME. BUT RIGHT NOW, WE NEED TO GET AWAY FROM HERE, FIND KAZAN, AND MAKE SURE NO ONE ELSE GETS THE ARTIFACT.
WE?
OF COURSE WE.
WE'RE A TEAM.
YOU HAVE FAILED VOSS AYRES.
I WILL NOT.

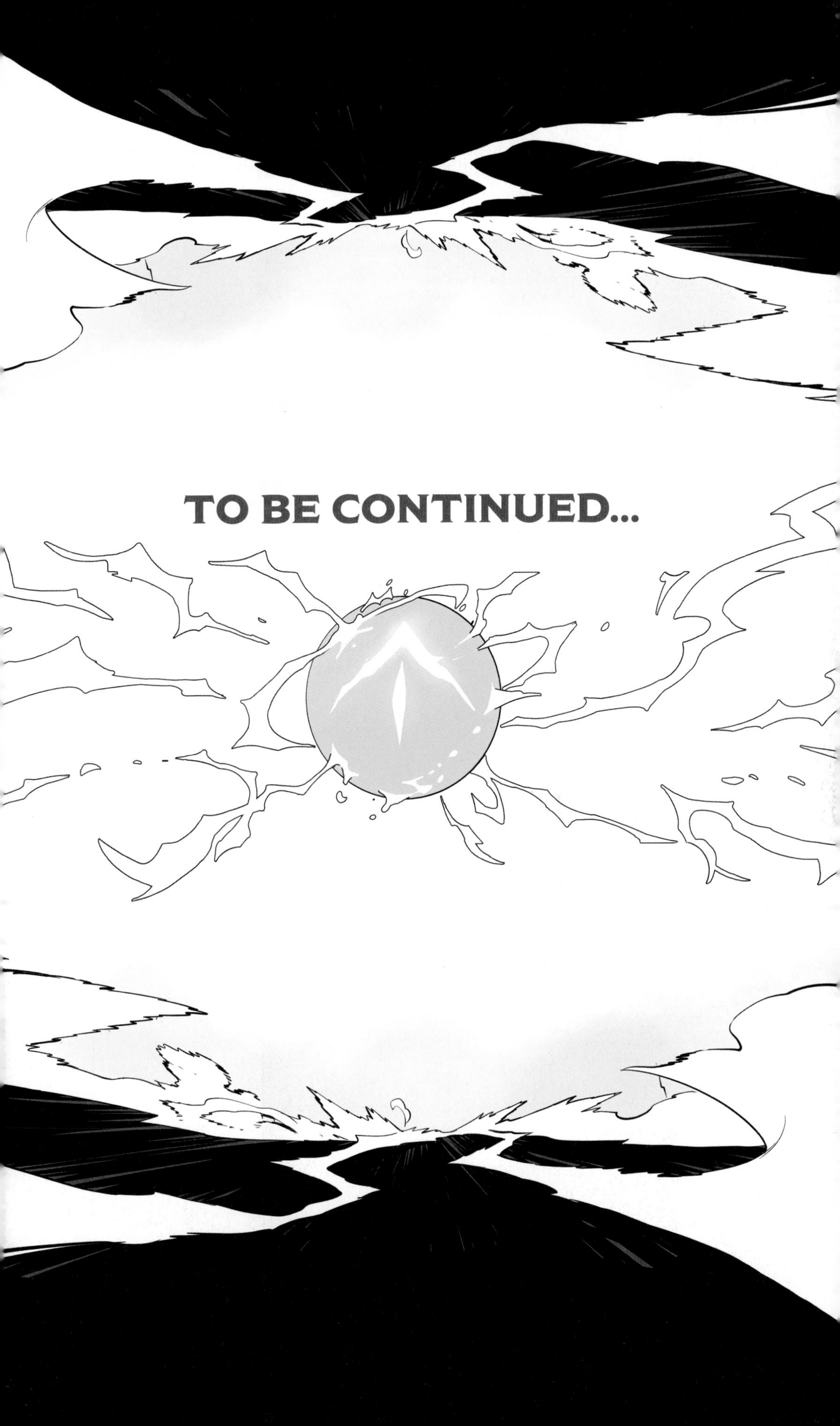
TO BE CONTINUED...

FOR MORE TALES FROM ROBERT KIRKMAN AND SKYBOUND

KIRKMAN • OTTLEY • WALKER • FAIRBAIRN
INVINCIBLE
VOLUME TWENTY-FIVE
THE END OF ALL THINGS
PART TWO

VOL. 1: FAMILY MATTERS TP
ISBN: 978-1-58240-711-1
$12.99

VOL. 2: EIGHT IS ENOUGH TP
ISBN: 978-1-58240-347-2
$12.99

VOL. 3: PERFECT STRANGERS TP
ISBN: 978-1-58240-391-5
$12.99

VOL. 4: HEAD OF THE CLASS TP
ISBN: 978-1-58240-778-4
$14.99

VOL. 5: THE FACTS OF LIFE TP
ISBN: 978-1-58240-554-4
$14.99

VOL. 6: A DIFFERENT WORLD TP
ISBN: 978-1-58240-579-7
$14.99

VOL. 7: THREE'S COMPANY TP
ISBN: 978-1-58240-656-5
$14.99

VOL. 8: MY FAVORITE MARTIAN TP
ISBN: 978-1-58240-683-1
$14.99

VOL. 9: OUT OF THIS WORLD TP
ISBN: 978-1-58240-827-9
$14.99

VOL. 10: WHO'S THE BOSS TP
ISBN: 978-1-60706-013-0
$16.99

VOL. 11: HAPPY DAYS TP
ISBN: 978-1-60706-062-8
$16.99

VOL. 12: STILL STANDING TP
ISBN: 978-1-60706-166-3
$16.99

VOL. 13: GROWING PAINS TP
ISBN: 978-1-60706-251-6
$16.99

VOL. 14: VILTRUMITE WAR TP
ISBN: 978-1-60706-367-4
$16.99

VOL. 15: GET SMART TP
ISBN: 978-1-60706-498-5
$16.99

VOL. 16: FAMILY TIES TP
ISBN: 978-1-60706-910-2
$16.99

VOL. 17: WHAT'S HAPPENING TP
ISBN: 978-1-60706-911-9
$16.99

VOL. 18: DEATH OF EVERYONE TP
ISBN: 978-1-60706-912-6
$16.99

VOL. 19: THE WAR AT HOME TP
ISBN: 978-1-60706-992-8
$16.99

VOL. 20: FRIENDS TP
ISBN: 978-1-63215-272-5
$16.99

VOL. 21: MODERN FAMILY TP
ISBN: 978-1-63215-511-5
$16.99

VOL. 22: REBOOT? TP
ISBN: 978-1-63215-815-4
$16.99

VOL. 23: FULL HOUSE TP
ISBN: 978-1-5343-0361-4
$16.99

VOL. 24: THE END OF ALL THINGS PT. 1 TP
ISBN: 978-1-5343-0322-5
$16.99

VOL. 25: THE END OF ALL THINGS PT. 2 TP
ISBN: 978-1-5343-0503-8
$16.99

ULTIMATE COLLECTION HC 1
ISBN: 978-1-58240-500-1
$34.99

ULTIMATE COLLECTION HC 2
ISBN: 978-1-58240-594-0
$34.99

ULTIMATE COLLECTION HC 3
ISBN: 978-1-58240-763-0
$34.99

ULTIMATE COLLECTION HC 4
ISBN: 978-1-58240-989-4
$34.99

ULTIMATE COLLECTION HC 5
ISBN: 978-1-60706-116-8
$34.99

ULTIMATE COLLECTION HC 6
ISBN: 978-1-60706-360-5
$34.99

ULTIMATE COLLECTION HC 7
ISBN: 978-1-60706-509-8
$34.99

ULTIMATE COLLECTION HC 8
ISBN: 978-1-60706-680-4
$34.99

ULTIMATE COLLECTION HC 9
ISBN: 978-1-63215-032-5
$34.99

ULTIMATE COLLECTION HC 10
ISBN: 978-1-63215-494-1
$34.99

ULTIMATE COLLECTION HC 11
ISBN: 978-1-5343-0045-3
$34.99

ULTIMATE COLLECTION HC 12
ISBN: 978-1-5343-0658-5
$34.99

BIRTHRIGHT
WILLIAMSON BRESSAN LUCAS
VOLUME TEN
EPILOGUE

VOL. 1: HOMECOMING TP
ISBN: 978-1-6321-5231-20
$9.99

VOL. 2: CALL TO ADVENTURE TP
ISBN: 978-1-6321-5618-1
$12.99

VOL. 3: ALLIES & ENEMIES TP
ISBN: 978-1-6321-5970-0
$12.99

VOL. 4: FAMILY HISTORY TP
ISBN: 978-1-5343-0198-6
$12.99

VOL. 5: BELLY OF THE BEAST TP
ISBN: 978-1-5343-0561-8
$12.99

VOL. 6: FATHERHOOD TP
ISBN: 978-1-5343-0498-7
$14.99

VOL. 7: BLOOD BROTHERS TP
ISBN: 978-1-5343-1053-7
$14.99

VOL. 8: LIVE BY THE SWORD TP
ISBN: 978-1-5343-1368-2
$14.99

VOL. 9: WAR OF THE WORLDS TP
ISBN: 978-1-5343-1601-0
$14.99

VOL. 10: EPILOGUE TP
ISBN: 978-1-5343-1948-6
$14.99

BRANDON THOMAS • KHARY RANDOLPH • EMILIO LOPEZ
EXCELLENCE
VOLUME TWO
THE PRESENT TENSE

VOL. 1: KILL THE PAST TP
ISBN: 978-1-5343-1362-0
$16.99

VOL. 2: THE PRESENT TENSE TP
ISBN: 978-1-5343-1862-5
$16.99

ROBERT KIRKMAN
CHRIS SAMNEE
FIRE POWER
WITH MATT WILSON AND RUS WOOTON
VOLUME 3: FLAME WAR

VOL. 1: PRELUDE OGN
ISBN: 978-1-5343-1655-3
$9.99

VOL. 2: HOME FIRE TP
ISBN: 978-1-5343-1718-5
$16.99

VOL. 3: FLAME WAR TP
ISBN: 978-1-5343-1908-0
$16.99

JUSTIN JORDAN
NIKO HENRICHON
REAVER
VOLUME TWO
THE GRIM AFTER

VOL. 1: HELL'S HALF-DOZEN TP
ISBN: 978-1-5343-1682-9
$16.99

VOL. 2: THE GRIM AFTER TP
ISBN: 978-1-5343-1903-5
$14.99

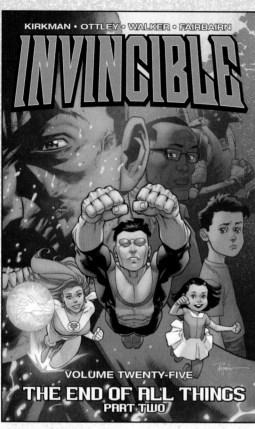